PRAISE FOR
Lost in the Summer of '69

"Buckle up. Eliza Knight delivers a delightful ride where memories and melody meet possibility. *Lost in the Summer of '69* follows three generations on a road trip through first love, second chances, and endless discovery. A heartfelt story that reminds us it's never too late to find yourself and rediscover the ones you love most."

—Meagan Church, *New York Times* bestselling author of *The Mad Wife*

"*Lost in the Summer of '69* quickly whisked me away with its heartwarming nostalgia and familial charm. Propelled by an adventure-packed road trip and the ever-hypnotic lure of music, Knight's delightful multigenerational tale presents an exploration of relationships, identity, and second chances—at any age. An endearing read to be savored, then shared with family."

—Kristina McMorris, *New York Times* bestselling author of *Sold on a Monday* and *The Girls of Good Fortune*

"An epic road trip linking three generations of women, Eliza Knight's *Lost in the Summer of '69* is an ode to music, family, and the importance of chasing your dreams. Readers will love this atmospheric and poignant novel!"

—Chanel Cleeton, *New York Times* bestselling author of *An Infinite Love Story*

"*Lost in the Summer of '69* tells the inspiring, nostalgic, multigenerational tale of three women who discover the power within themselves and learn that coming of age can happen at any age. Eliza Knight's sixties-era novel celebrates music, female resilience, and the strength of mother-daughter bonds, taking readers on a journey they won't soon forget."

—Marie Bostwick, *New York Times* bestselling author of *The Book Club for Troublesome Women*

"The best road trip you'll take this summer. I was happily *Lost in the Summer of '69* with three generations of women who captured my heart on every page. Journeying through music festivals during the pivotal summer of free love, the story follows a rocker grandma, her 1960s housewife daughter, and the free-spirited granddaughter who discover who they're meant to be, rather than who they think they ought to be… For anyone who loves to escape on a beach with a great book."

—Brooke Lea Foster, bestselling author of *Our Last Vineyard Summer*

"*Lost in the Summer of '69* is the multigenerational, bucket list, road trip, summer concert novel I never wanted to put down."

—Lynda Cohen Loigman, *USA Today* bestselling author of *The Love Elixir of Augusta Stern*

"Playful, poignant, and surprisingly powerful, *Lost in the Summer of '69* is the perfect road-trip novel, a heady blend of sun-drenched nostalgia and the summer sweetness of a melting Popsicle… Told in Knight's warm, intimate voice, this story of love and transformation—and a bit of rebellion—will appeal to fans of *Daisy Jones & the Six*."

—Donna Jones Alward, bestselling author of *When the World Fell Silent*

"An emotional, uplifting story… You'll smell the patchouli and warm beer and feel the mud squelch between your toes as you read this nostalgic, sensory, and joyful novel."

—Gill Paul, *USA Today* bestselling author of *Scandalous Women*

Lost in the Summer of '69

A NOVEL

Eliza Knight

sourcebooks landmark

The characters and events portrayed in this book are fictitious or are used fictitiously. Apart from well-known historical figures, any similarity to real persons, living or dead, is purely coincidental and not intended by the author.

Published by Sourcebooks Landmark, an imprint of Sourcebooks
1935 Brookdale RD, Naperville, IL 60563-2773
(630) 961-3900
sourcebooks.com

Cataloging-in-Publication Data is on file with the Library of Congress.

Printed and bound in the United States of America.
POD

For the women whose names we carry, whose stories we remember, and whose choices made space for our own.

What lips my lips have kissed, and where, and why,
I have forgotten, and what arms have lain
Under my head till morning; but the rain
Is full of ghosts tonight, that tap and sigh
Upon the glass and listen for reply,
And in my heart there stirs a quiet pain
For unremembered lads that not again
Will turn to me at midnight with a cry.

Thus in the winter stands the lonely tree,
Nor knows what birds have vanished one by one,
Yet knows its boughs more silent than before:
I cannot say what loves have come and gone,
I only know that summer sang in me
A little while, that in me sings no more.

—EDNA ST. VINCENT MILLAY,
"WHAT LIPS MY LIPS HAVE KISSED, AND WHERE, AND WHY"

PROLOGUE

Stomp the Intro

SUMMER 2019

NORA PERCHED ON A WICKER LOVE SEAT ON THE BACK patio of her daughter's house, steam curling from her cup into the early spring air. The garden was quiet—until it wasn't. Nora tucked a silver-nearly-white strand of hair behind her ear. Inside, there appeared to be an argument brewing between Anne and her teenage daughter, Ellie.

While it was probably inappropriate to smile, Nora couldn't help doing so. At Ellie's age, she and her own mother had had a few knock-down, drag-out fights over stupid things like boys, length of skirts, and music. And later, she'd listened to Anne stomp off just the same. Time softened the edges, but it never dulled the echo.

She leaned toward the window, snooping, because at her age, a little drama always provided a bit of a thrill.

"Why not?" Punctuating the ever-present *why* was the stomp of a foot.

Nora tsked. Didn't Ellie know by now—at seventeen—that stomping one's foot was simply silly? And with Anne, a prosecutor for the state, that it would get her nowhere?

Anne's words were muffled through the window, no doubt spoken in the calm, cool, collected manner she'd used since she was two and made a very sound argument to her mother about why she should be allowed to stay up later than her usual bedtime. And it wasn't because she wasn't tired; it was because if she'd gone to bed on time, she wouldn't have been able to warn the cow not to jump over the moon—he'd break his legs on the fall down to earth.

Nora had agreed and let her stay up an extra ten minutes.

The argument grew louder, their voices trailing closer, and then Anne was out on the back porch, arms crossed over her slim chest, tapping her foot in impatience, and Ellie stood beside her looking very much like a younger, identical version. Their raven-colored hair was reminiscent of Nora's beloved late husband.

"My, what have I done to warrant the wrath of my two favorites?" Nora worked hard to hide her smile.

"She wants to go to that Woodstock revival concert with her friends—camping and all! Mother, please tell Ellie she can't go." Anne rolled her eyes as if the idea was offensive.

"It's not even that big of a deal!" Ellie's voice cracked. "Everyone else's parents said yes."

Nora cocked her head, staring at Anne. Had her daughter really forgotten about Nora's epic summer adventure in the summer of '69 when she'd gone to Woodstock herself? From the confused look on her face, apparently, she had. "No."

"See," Anne said, gesturing toward Nora. "Your grandmother said no."

Nora chuckled. "Oh, Anne, I meant no I won't tell her she can't go."

Anne's mouth fell open. Nora was certain to get a lecture later about allowing Anne to parent on her own, but then she'd remind Anne—again—that inviting Nora into the debate came with consequences. Not every argument needed a witness.

"Mother!" Anne's voice held a warning edge.

"I'll take her," Nora said with a firm nod, eager to enjoy the evergreen sounds of rock and roll, to relive that amazing summer that had changed her life.

Anne's eyes practically bulged. "You can't take her to Woodstock; that's crazy. Don't you remember what happened in 1999, the last time they tried to revive that festival?"

Nora laughed a little louder, spilling droplets of tea until Anne took her cup and set it on the cedar table. Woodstock 1999 had been an utter disaster, that much was true. But maybe this time around, the organizers had taken a few pointers from Lilith Fair in the '90s, which had been all about hope and comradery, well, and female empowerment. Nora and Anne had gone to the Lilith Fair show at the Jones Beach Amphitheater in celebration of Anne's recent law school graduation, and Nora still had a picture of them, smiling with Sarah McLachlan singing onstage in the background, taped to her refrigerator twenty years later. A snapshot reminder of who they were.

"What is so funny?" Anne demanded.

"Oh, Anne, my darling girl, have you forgotten what I told you about your great-grandmother?"

Anne narrowed her eyes, and Nora could practically see her rolling through the files she kept alphabetized and in chronological order in the coils of her brain.

"Ellie," Nora said, patting the seat beside her. "Let me tell you a story about my grandmother, and how she got lost in the summer of sixty-nine. That summer changed everything for me. And maybe it will for you too."

PART ONE

California Dreaming

SUMMER 1969

CHAPTER ONE

ELEANOR BELL STRICKLAND HAD ALWAYS BELIEVED IN omens. Signs. Little winks from the universe. And tonight, sitting alone in her dimly lit living room, she couldn't help but wonder if turning sixty-nine in the year 1969 was some kind of cosmic joke. A cruel, poetic symmetry.

Her fingers sank into the royal-purple velvet of the couch, the fabric rich and smooth beneath her touch. A jazz record spun on the record player in the corner, its low, scratchy hum curling into the air like cigarette smoke. Overhead, the chandelier she'd found at a flea market decades ago cast jagged shadows against the walls, flickering like ghosts of old laughter, old arguments, old love.

On the mantel, next to the portrait of herself in her twenties—hair swept up, eyes burning with the certainty of youth—was the photograph of her wedding day. A black-and-white relic of a life that had once been brimming, roaring, unstoppable. She stood and brought the picture back to the couch, tracing the edge of the frame with one trembling finger. If only he were here. If only she could turn her head and see him standing in the doorway, smirking at her dramatic sentimental streak the way he always had.

But the room was quiet. Too quiet. And for the first time in her life, Eleanor felt something slipping—something she had spent years clinging to. The fierce, electric hum of life that had always run through her veins. Ebbing now, just slightly, just enough to make her wonder…

Was this what it felt like to fade?

Sixty-nine in 1969. Her golden birthday. That was supposed to mean something—supposed to be special. She and Henry had always talked about doing something big this year, something grand. A trip back to Malibu, where they'd spent their honeymoon tangled in salt air and endless, impossible love. Or maybe New Orleans, where the jazz clubs pulsed like a second heartbeat, where she could finally dance in a place that made music feel like magic.

But fate, as always, had its own sense of humor. And not the kind that made you laugh.

Henry was gone.

One minute he was there, humming some off-key tune while shaving, teasing her about a gray hair she absolutely did not have. The next—just…gone. Vanished into the abyss, leaving her stranded in a life that suddenly felt too quiet too still.

Age was a cruel joke. Death was a bully. It snatched, it sneered. It took what it wanted and left you holding nothing but a hollowed-out heart and a collection of what-ifs.

And now, on this golden day, she was left sitting here, staring at the ghost of a life they'd planned. Wondering how, exactly, she was supposed to celebrate when half of her had already been buried.

Eleanor forgot why she'd sunk so heavily onto the worn velvet of her purple couch, why a slow, creeping melancholy had wrapped itself around her shoulders like a too-familiar shawl. But then her gaze fell again to the slip of paper trembling in her lap, the inked scrawl of her doctor's handwriting etched sharp and final. The pamphlet she held that started a ticking time bomb to the end. And the mourning of what was written there came back all over again.

Dementia. Early signs.

The words blurred at the edges, but their meaning stayed razor clear.

She exhaled—long, slow—and let her gaze drift beyond the paper, toward the taxidermy peacock perched on the painted brick hearth. Its iridescent feathers shimmered dully in the afternoon light, glass eyes staring back with a secret only she knew. Henry had never asked about it, and she'd never offered the truth: that the peacock was a gift from a lover, a young man with calloused fingers and a fedora tilted on his head, a lifetime ago when her days were stitched with electric possibility.

Back when she still believed she could set the world on fire.

She had wanted to be a star once. Could play the drums, strum a guitar and a banjo—but her real instrument had always been her voice. Sweet, clear, a little wild around the edges. That's what they used to say. That's what *he* used to say. *Eleanor Bell, with a voice that rang like a bell.*

She'd been a musician ahead of her time, chasing rhythms and riffs the world wasn't ready to hear in the 1920s.

Her fingers, still elegant despite the years, released the papers, letting them fall to the floor like an afterthought. She stood, feet aching from the heels she'd kicked off, but back straight, and crossed to the record player. Gently, deliberately, she lifted the record from its spindle, set it aside, and replaced it with something with a little more pulse.

Jimi Hendrix.

As the first notes of "Purple Haze" crackled to life, the chords curled around her like smoke. A faint smile came to her lips. This room, this purple couch—it had all been shaped by the echoes of a song, by the girl she used to be.

That girl wasn't entirely gone yet.

With no one here to watch, Eleanor let herself be that girl again. Fingers strumming invisible chords in the air, she twirled through her living room, legs kicking, hips swaying, her body bending and flowing as if she were one more instrument in the band. The music surged through her, wild and free, and she moved like she'd never stopped, like the aches and pains of age didn't exist.

Certainly not how anyone imagined a grandmother should dance—not her daughter, not her granddaughter, and definitely not the friends she swapped casserole recipes and polite conversation with. But they'd never known her secret.

The secret she'd tucked away for the past four decades, folded between grocery lists, laundry, and dirty diapers.

That Eleanor Bell, if the world had let her shine, would have been wild and free—a musician with an unforgettable voice, a wild style and a long list of lovers. Someone who stayed on the stage and evolved as the music did. Maybe even now, she would've been the greatest damn rocker of all time.

Close behind the bully death was time, and time had stolen so much from her.

She spun faster, her laughter caught in her throat, feet skimming across the floor like those of a woman half her age. She let herself believe she had no cares, no doctor's words sitting heavy on her chest, no shadow creeping in to steal the edges of her mind.

But the fact lingered there anyway. Just out of reach. Soon, maybe tomorrow, maybe years from now, her memories would begin to slip like a broken record. Memories of her husband's hand in hers. Her daughter's first cry. The warm weight of her granddaughter curled beside her on Sunday mornings.

And perhaps worst of all—the flashbulb moments she'd hoarded for herself, the ones she replayed when no one was watching. Bright lights, sticky bar stages, the roar of a crowd. The nights before she'd been a mother, a wife. When she had been the Bell of Wartime Music. Sought after, cheered for.

She feared the loss of those memories, of being on the road, a young singer, a budding star. Moments she'd cherished over the last decades raising a family. Moments she'd relished in the night when no one was paying attention or when she was knee-deep in laundry or dirty diapers. Those memories had kept her alive and kept her going. Nights when the hot spotlight of the stage lights had warmed her skin.

To lose those felt like the end of the world. The door closing on a dream.

By the time Jimi crooned his final line, her chest was heaving, sweat beading at her temples. A nostalgic smile on her lips, she was breathless and a little dizzy, as though the song itself had transported her back to who she used to be. At her feet, Roxy yapped and twirled, the little Chinese crested equally giddy. Eleanor scooped up the dog, burying her face against her soft tuft and warm, hairless skin, holding on as if she could bring time to a halt.

"What's that you say, Roxy?" Eleanor asked the little dog in her arms. "You think I should return to my roots, become a star again?" She scratched behind Roxy's ear, staring into her devoted brown eyes as if that would give her the answer. Heat tunneled up her spine. "Me too."

The thought of striding onto a stage, a guitar slung across her shoulder, silver hair wild, her wrinkled and veined fingers plucking out chords as naturally as breath, made her laugh out loud. Her voice might be raspier now, might creak like old floorboards, but damn if she didn't believe it could still hold a crowd spellbound.

Maybe she needed to prove it to herself, that the Bell of Wartime Music had not left her completely.

Putting down the dog, she padded in her stockinged feet through the house, the wooden floor cool beneath her nylon-covered soles, to her bedroom. Past the massive gold-framed bed draped in silk sheets, rumpled and untouched. She'd stopped making the bed after Henry died, afraid smoothing the sheets might erase the dent he left behind. Past her mirrored vanity, cluttered with elegant little bottles: Chanel N°5, Shalimar, Joy by Jean Patou. Scents that once clung to her pulse points, to the folds of her blouses. On the nightstand sat a crystal ashtray, a lipstick-smudged cigarette extinguished but forgotten from the night before.

She bypassed all of these things as if they didn't exist.

Instead, she crossed to the closet, sliding open the heavy doors. Cool air wafted out, laced with cedar and the faint traces of Henry that grew weaker with each passing day. She pushed aside rows of silk blouses and sequined dresses until her fingers brushed something solid—the smooth wood handle of her guitar, tucked away behind decades of careful appearances.

She pulled the Gibson L-00 free. Her fingers danced over the rounded shoulders and narrowed waist of solid spruce, admiring that the sunburst finish had hardly faded. The dark outer edge had a nick on one side, barely noticeable because of the appealing honey-colored center, which drew the eye. But she remembered how the nick had gotten there. A kiss that made her jerk and hit her beloved instrument against a microphone stand.

Her thumb grazed the chords' steel wire, eliciting a soft hum that broke the stillness of memory. Eleanor closed her eyes, letting the vibration of the chords ricochet from her fingertips up her arms.

Roxy barked at her feet, pulling her from her memories. Her tail wagged furiously, demanding Eleanor sing.

Eleanor flipped the guitar over, giving it a gentle shake. A tiny, folded note fluttered to the floor, landing like a forgotten promise on the thick shag carpet of her closet.

She crouched, the guitar resting against her knee, and unfolded the yellowed paper, careful not to rip the aged edges. Three words stared back at her, ink slightly smudged.

Until next time.

Her breath caught. The memory washed over her like a swell—laughter backstage, a whisper in her ear, the scent of cigarette smoke and the leather of an old aviator jacket. She smiled, her fingers moving instinctively, languidly, over the strings, coaxing out a lazy melody.

There had never been a next time. She had met Henry, fallen in love. And she'd tucked the note inside the guitar, unable to bring herself to throw it away. Even as she traded away the possibility it hinted at—traded it for family, responsibility, the safety of routine.

That was a choice. A life of stardom and love versus stability and heart.

But standing here now, the weight of the guitar in her hands, the taste of old perfume still clinging to the air, she wondered, if life was about to slip away from her, piece by piece—why couldn't she revisit old choices, decide how life ended?

Why couldn't she make the rest of her *until next time* be right now?

Yesterday, she'd spotted an article folded in the corner of the newspaper, nearly overlooked. The Newport Pop Festival. California. Next week.

All the way across the country, but something about the idea of a music festival buzzed beneath her skin, lit her up like stage lights.

If she packed now, she could be there. She could walk among the crowd, guitar slung across her back, maybe even find a stage where no one cared how old she was or how many years she'd spent stringing laundry instead of chords. The Bell of Wartime Music could make one last appearance.

The thought made her pulse quicken.

But then doubt slithered in—could she make it in time? She couldn't recall what the calendar on the wall in her kitchen marked neatly in her daughter's handwriting said. And she didn't really care.

Flying seemed safest. She had enough money tucked away to buy a plane ticket without blinking. Maybe that would keep her from getting turned around, ending up in the wrong city or on the wrong coast. Driving across the country alone… That felt like tempting fate. A week on the road might be one detour too far for her fraying memory.

The doctor hadn't given her a timeline. First, it had been little things—misplacing her keys, standing in the cereal aisle when she meant to be lighting a candle for Henry at church. Picking up the phone and not recognizing the voice on the other end—her own daughter.

No one could say when the gaps would widen, the pace would speed up, memories and everyday functions would vanish and stay gone for good.

She shook the ugly thoughts away, banishing them like smoke.

She wouldn't give the forgetting, the diagnosis, any more space. Not today.

Instead, she focused on the festival. The hum of guitars in the distance, the thrum of bass vibrating through the soles of her shoes, voices rising into the summer air. A chance to be Eleanor Bell again—the girl who'd never needed permission to be loud.

Eleanor wanted her song to stretch into one endless chord shimmering beneath the California sun.

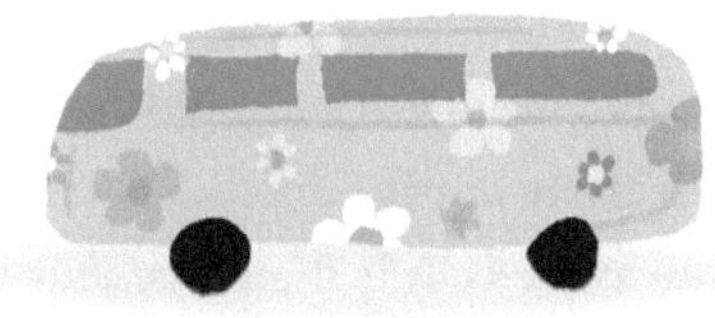

CHAPTER TWO

WITH A SIGH OF FRUSTRATION, LEANNE MILLER SET the phone back in its cradle and pressed her fingers to her temple.

She'd been calling her mother for hours, and despite her continued dialing, there was no answer.

Her mom was supposed to have gone to a doctor's appointment that morning, then stopped by for dinner and birthday cake—simple, straightforward plans. But Eleanor hadn't shown up. And now the silence on the other end of the line felt heavy.

Leanne glanced toward the brass starburst kitchen clock, its second hand ticking far too loud in the quiet house. The clock itself was in stark contrast to her rigid life. The beams of light catching on the brass radiated promising hope, when she felt none. Dean was "working late" again, somewhere behind glass walls in Manhattan, and when "working" meant nursing an after-hours cocktail instead of coming home. Upstairs, the floorboards creaked faintly with the movement of her daughter, Nora, around her room, fine-tuning yet another packing list for Yale.

Leanne crossed to the bottom of the stairs and called up, forcing her voice to sound light. "I'm heading to Grandma's. Want to come?"

A pause. Then her daughter's voice floated down. "No, thanks."

That was it. No explanation, and no question as to why Leanne was going. Just a polite decline from a girl teetering on the edge of adulthood, already halfway out the door.

That made sense and was as it should be, but it still made Leanne ache a bit. She rested her hand on the banister, fingers curling around the polished wood. The house felt too big tonight—echoing with the quiet absence of a daughter ready to fly the nest, a family she could feel slipping through her fingers, and the steady ticktick of the clock, its secondhand slicing through the quiet like a metronome. Dean logged hundred-hour weeks, rarely making it home in time for dinner, sometimes not bothering to come home at all. The office couch had become his second bed.

Once Nora was gone, there'd be even less reason for him to make an appearance.

Leanne—on the verge of becoming an empty nester—tried to imagine feeling even more alone and couldn't.

Slipping out the front door, Leanne climbed into her tidy station wagon, the leather seats still warm from the late-afternoon sun. She started the engine, flipping on the headlights with fingers cold from nerves. The haloed resonance floated off the brick of her house. She backed slowly out of the driveway, slamming on the brakes as one kid and then another darted behind her car. They were still at it—playing kick-the-can in the middle of the cul-de-sac, their laughter and apologies echoing through the warm summer air, punctuated by distant calls of mothers summoning them home for dinner.

The drive across the New York City suburb of Ossining took less than ten minutes. Leanne wound past leafy streets and colonial houses with tidy lawns, until she reached her mother's unassuming home. From the outside, the residence looked just like everyone else's. It was only once you stepped through the doors that Eleanor's style collided with polite society.

Immediately, Leanne noticed the garage door was left open and empty. No sign of Eleanor's car.

Leanne cut her engine and climbed out of the Buick. Cicadas buzzed in the trees, and the sky dimmed from a burnt orange to a bruised lavender haze. She could almost picture her younger self arriving home after school or piano lessons. The front porch light wasn't on, but the faint scent of incense drifted out through an open window. The door creaked open beneath her hand as she knocked.

Leanne frowned, her chest tightening. A few weeks ago, her mother had stopped locking the door, insisting she simply forgot. Even had the audacity to joke, saying, "No one's going to rob an old woman." But to Leanne, leaving the door unlocked was an open invitation for disaster, even if her mother did live in a nice neighborhood.

She stepped inside, her kitten heels muted against the thick carpet. The house hit her like it always did: a time capsule of chaos and charm, its scent a mix of incense, old records, and something floral—jasmine or rosewater, she could never tell.

The living room unfolded in front of her—cluttered and colorful, layers of velvet throw pillows, tapestries hanging crookedly, ashtrays balanced precariously on stacks of books. Records leaned against the wall alongside framed black-and-white photos from decades past that she recognized and several that she didn't: young musicians with sly smiles, concert posters peeling slightly at the edges. She picked up one of the posters, reading the headline: *The Bell of Wartime Music.* Beside the advertisement was a photo that looked very much like a younger version of her mother.

Leanne turned in a slow circle, taking in the disarray. Her mother wasn't a neatnik, but this was...unlike her.

No one would guess a sixty-nine-year-old woman lived here. Instead, the space felt like it belonged to someone decades younger—an artist in their twenties chasing freedom.

Or someone desperately trying to hold on to their memories.

A bohemian fever dream of clashing musical eras—1920s big band met with 1960s rock and roll.

Leanne stood there, taking it all in, worry gnawing sharper at her ribs. Her mother's world seemed stitched together by threads fraying just at the edges—beautiful, yes, but fragile in ways Leanne could no longer ignore.

"Mom?"

Her voice echoed softly through the house, but no answer came. Not even the familiar pitter-patter of Roxy's feet. The strange little dog usually bounded out of the bedroom at the sound of company—but tonight, nothing.

The silence prickled along Leanne's limbs.

Stepping farther inside, she scanned the space. Besides the addition of the photos and old posters, everything appeared the same—comfortably cluttered, charming in that haphazard way only her mother could pull off. Moving to the kitchen, she let her hand brush over the pastel-pink refrigerator, the early 1950s model her mother had insisted on keeping even when the rest of the world moved on.

Mismatched mugs filled the glass-fronted cabinets—some chipped, some with old logos and designs faded from decades of use. Leanne reached up, opening the door, and straightened one absent-mindedly, her finger brushing over the musical chords painted there. That had been her favorite one as a child, and she recalled many nights of tea or hot cocoa, curled up under a blanket reading a book.

Her gaze flicked to the pink refrigerator, where a memo was tacked up by a magnet in the shape of a guitar. Eleanor Bell's initials were monogrammed in swirling purple ink at the top of the white paper. The handwritten note was unmistakably hers in black fountain ink: *Don't trust the milk.*

Leanne squinted at the oddball message, her brow knitting in puzzlement. Don't trust the milk? What did that even mean? Was it a reminder? Some sort of joke?

Leanne tugged the metal handle, opening the fridge to see a carton of milk with an expiration date of next week. The cryptic note made no sense, like so many things her mother had been saying lately.

Her unease deepened.

She made her way to the bedroom. The bed was unmade, and the ashtray on the nightstand held a lipstick-smudged cigarette burned down to the filter. The closet door hung open, a sweater sleeve drooping out, a blouse crumpled on the floor. Leanne scanned the contents of the hangers, most of the clothing dating back to her childhood.

And then she noticed the empty space on the top shelf—the suitcase was gone.

A cold ripple worked its way around every vertebra in her spine.

Between the strange, rambling jottings and her mother's missing suitcase, something was wrong, really wrong. She began riffling gently through the disarray of her mother's things, scanning for a scribbled message, a list, anything to explain her absence. The speed of her search and the sense of dread inside her both accelerating as the bedroom proved disappointingly devoid of any clues.

The bathroom was the same story. A half-empty bottle of champagne on the edge of the tub. A mirror smudged with the sort of cryptic lipstick messages her mother was always leaving herself—*Shine on, Eleanor*—but no toothbrush in the holder. The shelf where her mother's favorite perfume usually sat was empty.

Leanne's pulse quickened.

Her mother had left town without telling her. Not even a note.

That wasn't like Eleanor. Despite being free-spirited, she always let Leanne know when she was traveling and called to check in. This... felt off.

Leanne walked back toward the family room, her stomach twisting.

That's when she spotted the paper, lying half crumpled on the floor near the record player. She bent to pick it up.

Her eyes scanned the heading.

Her mother's name was typed neatly at the top followed by: *Dementia. Early Signs.*

Below was a short note from her mother's doctor explaining the symptoms, the progression, and stating Eleanor's official diagnosis. The doctor noted that Eleanor should speak to her family soon about care.

Leanne's chest tightened. Her mother was losing her memories. But more than that, at this moment, she was physically lost too. Vanished from the house without a trace of anything other than her past.

There'd been signs of Eleanor's forgetfulness, of senility, creeping in—lost keys, missed appointments, odd comments. After overhearing one of her friends at a Tupperware party discussing her own mother's dementia diagnosis, Leanne had rushed to the library to find a book. But there wasn't one, only the librarian suggesting a title on aging that had a small chapter on senile dementia and a doctor from the 1800s called Alzheimer. She'd even called her own doctor to ask him questions about it. However, the information she'd discovered had been part of why Leanne had pushed her mother to visit the doctor in the first place. But seeing the diagnosis—*dementia*—in black-and-white made it heavier. Real. More final. Like the ground had shifted beneath her feet.

With an official diagnosis, things were going to change. At first it would be little things. Forgetting. Repeating conversations. Misplacing keys. But it would progress into possibly getting lost. Mood swings. Confusion. Delusions. Unable to dress herself or recognize her family. And near the end, she'd need full-time functional care and possibly be unable to communicate. The notion that her mother would one day be a shell of the lively woman she was terrified Leanne.

It also meant that soon her mother wouldn't be able to live on her own. They'd have to make space for Eleanor at their house. And while Leanne might be sending a child off to college, she'd be responsible for another person.

Leanne swallowed hard and crossed to her mother's phone. Pulling a notepad toward her, she scribbled quickly:

Call me, Mom. Leanne

She left it by the receiver, trying for hopeful. Maybe Eleanor had just run out to buy a new toothbrush. Perhaps she'd impulsively thrown out the old suitcase like she did when she got tired of things or didn't like the color.

Leanne clung to that thought, though unease kept buzzing beneath the surface.

Her mother wouldn't leave without telling her. She just knew it.

When Leanne arrived back home, the glow of the Zenith television lit up the family room. She set her purse down on the console by the door, then glanced over at her daughter. Nora's eyes were fixed half on the flickering black-and-white screen and half on her own bare feet, propped on the coffee table, as she painted her toes. She was watching *I Dream of Jeannie.*

"How's Grandma?" Nora asked without looking away from the brush putting bright pink polish on her left big toe.

Leanne studied herself in the entryway mirror, sliding a loose hair back into place. "She wasn't home." Leanne tried to be nonchalant but was afraid the pronouncement revealed the anxiety warring inside her body. Her gaze lingered on her daughter—so young, so sure the world would always stay the same. She wished it would, just for her.

Nora finally glanced up, eyebrows knitting as she shoved the nail polish handle haphazardly back into the jar. "Where is she?"

Leanne hesitated, the words catching in her throat. How could she answer without setting off the same alarm bells in her head, inside Nora's? "I don't know. Maybe…she went on a trip."

The explanation sounded hollow, ridiculous. And ominous. Dramatically ominous, if she was being honest.

Nora snorted, eyes wide, her smile wry. She shook her head, blond hair falling into her eyes as she swept it away with the ease of an unbothered teen. "You're joking."

Leanne forced a smile, though her stomach knotted tighter than her apron strings before she hosted Dean's partners for a dinner party. She was glad that Nora thought she was joking, even if she wasn't. "Sounds crazy, doesn't it? But I'm not."

Nora shrugged, her attention already drifting back to the TV and a second coat of Revlon's Pink Sugar. "I am sure she just ran to see a friend and she'll be here for us to sing happy birthday to her soon. When's Dad coming home?"

"Soon." The lie fell easily from her lips. And Nora seemed willing to believe it, because she just kept on painting.

Leanne moved into the kitchen before Nora could ask any more questions. The room's decor was in stark contrast to her mother's pink. The Miller cabinets and counters were a respectable ivory. A perfect replica of Julia Child's Queen of Sheba chocolate cake sat on the cake stand beneath its glass dome, waiting for Eleanor's celebration.

She needed to telephone Dean, her fingers itching to reach for the phone. She picked up the receiver, twisting the cord tightly around her index finger—a nervous habit she hadn't outgrown since her teens. His secretary answered, brisk but polite, and transferred her without question.

Dean always took her calls. No matter how late he worked or how many nights he spent in the city. She supposed that counted for something.

"Leanne?" Dean's voice was curt and hurried on the other end of the line. "Everything okay? I've got a meeting in a minute."

Leanne pressed the receiver tighter to her ear, her eyes drifting closed for a minute as her chest tightened with longing. Longing for the time when he actually worried about her. Cared about her. Wanted to talk to her. "My mother's gone somewhere."

There was a pause on the other end that lasted a thousand years. Finally, he said, "Like the grocery store?"

Leanne swallowed, forcing her voice steady. "Only if people take suitcases to the grocery store." The absurd image of a line of people hauling their suitcases by the handle through produce flashed in her mind.

Dean exhaled rather audibly—whether it was a sigh of concern or annoyance, she couldn't tell. "Let me get this straight. You think your mother stood you up for her birthday?"

"Maybe. I'm going to call a few of her friends. She might have told them something. It's possible I missed her message." Leanne blamed herself even if she knew she wasn't at fault here. "But, Dean, I think she may have gone on a trip. Out of town."

Before today, Leanne would have said with confidence that her mother wouldn't have up and gone on a holiday without a word. But after visiting the house, seeing the weird notes and disarray, discovering the diagnosis lying on the floor. She couldn't confidently rule it out.

"Okay. Let me know if you need anything." He was already slipping away, distancing himself from her and her concerns. The evidence was in his tone, even in the way his voice drifted.

Leanne hung up, the phone heavy in her hand.

She spent the next hour dialing every name she could think of—her mother's oldest friends, neighbors, anyone who might have seen Eleanor. Each conversation ended the same: polite concern, but no one had heard from her. No one knew where she was.

By morning, when her mother's house was still empty, the sheets on the bed still rumpled from two nights before, panic began to bloom in Leanne's chest. A panic that was impossible to ignore.

She called the police, who told her she was overreacting and refused to put in a report. Leanne did one more sweep of her mother's house, and she found a piece of crumpled paper in the trash she hadn't seen before. This couldn't be real. And yet there it was in black-and-white: *The Pink Flamingo, Los Angeles, California.*

"Oh, God, California? Really, Mom?"

Scribbled beneath the name of the motel were a few things that looked like maybe…songs? Leanne had no idea, but she knew one person who might. Her daughter.

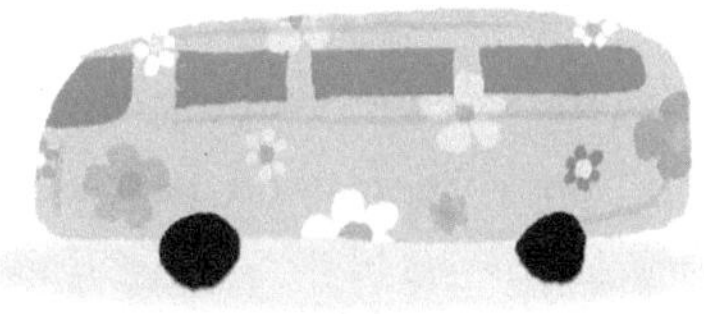

CHAPTER THREE

NORA SMOOTHED THE FINAL PHOTO ONTO THE COLlage, her fingertips lingering on the corners like she could press the memories into permanence. A memory already slipping, soft around the edges—like a Polaroid left too long in the sun.

A snapshot of her and her friends, sunburned and half drowned from their graduation canoe trip, grinning like they'd conquered something bigger than just high school. They'd just spent a few days pretending the next step toward the real world wasn't waiting right around the corner, ready to slap them with tuition bills and disappointing boyfriends. At least they had the entire summer to savor before college and adulthood had them bowing out of a party at the lake in favor of a decent bedtime.

The entire summer was planned out for her and her friends. Beach time, shopping, convincing their parents to let them attend a music festival, and plenty of girl time gossiping about celebrities and swooning over Dustin Hoffman and Bobby Sherman.

In the background, the Beatles' *Abbey Road* played on the record player she'd gotten for her sixteenth birthday, and she hummed along.

Her mom had come along on the graduation trip, labeled the designated "cool parent"—meaning she brought bologna sandwiches in wax paper and kept to the sidelines with a quiet, practiced smile. Nora appreciated that her mom understood her need for independence. But sometimes, just sometimes, Nora wished she didn't. Wished she'd stepped in a little more, asked a few extra questions, and acted like she actually wanted to know what was going on in Nora's life instead of just standing at the edges, looking…tired.

Not a tiredness sleep could cure, but one that settled deep in the bones—like carrying something heavy for too long without knowing how to set it down. God, she hoped she never ended up like that.

Had her mom even realized this was Nora's last summer at home? The last summer before she was supposed to go off and become someone entirely new—someone smarter, bolder?

Nora flopped onto her bed. Absent-mindedly, she traced the soft floral pastels of her bedroom wallpaper. The delicate pattern was a relic of her childhood, peeking out from behind tacked-up posters of rock bands she loved and magazine clippings of movie stars. The whole room felt like a silent tug-of-war between the girl she used to be and the woman she was trying to become.

She'd suggested redecorating once, floating the idea like a test balloon, but her mom had just given her a look—not quite a no, but something even heavier. Like the thought of changing Nora's room was too much, as if tearing down the girlish wallpaper and repainting would make her leaving all too real. And so, the flowery wallpaper remained, along with the unspoken weight of her mother's sadness.

Without considering why, Nora got up and began taking down the faded bits of celebrity-worshipping newspaper. There was a postcard on her wall, a snapshot of her and Grandma from that trip they'd taken together. They'd gone to London for her sixteenth, and Nora remembered the excitement of traveling abroad—how the air smelled like adventure, and rules felt optional. Nora plucked it down, flipping it over to reread the message scrawled in her grandmother's tight, looping script. *For my fearless girl—always choose the scenic route.* A grin tugged at her lips. Grandma's words were always sharp and clever like she was letting you in on some secret joke. She wasn't a rule follower.

If only her mother had inherited even half of that free, peregrine spirit. Nora had brushed off her mom's suggestion that Grandma had gone anywhere more exciting than out to run an errand. But now that Eleanor still hadn't turned up, Nora hoped she was wrong. That Grandma was off gallivanting on a fabulous solo adventure—drinking wine in Italy, riding camels in Egypt, or attending a concert for that new band Led Zeppelin. Wouldn't that be a hoot? Meanwhile, her mom was downstairs, wringing her hands, acting like a sixty-nine-year-old woman needed a permission slip to live her life.

Classic Leanne Miller, trying to control what was never meant to be contained.

Nora put the postcard back on the wall. Grandma would be fine. She always was.

Fall was coming; then she too could escape. Leave this wallpapered suburban fishbowl and begin her freshman year at Yale.

Yale. As in centuries-old, buttoned-up, boys'-club Yale.

For the first time in its storied, pipe-smoke-scented history, they were admitting women into the undergraduate program. A handful. A whisper of estrogen in a sea of testosterone and tweed.

She was fully aware she'd be one of the few. One of the first. And she was so ready for it. She could practically taste the dry, musty air of Sterling Memorial Library.

Nora had the grades, the ambition, and a bookshelf lined with Austen, Baldwin, and Simone de Beauvoir to prove she could hold her own. She'd clawed her way into the Ivy League with nothing but determination, a dictionary, and the lingering sting of every boy who ever told her she talked too much while she silently corrected their grammar in her head.

She wasn't scared. Not of being the only girl in a lecture hall full of men. Not of professors who might pat her on the head instead of taking her seriously. And not of going it alone, with no best friend from home to soften the edges of the unknown.

She was ready. Thrilled, even.

But until then, there were the long, humid days of summer. One more season of borrowed time with Kelley and her other friends. A summer to get sunburned noses and tell inside jokes. Kelley was planning another trip to the lake that Nora didn't want to miss—skinny-dipping optional, sneaking boys in, stealing cigarettes from older siblings, maybe sipping her first beer sitting in the sand. She'd been too focused on grades to try it on Friday nights. One last epic summer trip before everyone shipped off to college or, in the case of some boys, overseas to fight in Vietnam.

Below, a door slammed, pulling Nora from her fantasy of a shirtless older boy, sitting beside her on the dock offering her a sip of his Miller High Life.

Nora listened to the rhythmic staccato of her mother's heels clacking against the foyer tile—purposeful, perfectly timed, like a dozen punctuation marks.

Nora picked up her journal and pen, twirling the pen cap between her fingers, the blank page glaring back. The paper was slightly warped from the summer humidity. She flipped through older entries. Most of them were rants, partial poems, or lines she swore she'd one day use in a novel no one would be allowed to read until after her death.

Going back to today's page, she tapped the pen against her chin, then scrawled:

Summer of 1969. Still stuck in suburbia.

As a student at Yale, she officially planned to go into marketing like her father, though she wanted to write copy for shiny ads rather than sell them. That's what she told her parents, anyway. It was the easiest way to explain the minor in English she planned in addition to her major in business and communications.

But the truth was, she wanted to write fiction. Invent lives, rewrite endings. Create female characters who didn't smile when they didn't want to.

She wasn't sure her parents would understand that—or, worse, they would understand and try to kill the dream slowly with phrases like "backup plan" or "don't get your hopes up."

So, she told them what they wanted to hear, because placating them had become a second language.

A soft knock, followed by the door creaking open, and her mother's face appeared, eyes heavy and posture tight.

"Did Grandma call while I was out?" Leanne's voice was barely above a whisper.

Nora lowered her pen. "You mean while you were at her house again?"

She didn't mean to sound sharp. Okay, maybe she did. Her mother had been spiraling over this for days now, and Nora couldn't decide if it was genuine concern or another way for Leanne to control things that didn't want to be controlled.

"She's still not home, Nora. It's been three days." Leanne stepped into the room fully now, arms crossed. "I called the police. They didn't seem particularly interested."

Nora rolled her eyes. "Grandmothers are allowed to disappear if they want to. She probably just needed space. She's kind of a free spirit, ya know?" Nora recalled afternoons of dancing barefoot in a patch of dandelions, followed by singing sessions around a campfire with marshmallows crisping on long sticks foraged in the yard. Her grandmother had always seemed to be so free and yet so…trapped.

Leanne let out a long, uneven breath. "It's just that—" But her mother's lips tightened as her demeanor shifted.

Nora sat up straighter on the bed, the sarcasm draining from her throat. "What is it?" she asked. "Is there something wrong with Grandma?"

Her mother rubbed her temple, pressing her fingers hard into the skin like she could force coherence into her thoughts. Then, slowly, she looked up.

"She's not well," Leanne said. "Not mentally. I found a note from the doctor's office at her house. She's been diagnosed with dementia. I think…I think we need to find her."

Panic pressed against Nora's ribs. *Dementia?* "Where would we even start?"

"California. I found this note crumpled in the trash at her house." Leanne's voice was tight. She held up a torn scrap of paper, the margin jagged like it had been ripped from a larger thought.

Nora scanned the slanted, unmistakable handwriting. The identical looping cursive that Eleanor had signed her name within every hand-painted birthday card and the postcard on her wall. *The Pink Flamingo.*

Nora wrinkled her nose. "What's the Pink Flamingo?"

"A hotel in California." There was an edge to her mother's voice, like she might just crack at any minute.

"Why would Grandma write down the name of a hotel in California?"

Leanne's mouth tightened, the line of her lipstick disappearing, and for a second, she looked like she might cry. "I think it has something to do with the songs."

Nora looked down again. Below the hotel name, her grandmother had scrawled a short playlist: *Purple Haze. Proud Mary. With a Little Help From My Friends.*

Nora's chest gave a small thump. "I love those songs."

"Any idea what they have to do with the Pink Flamingo? Or California?" Leanne's eyes shimmered, and she wiped at them quickly, as if acknowledging her emotion might make it worse.

Nora didn't comment. Her mother hated being seen while unraveling.

Instead, she hopped off her bed and crossed the room, grabbing the latest issue of *Rolling Stone* from her desk. The cover was already curling from overuse.

"Yeah. I think I do." She flipped rapidly through the glossy pages until she reached what she'd been obsessing over the day before: a two-page spread filled with names, bands, bright colors, and promises of noise and liberation. There was no way her parents would let her go, but a girl could dream.

"The Newport Pop Festival. It's starts later this week in California."

She held the magazine open, showing her mother the full-color ad she'd practically drooled over, tracing the band names like prayers. Janis Joplin. Jimi Hendrix. Creedence. Joe Cocker. The Byrds. The gods of music, and the concert was the altar at which the fans could worship them.

"There's another one at the end of summer," she added, chewing her lip. This was the one she'd been banking on attending. "Woodstock. But that's in New York." Her voice dropped, wistful. Half her graduating class planned to be there. Some of them planned on wearing "Make Love, Not War" T-shirts in protest of their friends being sent to fight in Vietnam. She, Kelley, and the others were already planning a campaign to attend. They had to be strategic, their parents so strict about where they went and with whom. Most of the time, Nora's mother called the bands she loved "heathens."

Leanne stared at the ad, her lips parting slightly. "That's a lot of festivals."

"You don't really think Grandma went to one, do you?" Nora asked, the question hanging between skepticism, awe, and hope. If her grandmother knew she had dementia, why would she risk it? The woman was smart—there had to be some reason…

Leanne didn't answer right away. She stared down at the note again, the shaky handwriting, the songs—like breadcrumbs leading to some secret version of her mother she'd never been able to follow.

"She loves music," Leanne said finally, almost to herself. "She always has. Maybe she felt like after the visit with the doctor that she had to do this. I think she…I think she really went to California. Her car is still gone. God if she drove…"

Nora didn't know what to say. It wasn't just the idea of Eleanor going rogue that stunned her—it was the strange gleam in her mother's eyes. Fear. Determination. Maybe a little envy. There was an uncontrolledness about it that had Nora standing up a little taller.

"I need to go after her." Leanne squared her shoulders as if expecting her daughter to say she was crazy, and maybe she was a little bit. "She's not safe alone."

Nora didn't argue. She just nodded slowly, watching her mother like she'd suddenly become someone from a different planet.

Or maybe just someone who finally realized her mother had a whole secret side of herself that Nora wasn't privy to.

"I'll see if Dad wants to go," her mother said, disappearing down the hallway.

Not an hour later, there was another knock at the door. Softer this time. Hesitant.

Leanne peeked her head in. "Any chance you want to go on a road trip?"

Nora stared at her for a long second. "A what?"

"A road trip. To California. To find Grandma."

A road trip.

With her mother.

To track down her possibly-losing-her-mind, possibly-rock-fanatic runaway grandmother.

Across the country. In the summer heat. In a station wagon.

Or she could be at the lake with Kelley and the girls, drinking ice-cold Coca-Cola, talking about boys they didn't really like, and making memories to last her through the fall and winter at Yale until break.

This was not how she'd seen her last summer going, and she felt guilty for being disappointed. She should care about her grandmother; she should want to help her mother. And yet, she was just barely eighteen and had a whole fun summer planned with her friends. Then again… This was a chance to possibly go to a music festival she'd never dared to think her parents would let her attend.

Nora glanced at the photo of herself with her grandmother in front of Tower Bridge in London, recalling the excitement, the pure joy of that moment. "When do we leave?"

CHAPTER FOUR

ELEANOR HADN'T EXPECTED BUYING A PLANE TICKET to be so easy.

She simply walked up to the Pan American airline counter and paid in cash—an entire wad of bills she'd kept tucked in a handkerchief drawer in the back of her closet. The woman behind the counter barely paid her any attention. Within minutes, Eleanor was holding a ticket to California. No complications.

Almost too simple for something so…monumental.

She boarded the plane with her guitar, hoisting it carefully into the overhead rack with the help of a flight attendant and whispering a silent prayer that, even though it was in its hard case, it wouldn't get crushed mid-flight. Then she slid into her window seat, where she was soon joined by a young man in a narrow tie and a college-aged girl wearing bell-bottoms and wire-rimmed glasses. The girl reminded Eleanor of Nora—not so much in looks but because she radiated the same quiet, restless ambition.

For a fleeting breath, guilt threatened to bubble up inside Eleanor. She pictured her daughter arriving at the house, trying to make sense of where she'd gone. But the feeling passed. Eleanor had spent the majority of her adult life doing for others, making sure Leanne felt secure and loved. Now it was time to do something for herself.

She unwrapped a peppermint and popped it into her mouth, the cool sting spreading across her tongue. She offered the tin to her seatmates. The businessman accepted one with a nod of thanks. The girl declined, flipping a page in her book, lost in whatever world was printed in her lap.

The plane taxied down the runway at about four thousand miles per hour. Eleanor gripped the armrests as if that might stop the impending crash. She hadn't remembered until right now—this was her first time flying.

The thought startled her. The process had felt so smooth, so shockingly easy, that she hadn't even stopped to realize she was doing something she'd never done before.

The engine's roar built to a howl, rumbling the blue-cushioned seat beneath her. Then they lurched forward, tilting up into the sky.

She was airborne.

For the first time in decades, she felt the sharp ache of possibility crack open inside her.

Was she flying back in time—to a version of herself she'd never gotten to fully become? Or forward into a future that still had room for change?

Maybe both.

The young man beside her must have noticed her white-knuckled grip on the armrest. He reached over and gently patted her hand.

"You okay, ma'am?"

She turned to him, blinking. Then she smiled. A real one. Wide and a little wild.

"Never better," Eleanor replied.

"Where are you headed?" the young man asked, his voice easy, casual.

Eleanor shifted in her chair, her lips twitching. "Newport Pop Festival."

Saying it aloud for the first time was freeing and a little rebellious, and his reaction was worth the admission.

His eyebrows lifted, a grin hitching the corner of his mouth. "Are you meeting someone there?"

Eleanor tutted, giving him a sidelong glance. Did he really believe the only way it was possible for her to attend the festival was with someone else? Likely, he thought someone younger. "You sure do ask a lot of questions."

He blushed slightly, caught off guard by her bluntness, and chuckled. "Just curious, ma'am. Can't quite picture my grandma heading to a pop music festival is all."

"Well," she said, unwrapping another peppermint, hoping to settle her stomach, "maybe you should ask your grandma if she's a fan of Jimi Hendrix."

He grinned. "I think I will—soon as I get off this plane." There was a brief pause before he asked, "Do you play music?"

"I did," Eleanor said softly, her eyes drifting to the clouds beyond the window, noting one resembling a rabbit. She loved to look at the clouds and imagine the possibilities of what creatures might float by—a game she'd played with Leanne when her daughter still allowed herself to have an imagination.

Unbidden, her fingers tapped against the armrest, itching as if they could still feel the fingerboard beneath them. She thought back to fairgrounds shows and vaudeville stages, the weight of a guitar strap across her shoulders, the way a song once flowed from her like water.

"Do you still?"

A beat. Then, "I think I do."

He tilted his head, bemused. "Think?"

For a second, Eleanor faltered. The memories blurred—not lost, but jumbled. But then she saw herself, just yesterday, standing in her closet, pulling the old Gibson from its hiding place, her fingers brushing the strings. She remembered the way it had come back to her—like muscle memory, like breath.

The girl who played had never really left. She'd just been quiet for a while.

"I do," she said finally, with more conviction. "I do play."

"I'm sure you're wonderful."

Eleanor smiled at that, surprised by how much she wanted someone—anyone—to hear her. "Would you like to hear me play?"

"Are you performing at the festival?"

She laughed, warm and unguarded. "I doubt they've got a spot saved for me."

"I heard there's going to be a free stage for anyone who wants to jam," he said. "You could sign up."

Eleanor raised an eyebrow, amused. "That so?"

He nodded, earnest now. "Absolutely. You should do it."

She let the thought settle like a stone dropped in water. An open mic. A crowd. A chance.

Why shouldn't she?

She looked out the window again. The sun was just beginning to dip, casting golden light across the airplane's wing.

"I just might," she said.

"Do you have your guitar with you?" the young man asked.

Eleanor tilted her head, narrowing her eyes. "How do you know I play guitar?"

He nodded toward her hands. "The pick," he said. "Dead giveaway."

She looked down at her fingers, where she held on to her old chestnut-colored guitar pick, with "The Gibson" engraved on one side, worn down from her thumb rubbing across it. She smiled.

"Well, aren't you observant."

"Let's hear it then, ma'am."

Without hesitation, Eleanor stood, reaching into the overhead storage rack and pulling her guitar case down, careful not to jostle it. A muffled bark erupted from underneath the seat in front of her and inside her half-zipped carry-on bag.

Heads turned in her direction.

Roxy. Whom she'd snuck onto the plane…

She bent down to the soft tote just enough to peek inside. "Shh," she whispered. "You're a stowaway, remember?" She handed her dog a biscuit from the outside pocket, and Roxy greedily gobbled it up.

Passengers craned their necks, a few smiling, some shaking their heads, but Eleanor was already kneeling in the aisle. She opened the guitar case and ran her hand along the smooth wood—mahogany darkened by age, the scent of worn lacquer and tobacco still clinging faintly to the grain. Her fingers lingered over the delicate inlay of the name carved into the headstock: *Euterpe*. She'd named the guitar decades ago, after the Greek goddess of music, back when she believed naming things gave them power.

"What do you want to hear?" she asked, tuning the Gibson with deft, practiced fingers.

"'Twinkle, Twinkle, Little Star'!" shouted a child from a few rows back.

Eleanor laughed, nodding. "All right, maestra."

She plucked the familiar notes, slow and sweet, giving the nursery rhyme a gentle blues twist. The cabin filled with giggles and scattered applause. A chorus of other requests followed—"Old MacDonald," "The Itsy Bitsy Spider"—and she played each with theatrical flair.

Then someone called out, "Something classical!"

Eleanor smiled with pride, her mind percolating for a second, and then she easily shifted into the opening bars of Beethoven's "Für Elise"—Henry's favorite. Her fingers danced along the strings. The melody rang out crisp and bright, her years of playing whispering through every note, every night of playing in the twilight with lightning bugs dancing around. The contrast between the playful children's songs and the structured elegance of Beethoven lifted her heart along with the memory she wished to freeze in front of her like a picture.

And then—without thinking, without asking—she eased into something more modern.

"Piece of My Heart," originally recorded by Erma Franklin, and recently covered by Janis Joplin. The chords emerged, fierce and electric. The song had been a regular companion on the radio lately, Janis and Erma both having the kind of voices that made you feel like your ribs were cracking open just to make room. Eleanor didn't have sheet music; she didn't need it. She'd played this one alone, countless nights in the dark, until the shape of it lived in her bones.

Someone in the back of the plane stood and belted out the chorus:

"Take another little piece of my heart, baby!"

Another voice joined. Then another. Before long, the entire back half of the plane was humming and clapping along. Eleanor kept strumming, her heart soaring with every note, the whole cabin echoing with a chorus of strangers who suddenly felt like a band, like the audiences she missed playing for.

By the time they touched down, she had half a dozen new friends, three promises to find her at the festival; and one woman who asked for her autograph—"just in case."

All that was left now was figuring out how to get onstage.

That part, Eleanor suspected, might take a little more magic.

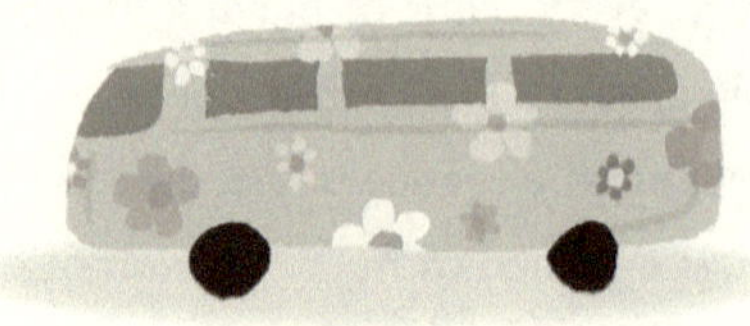

CHAPTER FIVE

IT HAD BEEN DEAN'S IDEA TO TAKE THE LINCOLN Continental.

Leanne had assumed they'd hop on a plane and chase her mother to California with tickets booked and bags checked, like reasonable people. But Dean, ever the strategist, had offered something different.

"If your mother drove cross-country, you might run into her along the way. Besides, this is the perfect chance to get Nora alone," he'd contended. "Talk to her. Really talk. About her future."

An unexpected suggestion from a man who spent most of his life behind glass walls in Manhattan. Dean was distant on the best days—home in body, absent in almost every other way. But he wasn't wrong.

There had been a growing silence between Leanne and Nora for months. A cold draft of emotional distance neither of them seemed willing to name. At the end of the summer, Nora would leave for Yale, beginning her launch into life. The part where she peeled away. The part where she figured out who she was and wanted to become. The part where she might find a reason never to come home again.

Leanne wasn't ready for that.

She was proud that Nora would be among Yale's first class of women—making history just by unpacking her books. But that pride wouldn't keep Leanne warm at night. Pride wouldn't replace the sound of her daughter's footsteps overhead or the giggles as she gossiped with her girlfriends on the telephone.

Leanne carried her suitcase down the stairs, the worn handle warm in her trembling palm. A trace of Aqua Net and pressed linen lingered in the hallway, the scent of them setting off into the unknown. The more time that passed without knowing what had happened to her mother, the less Leanne was able to quell the shaking of her hands.

Dean was waiting at the door—buttoned-up, unreadable. He took the suitcase from her without a word and carried it to the trunk of the cherry-red Continental, the chrome grille catching the early morning light like a sneer.

"Remember," he said, closing the trunk with a solid thunk. "This is a great opportunity."

Leanne nodded. What she really wanted to do was ask: *When will* you *take the opportunity to get to know your daughter?*

Or better yet: *When will you make time to know me again?*

But she didn't say any of it. She never did.

They hadn't been on a vacation in years. Hadn't been on a date in nearly as long. He was already walking away, checking his watch, silently declaring that handling this situation was just another box to tick in a day full of needed checkmarks. Meanwhile her mother could be dead in a ditch.

Leanne lingered on the porch, breathing in the scent of summer and possibilities, trying to quell the pounding of her heart behind her ribs. She refused to indulge in bitter thoughts about her husband or terrifying thoughts of her mother. Not when she was about to embark on a cross-country road trip with her daughter. Because as much as she hated to admit it, Dean was right. This was an opportunity. Maybe it was her last real chance to close the growing gap between her and Nora. And, they were going to find her mother in one piece. Resolute on those two things, she went to stand beside, but not really next to, her husband and the car.

The front door swung open, and Nora bounded out and down the porch steps, suitcase in hand, canvas backpack slung over a shoulder. She looked up at her parents, her smile flickering as she sensed the tension in the air.

Were they really that obvious?

Leanne slid toward her husband, slipping her arm through his and resting her head lightly on his shoulder. The gesture felt stiff and performative, like something from a magazine ad: "Perfect Family Sends Daughter Off in Style."

"Do you have to do that out here?" Nora muttered, rolling her eyes and stuffing her suitcase into the trunk.

As she tossed her backpack onto the front seat, Dean stepped away from Leanne and held out his arms. "Come here, kiddo."

Nora sank into the embrace automatically, the way she had since she was small. Her cheek pressed against his lapel, her eyes softening, the mask slipping ever so slightly. Leanne saw the trust there. The simplicity. For better or worse, Dean loved their daughter.

"Be safe," Dean said over their daughter's shoulder before letting go of Nora. "Call me as soon as you arrive at the first hotel. If anything goes wrong, you know what to do. I've got a full map in the glove box and a list of approved hotel stops. All organized."

Leanne nodded. She was quietly grateful Dean had asked his secretary to pull everything together, because she just didn't have it in her.

In a practiced move that came with nearly two decades of marriage, she reached up and smoothed a hand over Dean's sharply tailored shoulder. His ever-present suit jacket was pressed to perfection, buttoned high, collar crisp, tie knotted with surgical precision. Dean wore his clothes like armor—always had.

What would happen if he loosened his tie? Would the man beneath all that structure unravel?

Then she glanced down at herself—nipped-in waist, pale linen dress, the familiar cool weight of pearls against her collarbone. She was no better. Buttoned-up in her own way. Contained.

Maybe this trip wasn't just about finding her mother.

Maybe it was about finding herself.

Dean dangled the keys before her, the metal glinting in the early sun. "Remember to go easy on the clutch," he said. "And if you want to put the top down, take a look at the manual—I highlighted the pages with pictures."

Leanne nodded. "We probably won't take the top down," she replied, shaking her head with a rueful laugh.

The top of the car, she suspected, would stay just as tightly fastened as her belt. As buttoned-up as her marriage.

Nora tapped the roof of the Lincoln with her palm. "Don't worry, Dad. I fully plan to make Mom drive with the top down all the way through the Midwest. I want to feel that sun on my skin. If I'm going to be trapped in a car, I'm coming back with a tan."

Leanne laughed—her voice a little too high, a little too forced. She could already feel the arguments waiting to unfold like road maps across the plains. Nora had agreed to go on this trip with her, but Leanne knew what her daughter was giving up—one last summer with her friends.

Maybe Leanne needed to start making concessions now, in gratitude for her daughter's sacrifice.

"I might be persuaded to let you put it down," she said, smoothing her skirt with a small smile. "Once or twice."

Nora raised an eyebrow. "Oh, really? I'll believe that when I see it."

She climbed into the passenger seat and slammed the door with purpose.

Dean leaned in for a goodbye kiss. Leanne offered him a polite peck—brief, closed-mouth, practiced.

When was the last time they'd kissed like they meant it? Probably sometime around the Eisenhower administration. Or was it Truman? She couldn't remember. Maybe not since Nora was conceived.

Dean stepped back with a smile that was more habit than heat. "Enjoy the trip. I hear Nora's packed *The Godfather* for the road."

"Yes, I packed a book too," Leanne said, mildly amused.

"I trust you're packing something more…refined."

Leanne turned her back to him, slipping into the driver's seat. She didn't bother answering. Let him believe she packed *Good Housekeeping* if it helped him sleep better at night.

In truth, *The Love Machine* was buried deep in her purse—bold, dog-eared, and buzzing with a female energy she'd long since personally repressed.

He'd always been dismissive of her reading choices—calling them trash, lowbrow, fantasy nonsense. If Dean had acted even remotely like Jacqueline Susann's smoldering anti-heroes, maybe she'd give him more than a goodbye peck on the lips.

She adjusted the mirror and started the engine as Nora began flipping through the opening pages of *The Godfather*, her long legs propped on the dash like she had all the time in the world.

Then Leanne pulled out of the driveway, a quiet, intrepid thrill humming beneath her pearls.

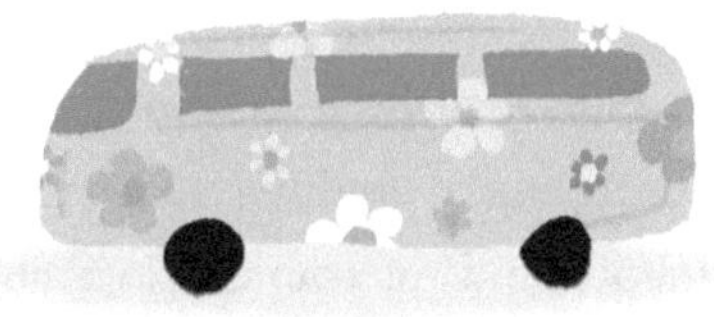

CHAPTER SIX

NORA WATCHED HER MOTHER'S TIGHT AND AWKWARD hands on the steering wheel—as if she'd never driven a car before. She wanted to ask what she was worried about, but she bit her tongue. The answer was obvious. While Nora believed her grandmother had gone off on a grand adventure, her mother believed Eleanor had likely been abducted or worse. Besides, they were only fifteen minutes into at least a three-day road trip to California, not to mention the ride back. The last thing Nora wanted was to spend the entire drive locked in silent warfare over something dumb.

Reaching forward, she switched on the radio. The dial buzzed and clicked, then settled into the warm hum of rock and roll—Jefferson Airplane's "White Rabbit"—pouring from the speakers in scratchy stereo. Nora braced for a groan, a sigh, a predictably passive-aggressive comment about "noise" or "those drugged-up musicians."

But none came.

In fact, looking over at her mom out of the corner of her eye, Nora would almost swear she saw her mother's lips twitch upward.

They were chasing Eleanor just like Alice was chasing the white rabbit, like the song lyrics…

The truth was, Nora had been kind of pissed about this whole thing. Her mom dropping everything to chase Eleanor across the country felt…dramatic. And, of course, Nora couldn't say no. That would've made her the selfish one. The ungrateful daughter. The one who let her possibly senile grandmother vanish into the California sunset with nothing but a playlist and a dream.

Kelley had been as disappointed to hear Nora tell her she wasn't going to the lake this weekend as Nora had been to tell it. The only consolation was that she was going to a music festival, maybe more than one, and Kelley wanted a picture of Nora near the stage.

Watching their neighborhood slip past the windows—sprinklers hissing, boys on bikes weaving between driveways—something shifted. Nora had never admitted it out loud, but the idea of seeing Janis Joplin or Joe Cocker in person made her stomach flip. She'd read about them in *Rolling Stone* and studied their photos like they were gods. And now she was heading west, toward the sound.

She tapped her fingers along the dashboard in rhythm with the song, her voice soft at first, then growing louder with the chorus. Her mother said nothing—but the nascent smile on her lips grew.

Maybe this wouldn't be completely terrible.

Or maybe it would. By the fourth song, Nora felt the familiar itch of restlessness. She picked her copy of *The Godfather* back off her lap where she'd laid it, running her fingers over the black cover and gold lettering. She was still shocked that her mom had agreed to let her read it aloud on the road. It wasn't exactly *Little Women*.

She'd first picked it up last year in English class during their "choose-your-own-book" unit—a rare rebellion from the usual syllabus of dead British men. Her teacher hadn't exactly been thrilled.

He had likely expected Austen. Maybe Woolf. Possibly something "respectable," like *To Kill a Mockingbird* or *A Room of One's Own.*

Instead, Nora had slapped down a Mafia saga full of blood, sex, betrayal, and men who made decisions with their fists. It was dark. Violent. Raunchy. And absolutely intoxicating.

The teacher, Mr. Boone, had raised an eyebrow. "Are you sure, Nora?"

She'd nodded without flinching. "Positive."

Because what she loved wasn't just the crime or the swagger—it was the storytelling. The pulse of it. The way the book moved—no frilly subtext, no polite metaphors. Just pure power in every sentence. *The Godfather* was the first book that made her feel like storytelling could be dangerous.

And she'd started a trend.

By the next day, two other students had walked in with their own dog-eared copies, Mafia-style grins as they slid the paperbacks onto their desks like contraband. Mr. Boone had bristled, clearly rattled by the sudden literary mutiny, and Nora was sure he'd scrap the whole assignment, and reimpose top-down order.

But in the end, he'd let it stand.

Now, curled into the passenger seat of an outlandish red Lincoln Continental rumbling west on the highway, she cracked open the book to page one and prepared to narrate the story aloud.

She just hoped she wouldn't get carsick. Reading in the car had never bothered her when her dad was driving. But her mother's style behind the wheel was...different. As if on cue, her mother changed lanes in a not so smooth fashion.

"Ready for me to start?" Nora asked, looking over at her mom and wondering for a second whether there was more to the woman behind the wheel than tight waistbands and Jell-O molds, and coming to the conclusion there wasn't.

Leanne glanced over with a glint in her eyes that Nora hardly recognized. It hit her with a weird sort of nostalgia, like a half-remembered winter evening. Snow piled high outside, cocoa cooling beside the fire, and her mother reading aloud from a library book while she curled under a blanket. Before things got more complicated. Before everyone got so tired.

"I am ready." Leanne's voice was mischievous but at the same time almost conspiratorial. "But first, I want you to see what I brought." She nodded toward her purse, nestled between them on the bench seat.

Nora raised an eyebrow and reached over, flipping open the clasp.

Nestled among tissues, a compact mirror, a tube of lipstick, and a roll of Certs peppermints, was a hardback with a cracked spine. Drawing it out, Nora inspected the cover like it might singe her fingers. *Holy crap.*

There was a close-up photograph of a man's hand clasping a woman's, the image tight and intimate. Something about how his fingers curled around hers—possessive, urgent—made Nora's face go hot.

There was no mistaking the intent.

It wasn't just a handhold.

It was sex.

Angsty, glossy, unapologetic sex.

Her eyes drifted to the ring on the man's finger—bold, gold, and centered with a strange symbol she recognized immediately from her world history unit: the ankh, the ancient Egyptian sign for life. Eternal life. Fertility. Vitality.

On the cover model's hand, though, it didn't feel sacred.

It felt carnal.

Like a promise.

At the top of the cover, Jacqueline Susann was stamped in bold, black, uppercase letters—like the author was daring you to judge her.

Just below the photograph, in a sultry serif font, sat the title: *The Love Machine*.

Nora swallowed. For a book her mom had casually thrown into a road trip bag, this thing was…loaded. And she thought she was being rebellious with *The Godfather*.

"Mom, you're kidding." Her voice carried the packed, dramatic weight of a teenage girl who had just discovered she was trapped in a car with her mother—and her mother's racy romance novel. Nora looked across at her mother as though she'd just confessed to smuggling something indecent across state lines.

Leanne laughed, the same full, unbothered laugh that used to echo through the kitchen when she was baking or dancing to Dusty Springfield on the radio. "Don't knock it till you try it, hon. I promise—we'll get through *The Godfather* first, but that one's next."

Nora groaned, flopping back in her seat like a martyr.

Except…

She wasn't entirely uncurious.

Because truthfully?

She had seen the book before—on her mother's nightstand more than once, the cover half hidden under *Good Housekeeping*. She'd even flipped through it once while her parents were at a dinner party—going just enough to hit a page that made her cheeks burn and her pulse race. The idea of reading it in front of her father was mortifying. But here, with just her mother and a long stretch of highway?

If her mother was game, she'd play along.

After all, what eighteen-year-old girl headed off to college wasn't curious about something called *The Love Machine*?

She smirked. "Fine. But I'm doing voices."

"I'd expect nothing less," Leanne replied, almost serious. "But first—the Mafia."

Nora opened the book to read, smoothing down the pages with her palm.

"A quote from Balzac: 'Behind every great fortune there is a crime.'" She paused, glancing out toward the cars that sped past them. "Do you think that's true, about fortune and crime?"

This was something she'd wanted to ask in class but had been afraid her teacher would think it was a silly, immature question.

"No." Leanne gave a subtle shake of her head. "Some people earn their fortunes honestly."

"But are those fortunes considered great?"

Leanne shrugged. "Depends on your definition of great."

"My teacher said the inclusion of the quote was a critique of capitalism."

"Hmm." Leanne adjusted her grip on the steering wheel. "I can see that. Maybe Balzac meant that enormous wealth—the kind that builds empires—usually steps on someone along the way."

"He was French," Nora added, half grinning. "And they did have that whole revolution thing."

Leanne laughed. "True. But he might also have meant that success where no account is offered of how it was earned can conveniently hide a crime. Depends on the translation, I guess."

Nora tilted her head, a little surprised. "That's...actually a good point."

Leanne shrugged, giving a half smile. "Actually? But thanks. And since we're diving into a Mafia novel, let's just say for the purposes of examining the quote in context, that we're talking high-stakes crime."

Nora grinned. Her mom actually seemed excited about the book. Maybe even...interested.

"All right, Mrs. Miller," Nora said with mock formality. "Let's do this."

Leanne glanced sidelong in her direction. "All right, Miss Miller. Proceed."

Nora cleared her throat, sitting up straighter. "'Amerigo Bonasera sat in New York Criminal Court Number 3 and waited for justice; vengeance on the men who had so cruelly hurt his daughter, who had tried to dishonor her.'"

The words spilled from her lips effortlessly—she'd read this page so many times it had practically imprinted on her brain.

She didn't say it out loud, but every time she read that line, she wondered what it would feel like to have a father who wanted vengeance for her. Who burned with fury at the thought of her being harmed. Who couldn't stand the idea of someone touching her without love.

She knew her father loved her. That wasn't the issue.

The issue was…sometimes she wondered if she existed to him when she was out of sight.

And worse—if her mother did either.

CHAPTER SEVEN

THE HOT, DRY CALIFORNIA SUN BEAT DOWN ON Eleanor's shoulders, baking the dust into her skin and warming the crown of her scalp through her wide-brimmed straw hat. She'd chosen a sundress that morning—white cotton, patterned with faded yellow flowers. She wanted to fit in a little more with the crowd.

They meandered the dirt path, Roxy trotting on a thin leash at her side, her petite, hairless but fabulous body full of spunky energy. Eleanor's guitar was slung over her shoulder, strap pressing into her collarbone with a familiar weight—like an old friend leaning against her after too many years apart.

A thrill traveled through her limbs as she stepped on the free stage erected for impromptu jams. Her fingers itched. Her chest lifted. Decades had passed since she'd been in front of a crowd, felt the rush of anticipation ripple across her skin like an applause. The nerves she'd thought would freeze her throat didn't show up, thank goodness. *Like old times, Eleanor. You're the Bell of Wartime Music.*

The audience wasn't an audience yet—just clusters of young people sprawled across the grass, their feet bare, denim bell-bottoms grass-stained, cigarette smoke curling above their heads like question marks. They laughed with the loose easiness of the young and unburdened.

Eleanor wished, for a beat, that she could have laughed like that in her twenties—after she'd given up on her dreams. That she hadn't spent so much time stitching herself into the tight hemline of duty. That she'd let her soul sing rather than bottling it up.

But she'd tried, hadn't she? Her husband had always known music was in her—had even encouraged it initially. But over the years, his encouragement turned into tolerance, and then expectation took over. Housework. Dinner. Shopping. Childcare. Manners.

Here, though, no one knew her name.

Just an old lady with a guitar and Roxy and no responsibilities except for keeping herself and her dog fed and in the shade.

Her flight had landed late the night before. By the time she'd taken a cab to the motel and collapsed onto the bed, she was too tired to do anything but sleep. Despite the time difference from New York to California, she still woke up long past her usual hour, but she didn't feel guilty about it as she usually did at home. She felt…rested. Recharged. Even the motel's stale continental breakfast—lukewarm coffee, a blueberry muffin, and a hard-boiled egg—had tasted better than any breakfast she remembered having for a while. Someone on the plane mentioned the open mic sign-up happening on the festival grounds that morning.

More than one person had to give her directions as she kept getting lost, but she eventually she found the right tent. The woman at the sign-up table hadn't even blinked at her age.

That, in itself, was its own kind of grace.

And now here she was, stepping out onstage. It wasn't a prime-time slot. Just a chance to perform for the early birds staking out their patch of grass before the three dazed days of "real" concerts began.

Eleanor stepped up to the microphone, her fingers grazing the cool metal, the weight of it familiar and foreign all at once, like being in the spotlight—with both the excitement and the dread that accompanied performing for a crowd.

"How's everybody doing this morning?" she asked, her voice slightly higher than she intended.

A few halfhearted responses floated up from the lawn, but most of the crowd was still busy with their granola bowls, apples, or morning cigarettes. The scent of clove smoke and suntan lotion drifted through the air, blending with the faint sweetness of patchouli.

Eleanor bit her lip, wondering if she could go through with this. Almost fifty years had gone by since she'd stood on a stage. Singing in the living room at Christmas or humming to herself while folding laundry wasn't the same.

She considered walking off. Just stepping back down and pretending she'd come up by mistake. What was she doing here, anyway? At her age?

Leanne would have a heart attack if she saw her here. Eleanor swallowed, wondering if she'd made a mistake. Maybe some dreams weren't worth reliving.

She glanced out over the crowd. A patchwork of brightly colored nylon sleeping bags, cross-legged youths, and transistor radios scattered like seashells on the grass. The sun rose behind them, casting the scene in a warm, golden haze. A slight breeze lifted the hem of her sundress and danced across the chords beneath her fingers.

This was the moment. *Her* moment. If she couldn't do it now—here, in California, guitar in hand and no one to answer to—then she never would. And she might as well go home.

"Sing!" someone shouted, laughing. A few others joined in with chuckles and spunky encouragement.

Roxy gave a sharp little bark at her ankle and nudged Eleanor's leg with her wet nose. That tiny nudge was enough.

Eleanor inhaled. Exhaled. Let her fingers settle on the strings.

She strummed a few soft chords, testing the resonance, the rhythm. Then she began to sing the song she'd written on the plane—scribbled onto a cocktail napkin. A song about endings and beginnings. About loss and reinvention. About loving fiercely and letting go gently.

At first, the crowd barely noticed. Then something shifted. As she finished the first verse, conversations faded out of the background noise. Heads turned. A couple in the third row began to sway in time with the melody. A young man with a joint in hand closed his eyes.

So Eleanor kept going.

Her voice grew stronger. Her foot tapped the worn wood of the stage. Her spine straightened and she leaned into the microphone, her breath catching fire on the lyrics. The sound came from somewhere deep—bone-deep, soul-deep. Not just singing anymore.

This was remembering.

Her fingers danced over the strings like they were part of her—an extension of memory, longing, and youth that lingered in the recesses of her tangled brain. The energy from the crowd buzzed in her skin. Filled her. Lifted her. Made her feel timeless.

Suddenly, she wasn't Henry's widow. Wasn't Leanne's mother. She wasn't sixty-nine, with wrinkles etched around her eyes and mouth. Her memories weren't fading.

She was Eleanor Bell. A woman with a voice and a Gibson L-00.

The crowd erupted as she strummed the final chords, the last note hanging like a secret in the warm morning air.

First came the applause. Then cheering. Then, a smattering of people rose to their feet.

And then—unexpectedly—calls for an encore.

Eleanor's breath caught, stunned. The half dozen performers who'd gone on before her had received scattered polite claps and a few nods. But this—this was different.

The skeptical side of her wondered if they were just humoring her. An old lady with a guitar.

But when she scanned the faces in front of the stage—sun-kissed, wide-eyed, grinning—she didn't see pity. She saw interest. Joy.

She leaned into the mic, breathless but smiling. "Another?"

"Encore! Encore! Encore!" Listeners chanted back in unison, clapping in time.

Eleanor grinned.

The first song had been written in a rush of urgency—scribbled across the sky between New York and California. But the next song… The next one was different.

Old. Older than some of the kids standing looking up at her on the stage.

She hadn't played it in nearly fifty years. A song from a time when she still believed her whole life was stretched out like a ribbon of possibility. A song she had written for someone she'd loved. Briefly. Fiercely. Someone lost to her. The man who had once handed her a note with only three words: *Until next time.* But they never had a next time.

She stepped closer to the mic, adjusting her grip on the guitar.

"I wrote this song a long time ago," she said, her voice warm and steady. "For a man."

The crowd laughed with her, easy and open.

"But also," she added, "for me."

Cheers rang out, more sincere than before. And then, she began to play.

The opening chords came slower this time—gentler. Her voice entered low and soft, growing with each verse. There was something raw about the performance. Not polished. Not perfect. But true. Because she was singing from a place so deep it didn't have a name.

By the time the final chorus came, her voice was trembling with emotion—years of love and loss threading through the melody. Tears slipped down her cheeks, but she didn't stop. Not this time.

When the last note faded, she stepped away from the mic. The silence held for a beat longer than expected before the crowd exploded into cheers again. Someone tossed a flower toward the stage.

She gave a slight curtsy—half embarrassed, half triumphant.

They shouted for another encore. But this time, Eleanor simply smiled and walked off, the flower tucked behind her ear, the guitar still humming softly in her hands, Roxy beside her with a little bounce in her step.

She was emotionally drained.

But also—alive.

"That was amazing. Oh my gosh—I can't believe you're not already on the lineup for this festival."

The words hit Eleanor like a warm breeze—unexpected and entirely welcome.

She turned. The woman speaking was young, maybe mid-twenties, with freckled cheeks and a clipboard tucked under one arm. A red bandanna was tied around her head in that effortless way only girls born after World War II seemed able to master. She scribbled something on the form in her hand, glancing up.

"What's your name? Where can we reach you?"

The question surprised her, and her gaze unfocused for half a breath. No one had asked her that in decades—not like this. Not as someone to book, someone to want.

"My name is Eleanor…Bell." She wasn't entirely certain why she left off her married name, Strickland. Only that she wanted to be the Bell of Wartime Music again. "I'm staying for the whole festival," she said, adjusting her guitar strap on her shoulder. "I'm at the Pink Flamingo. Room seven."

The woman nodded, jotting it down.

With a sudden burst of confidence, Eleanor added. "I'll be on the lawn listening to music. If you need me just say my name into the mic and I'll come running."

The girl glanced up from her clipboard, meeting Eleanor's gaze with a self-assured smile. "I just might."

Roxy gave a high-pitched bark, her little legs prancing in place.

Eleanor glanced down. "What do you say we get something to eat, hmm?"

Roxy's ears perked, and she let out another bark, clearly in agreement.

Truthfully, Eleanor wasn't hungry. Not really. What she needed wasn't food so much as a moment. A moment to step away from the stage, from the adrenaline still buzzing under her skin, and to…digest.

Because something had shifted.

Eleanor had stepped onstage as a memory, but she'd stepped off it as a musician.

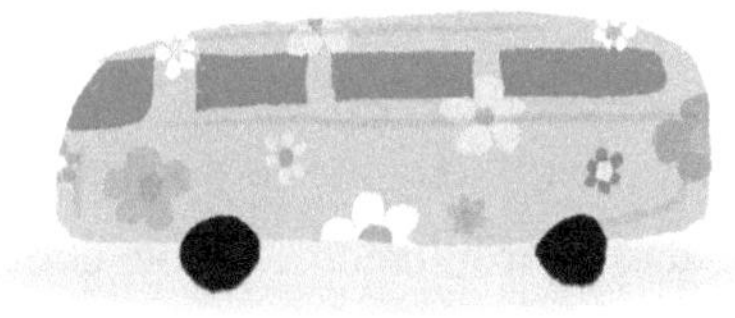

CHAPTER EIGHT

LEANNE SHOULD HAVE PAID MORE ATTENTION TO THE route.

Though they'd left just after sunrise, they didn't pull into the Howard Johnson's Motor Lodge until well after sunset—bone-tired, bleary-eyed, and running on fumes. Dean's secretary—ever efficient, never intuitive—had mapped out an itinerary that called for more than eight hundred miles on the first day. New York to Chicago in a single shot. On paper, it looked tidy.

In reality? Utter hell.

She should have gone with her gut and boarded a Pan American flight. The last person she knew who'd decided to take a cross-country road trip was a decade ago when their neighbors down the street had piled all their kids in the car for a Route 66 adventure from New York to Arizona. And Leanne was pretty certain Cheryl had said it was the biggest mistake of her life. Remembering that twelve hours ago would have been good.

They'd stopped once for watery coffee and a blue plate special at a truck-stop diner somewhere outside Cleveland. The eggs had been rubbery, the toast cold, the butter like paste. Both of their stomachs had protested ever since. The only other sustenance came in the form of hamburgers from McDonald's speedy-service drive-in, and Cracker Jacks and potato chips that Nora picked up at a gas station and tossed casually onto the dashboard like they'd be enough to carry them through Illinois.

They weren't.

By the time they stumbled into the motel lobby, both dragging overstuffed suitcases behind them, Leanne felt like her bones might crack, and Nora was walking like hers already had.

"Miller," she said to the woman behind the desk, voice hoarse.

The clerk—a woman with bright blue eyeshadow and a teased beehive—flipped through the reservation ledger, then reached behind her to pull a key, dangling from an oversize orange tag, off a wooden hook.

"Room number six," she said, with the tone of someone who hadn't slept in two shifts.

Leanne took the key and gave a nod of thanks.

As they turned to go, the clerk called out, "Breakfast is from seven to nine. Sharp. If you want it."

"What's for breakfast?" Nora asked, swaying where she stood half asleep on her feet.

The woman shrugged. "We have a wide variety. Eggs, bacon, hot-cakes. A Toastee Club."

"I'm getting all of that in the morning," Nora said with a laugh.

They made their way to the room, walking past brightly painted orange doors under a buzzing neon strip of light. When they reached number six, Leanne unlocked the door and stepped inside, flipping on the light, which flickered then solidified, revealing a clean room with teal curtains, matching chairs, and two beds with vibrant carroty bedspreads. A television stand was in the corner.

Leanne let out a long breath she didn't know she'd been holding and slipped into the motel bathroom and flicked on the overhead light, which buzzed faintly yellow. She turned on the tap and splashed cold water on her face, attempting to wash away the strain of hours on the road. Her skin felt tight and travel-worn, like she'd been living inside the car's upholstery. How in the world was she going to climb behind the wheel again in the morning?

She used the toilet, dried her hands on a fresh towel, and took one last look at herself in the mirror—faded lipstick, tired eyes, and hair that had started to fall from its pins.

When she emerged, Nora was curled on the bed. "Look, a remote!" she said, flipping channels with the black box they didn't have at home. "Oh my gosh, *The Ed Sullivan Show*!" Nora rolled onto her stomach, suddenly awake. Her feet kicked lazily in the air, crossed at the ankles, her chin resting in her palms. She looked impossibly young—like the girl she used to be before college acceptance letters, eyeliner, and existential sighs.

Ed Sullivan introduced a comedian, his voice as energized as his wave for the audience to welcome the entertainment. The studio audience clapped on cue.

"I'm going to find a pay phone to call your dad," Leanne said, reaching for the room key.

Nora nodded, barely looking up.

Leanne stepped out into the night and headed for the front desk.

"Where's the pay phone?" Leanne asked the woman at the desk.

Looking up from the *TV Guide* she was reading, the clerk hooked her thumb over one shoulder toward a window. "Just around the side."

"Thanks." Leanne nodded and headed outside. The air had cooled slightly, though the pavement still radiated the day's heat. A buzzing neon sign above the lodge cast a glow over the parking lot.

She rounded the corner, passing another family finding their way in late on the road.

The red-painted phone booth stood in a pool of light from a distant streetlamp. Leanne grabbed the handle and gave the door a tug.

Not even a budge.

"What in the world..." she muttered, tugging harder this time.

From inside came a low, guttural groan.

Leanne froze, goose bumps rising on her arms.

She stepped closer, squinting through the foggy glass. Her eyes adjusted slowly to the shadow inside. A man was lying curled on the booth floor, his knees drawn up, one hand clutching the receiver as if it were still connected to something—or someone.

"Are you okay?" she called, tapping the glass with her knuckles.

No answer.

Only another low groan.

Her pulse kicked up, sharp and sudden. She considered running back to the room, grabbing Nora, telling the motel attendant, doing something, anything.

"Jush leave me alone. Shtopp hitting me."

The man's slurred voice inside the phone booth was thick with alcohol and confusion. He flopped an arm against the glass, smacking his palm to the door with a dull slap that had Leanne flinching.

"I just need to make a call," she said, teeth clenched. "Think you can step out for a minute? I'll be quick. Promise."

He answered with a groan and a raised middle finger, his body folding deeper into the booth's corner like he was trying to disappear into the floor.

Leanne sighed sharply through her nose. She turned on her heel and marched back to the motel lobby.

The clerk smiled. "Did you find it?"

"Is there another phone I can use? Inside? There was someone… indisposed outside."

The clerk wrinkled her brow. "Oh, dear me." She bit her lip, glancing at the sign tacked on the wall that said PATRONS MUST USE PAY PHONE. "I'm not supposed to…"

"It's fine. I'll call my husband in the morning. But you ought to get someone to help the fellow out of the booth outside."

"If you're quick," the clerk said, lifting her telephone up onto the raised part of the desk.

Leanne shook her head, too exhausted to try.

She returned to the room, her key clicking in the lock. Inside, the glow of the television filled the dark, and Nora was exactly where she'd left her—stretched out on the bed, face lit up in the soft flicker of the black-and-white screen. Only now instead of watching *Ed Sullivan*, she was watching *Bewitched.*

Leanne recognized it immediately. Nora was giggling as Samantha twitched her nose and made the dishes fly into the sink.

Leanne pulled her dress for the next day out of her suitcase and hung it from the doorframe, hoping gravity might handle the worst of the wrinkles. She peeled off her stockings, changed into pajamas, and scrubbed the day off her face and dried it with the motel towel, which smelled faintly of pine and mildew.

She crawled into bed just as Samantha Stephens wiggled her nose and made a pile of dirty dishes disappear with a twinkle and a chime.

If only, Leanne thought.

If she had magical powers, she might've managed less stress about spotless house and dinner on a loop and instead found a hobby she could enjoy. Gotten more books from the library and spent endless hours reading.

She turned slightly to look at Nora—her daughter still giggling, her hand fishing out the last sticky caramel-covered peanut from the Cracker Jack box.

Please, Leanne thought, *let her have more options than I did.*

Yale was Ivy League. A degree from Yale meant job security. More choices for Nora.

Leanne hadn't the opportunities afforded to Nora. Her education had been a secretarial course. Getting hired depended less on your skills and more on whether the man behind the desk thought you'd look good typing in heels.

Nora's future would be completely different. Her daughter wanted to go into advertising like her father. A job that would allow her to use her creativity and receive a paycheck.

Leanne hoped her daughter would be happy.

Nora had always been creative—sketching in the margins of her notebooks, writing stories on the backs of napkins. Leanne had encouraged it when she could. But Dean? He thought it was a phase. That she needed something "practical." A real plan.

She couldn't blame Dean, not really.

He wanted Nora to be able to support herself—if it ever came to that. Not that either of them believed it would. Dean thought it was only a matter of time before Nora got married, just like Leanne had. College was a stepping stone, not a destination. Eventually, the degree would grow xanthic in its frame, collecting dust above the washer and dryer while Nora kept house and raised children.

Just like Eleanor. Just like Leanne.

Leanne didn't want Nora's fire to be dimmed by duty. Not the way hers had been. Not the way, now that she considered it, her own mother's had as well, if, perhaps, not as obviously.

Leanne pulled the covers up to her chin and closed her eyes.

She wasn't sure what was waiting for them in California. She wasn't even sure she'd recognize her mother when they found her. *My God, please let her be okay.* Every stop they'd made, she'd asked if anyone had seen an older woman with a hairless dog, but all she got were quizzical looks and slowly shaking heads. She told herself that no news was good news.

Leanne rolled away from the flickering television and stared at the wall, her eyes settling on a hairline crack in the wallpaper. A narrow little fissure that begged to be scratched with a fingernail. Peeled back. Exposed.

She had the sudden urge to do it.

To tear it down.

To see what was underneath.

Because the real question wasn't about Dean or the job market or how many female undergrads Yale had finally agreed to admit.

The real question, the one whispering at the back of her mind, was why shouldn't Nora get to do what she wanted?

Why shouldn't she have a career and a life of her own choosing? Why shouldn't she skip the housewife part entirely if she wanted to? If she could?

She thought about the road trip. About what it meant—not just miles logged in a Lincoln Continental but the space it created. For conversation. For discomfort. For possibility. They were unraveling, bit by bit, the old stitched-together assumptions of their lives.

All while pursuing Eleanor Bell Strickland, the runaway grandmother.

Something had cracked in Eleanor too—made her pack a bag and walk away from everything she'd known with little clue as to where she'd gone.

Was it the dementia? Or was it something bigger.

Something truer?

The last flickers of lucidity? Or the first real act of clarity her mother had made in decades?

Leanne stared again at the crack in the wallpaper.

And wondered how many of them it would take to finally peel everything back.

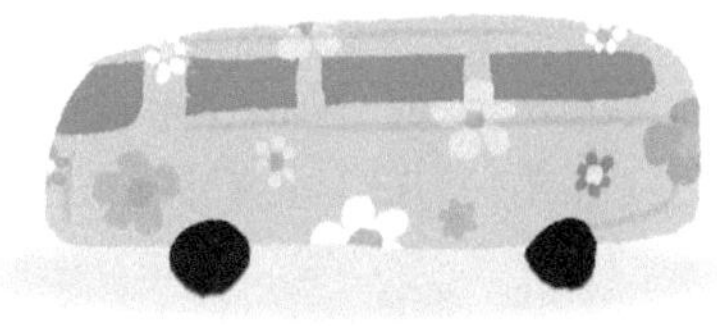

CHAPTER NINE

BLEARY-EYED AND STILL HALF ASLEEP, NORA MADE HER way out to the Lincoln. She popped the trunk, tossed her overnight bag inside with a thud, and slid her backpack across the wide leather front seat. She couldn't believe she had to spend another entire day in this car with her mother. Right now, Kelley and the girls were probably lying out and getting a suntan, gossiping about the hot boys at the lake.

A few rogue popcorn kernels from the night before clung to the upholstery. She brushed them away with the back of her hand, along with her jealousy, before climbing in, letting the door slam shut behind her.

The motel's breakfast had been delicious. She'd opted for a stack of hotcakes doused in syrup, and her mother had a meager meal of toast and a poached egg.

A few miles down the road, her mom pulled into a gas station—one of those sun-bleached, two-pump places with a rusted Coke machine out front and oil-stained concrete beneath the tires.

"I'm going to try the pay phone here." Leanne rolled down the window to signal the attendant. "The one back at the motel was occupied."

"Occupied?"

Her mom hadn't mentioned anything about that last night.

"Dad's going to be worried." Nora glanced at the station's clock tower, its hands frozen at 8:32. Broken. Of course. "We were supposed to call him."

Leanne nodded. "I'll call him now. There was a drunk guy passed out in the booth last night. I didn't feel like dragging him out. He was…not exactly polite."

"What did he say?"

"It's not what he said. It's what he did. The middle finger." Her mother's tone was full of indignation, as if she'd never been flipped the bird before.

Nora snorted, unable to help herself. "Classic."

Leanne waved to the young attendant, who'd just appeared wiping greasy fingers on his smudged jumpsuit. "Fill it up, please."

Then her mother crossed the lot toward the phone booth, her skirt fluttering slightly in the breeze, perfectly manicured fingers steadying the purse on her shoulder. Nora watched her enter the booth, the glass door squeaking closed behind her. Then she twisted around in her seat and rummaged through her backpack for her copy of *The Godfather*. They'd only made it through less than an eighth of the book on yesterday's drive before her eyes started to cross, and the words blurred into one long, masculine monologue of power and blood. But the one line she couldn't forget was about Sonny's giant…penis.

Was it possible for a penis to be that big? She and Kelley had spent a considerable time discussing that question. What she wouldn't give right now to call Kelley from the pay phone and tell her that road trips weren't all they were cracked up to be.

Nora unearthed the book and settled into the leather seat again. The gas station attendant leaned against the open window on the driver's side.

"Where you two headed?" he asked, chewing on a toothpick.

"California," Nora replied, not really in the mood to elaborate.

She was too busy trying to find her place in *The Godfather*. At this point, the pages were a minefield of creases—evidence of all the times she'd read it, reread it, and folded down corners like breadcrumbs. Figuring out which turned-down page was the one she needed at the moment was tricky.

Some literary purists considered dog-earing a cardinal sin, but Nora didn't care. Preserving books wasn't why she read them. She read them to live inside the pages, no matter how battered.

Having found the page, Nora glanced toward the pay phone. Her mother was still inside, one hand pressed to her temple and a pinched look on her face that was visible even from this distance.

Nora sighed.

She spent a lot of time *not* looking at her parents. Not really. Their marriage had always felt like background noise, but the background noise to a suspense movie, not Mayberry. Nora experienced their relationship via tension humming through the walls, snatches of clipped conversations, and the way her mother poured wine increasingly often after dinner. Sometimes, Nora wished she had a sibling—someone to roll her eyes with across the room or to whom she could say, *Did you hear that too?*

But she didn't.

And it wasn't like she would tell her friends that her parents' marriage seemed less than happy. That was "family business."

The sharp crack of the pay phone receiver slamming into its cradle across the parking lot made her jump. Leanne shoved the door closed and marched toward the Lincoln, her mouth set in a firm line as though she were late for a meeting that she didn't want to attend.

Nora sat up a little straighter. "How's Dad?" she asked, worried she was about to hear something she didn't want to know.

Leanne pulled open the door and exhaled loudly. "Couldn't get the phone to work. Every time I picked it up, the operator would ask, 'How can I direct your call?' But no matter what I said, she kept repeating herself like my end was muted."

She slid into the driver's seat, shaking her head, her lips pressed into the thin line. "I even tried unscrewing the mouthpiece. Nothing. Like it was jammed."

"So…you didn't talk to him?" Nora tried to keep the irritation out of her voice, but it felt like her mother wasn't trying hard enough. First the guy last night, and now the phone not working?

Leanne shook her head, and for a moment there was a sheer look of panic on her face that had Nora's heart skipping a beat. "I'll try later—maybe when we stop to eat at a diner."

Nora nodded, keeping her opinion to herself.

The gas station attendant finished filling up the car. "All done, ma'am." He gave her the total, and Leanne handed him some folded bills from her purse.

"You didn't happen to see an older woman drive through here a few days ago? She would have had a hairless dog with her."

The gas station attendant laughed, then stopped when he stared at Leanne's serious expression. "No, ma'am. So sorry. Never heard of a hairless dog…" he trailed off as he walked away counting the bills.

Leanne's lip quivered, but she sucked in a breath and tucked a loose tendril of hair behind her ear. "I'm hoping these pay phone mishaps are not a trend. Your father's going to be worried sick," she said as she turned the key in the ignition and the engine came back to life. "And if I don't hear something soon about your grandmother…"

Nora nodded, her fingers sliding over the book still on her lap. "We're going to find Grandma. No news is good news, remember? And Dad has our itinerary. If he's worried, maybe he'll leave a message at our next hotel." She shrugged.

"Hopefully it doesn't come to that." Leanne adjusted the rearview mirror, smoothed a hand over her hair gone slightly wild from the wind, and then pulled the car back onto the road.

She tapped *The Godfather* on the seat beside Nora as they merged, joltingly, back onto the highway, the morning sun flaring through the windshield. Nora reached for her sunglasses she'd tossed onto the dash before they were crushed forever under someone else's wheels.

"Want me to drive?"

Her mother shook her head. "Shall we continue with the Mafia underworld? Maybe hearing about crime will stop me from committing one."

Nora laughed, surprising herself. "That frustrated, huh?"

"Nothing a little crime fiction can't fix."

Nora began to read, falling back into the story's cadence—Don Corleone, criminal justice, loyalty, and blood. She could feel her mother watching her out of the corner of her eye. Normally she'd roll her eyes and ask her mother what she was staring at, but this time, she wasn't as irritated as she'd expected to be. That was a real shock.

She realized in a flash of insight that, though they'd only been on the road for about twenty-four hours, something felt...different. Not entirely comfortable, not yet. And she was still irritated she was missing out on her summer with her friends. But she'd expected more arguing. Instead, it felt easier. Like the edges between them had started to soften.

She stopped reading, staring out the window at a row of farmland rushing by. And suddenly, a pang hit her in the chest—sharp and unexpected.

In a few months, she wouldn't be riding in a car with her mother. She'd be in a dorm room. Eating in a dining hall. Figuring out where to do her laundry and how to navigate a campus that still wasn't quite sure what to do with its first class of female undergrads.

For the last eighteen years, it had mostly been the two of them. Sure, she'd gone to sleepovers, had weekends away, and a whole week at the lake after graduation. But she'd always come home again. Even when she was annoyed with her mother's existence.

She closed the book and set it in her lap.

"Mom," she said softly, "can I ask you something?"

Leanne glanced at her, hands at three and nine o'clock on the wheel. There was a flicker of concern at the corners of her eyes. "Of course."

Nora hesitated. "Did you know it was the last time you were going home? When you left?"

Leanne let out a small laugh, taken aback by the question. "I just went home a few days ago."

"No, I mean—" Nora looked out the window again, trying to find the right words. "I mean when you left home. To live somewhere else. Did you know it was the last time? That you might visit but you wouldn't be living there anymore?"

Leanne was quiet. She bit her lip, then nodded slowly. "Yes. I think I did. I'd known for a while. That it was time."

She glanced sideways at Nora. "Are you…?"

But she didn't finish the question.

Nora shrugged, her voice quieter now as she voiced what had been on her mind for weeks. "Just thinking I might want to come home before Thanksgiving. For a weekend or something."

Leanne's hand tightened slightly on the wheel, making Nora's stomach imitate the movement.

"You can come home anytime you want, Nora," she said. Her voice was steady but soft, and instantly Nora's muscles relaxed.

Leanne's voice held the weight of her earnest expression. "Our house is your house. Always."

Nora nodded, looking back down at the book in her lap. But she didn't open it. She was suddenly filled with emotion. No matter how much they'd butted heads the last year, her mother still wanted her to come home.

She just sat with her mother's words.

Absorbing them along with the sunlight, the silence, and the soft vibrations of the engine.

She wanted to remember the feeling of her mother beside her, just driving.

CHAPTER TEN

A KNOCK AT THE DOOR STARTLED ELEANOR FROM SLEEP.

She sat up in bed, disoriented, her breath caught in her chest like a question. Unmoored, she swiveled her head slowly back and forth. Didn't recognize the room—didn't know where she was, what day it was. She didn't even know who she was. Waves of panic washed over her as the pale motel wallpaper swam before her eyes, warped in the dim morning light.

But then, like a camera lens adjusting its focus, her identity and memories came rushing back.

The stage.

The spotlight.

The roar of applause.

Her own voice, rising up like a soul finally unlocked from its vault.

But so too had the gloriousness come with a sense of overwhelming sadness. That was the strange thing about memory lately: It wasn't chronological anymore. But musical. Emotional. Came back in flashes and tones.

Roxy jumped off the bed with a soft thump. Her tiny feet clicked across the floor as she trotted to the door, claws scratching at the bottom panel just as the knock sounded again.

Eleanor pushed the covers aside, realizing with a faint jolt that she'd fallen asleep in her dress from the day before. The fabric was wrinkled now, the hem twisted around her knees, and the faint scent of sweat and lavender clung to the cloth like perfume and memory.

She padded barefoot across the room and cracked the door open.

A young man in a front-desk uniform stood there, holding up a folded piece of paper.

"Eleanor Bell?" he asked, polite but hesitant.

"Yes?" Eleanor blinked, trying to rid the sleep—and the fog—from her eyes.

"I've got a message for you." He handed her the slip of paper. His eyes lit up suddenly. "Shep Moon."

The name landed in her ears like a whisper, hinting at something she should remember.

"Shep Moon," she repeated aloud, but it came out more like a question than a statement.

Something in her stomach fluttered—recognition? Or was it just the lyrical cadence of the name that suggested someone worth knowing?

Shep Moon.

Wasn't that the musician Nora had mentioned once?

Claimed he played guitar like nobody's business. And of all the ridiculous things to say, Nora claimed Shep Moon gave Jimi Hendrix a run for his money. When she'd asked if Nora had a crush, her granddaughter had scoffed and said he was too old, but from the picture Eleanor saw, he wasn't old at all. Probably late thirties or early forties. But she supposed to any eighteen-year-old, that was elderly.

What in the world would Shep Moon want with her?

Eleanor held out a hand and took the slip of paper, covered with messy, unfamiliar handwriting from the clerk. She murmured her thanks before closing the door and clicking the lock firmly into place.

Leaning back against the wood, letting the solidness hold her up.

She looked down at the note again, her hands trembling.

Shep Moon requests your presence onstage to sing his first number, Rising Tide.

Eleanor's heart pounded behind her rib cage, her fingers trembled against the paper that she held in her hands. She stared at the words, expecting them to rearrange themselves. A musician wanted her onstage with him. Not as a fluke. Not as a nostalgia act.

As a performer.

Was this real? She wasn't always sure anymore what was real and what were figments of her imagination.

She pressed a hand to her arm. The skin—soft, papery, the elasticity of youth vanished—warmed slightly under her touch. She didn't dare pinch herself or risk a bruise, which happened too easily these days. But this wasn't a dream.

In a dream, she wouldn't be able to see the delicate blue veins beneath her skin. The fine age spots. The realness of time.

No, dreams didn't look this lived-in.

She rushed to change her clothes, moving with a giddy urgency she hadn't felt in decades.

She chose another floaty dress—this one light teal with a daisy pattern—something that felt in fashion for the festival scene. Standing in front of the bathroom mirror, she started to twist her hair into a bun, then let it drop long and loose around her shoulders again. Something she never would've done back home. Something a woman of her age wouldn't ever do in public. But right now, she didn't care what a woman her age should or shouldn't do.

Roxy danced around her feet, tail wagging as Eleanor clipped the leash onto her collar.

"Ready?" Eleanor asked.

The dog barked once, as if to say, *Finally.*

Eleanor swept out of the motel room, feeling ten years younger. Then stopped short.

She didn't have a car.

Of course, she didn't.

She turned back toward the front desk, her sandals tapping against the hot concrete. She was halfway to asking the sleepy clerk to call her a cab when a young woman in cutoff denim shorts and a gauzy white tank top caught her eye. Was she the same one who'd stopped her coming offstage the day before?

The girl was leaning against a beat-up silver VW bus with flowers painted on the side and a peace sign hanging from the rearview. She was eating a peach, juice dripping down her wrist. When she saw Eleanor, she broke into a wide, fruit-juicy smile—like she'd been waiting for her all along.

"Eleanor, right?" the girl called out. "You were amazing yesterday."

Eleanor's eyes widened, thrown off. "Oh. Thank you."

"Mr. Moon asked me to come for you," the girl said, pushing off the bus. "You made such a huge impression yesterday when you were singing during the open mic time, and he thought it would be really fun to open the show with you today."

Just like that.

No hesitation. No questions about how she had even gotten here.

"Everyone's talking about you," the girl continued, dropping the peach pit to the ground and opening the van's passenger door for Eleanor, before climbing into the driver's seat.

"Talking about me?" Eleanor laughed, attempting to brush off her embarrassment as she climbed in and put Roxy on her lap.

"You've got a lot of talent." The young woman glanced over at her, turning the key in the ignition, the van's engine rumbling to life. "Where've you been hiding all these years?"

Eleanor smiled softly, eyes out the window. "At home."

The girl tilted her head, clearly not understanding.

"Home" didn't mean much to someone like her, Eleanor supposed. She looked at the young, wild woman, who wore her liberation like women of Eleanor's generation wore perfume. She likely lived out of a van, probably hadn't done a load of laundry in a washing machine in weeks, and used the word "free" like a religion.

To Eleanor, home had meant something very specific.

A husband.

A child.

A calendar filled with things that didn't include her name.

"Well," Eleanor said, smoothing her dress as a cue to change the subject. "Let's get going then."

She didn't want to explain it. Not the detour of her life. Not the reasons she'd stopped singing. And certainly not the sharp, terrifying truth that she was on borrowed time. That the memories were already slipping, slow and quiet like tides pulling back before anyone noticed they were gone.

Liberation, she quickly learned, came with a lead foot.

The girl drove like she was in a race no one else had entered. The van screeched through a turn into the festival parking lot, and Roxy let out a yip from Eleanor's lap, claws scrambling for traction.

"Good heavens," Eleanor muttered, clutching the seat belt, which didn't latch. By the time they came to a stop, her knees were shaky, and her hair had gone wind-wild.

She stepped out onto the dusty grass, trying to compose herself. "Thank you for the ride, dear," she said politely, then added silently, *Never again.*

"Right this way, Miss Bell," the girl said with a grin, clearly unfazed.

Eleanor followed her across the field, past a tangle of tents, food trucks, and barefoot festivalgoers dancing.

When they reached a massive canvas tent near the side of the main stage, the girl flung the flap open and gestured grandly. "Welcome backstage."

Inside, the light shifted—filtered through canvas, golden and dim. The smell hit her first: burned coffee, body odor, and something sweeter, more herbal.

Marijuana.

Men and women lounged on cots or sat—some on ground, others on a collection of mismatched chairs—sipping from enamel mugs and strumming guitars. A girl was braiding another's hair. A boy with no shirt and too many bracelets was tuning a bass.

Eleanor stepped carefully over a tambourine.

She stood in the middle of the tent, one hand lightly gripping Roxy's leash, watching the crowd move around her like a tide she wasn't a part of.

"Eleanor!" The voice came from the back of the tent—a rich, bright tenor that cut through the haze.

A man rose from where he'd been crouched, tuning a guitar. He set his instrument down with reverence and moved toward her.

His shirt was a flowing, ruffled affair, open nearly to his navel, exposing a smooth chest lightly dusted with sandy hair. His jeans clung to him like a second skin. His feet were bare, toes ringed in dust.

He moved like he owned the earth he walked on.

Eleanor was jarred by his presence, his energy. There was something about the chiseled angle of his jaw, the curve of his mouth, those sea-glass eyes—green with a halo of blue, etched with just a hint of age lines.

He wasn't entirely unfamiliar. She remembered seeing him in a magazine. A copy of *Rolling Stone* that Nora had held out for her—with a full spread of this very man, Shep Moon, dubbed the Great Guitar God.

He stopped in front of her, all easy energy and effortless edge.

Silver rings glittered on nearly every finger. Beaded and leather bracelets stacked up his wrists. He reached up, sweeping back a mess of sun-kissed curls, then removed his floppy felt hat before offering her a theatrical bow.

"You are even more radiant up close than onstage," he said with a grin that could melt a vinyl record.

Eleanor felt a jolt of something. Not just attraction—though, God help her, that too—but recognition. Of joy. Of being young and chosen. Of being seen.

Stretched out in front of her was his offered hand, and she took it. His palm was warm, rough with the callouses of someone who lived in music.

Time slid crabwise, along with her fingers curling into his. She was no longer in a festival tent in California. She was somewhere else—someone else. Holding the hand of a boy she had once promised everything to.

Someone she'd lost.

"Are you ready to sing with me, Ellie?" he asked.

The nickname hit her like a bell rung from deep inside her chest.

Ellie.

No one had called her that in decades.

Her lips parted, but no words came. Just that odd, heart-shifting ache.

Because she had heard that voice before.

Because someone else had once said her name just like that.

And because, for the first time in a long time, she wasn't entirely sure if this moment was new—or a memory so real it seemed new.

"I've been waiting to," Eleanor said, her voice suddenly steadied by soul-enriching memories.

Shep didn't seem thrown off by her answer. He gave her an easy smile and said, "Well, today's the day." He gave her hand a playful squeeze before letting go. "Now, let's get practicing so we can go out there and blow this joint straight to the sky."

He turned, his bare feet moving confidently across the carpeted tent floor. With one hand, he plucked his guitar off its stand and, with the other, gestured for her to follow.

Eleanor drew in a steadying breath. The same type of relaxing breathing she'd told her daughter to do when she panicked over a test score. Only this wasn't school, and the score certainly mattered. Her pulse galloped, her fingers tingled. But it wasn't just nerves. It was a feeling of pure aliveness.

The back of the tent had been sectioned off with colored scarves tacked to the canvas, giving the illusion of a separate space. It wasn't much—just a folding chair, a milk crate, and a few instrument cases stacked like suitcases in a forgotten train station. But Eleanor saw it for what it really was—a portal.

To before.

To possibility.

To a version of herself she hadn't been or even seen in decades.

Shep plopped onto the milk crate and began to strum, humming softly under his breath as he tuned. Then he looked up, his expression gentle. "You good with harmony? Or do you want to lead?"

Eleanor's head jerked, taken aback. "You want me to lead?"

"I asked you to sing with me, didn't I?" he said, eyebrows lifting. "What kind of fraud would I be if I put you onstage and didn't let you shine?"

She laughed, floored by the sheer absurdity of it, and yet…not absurd at all.

Because somewhere in her bones, she remembered not just music but the feeling of being chosen.

"I can lead," she replied softly, wishing she had the gumption to ask *Why me?* but afraid doing so would break whatever spell was at work here.

"That's what I'm talking about." Shep leaned forward, passing her a small lyric sheet, handwritten and smudged with coffee rings. "'Rising Tide' is a duet I wrote last winter about forgetting and remembering. Figured it might suit us after hearing your song yesterday."

The first line of the song swam before her eyes: *Now's not the time for forgetting. Now's the time for love.*

Eleanor's chest swelled, tightening with emotion, with reverence and hope.

There was truth in the line. She'd lived it once.

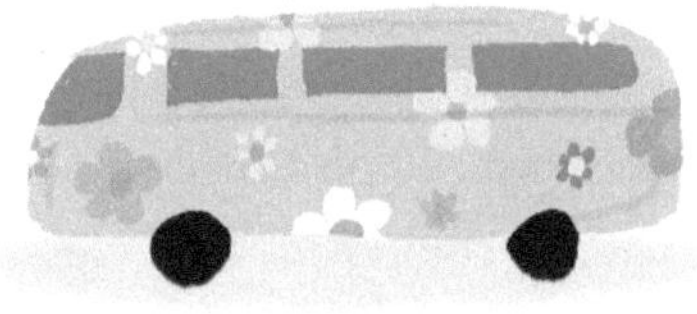

CHAPTER ELEVEN

IF DON CORLEONE COULD TAKE A BOLT OF LIGHTNING striking his friend as a personal insult, then Leanne was absolutely allowed to take this flat tire as one.

Standing on the side of a nearly deserted stretch of Illinois highway, hands on her hips, she glared at the back passenger side of the Lincoln Continental, certain it had betrayed her.

Which, honestly, it had.

The tire was fully deflated—pancaked, useless. She gave it a swift, pointless kick, the toe of her pump thudding against the rubber. The black smudge of dirt left behind on the creamy leather of her shoe added insult to injury. The dusty heat shimmered off the road, and a trail of sweat slid down her spine.

Of course, this would happen.

They hadn't even reached Iowa yet, and already this trip was veering wildly off course. Two broken pay phones, two missed calls to her husband. And, of course, the purpose of the trip itself—searching for a mysterious mother who had disappeared into thin air with no trace in sight—suggested chaos. A flat tire on a stretch of highway where there was literally nothing but road and land for as far as she could see, seemed entirely appropriate to their voyage into the unknown.

Nora climbed out of the passenger side, her book still clutched in one hand, sunglasses perched on her nose. She closed the door and leaned against it, calm and composed, arms crossed over her chest.

"Looks like we'll have to change it," Nora said flatly—like it was the most obvious thing in the world.

Leanne gritted her teeth.

Where the hell was Dean when she needed him? He was the one who always knew what to do in situations like this. Even as he disappointed in other areas, he was good in a crisis. A man with backup plans and the appropriate tools tucked in the trunk. She was the one with pearls and a manicure. The one who'd never driven more than a few miles beyond the suburbs without someone else behind the wheel or within reach of a phone.

She blew out a breath.

"I don't know how to change a tire," she admitted, the words tasting half defiant, half defeated. "I've never had to."

"Seriously?" Nora raised her eyebrows over the top of her sunglasses.

"Now would not be a good time for you to point out my shortcomings," Leanne snapped.

Nora frowned, then bent down and set her book carefully in the back seat, then straightened and cracked her knuckles. "Good thing Dad showed me how, then."

Leanne stared at her for a beat. Leanne should've felt ashamed. Instead, as her daughter stepped forward, calm in crisis, unfazed by the blistering sun or the ruined plans, she felt...something else.

Pride.

Admiration.

Along with that bittersweet ache that comes with realizing your child might already be braver than you ever were.

Leanne held out her hand. "I'll hold your sunglasses."

"Deal," Nora replied, handing them over like a torch.

Leanne watched Nora head to the trunk and begin to take things out. She had asked her husband a couple of times to show her how to change a tire—usually after a long drive or an ominous crunch on gravel. She'd voiced her concern plainly: *What if I run over a nail? What if I'm stranded somewhere?*

But Dean always waved her off. Reinforced the idea that she was never far from home. That she was safe.

And yet—he'd taught Nora?

The contradiction stung, even as she was grateful he had, or else they'd be screwed right now.

"All right," Leanne said as Nora approached the flat with a jack in one hand and a tire wrench in the other. "Maybe you can show me how to change a flat while you're at it. And I'm sorry I snapped at you."

"Sure, Mom." Nora smiled. She wasn't gloating, but she was proud. Proud of knowing something her mother didn't.

Leanne didn't take it personally. She wanted Nora to feel confident. Her daughter had always been a little cautious when it came to her own brilliance. And suspicious of compliments—especially from her mother.

Every time Leanne praised her, Nora brushed it off with *You're only saying that because you're my mom.*

But Leanne saw her daughter as having a once-in-a-lifetime kind of mind. A force still forming.

Nora set the jack and the wrench down next to the car. "Let's go get the spare."

This time the two of them went to stand behind the trunk together. The full-size spare lay there under a thin layer of dust.

Nora grabbed one side of the spare and tried to lift it. Apparently, it was heavy because she didn't even get it high enough to rest it on the edge of the trunk opening.

Leanne hesitated to step forward, not wanting her daughter to think she didn't believe she could do it. Then Nora glanced up and mouthed an exaggerated "Help."

Leanne placed her hands on the other side of the tire and braced her knees to lift.

"On three," Nora instructed.

Between the two of them, they managed to get the tire out and set it on the roadside like a moon rock. Nora rolled it along and leaned it on the car just beyond the flat.

"Let's get started." Nora looked at Leanne. "First, you have to loosen the lug nuts before you jack it up. Otherwise, the wheel just spins." Nora made a looping gesture in the air with her finger and then by her temple with her tongue sticking out.

Leanne laughed, watching closely as her daughter loosened one nut and then stepped back and gestured for her mother to do the next. Leanne's hands felt clumsy, but she followed Nora's instructions and got not one but two nuts off before Nora jumped back in.

Together, they cranked the bumper jack until the heavy Lincoln lifted just enough for the flat to dangle slightly off the asphalt.

They worked in a rhythm that felt natural. Nora positioned the iron, and Leanne helped with the nuts. The spare was fitted in its place, the nuts hand-tightened and then fully secured with the wrench once the car was lowered again.

When they finished, Leanne stood up, brushing dust from her skirt and catching her breath.

"Well," she said, "that wasn't so bad. Thank you."

"You did it." Nora gave her the kind of smile that Leanne wanted to fold up and save in her wallet forever. A smile infused with respect and even pride. "Now if we get another flat, you can change it all by yourself. If you want."

Leanne gave a tired laugh. "Let's hope that doesn't happen."

They drove the next few miles on the dummy spare—just wide enough and safe enough to get them off the shoulder—and exited toward a flyspeck gas station where they could get a new tire installed.

A single bell rang overhead when they pulled in.

The young man working the pumps leaned into the window and said, "Mechanic's out for lunch. Be about forty-five minutes."

He pointed across the road toward a low-roofed diner, the sign half lit, advertising "Hot Sandwiches & Cold Pie."

"Well," Leanne said, eyeing the building. She held up her hands, blackened from changing the tire. "Shall we trade tire grease for grilled cheese?"

Nora chuckled. "Sure, if they have milkshakes."

As they ate their sandwiches in the diner—egg salad for her, grilled cheese for Nora—Leanne watched the men who came and went at the gas station, trying to guess who the mechanic was. But as she and Nora made their way back across the street and then the sunbaked lot to the station, she admitted she wasn't sure if the man had come back at all.

"He's back now," the attendant said, waving a hand. "Told him to take care of your tire already. Should be done in a jiff."

"Thanks." Leanne gave him a smile. It wasn't until they climbed back into the Lincoln and pulled onto the road that she glanced at the clock. Almost three hours gone. *Damn it.* She wondered if they'd make their next motel. Or if they'd have to give up and get a different place.

They drove in silence for a bit, dust curling behind them on the highway.

Nearly an hour later—Nora asleep with her head tipped against the window—Leanne realized something was wrong. Not with the car this time but with where they were.

The mile markers looked unfamiliar. The terrain wasn't right. They were headed west, yes—but not toward the coast.

"Oh, no," she muttered aloud, pulling over to check the map. Her stomach twisted.

They'd taken the wrong highway. Somewhere near Des Moines, they'd veered north. They'd been driving in the wrong direction. For an hour.

Between her mistake and the tire, they were five hours behind.

Rather than arriving in Los Angeles tomorrow night, they were more likely going to be getting there two days from now. *Double damn it.*

The next two days on the road, between Leanne's panicking over her mother, being unable to reach her husband, and Nora's sulking about missing the majority of the festival, the car ride was silent and sullen.

By the time the Lincoln rolled into the neon-lit lot of the Pink Flamingo Motel, the dashboard clock read 12:57 a.m. and they'd not exchanged a word in at least eight hours.

The sign flickered VACANCY in hot pink cursive. The building itself was stucco—faded blush with turquoise trim. Plastic flamingos dotted the patchy front lawn, glowing ghostly under the lights.

Neither of them said much, dragging their exhausted bodies from the car as if they weighed a thousand pounds each. They checked in with the night clerk, who had pink curlers in her hair and a black-and-white TV flickering behind the desk.

"Any chance you've seen an older woman with a dog?" Leanne asked.

The clerk glanced up, squinting her eyes. "Can't divulge the identity of our guests unless you're law enforcement."

"Understood, but she is my mother. I'm looking for her."

"Not since I started my shift this afternoon. Can't say whether she was here before that. I was out sick."

Leanne nodded and muttered a thank-you, trying not to let her frustration show. Only because of her sheer exhaustion did she not bang her hand on every door of the motel to see if her mother opened one of them.

Once inside their room, Nora collapsed first, face down on the pink flamingo comforter, while Leanne only halfheartedly washed her face and brushed her teeth before flopping down on the second bed.

Since they were running a little behind schedule, they'd missed their chance to go to the festival today. But at least they'd made it to California, and the festival was still going on tomorrow. Leanne fell asleep with the lights still on.

The following morning, they were up at dawn, eager, groggy, rushing to hit the road. And thankfully, Nora's spirits had lifted at the prospect of catching the last day of the festival. Leanne's was more like relief they'd made it and soon she'd have eyes on her mother.

Within miles of the Pink Flamingo, they were caught in the crawl of traffic—dozens of VW buses, station wagons, motorcycles, and flower-painted Beetles inching forward under a rising sun. Some drivers leaned out of windows, passing bottles or offering peace signs to strangers. A group of girls danced on the roof of a van up ahead of them, barefoot and glowing.

Demonstrators protesting the war marched alongside the trail of vehicles.

When Leanne and Nora finally got within sight of the festival and found a spot to park on the dusty grass shoulder, the sun was high overhead. They slammed their doors and jogged toward the gates.

Since they'd already missed the first two days of the concert, they were charged only six dollars for a day pass—though Nora had half-jokingly suggested they climb the fence, like a group of teenagers they'd seen scrambling over it at the back corner of the field.

"You think I came all the way across the country just to get arrested in California?" Leanne laughed breathlessly.

As they entered the festival grounds, they were hit by a wall of sound—drums, guitar feedback, laughter, and someone screaming joyfully in the distance. Leanne scanned every face for recognition but found none.

"Have you seen an older woman with a dog?" she asked each person who met her eyes. "About this big? Hairless?" She made motions with her hands.

All of them shook their heads.

Music pulsed from the stage, weaving through the scent of cigarettes, sweat, patchouli, and the unmistakable sharp tang of pot. Leanne had never smoked weed in high school, though she'd been offered some a few times at parties.

Tie-dye blankets covered the field like wildflowers, and everywhere people were dancing, swaying, spinning with their hands in the air like the music had loosened something inside them.

A guitarist launched into a solo as they entered the crowd. Would it be possible to sneak onstage and call her mother's name out over the microphone?

Leanne didn't recognize the name on the set list as it was belted out, but Nora started clapping, her face lighting up with recognition, her whole body moving to the beat. She shouted something over the music, but Leanne didn't catch the name.

The music had taken her daughter too.

Then, a shift—the next set was announced, and Leanne recognized the names Ike and Tina Turner, knew the song belted into the microphone.

And just like that, she too was taken in by the music.

Instinctively, she sang along, the lyrics tumbling from her lips like they'd been waiting there all these years. Her arms lifted in rhythm, her hips moving, laughter rising from somewhere deep in her chest. Letting go was not something Leanne usually allowed herself, but boy, did it feel good right now.

There was something liberating in this sea of strangers. Something unburdening. Here, she wasn't a wife or a mother searching for her missing mother. Here, she was just a woman alive in the moment.

The autonomy didn't last long. Guilt riddled her limbs for having even spared a moment in her search to sing.

Within minutes, Leanne unconsciously shifted to studying the crowd, her gaze scanning over the heads and shoulders, searching for her mother's face, light hair, and eccentric clothes. Concentrating on hearing just the slightest sound of her melodic voice—a voice she didn't realize how much she'd missed until now.

But she couldn't find even the slightest hint of her mom. Admittedly, given the crush of bodies and sound, she might not have been able to spot her.

"Hey there!"

A man brushed past, singing loudly, one hand raised for a high five, jostling Leanne to the side. Dressed in a purple wizard hat, slouched at an angle, and a silver-stitched cloak thrown dramatically over bare his shoulders. Bell-bottoms. No shirt. Magical runes painted in ink across his chest. Leanne did a double take at his getup as if she'd inhaled too much secondhand marijuana smoke.

He looked like a lunatic. Or a legend.

Then, without hesitation, Leanne slapped her palm to his. "Have you seen an older woman with a hairless dog?"

He nodded and grinned at her, then turned to Nora. "What'd you two think of Grandma?"

Both Leanne and Nora froze. The first clue that Eleanor might be here.

"I'm sorry—what?" Nora's eyes narrowed.

"Grandma." The man spun in a circle, cloak flaring behind him. "Rock-and-Roll Grandma was freaking awesome. Played a set earlier with Shep Moon. Made the crowd go wild. Gave him a run for his money! And the dog is hilarious looking."

"Shep Moon?" Nora gasped, starstruck.

"The one and only." The wizard wiggled finger guns at them before twirling and disappearing into the crowd's haze of cigarette smoke like a spell had swallowed him whole.

Leanne and Nora stared after him, maybe in shock, before their gazes met, their lips pressed together to hold in their laughter.

"Do you think…?" Nora's skeptical tone softened into awe.

Leanne looked out at the crowd, at the swaying bodies and the shimmer of heat on the stage. At the way Tina Turner had just kicked off her heels and was dancing like fire itself.

"Before now?" she said. "I'd have said no."

She turned to her daughter, the beat of the music thudding beneath her feet like a second heartbeat.

"But we just drove across the country chasing Grandma…and now we're standing in the middle of a field, high-fiving wizards and listening to Tina Turner." She laughed, shaking her head. "At this point, anything's possible."

Nora beamed, eyes full of something close to wonder.

Leanne glanced back toward the stage—imagining Eleanor there, hair loose, hips swaying, voice rising. Imagining her mother not lost or slipping away but soaring—belting notes next to a rock star like she'd been born to be.

If the Grandma the wizard-man mentioned was her mom—and it sounded like she was—then Eleanor was fine. Safe. Having a good time, even.

Leanne wasn't sure what her vision or the strange festivalgoer's words meant, or the sudden sense of calm that overtook her.

But surely, they meant something.

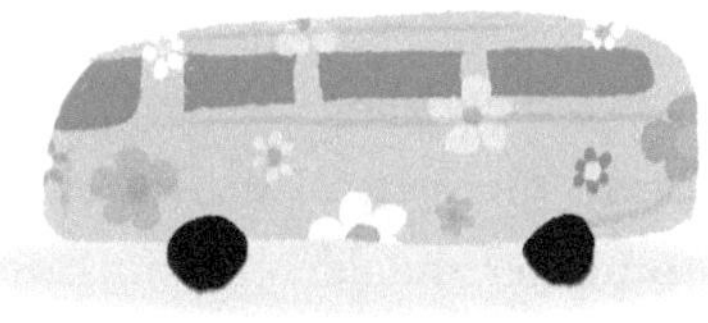

CHAPTER TWELVE

"ARE YOU THIRSTY?" NORA BRUSHED HER SWEATY HAIR off her forehead. She and her mother had been dancing for nearly an hour, swept up in the music, the heat, and the sheer strangeness of it all.

The panic her mother had over finding Eleanor had tempered somewhat when they learned that she'd been here, that she'd been singing, and that she was apparently safe. Nora was grateful for that bit of information, not only because knowing her grandmother wasn't in a ditch somewhere was of course good news but also because her mother had finally let loose a little.

Leanne nodded, lifting her hair away from her damp neck. "Want me to grab us sodas?"

"I've got it," Nora said quickly. "You keep an eye on the stage in case Grandma makes another appearance."

Her mother smiled, wistful and soft, her gaze lingering on the crowd. Nora followed it for a second, wondering what it would feel like to find out your mother had disappeared…only to reappear onstage with a guitar and a rock legend beside her?

Was that something that even the nonconformist Eleanor Bell would do?

And yet—if not her, then who?

Nora wove through the press of bodies, sweat sliding down her spine, the sun sharp on her shoulders. She'd definitely be pink with sunburn by evening, maybe even peeling in a few days. Not that she cared. Sun was part of the story now. She couldn't wait to tell Kelley all about this. While she was still sad to miss out on the weekend at the lake, it seemed like they were going to be headed home soon with her grandmother, and she wasn't going to miss the whole summer like she thought.

She passed a couple kissing in a hammock strung between two trees. A girl with a daisy-chain crown offered her a sip from a jug of something amber colored. Nora shook her head politely and kept moving. Her sandals kicking dust with every step.

And to think Grandma might be the story's main character.

She remembered her grandmother playing the guitar when she was little. A silly song about pancakes and pirates. She must have been six, maybe seven, dancing barefoot on the carpet while Eleanor strummed and sang in her smoky alto voice.

The memory felt blurry around the edges—like an old photograph, forgotten until it resurfaced and one realized it was important all along.

Growing up, she'd never really understood her grandmother. Eleanor was half elegant, half nonconformist. Pearls around her neck and bare feet. Her house smelled like lemon polish and sandalwood some days, like incense the rest of the time. She kept issues of *Vogue*, *Good Housekeeping*, and *Rolling Stone* on the same coffee table.

Nora used to think it was eccentricity.

Now she wondered if maybe it was just…expression.

She reached the row of food stands and vending carts, the air thick with the smell of popcorn, grilled onions, and something fried.

Somewhere behind her, music rose again—a new set, a new voice. But she could only think about her grandmother's hands on the guitar. The way she used to hum while pushing Nora on a swing. The way her voice had a rasp to it that made even the word "Tuesday" sound like the beginning of a ballad.

Maybe Nora didn't know her grandmother as well as she thought.

Maybe none of them did.

As she stood in line for a soda, craving that crisp bite of Coca-Cola against the back of her throat, a boy—maybe her age, maybe a year or two older—turned around in front of her. He had white teeth and a small chip to his incisor that made his smile more interesting than perfect. "Great concert, right?" His voice was easy and warm.

Nora looked at him more closely. He wore a white button-down like what her father wore with his suits, only rumpled, and this guy's sleeves were rolled to his elbows. It was tucked into slim-fitting jeans that weren't quite bell-bottoms but nodded in that direction. A leather satchel hung across his chest. Unlike most of the festival crowd, he wore no fringe, no face paint, no visible flower crowns—but somehow, he still fit. Like someone who knew who he was without needing a costume to say it.

In his upper shirt pocket, a harmonica popped out beside a notebook and pencil.

"Yeah, so far." Nora brushed hair from her face. "We got here about an hour ago, but I'm loving it."

He raised an eyebrow. "So you missed Grandma, huh?"

There it was again—that nickname. That strange, reverent tone everyone used when they said it.

"We did," she admitted. "But I heard she was amazing?"

"Maybe even the act of the day," he said, laughing. He patted the notebook in his pocket. "Got it all written down. Front-row view."

"Are you a journalist?" she asked, intrigued.

"Hoping to be. Right now, I'm an intern for the summer at the *San Francisco Chronicle.* Out here chasing a story on the next wave of musical stars. And I think I might've just found one." He held out a hand. "Name's Joe."

"Nora." She shook it—firmly, confidently, and quickly.

He grinned again, cocking his head like he was sizing her up.

"You strike me as the kind of girl who drinks black coffee and reads Sylvia Plath." He tapped his lower lip, eyes scanning over her with studied practice. "But here you are…waiting in line for a soda. Is this your plot twist?"

Nora lifted an eyebrow, trying for nonchalant even as her belly was filling with butterflies. "Impressive guesswork. What does my soda order tell you about my tragic backstory?"

"Ah, that depends." A twinkle entered his eyes, mesmerizing her, and Nora had to straighten herself up or risk falling for his charm.

"Oh, yeah?" she asked. "On what?"

"Well, if you order root beer, you're nostalgic. If you order Sprite, you're avoiding commitment. And if you order a Coke, you secretly long for Parisian cafés but are stuck in a world of diner booths—and I would know. *Je suis en partie français, mademoiselle.*" He winked. "Or maybe you just really wanted a soda, and I'm overanalyzing. But where's the fun in that?"

Nora didn't answer. Instead, she stepped forward in line, smile tugging at the corner of her mouth.

"Three Coca-Colas, please," she said to the vendor. The teenager in a tank top handed her the first sweating bottles of soda from a galvanized tub packed with ice.

Nora could feel Joe watching her as she took the next two and the glass bottles clinked together in her hand. She handed over the money, grabbed the drinks, and turned just enough to throw him a glance over her shoulder.

"What does this say about me?" She held up the three sodas.

"That you're here with someone." He narrowed his eyes for a moment, then smiled when she didn't reply. "And that you're a mystery I've already started writing about."

"For the sake of accuracy in your exposé?" Nora said, with a challenging lift of her brow. "I prefer Woolf to Plath."

Joe's grin widened, and he said, "Ah-ha." He made the phrase sound as if he'd just discovered a significant secret. Reaching into his shirt pocket with dramatic flair, he pulled out a stubby pencil and worn notebook. As he eyed her, he licked the tip of the pencil with exaggerated seriousness and began to narrate while he scribbled.

"Developing story: Subject prefers Woolf. Possible influence of stream-of-consciousness on worldview. Coca-Cola preference remains unexplained. Mystery deepens. Must investigate further."

Nora rolled her eyes, thrusting one of the ice-cold bottles toward him. As he took it, their hands brushed. Cool condensation slipped between their fingers—briefly, but long enough to send a jolt up her arm.

"Careful, Joe the Journalist," she said lightly. "Some mysteries don't want to be solved. For example, Woolf is only my preference in classics. Right now, I'm digging Mario Puzo."

He didn't flinch. Didn't break eye contact.

"That just makes this a mystery more worth chasing."

Something about the way he said it—low and casual like he hadn't even meant to charm her—made her pulse spike in her throat.

Without another word, Nora turned away and waded back into the sea of strangers. Her heart pounding louder than the music, sharper than the sunlight bouncing off the Coca-Cola label.

Of all the boys she'd met in high school—yearbook committee boys, football players and honor society boys, and the boy who'd kissed her at junior prom with a mouth full of ginger ale—none of them had made her feel this way. Like she was the interesting one. Like someone had seen inside of her, not past her.

Joe the Journalist.

The name stuck in her mind like the hook of a song. She didn't turn around to see if he was watching her go. But she hoped he was. And she couldn't help but wonder…

Would she see him again?

PART TWO

Mile High Riff

SUMMER 1969

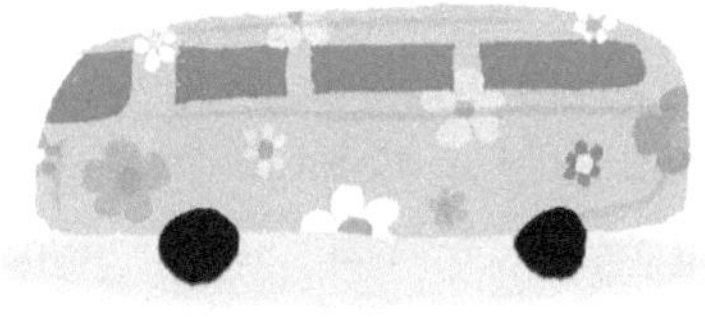

CHAPTER THIRTEEN

"ELEANOR?"

Her eyelids fluttered at the sound of her name.

Sitting cross-legged on the grass, Roxy curled in her lap like a warm little snuggle bug, Eleanor had drifted somewhere else—halfway between memory and music. The bodies swaying around her were moving like waves, smoke curling in the air, the sun smudged behind a veil of cigarette haze. The music was loud, something bluesy and familiar, but it came in muffled—like hearing through water.

She looked down and noticed her cigarette—burned halfway through, the ash long and curling like a gray snake. One wrong move, and it would tumble onto her skirt.

"Eleanor?" the voice called again, closer now.

She squinted up, half blinded by the sun.

A man stood over her, body haloed in golden light. His face was flushed, and he looked a little breathless, smiling at her in that startled, unbelieving way—like he'd found something precious he thought he'd lost.

There was something so familiar about him. The curve of his jaw. That thick, unruly hair. The bow-shaped lips.

"Is it really you?" Eleanor wiped her eyes. "Jet?" she asked softly.

A name she hadn't spoken aloud in decades. Jet was the boy she'd met one summer at a music festival near her hometown. The way he'd played the banjo had been soul exposing, and the way he'd kissed her had been a high note. They'd sung together onstage once—just once—before she'd gone back to her last year of high school and he went wherever boys like him went…everywhere.

"Jet's my uncle," he said, laughing. "Did you know him? Wouldn't that be something. He was a great musician."

Eleanor wrinkled her brow at the sound of his voice. Husky, deep, and sensual. But different. Memories unfolded in her mind like a movie reel. Jet's face blurred in the recesses, fading out. Uncle? What was he talking about?

She stared at the man in front of her, a buzz of unease under her ribs.

He extended a hand.

She hesitated, then slowly unwrapped Roxy's leash from her wrist and placed her hand in his palm. Roxy squirmed a little as Eleanor set her gently on the ground.

With a gentle tug, he pulled her to stand on uncertain legs. Their hands lingered for just a fraction longer than friends' would before he let go.

The man—she wasn't convinced he was Jet anymore, as he looked a bit older than she first thought—let out a low whistle. "That performance of yours was impressive, Ellie."

Ellie. She hadn't been called that in years.

"You've seen me do it a thousand times." The words slipped out before she realized what she was saying.

The man beside her looked puzzled, his head cocking to the side, brows drawn together, mouth opening just slightly. There was no recognition in his eyes. Just confusion. And now concern.

And that's when she knew for certain.

This wasn't Jet.

And she wasn't nineteen.

This wasn't the county music festival just outside her hometown. Nor was she dressed in her school uniform after having snuck off to perform. Worst of all, she wasn't in love for the first time.

Instead, Eleanor was standing in the middle of a field in… *Where were they?* Her knees ached. Her hands—she looked down at them—were thin and veined and spotted with age.

Only a few days ago she'd missed the celebration for her sixty-ninth birthday because she'd run away.

The realization came down like a soft collapse, deflating the hope she'd felt just seconds before.

"Oh," she whispered, her voice caught on the wind.

The last lines of "Proud Mary" faded from somewhere in the distance, followed by the crowd cheering for the next act. A girl danced by in a yellow fringe vest, a tambourine trilling with each bounce against her palm.

"I don't remember the mountains being so tall," Eleanor murmured, squinting at the hazy, jagged horizon.

The young man turned, following her gaze. "Denver caught you by surprise?" There was a bit of surprise in his tone too.

She nodded absently. Denver… They weren't in California anymore. Eleanor suppressed a shiver at not remembering how she'd gotten here or where she was. Her mind flashed to the appointment with her doctor. To his prognosis. The words had tumbled from his mouth in a cloud of nonsense that she still hadn't parsed.

More than Denver caught her by surprise. So did time. But she didn't say this part aloud. There were some things she needed to keep to herself. Yet somehow her expression must have conveyed her confusion.

"We're in Mile High Stadium," the stranger said gently. "Remember? You rode here with me in the van. Me and the band."

"Oh," she said, laughter softening her slipup, she hoped. She shook her head lightly like she was brushing off a cobweb. As if it were just a silly, momentary lapse. Not the reality, that she couldn't remember any of the drive. Couldn't remember climbing into his van. Couldn't even recall his name until—

Shep.

Yes. That was it. Shep.

The resemblance to Jet was uncanny, but she wasn't about to confess to knowing Shep's uncle. That would break two of her rules. One, a lady never kisses and tells, and two, a lady never reveals her true age. At least she'd come back to the present.

But the rest? A haze.

"You okay?" He studied her, his voice lined with something like worry.

Eleanor tried to brush off his concern with a pat to his arm, her touch warm and practiced. The same pat she'd given Henry, Leanne, and Nora when she was proud of them, comforting them, walking past. The same one she gave Roxy when the little dog was twirling in a circle. A touch that spoke louder than words. A touch that held depth.

"I'm doing just fine, honey." She mustered a smile, hoping it stuck.

His hand covered hers, brows wiggling, giving her a cheeky, teasing look. "Oh, you're flirting now? Don't hold out on me, Ellie. Give me all you've got."

Heat filled her cheeks, and she playfully swatted his hand away.

Ellie. The nickname still made her heart hiccup. Two syllables, so personal, echoed from a time when someone else used to say it—whispered behind a stage curtain, wrapped in the sweet heat of summer and possibility.

But she didn't want to think about that. She didn't want to think about the part where she had forgotten—*again*—where she was. Or the sharp, terrifying emptiness that opened up when a name or a thought slipped away like it had never existed at all. The truth was, Eleanor hadn't been completely honest with her daughter or the doctor about how things were progressing with her. She'd told them the bare minimum too afraid to face the truth of how fast she appeared to be slipping away.

"Want to sing with me again?" Shep asked. "Last time, we were a real hit. Got the crowd going."

Eleanor looked past him to the field, the heat warping the distance, bodies packed in tight. The late-June sun pulsed against a chaotic wash of sound—drums, shouting, someone tuning a guitar far too loudly. Tie-dye bled into camouflage. Shirtless men threw Frisbees across clusters of half-pitched tents. This wasn't like California. There, the festival had felt dreamy. Loose and golden and strange in a beautiful way.

Here, there was tension beneath the joy. Electricity. Like something might crack open at any second.

Still, she nodded. "Yes."

Shep took the cigarette from her fingers, flicked off the long, crumbling ash, and handed it back to her with a quick glance. His expression said what he didn't: *You okay with doing this?*

"Don't want to burn yourself," he murmured.

Eleanor nodded again, more to herself this time. She had to focus. The forgetting was getting worse. The doctor had warned her that there was no telling how quick or slow the progression would be. And she didn't want to tell anyone she felt like she'd been caught in a rip current—one minute standing in the surf, the next yanked under. Her doctor had stressed the importance of rest and nutrition, both of which she wasn't getting enough of.

But she wasn't going to let some diagnosis pull her away. Not yet.

She had things to sing. A story to finish. A life she wanted to leave her way—with music, with meaning, with fire.

Shep handed back Roxy's leash.

Automatically, Eleanor slipped her hand into her skirt pocket, fingers brushing over the familiar rustle of dog treats. She pulled one out, crouched slowly, steadily, and fed it to Roxy, whose tiny tongue gave an enormous lick against her palm.

Her memory might be dependably undependable, but she hoped her instincts weren't. She was counting on that.

"We've got about an hour before our set," Shep said, checking his watch. "Want to take a nap in the tent? I know I'm exhausted."

Eleanor was surprised at how heavy her limbs felt at the suggestion. As if she'd walked all the way from New York to California to Denver. But then her stomach gave a hollow growl.

"I could really use a sandwich," she said. "I don't think I've eaten all day."

"And a coffee," he added. "I could use one of those."

She followed him toward the tent, his hand warm and solid around hers.

Shep looked every inch the rocker—denim vest, guitar pick necklace, fingers calloused and ink-stained—but he was far from the wild type Eleanor might've expected in this world of late nights and hazy clouds. He didn't drink. Didn't smoke marijuana, even when he passed it around to others. He smoked cigarettes, sure, but in moderation, like it was more rebellion than habit.

She liked that about him. That he was steady. That he noticed things, like when she hadn't eaten.

He reminded her of Jet—not the blurry version from her slipping memories but the real one. The one who'd carried her guitar across gravel lots and always remembered how she liked her tea—two lumps of sugar and a splash of cream.

Inside the tent, the air was cooler, dimmer. A folding table had been set up with prewrapped sandwiches, bottles of cold Coca-Cola sweating in a metal bin of ice, and a tin of mismatched chips and cookies.

"No coffee, I guess," Shep said with a chuckle. "Will a Coke do?"

"That'll do just fine," she said, coughing gently into her fist. Her chest felt a little tight—just enough to make her notice her breath.

"You'll get used to the altitude soon." Shep cracked open a bottle and handed it to her. "I had the same thing the first time I played here last year. Thin air messes with you."

"Groovy," Eleanor said the way Nora did, then smirked. "So, how long until I stop feeling like I'm in the middle of a space race but forgot my oxygen tank?"

Shep barked a laugh, biting into his roast beef sandwich, a bit of horseradish sitting at the corner of his mouth until he wiped it away.

"Is that where you're headed next, Ellie? Leaving the music world for a life in space?" He grinned, lopsided. "Didn't peg you for an astronaut groupie."

"And I didn't peg you for a grandma groupie," she shot back without missing a beat.

That got him. His grin widened around a mouthful of bread and roast beef. She took a long sip of the cold soda, the bubbles fizzing sharp at the back of her throat. With each swallow she started to feel a little more like herself. A little more here in the present.

Her laughter surprised even her. It felt good to laugh like that again. Her chest still ached faintly. But her heart? Her heart felt clear.

"What can I say, doll?" He swallowed. "I dig a gal with a little experience and a lot of charm. Some guys are chasing the hopeful moon landing. I'm just over here appreciating you've already been to the stars."

Eleanor's mouth nearly dropped open—would have if she hadn't just taken a sip of Coca-Cola. She swallowed, the bubbles popping over her tongue. "Oh, you devil. Keep teasing like that, and I'll forget my manners." She kept her voice low and playful. Where had that come from? This flirtatious side she hadn't felt in years… It was like a spark jumping from an old wire.

Shep winked at her, slow and shameless, enough to make her already weak knees wobble.

"Well, now," he said, leaning in just a little, "I wouldn't want to be responsible for that…or would I?"

Before she could respond, a voice called out behind them.

"Shep, it's time."

Eleanor turned, blinking into the dimmer light of the tent—and recognized Megan. Her heart lifted.

The same young woman who'd picked her up at the hotel in California. The one with the too-fast van and the floaty tank top. Eleanor remembered gripping the dashboard while Megan raced through traffic like a game of chicken. At one point she'd taken a turn so hard, the dice had come right off the rearview mirror and hit the drummer in the forehead.

"Any chance," Eleanor said, squinting with mock suspicion, "you drove us from California all the way here to Denver?"

The girl laughed and wagged a finger. "You're funny, Ellie. You know I did."

Eleanor chuckled, smiling wide—covering the flicker of anxiety in her chest. She didn't know. Not really. But she remembered how the van fishtailed onto gravel and how Roxy had whined the whole drive like she'd been on a roller coaster.

Maybe it wasn't that she'd forgotten.

Maybe she'd just blocked it out.

No wonder the memory had gone missing—self-preservation, plain and simple.

"You're a menace behind the wheel, you know that?" Eleanor said, lifting her soda bottle in salute.

The girl grinned and gave a proud shrug. "Only when I'm awake."

CHAPTER FOURTEEN

THE SUNSET STRETCHED ENDLESSLY ACROSS THE HORI-zon, a molten ribbon melting into the road ahead. The radio fizzed in and out of focus as they moved close to the edge of the station's reach, but the Beatles still played through the speakers. "Here Comes the Sun," played and its gentle optimism was at odds with Leanne's growing unease.

They'd left California empty-handed that morning.

No Eleanor. No confirmation. Just rumors of an old woman who'd climbed aboard Shep Moon's tour bus after a surprise performance that had left the crowd buzzing. Leanne had dismissed the idea that the woman could be her mother—until she heard someone mention the hairless dog.

"A pip-squeak pooch with a beehive tuft of hair and a bark like bad feedback on an amp" had been the exact description.

There was only one dog like that. And only one woman bold enough to bring her onto a rock-and-roll stage.

Eleanor Bell Strickland. There'd been a sharp sense of relief that her mother was alive and well, and hopefully safe, along with the plummet of her stomach when Leanne realized the chase wasn't over and that they'd now have to figure out where Shep Moon and his band were headed with her in tow.

Leanne and Nora had stayed at the festival until every last tent had been taken down, searching for Eleanor with no success. At least a dozen people told her Shep's next stop was in Colorado. With no reason not to trust that, Leanne and Nora, after waiting until checkout to make sure Eleanor was one of the people leaving the motel the following day, had climbed back into the Lincoln Continental—its new tire humming over the asphalt, a full tank of gas beneath them, and miles to go. They'd pointed the car toward Colorado, where the Denver Pop Festival would start in five days.

Leanne was hoping that—as everyone said—the festival would be smaller and easier to navigate than the one they'd just left. That she'd have a chance of actually spotting her mother.

Six hours after leaving California, they started to pass signs for Las Vegas. In the distance, the lights of the Strip shimmered like a carnival dream against the deepening purple of the desert sky.

Beside her, Nora was pressed against the window, her face aglow in the reflected lights. No doubt upset to be missing even more of the summer with her friends than she thought.

Leanne stole a glance. So wistful. So young.

And then, without thinking, without planning it out, Leanne asked, "Should we stop in Vegas?"

The words hung in the air like smoke. She hadn't meant to say them. She didn't do spontaneous. Her life was a sequence of lists and quiet compromises. Where Eleanor had been whimsy and wonder, Leanne had been structure, predictability. Pressed pleats and presliced sandwiches.

Nora turned slowly, eyes wide. Looking at Leanne as if she'd rolled a joint and lit it with a match made of reckless spark.

"Are you serious?" Nora asked, cautiously thrilled.

A thrill rushed through Leanne in response—real and ridiculous. She smiled. Leanne had always been the kind of person who waited for life to happen.

There was a sequence, a proper order of things, that she'd been following since girlhood. Probably even before. Everyone grew up, went to school, found a respectable job, married well, kept the house clean, raised the child, wore the pearls, and paid the bills. No detour. No deviation. No dreaming beyond the edges of the script.

But everything was shifting now.

Nora was leaving soon. Off to Yale. Off to begin the rest of her life. And Leanne… She wasn't sure what came next. Her marriage? A question mark. Her mother? A mystery. The only thing she did know was that she was afraid of the empty spaces ahead.

So maybe it was time to do something wild. Or at least uncharacteristic.

Maybe it was time to embrace the now—just once.

She turned on her blinker and eased the Lincoln off the highway, merging onto the glittering stretch that was Las Vegas Boulevard.

"Dead serious," Leanne said, her voice firmer than expected. "We have five days until the next festival, and it will only take a couple days to get there. We know my mom is with the band and not lost alone somewhere. Why not?" She smiled again as her daughter's eyes widened.

They cruised down the Strip, neon blooming around them, lighting up the dusk in electric pinks, golds, and icy blues. Signs pulsed like heartbeats: The Sands. The Dunes. Stardust. Caesars Palace.

The street was a mix of contrasts—men in slick suits and women in cocktail dresses brushing shoulders with barefoot hippie girls in fringe vests and bell-bottoms. A saxophone player on one corner crooned something jazzy. The lights from the nickel slot machines spilled from open doors. Someone, somewhere, laughed too loudly. Somewhere else, someone cried.

This was the city of in-betweens.

"Frank, Dean, Sammy…they made it all look so glamorous," Leanne murmured, half to herself.

"There's a rumor Elvis is going to start performing here in July," Nora said, craning her neck to catch the glittering sign of the International Hotel slated to open in a week. "Too bad we're not coming back."

Leanne smiled faintly. *Too bad.*

Nora traced her finger over the gold lettering of *The Godfather* on the seat between them. "The Mafia's huge in Vegas, right?" Her voice was half serious, half amazed. "Do you think we'll see someone like Don Corleone?"

The city flickered outside their windows like it was alive—buzzing and hungry and full of secrets. And for the first time in a long time, Leanne wasn't just driving through it. She was in it.

"Well, I hope no one offers us a deal we can't refuse," Leanne said, putting on her best mobster growl, her fingers tented like a tiny don.

Nora burst out laughing. "If they do, you're handling the negotiations."

They cruised the Strip a few more times, taking in the wonder of the city, letting the neon blur past them like the frames of a dream. Showgirls in feather boas strutted down the sidewalk in a formation that was both tight and fluid at the same time, disappearing through the spinning doors of a casino. A man in a white tux leaned against a red Cabriolet out of the 1940s, smoking and watching the world go by with the confidence of someone who owned it. Sonny Corleone before the job had gotten to him? Leanne couldn't remember the last time she'd simply looked at life happening around her.

They chose the Sands for the night, drawn in by a glowing sign out front that read "Join us tonight in the Copa Room for a Legendary Show."

Inside the hotel, the casino floor buzzed like an elegant hive. Red velvet carpet softened their steps; shimmering chandeliers cast golden light over a crowd of men in tuxedos and women in sleek dresses, sequins glimmering like stars. Cigarette smoke curled through the air, mingling with an artificial floral scent, sweet and acrid.

They stood at the center of it all—mother and daughter, soaking it in.

"Is he famous?" Nora whispered, nodding toward a man in a silk ascot holding court at a blackjack table.

"He looks like someone who once dated someone famous," Leanne murmured back.

"Half the men in here look like mobsters."

"They might be."

They approached the man at the front desk in his tailored navy suit. He had a smile lacquered onto his face and a gold name tag gleaming on his lapel.

"Is there a pool?" Leanne asked, her voice breezy but hopeful, as the man slid a room key across the polished desk.

"Indeed, madam. A tropically styled pool deck just out back—with cabanas, cocktail waitresses, and palm trees," he said with a little flourish as if describing a personal oasis.

"Palm trees?" Nora echoed.

The man stared at her as if she'd asked if the rooms came with ceilings. "Of course. Imported from Palm Springs."

Leanne felt wonderfully, oddly giddy. Like she might just go for a swim tomorrow. Or order a cocktail before five o'clock.

Then, she sobered. "Where can I find a telephone?" It'd been nearly a week since she'd spoken to her husband, and if she didn't get through to Dean… Well, she wasn't sure what would happen. She'd had no success, but he certainly hadn't made any Herculean attempts to find her.

The man nodded toward a gold-framed hallway just off the lobby. "There's a row of booths just behind the elevator bank, madam. The operators will be happy to assist with long-distance."

She nodded her thanks.

After nearly a week had gone by, Dean was probably half worried, half irritated. Maybe she was underestimating him and he'd left a dozen messages at the hotels her itinerary had listed. If she'd called him earlier in the week, he might've told her to come home.

And she would have. But now? Now she wasn't sure she'd listen.

Once they were settled in their room and with Nora in the shower—singing something Beatles-adjacent behind the door—Leanne slipped out, her purse slung over her shoulder, her heels clicking faintly against the marble. The air downstairs was heavy with perfume and panic.

She found the row of pay phones, and several of them were empty. Slipping into one, Leanne picked up the receiver and pressed zero.

"I'd like to place a call to New York, please," she told the operator.

"Yes, ma'am. Number?"

Leanne recited her home telephone slowly. The operator quoted the charge of eight quarters. She dug cool, if slightly sticky from a melted peppermint, coins from the bottom of her bag and fed them one by one into the slot. *Click. Click. Click.*

She glanced at the delicate gold watch on her wrist, listening to the ringing on the line.

"No one appears to be answering your call, ma'am," the operator said after an eternity of trilling. "Would you like me to redirect to another number?"

Leanne hesitated. She didn't want to call the office. Not really. But if he wasn't at home, he was there. Always there.

"Yes, please," she said and gave the number for the firm.

The connection clicked.

Rang once. Then—

"Miller, Abrams and Associates," came a voice. Smooth. Sultry. Practiced.

Leanne stiffened.

Charlotte. Dean's secretary.

It wasn't just the voice. But the lilt, the overfamiliar way she always said "Mrs. Miller" like it was both a compliment and a warning.

"This is Leanne." Her tone was even, measured, and more controlled than casual conversation required.

"Mrs. Miller! So good to hear from you." The voice brightened too much, too quickly. "How's the travel going?"

"Quite well. And thank you again for putting together the itinerary," Leanne said, her voice clipped but polite.

"Of course," the secretary replied, voice syrupy. "My pleasure. I'm always happy to help. Dean—I mean, Mr. Miller—has been quite worried. He hasn't heard from you."

Leanne heard the slip. But she didn't say anything. She didn't have to. The flicker of nausea that hit her gut said enough. She didn't believe that Dean had crossed any lines…but the suspicion always lingered. She steadied her voice.

"May I speak with him, please?"

"I'm really sorry; he's already left for the evening," came the smooth reply.

Leanne's jaw tightened. "Then why are you still there?" The question was genuine—at first. But as the question left her lips, the edge intensified.

"Just finishing up some last bits of correspondence. Makes the morning easier."

The secretary's voice was easy, almost conspiratorial. As if she expected Leanne to bond with her over the weight of office work. To relate.

But all Leanne felt was the slow, cold curl of unease wrapping around her ribs.

"Well," she said, steel in her tone, "if you could let him know that Nora and I decided to stop in Vegas for the night, I'd appreciate it. I tried the house first—couldn't reach him."

"I certainly will, Mrs. Miller."

Leanne hung up.

She stared at the pay phone, fingers curled tightly around the receiver even after the line went dead. Her stomach churned with a queasy mix of regret and suspicion. She'd finally found a phone that was usable and called to reassure her husband she and Nora were okay. And what had she gotten for her effort?

She walked briskly back through the lobby.

As she moved past the lobby bar, a man with long hair, gold rings on every finger, and a purple velvet jacket raised his glass toward her. He resembled the groupie dressed like a wizard she'd seen in California.

"You look like you need a cocktail," he said, smiling.

Leanne stopped.

The last time a man said something like that to her, she was twenty-three and single. Something in his voice—teasing, yes, but kind—cut through the fog of her frustration. So instead of getting ruffled or indignant she said, "Maybe I do."

He signaled the bartender, and a moment later a bright pink drink was set in front of her. It was cold, far too strong, and precisely what she needed.

By the time she stepped off the elevator and returned to her hotel room, the last of her cocktail in hand, she was seething.

Not drunk.

Not dramatic.

Just done being the only one putting effort into her marriage. Though in truth, how much had she really tried lately?

"Ready for dinner and a show at the Copa Room?" Leanne asked, smoothing her dress and checking her earrings in the hotel mirror.

"Did you find out who's playing?" Nora turned from the vanity, applying a fresh swipe of rose-petal lipstick, then blotting her lips with a tissue she tossed on the bed. She eyed the half-empty cocktail in Leanne's hands but said nothing.

"Not yet," Leanne said. "But it's sure to be swinging—whoever it is."

"Swinging," Nora repeated with a mischievous grin, drawing out the word like it was their own private language now. Her daughter's smile full of amusement but something quieter as well—affection. For a second, Leanne forgot all the eye rolls, the slammed doors, the distance over the last year. The grumpy argument they'd had that morning getting back into the car. She was simply grateful. Grateful to be here with her daughter. On an adventure they hadn't planned in a city that shimmered like a mirage.

"Maybe it'll be Grandma," Nora deadpanned.

They both laughed. Sharp, spontaneous peals that surprised even them.

But then they caught each other's gaze.

And stopped.

A beat passed.

"What if it is?" Nora asked softly now.

"What if it is," Leanne echoed, barely more than a whisper.

Neon lights flickered like heartbeats outside the hotel window, and the Strip buzzed with the promise of strange, unforgettable things.

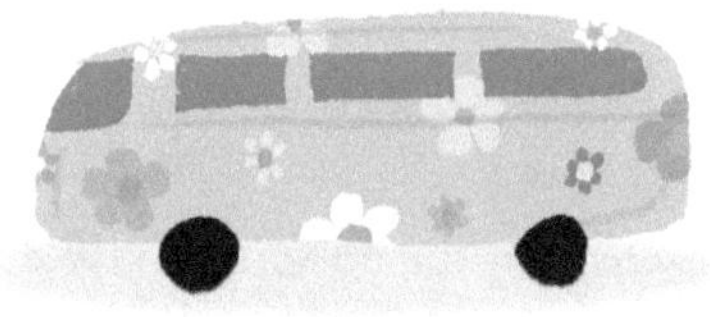

CHAPTER FIFTEEN

OVER COFFEE, LEANNE FLIPPED THROUGH THE NEWS stations to see if there were any reports of her mother, and coming up empty-handed, they once more decided no news was good news.

After a breakfast of bacon and sunny-side-up eggs with buttered toast, and a leisurely swim in the hotel pool, Nora and her mother climbed back into the Lincoln Continental, its chrome glinting under the morning sun.

Heat radiated in shimmering waves off the highway. Given the weather, they'd decided to try taking the top down. A surprisingly complicated task, given that neither of them had done it before. But after some tugging, and a few exasperated huffs, the valet jumped in to help and the roof folded away like an accordion, revealing an endless blue sky to Dean's leather seats.

They drove down the road, the wind tangling their hair, music blasting from the radio in competition with the whizzing air.

Nora dug into her backpack and pulled out her Polaroid camera. Clicking the knobs, adjusting the focus, she held it up to her eye, framing her mother behind the wheel—sunlight in her hair, head tilted back in laughter, singing like she had no cares in the world.

She pressed the button.

Click—whirr—shlunk.

The photo fluttered out the bottom, nearly snatched by the wind. Nora yelped and lunged, catching it just in time. She held it up, waving it gently in the air until the image began to appear.

She'd never seen her mother like this before. She wondered if her mother had really changed. Or had she, Nora, merely failed to look closely enough? Probably, she thought, it was a combination of both.

In the picture she held between two fingers her mother was not the household list maker or the voice reminding her to pack extra socks.

She was a woman, alive in her joy. *Free.*

Nora tucked the photo carefully into the glove compartment, not wanting to risk it flying off into the desert. It was important that her mother see it later. Important for her to see what Nora saw.

Another song came on the radio—one they'd heard at the concert just a few days ago, Three Dog Night's "Celebrate"—and Nora couldn't help herself. She started dancing in her seat, letting her arms catch the wind, hair whipping across her face as she belted out the chorus.

Her mom joined in, singing the lyrics at the top of her lungs.

When the song ended, Leanne pushed her hair back from her eyes and gave Nora a quick flash of a smile. Her hands stayed steady on the wheel, but her gaze was carefree, youthful, almost mischievous.

"Never thought I'd love that song so much," she said.

"Never thought I'd hear you sing it," Nora replied.

She looked at her mother again—really looked.

Not simply the woman who made her breakfast or reminded her about curfews. But someone who had once been eighteen too. Someone who'd had dreams and crushes and a favorite song. A girl who had danced like this once, with her whole life ahead of her. Maybe she should cut her mom some slack, because from where she was sitting, it seemed like her mom was doing the same.

"Did you date someone in high school?" Nora asked, keeping her voice casual, even if she felt quite the opposite.

They'd been driving for hours, the sun slanting lower across the sky, bathing the dashboard in gold. The wind carried music, and the faint scent of roadside dust and the open air made it feel safer to ask a question she'd never broached before.

Her mom had always just…been a mom. As far as Nora had ever been concerned, Leanne had skipped straight to adulthood like she'd never once been a girl who passed notes in class, had flirted with boys at school, or got butterflies before a dance.

Leanne laughed, eyes on the road. "Not just someone. A few someones, much to my parents' dismay, although I always thought your grandmother was a little proud."

Nora leaned her head back, smiling. "She would be. I think she'd be proud if she knew we were on this grand adventure."

"I think so too."

"Where did you meet Dad?"

"At an interview, actually," Leanne said. "I'd just finished secretarial school."

Nora gasped. "Don't tell me he was your boss."

"No, nothing like that." There was something abrupt about her mom's voice. Then she laughed and her mood went back to what it had been. "He was interviewing too. Not for the same position—he was there for something higher up. He was nervous."

"Solid," Nora said.

Leanne glanced at her daughter, clearly amused. "He made me a bet. Said whoever got the job second owed the other dinner. Then he asked for my number."

"Who won?"

"I did," she said, a flicker of pride lighting her face. "I got an offer in the interview and started work the next day. He got a callback the following week. So, we did end up at the same place."

"And where'd he take you for dinner?"

"A cozy little Italian place in the city. Red-checkered tablecloths. Pasta, wine. The kind of place where half the men looked like they belonged in *The Godfather*."

"Served by Don Corleone himself?" Nora teased.

"Could've been." Leanne's smile was wry as she teased back, "He had an Italian accent and kept muttering about a deal. I was just relieved there weren't bullets in our spaghetti instead of meatballs. Kidding."

Nora smiled, picturing her parents on a date surrounded by possible mobsters. Her mother, years younger, dressed up, sitting across from her future husband in a restaurant that smelled like garlic and danger. Would she have looked nervous or excited?

"Why do you ask?" Leanne slanted a glance.

Nora shrugged, but not casually. "I guess I've just never heard you talk about your past…past boyfriends or anything before Dad, really. Sometimes it just feels like you two have been together since birth."

Leanne nodded thoughtfully, but she didn't say anything else right away.

Then, after a beat, she said, "What about you? Any romance I should know about?"

"You know Jack, my prom date." Nora paused, tracing the rim of her leftover cup from breakfast. "He was…fine. But I told him I wasn't really interested in a long-distance thing. He wasn't either."

"Understandable. You want to concentrate on college, not a boy hundreds of miles away. I think I remember him saying he was joining the army."

"Yeah." Nora nodded, pursing her lips on a thought, hoping Jack would be far away from the fighting. "I'm hoping boys will be more mature in college and the relationships less...silly."

Leanne gave an assured nod. "They will be. Teenage boys are mostly just out to have fun. They have no responsibilities yet. They're just...sowing their oats, as the saying goes." Her mom's tone was matter-of-fact.

Nora raised an eyebrow, imagining the boys from kindergarten growing older and spreading a bag full of oatmeal. Then she laughed out loud. "I've never understood the correlation between breakfast cereal and, well...*that*."

Leanne chuckled. "It's a strange one, for sure." Their conversation broke as she tapped the paper map and asked if the highway ahead was their exit. After they were on another stretch of road, she said, "But once they get to college, something shifts. Most of them know what's coming. They've got to pick a major, finish their degrees, start a career. They're not boys anymore. Not entirely."

"But there'll still be parties." Nora planned to study hard during the week to keep her weekends free.

"Plenty of them. Mixers, bar nights, bad decisions. But underneath all their wild behavior, most of them know it won't last forever. They start to look around and think about what's next."

Nora gazed at the horizon, the car humming along the open road. She tried to imagine what it would be like—falling in love with someone you might actually marry.

"What if I don't want to think about what's next?" she murmured.

Leanne didn't answer right away. When she did, her voice was soft. "Then don't," she said. "Not yet. Just live, honey. Enjoy your classes. Make friends. And when you're ready for romance, you'll know."

"That makes sense," Nora said, turning the thought over.

All the high school boys she'd known had really only lived for two days a week—Friday night and all day Saturday. And if she was being honest, she had too. Especially Saturday mornings, when she could sleep in, listen to music, and not think about anything heavier than what record to spin first.

"Do you think I'll get to sleep in while I'm at college?" Nora joked, ready to lighten things a bit and veer away from romance.

"That depends." Her mother flicked on her blinker, pointing to a sign for a scenic overlook.

"On what?"

"I think everyone should get to sleep in on weekends. But you have to remember—you're at college for a reason. And it's not to catch up on your sleep."

"You mean to find a husband?" Nora asked, half joking…half not.

She fiddled with the Polaroid camera in her lap, spinning the lens idly. She could feel her mother's head swivel toward her—and when she glanced up, the look of sheer horror on Leanne's face was priceless.

Click.

She snapped the photo.

"I'd be okay if you let that one fly off in the wind." Leanne fluttered her hand toward the sky with a laugh.

"Oh no. This one's getting pride of place on my dorm room wall." Nora waved the photo in the air. "A reminder of my many responsibilities."

"Which don't include a wedding ring," her mother added firmly.

"Right. I'm not going to Yale to meet a husband," Nora said, more serious now. "I'm going to be part of something bigger. A shift in America. I want to graduate from an Ivy League, with honors. I want to start my life right."

Leanne didn't answer at first. Looking at her mom out of the corner of her eye, she noticed her lips pressed together, the corners twitching slightly, fighting emotion.

"I'm really proud of you, Nora," Leanne said finally.

Nora felt something warm rising and expanding inside of her. It wasn't that she didn't know her mother was proud of her before this moment, but more often than not her mom was closed off. There was something comforting about hearing her mom open up—it lifted Nora like a helium balloon. Nora smiled, staring at the slowly filling parking lot of the scenic overlook, her hand still wrapped around the warming Polaroid.

"Thanks, Mom."

Glancing at her again, Nora caught the soft look that slipped across her mother's face. Nostalgic. A little far away. An expression that might've led to tears if she let it.

Then her mom's expression went back to business. She clearly didn't want to end the conversation in a puddle of feelings. Pulling the keys from the ignition, she said, "Let's take some pictures."

As they climbed toward the fenced-off area, Nora said. "So…did I tell you about the hot writer I met at the festival?"

Leanne blinked. "Sounds like that could be an opening line for the sequel of *The Love Machine*."

Nora burst out laughing. "Maybe it could, but no. He was young—like, my age—and the pickup lines? Some of the worst I've ever heard."

Leanne raised an eyebrow, clearly intrigued. "Do tell."

For the first time in maybe ever, Nora felt her mother's openness, and she was excited to spill her secrets.

CHAPTER SIXTEEN

CREEDENCE CLEARWATER REVIVAL'S "BAD MOON RISING" crashed like a wave over the amped-up crowd. John Fogerty's voice rasped into the microphone. Sweat trailed down his shirtless chest and dampened the hair at his temples. Behind him, drums thundered. Guitars growled.

Eleanor tapped her foot at the brilliant storm of rhythm and heat and sound.

Eleanor stood just offstage, her fingers moving in the air, strumming an invisible guitar, reflexes guiding her along with the beat. She couldn't help herself—she knew the chords by heart, even if her hands weren't holding anything but the moment.

Up next was Shep's band. Which meant *she* was next.

They'd rehearsed her song all morning. One she'd written years ago and nearly forgotten until this tour brought it roaring back. Shep had insisted she take the lead, treating her like she was the headliner and he was just the backup.

It was sweet. Almost unbearably so.

The last chords of "Bad Moon Rising" rang out, the crowd

surging, shouting for an encore. The sound hit her like a gust of wind, and Eleanor's nerves lit up—not like the first time onstage, but still… sparks.

That familiar buzzing at the tips of her fingers, across her shoulders. Warning bells, maybe. But warning her of what, she couldn't say.

A tug at her elbow pulled her out of the nervous spiral. Shep's assistant, Megan, a willowy girl in bell-bottoms and a crochet top, held out Eleanor's Gibson L-00.

"Here you go." She tilted her head, studying Eleanor. "You okay?"

"Oh, I'm fine, deary." Eleanor brushed a hand through her hair before sliding the strap over her shoulder.

The guitar settled against her like a memory, the weight comforting. Familiar. Safe.

Like holding baby Leanne.

She hadn't expected to think that, but it came to her all at once—how her daughter had felt in her arms, heavy and warm. And how, the second she'd laid her in her crib, her arms had ached. Like she was putting part of herself down, even just for the night.

The Gibson was like that. A part of her. Something she loved beyond words. Something that remembered her, even when she forgot herself. And every time she'd had to put it away, she'd itched to go back and pick it up if only to hold it a little longer.

The band onstage launched into their encore, the lead singer whipping the microphone stand in the air like a lasso. For a split second, Eleanor thought he might actually toss it into the crowd and knock someone senseless. But instead, he planted it on the stage, raised a fist to the roaring audience, and shouted a final thank-you before disappearing with the rest of his band.

The emcee's voice boomed overhead, announcing Shep Moon and his band.

Eleanor hesitated on the side of the stage, a bolt of nerves making her whole body go rigid and causing her to forget how to walk. Shep's drummer and guitarists ambled onto the stage and began tuning their instruments, adjusting amps, and tapping cymbals. A cacophony of sound that was familiar and exhilarating. She wasn't sure if she should follow or run away. Did she really belong here?

The energy shifted inside her—less a feeling of being unmoored and more of being anchored. She had been invited. She wasn't an impostor here. Yes, she did belong.

Beside her, Shep rested a hand lightly on her arm, the pads of his fingers trailing to the small of her back. His voice was low and warm, and he leaned in close, his lips brushing the shell of her ear.

"You ready for this, Ellie?"

A thrill zipped up her spine—from the music, his touch, and the fact that this was *real*. The open mic had been exhilarating enough, but now… Eleanor sucked in a heady breath.

"I was born ready." A soft laugh escaped her, and she gave her shoulder a little toss like she was twenty again.

Shep lingered a beat longer, leaning into her, then murmured, "Do you how much I like you, Eleanor?"

Suppressing a shiver, she raised an eyebrow instead. This young man was such a flirt. "Enough to let me hijack your band for a night?"

His chuckle was low and gravelly, curling under her skin. "I must like you a whole lot, then."

Shep gave her hand a gentle squeeze—warm, grounding—and then he was gone, striding out under the lights to a wave of applause and cheers.

Eleanor stayed in the wings for a breath longer than she meant to.

Something held her there.

A memory flared—brief but bright. Another man. Another stage. Another lifetime. A voice whispering encouragement, a calloused hand tugging hers into the spotlight. Her heart thudded, not from nerves but from something more profound. A tether between then and now.

With a shake of her head, she smiled. This was a new stage. A new hand. She stepped forward at the same time Shep lifted his mic and grinned at the crowd.

"Folks," he called, "I've got a very special guest joining me tonight."

He extended his arm in her direction. And Eleanor Bell, guitar slung at her side, stepped tentatively, almost shyly, under the stadium lights, which cast a golden haze over her. At first, she hovered near the edge of the spotlight, blinking into the crowd.

But then she looked up. The sea of people, the swell of sound, the beating pulse of music—this was her shot.

A second chance.

A chance to reclaim a life she had once set aside.

A chance to honor herself, her voice, her art.

To be reborn, and live the dream she'd given up, if only for a moment.

Somewhere along the line, she'd been taught that a woman's worth was measured by what she did for others. How well she kept a home, how selflessly she raised her children, how patiently she supported a husband. And those things *were* important.

But she'd learned, sometimes painfully, that when a woman gave and gave and gave—and forgot herself in the process—no one truly saw her. Not even herself.

If she was going to love others well, she had to first love herself.

And so tonight, Eleanor Bell was loving herself—through song, through courage, through presence.

The drums behind her kicked into rhythm. The bass thumped steady. Shep stood at her side, smiling like he had all the faith in the world.

Eleanor's fingers found the familiar placement on the Gibson's strings, and she began to play. Words rose in her throat, shaped by melody, by memory. She and Shep sang the lyrics they'd practiced, their harmonies folding into one another like a heartbeat.

And then—it happened.

A note in her throat faltered. Her mouth stilled. Her fingers stumbled on the chords.

A single moment. A breathless pause.

Her mind went blank.

Her gaze on Shep, panic set in, making her hands go slippery. But his eyes were steady on hers. Eyes that reminded her of someone from long ago. Another life. Another man. Another stage.

She'd forgotten. Forgotten the words. Forgotten the chords. Forgotten herself.

But Shep kept playing. He deftly carried the next line, his voice wrapping around hers, guiding her back.

And just like that—it returned.

The lyric.

The chord.

The memory.

The song's inscape caught before it slipped away completely. To the audience, it was nothing. A hiccup in rhythm. A slight variation. But she knew. So did he. And for a second, fear bubbled in her chest. Had she disappointed him?

But then Shep stepped closer, their shoulders brushing, and gave her the softest nod. Not of pity. Of respect. Understanding.

And Eleanor kept singing.

At the song's end, Shep beamed down at her, eyes shining with joy. Not a flicker of doubt or disappointment in them. Whatever blip had happened mid-song, he'd either forgotten it or forgiven it. Maybe both. And she needed to do the same.

He leaned in and kissed her cheek, a soft graze of his lips, then raised her hand above their heads to the cheer of the crowd.

Eleanor curtsied low, then waved, smiling so wide her cheeks ached. She backed offstage, still riding the dizzy pulse of the performance, the guitar warm against her.

At the base of the stairs, Megan stood waiting, holding out a glass of water.

"Great job out there," she said. "There's someone who wants to talk to you."

A flicker of panic cut through Eleanor's euphoria. Had her family found her? Was this it? The end of her freedom?

The fear came fast—tight in her chest. Because she couldn't go back. Not yet. Not when she'd just remembered who she was. She couldn't say exactly why, other than she feared they would make her go home. Feared they'd make her give up what she'd already spent a lifetime missing.

But it wasn't Leanne or Nora waiting for her. Instead, it was a young man with a notepad, a press badge, and a spark in his eyes.

"My name's Joe, ma'am," he said, extending a hand.

"Nice to meet you, Joe."

Joe had an easygoing nature about him, putting Eleanor at ease. "I'd love to ask you a few questions—about your music, your story, all of it."

Megan handed Eleanor a glass of water, which she accepted with her free hand. "I'd be happy to answer."

"Do you ever watch Johnny Carson?" he asked.

She nodded, unsure of where this was going. "I have. On occasion."

"Well, you might want to tune in tonight. When I was watching last night, you came up."

"Me?" She couldn't help the surprise in her voice. "Why on earth would Johnny Carson be talking about me?"

Joe grinned, flipping open his notebook and skimming his finger over the page before tapping. "They're calling you the Dame of Rock and Roll after your performance in California. And surely after tonight, it's a name that will stick."

Stunned, Eleanor stared at him for half a beat. Maybe this was a dream, a hallucination. Any second now, she would wake up, sprawled on her purple velvet couch at home. But someone coughed a few feet away, and in dreams, did people ever cough?

Eleanor laughed softly, her fingers tapping against her arm as if it were her guitar. "'The Dame of Rock and Roll'?" She let the name roll off her tongue, feeling out the syllables. "I guess that's better than 'Rocking Grandma'."

Joe's eyes gleamed with mischief. "So, you like 'the Dame of Rock and Roll'?" he asked.

A sense of pride filled her, and she lifted her chin slightly. Despite the ache in her joints, the heat in her throat, there was a spark in her chest that hadn't been there in years.

"I think," she said with a smile, "it has a damn good ring to it."

"Good, because I gave it to them." He chuckled. "You hungry?" Joe tucked his notepad back into the pocket of his jacket.

"Famished."

"Well then," he said, already half rising, "what do you say I find you something to eat?"

Eleanor narrowed her eyes at him, amused. "If this is you trying to butter me up for questions, you don't have to. I'm happy to answer."

"The Dame of Rock and Roll is feisty," Joe teased.

She smirked. She'd never thought of herself that way, but now that he'd mentioned it… "You could say that."

Her gaze drifted to the cigarette in his hand—unlit, forgotten.

"Are you going to smoke that?" she asked.

He looked down as if he hadn't even realized he was holding it between his fingers. "No," he said. "Would you like it?"

"I would." She hoped doing something as simple as puffing on a cigarette would bring her back to earth.

He passed it to her without hesitation.

"Got a light?" she asked.

Joe struck a match, shielding the flame from the wind with his palm, and she leaned in. Eleanor took a long drag, the cherry flaring red in the low light. She held the smoke in her lungs for a beat, then exhaled slowly, watching the grayish curl drift toward the stars and seeing something different in her mind. Memories of other nights when she'd sung, followed by a cigarette and a boy with a match.

Her body still buzzed from the performance. Her voice still felt warm, alive. The music was still in her blood.

Joe watched her with the cautious awe of someone who knew they were witnessing something more significant than a good story.

"So," he said, voice soft, "what does your family think about you starting a singing career this late in life?"

Eleanor took another drag, the edge of her lips quirking into a smile. She thought of her daughter. Her granddaughter. The house. The years she'd spent in silence.

Then she looked him square in the eyes.

"I wouldn't say it's so much a new beginning as a return," she said. "And I believe it's never too late to do what you love."

CHAPTER SEVENTEEN

AFTER DAYS ON THE ROAD, LEANNE PARKED THE Continental in the only spot left—a crooked sliver of grass between two psychedelic-painted vans. The motor fell silent, and she just sat there for a beat, letting her joints recalibrate.

Road-tripping was not for the faint of heart. And when they finally got back to New York, she might boycott automobiles for the foreseeable future in favor of walking, even if it took her the entire day.

When she finally swung the door open and stepped out, her entire body groaned in protest. Knees stiff. Back sore. If she hadn't been driving for hours on end she might have worried she was suddenly ninety. The time on the road certainly had felt like longer than fifty years.

She stretched her arms over her head, twisting right and left from the waist up, feeling her muscles loosen. Music thundered from the stadium—deep, pulsing, relentless. Lights shot into the night sky like flares. The whole scene was alive, pulsating with energy.

She could only imagine the thrill of being on the inside.

And, allegedly, somewhere in that musical pandemonium, her

mother was singing and playing guitar. Performing like she was twenty, not nearly seventy.

How in the world was Eleanor doing all this? Leanne had barely survived a twelve-hour drive. She felt like she'd gone ten rounds on one of those vibrating belt machines—except instead of her hips having been slimmed, she felt like her organs had rearranged themselves.

Unlike her mom, Nora had leaped out of the car—camera swinging around her neck, her hair catching the glint of neon from the stage lights—all youthful bounce and forward momentum.

Leanne watched her daughter with a strange mix of admiration and envy. To be that young again. She shook her head ruefully.

"You all right?" Nora slowed just enough to glance back.

There it was again—that look. The one Leanne had started catching more and more. Not pity. Not concern. Something new.

Recognition? Acceptance?

It felt like Nora wasn't seeing just as a mom anymore. She was seeing a woman. One with a past, one who looked a little lost sometimes. Or maybe that was wishful thinking on Leanne's part. In fact it had been nearly twenty-four hours of complete pleasantness, and not a single argument or snide remark.

"I'm good," Leanne replied, smoothing her skirt. "Just a long drive."

Nora agreed, but her voice brightened. "But we're here."

She punctuated the sentence with a little hop and a squeal, already bounding toward the stadium gates, full of energy and wonder.

Leanne fished into her purse for cash, fingers brushing old receipts, a tube of lipstick, and a stray mint fallen from the Certs pack lying on top of the folded bills left over from pumping gas that morning. They'd been in such a hurry she hadn't bothered to put them back in her wallet.

Every time they approached a festival gate, she worried tickets would be sold out. That they'd be turned away at the last minute. That their chance to finally put eyes on her mother would disappear. So far, they'd gotten lucky. But still, the uncertainty made her stomach twist. From the looks of things, Mile High Stadium was already packed.

As they entered, she was immediately aware that this crowd felt different from the one in California. The atmosphere there had been mellow, almost dreamy—tie-dye and tambourines, patchouli and peace signs. Here in Colorado, she'd expected something similar—mountain air and mellow vibes. But there was nothing bohemian about this crowd. The energy was less euphoria and more edge.

On instinct, she stepped closer to Nora, brushing her hand against her daughter's in case she needed to grab hold. A strange protective urge that came from within rather than any outward urgency.

True to form, Nora appeared unaffected. She had her camera out, snapping candid shots of the scene—bare feet, shirtless guitarists, a girl with daisies woven into her hair. With wide, enthralled eyes, Nora rode the wave of the crowd, documenting every second to share with her friends back home.

While Leanne wanted desperately to feel the same way, to sway with the music and live in this carefree pocket of time, she couldn't shake the unease curdling in her stomach. The rock that had settled there, she admitted to herself, could have been the greasy burger they'd picked up off the highway. But more likely, it was the creeping worry that this would be the end of the trail. That her mother had vanished somewhere and they'd never see her again. That they were too late.

A man stepped in front of them, blocking the view and startling Leanne. But his massive grin disarmed her. He juggled five bright balls—red, green, yellow, blue, and orange—each arcing in a dizzying whirl above his head. They spun like planets. Hypnotic.

He grinned with every whirl, his face half hidden behind the blur of motion.

Something was familiar about him. Not just the artistry but the aura.

Beside her, Nora tilted her head, camera half raised.

"The wizard?" Leanne asked, squinting.

The mellow fellow laughed, tossing his arms wide and nearly sending a ball flying into the crowd.

"I am a wizard!" he declared. "A juggling wizard!" He turned in a full circle, tossing the balls high above his head and wiggling his fingers as if conducting a great cosmic spell. Somehow, he caught them all on the way back down.

One wrong toss and that rainbow would've smacked Leanne right in the face. Still, she found herself smiling despite the nerves.

"I thought I recognized him," she muttered out of the side of her mouth, curling her arm around Nora's and steering her out of the juggler's path. "Pretty sure I saw him in Vegas too."

Nora laughed, lifting her camera to snap another picture. Then she let herself be tugged along, the click of the shutter lost in the roar of the music.

Leanne's eyes drifted toward the stage. She didn't recognize the band. The musicians glistened with sweat, while their lead singer practically devoured the microphone like an ice cream cone. They were talented, but it was not the sort of music she'd ever play on the console stereo in the living room.

More importantly, there was no sign of Eleanor.

Nora danced without a care, arms high above her head, swaying with a rhythm. A smile played on her lips. She leaned close to her mother, pointing and shouting something about the drummer, but Leanne couldn't make it out over the clash of the crowd and music. An uneasy feeling gripped her like a vice.

Leanne scanned the crowd—hair flying, cigarettes dangling from lips, glass bottles clinking together. A couple was pressed against each other so tightly it made her blush, limbs entwined like ivy. Their kiss was slow and messy, full of hunger and complete abandon.

That kind of affection hadn't been an element of her marriage in years.

Leanne quickly looked away, the ache in her belly part longing, part memory. She thought of Dean. How once, she would've kissed him like that in the middle of a street if he'd ever allowed it.

Beside her, Nora followed her gaze. With a laugh that was more gasp, she lifted her hand in front of her mother's eyes like a blindfold. "Mom! Don't stare!"

Leanne laughed, tugging down her hand with a wiggle of her brows, trying to lighten the mood. "Do you think he swallowed her tongue?"

"He does look hungry." Nora raised her eyebrows up and down jokingly.

Then they laughed together—*really* laughed. Leanne felt like a bridge between them, strung with light, had appeared and they'd met in the middle.

Then, Leanne's laughter cracked, cut off as quickly as it had come.

From somewhere off to the right of the stadium came shouting. Not excited, not playful, but sharp. Angry. *Mom?*

"What's going on?" Nora asked.

The shouts grew to bellows, more and more people joining the fray. But she could see nothing, only hear them. Leanne's entire body tensed.

A ripple moved through the crowd. As if the fury of shouting rode the bodies of fans. A bottle launched overhead, arcing. Nora flinched, ducking and instinctively Leanne leaned her body over her daughter's.

People began to scatter. Their bodies bumping indiscriminately into one another. The air, thick with music and smoke just seconds ago, snapped taut like a wire.

Leanne grabbed Nora's hand, her voice cutting through the noise. "Stay close."

They shoved, joining the scattering crowd, barely making any sort of progress in the crush.

Then came the explosion.

A crack of sound and light—too close, too loud—and the air shifted. A thick, smoky film clouded everything, a fog that stung her eyes and burned the back of her throat. Her lungs screamed with each breath.

"What is that?" Leanne gasped while Nora coughed beside her.

"Tear gas!" someone shouted, voice cracking.

"Fucking pigs!" someone else roared with a rage Leanne had never experienced.

Panic surged. Bodies pressed in on all sides, the scent of sweat and marijuana strong. People shouted, coughed, and shoved. Leanne clutched Nora's wrist and yanked her close, trying to pull her toward the exit. Back to the Lincoln. Back to breathable air. Back to safety. But the crowd surged like a wave, crashing against them with no rhythm, no mercy.

She stumbled over something. A shape on the ground.

A person.

Leanne bent to help, but someone behind her shoved hard, and she toppled, landing on the fallen figure. Her knees hit the ground, her palms scraped, and the impact knocked the breath from her lungs.

"Mom!" Nora screamed, her voice ragged with fear.

Leanne looked up through the blur—of smoke, of noise, of movement—and saw only mayhem. Mayhem that made people forget which way was forward. Which way was out.

Every inhale was a struggle. Stinging tears blinded her.

And in that split second of fear, a terrible thought took hold. *This is how I die.*

This was how her mother would die.

Crushed under the weight of strangers. At a concert she'd never wanted to be at. Choking on tear gas while trying to save a daughter who shouldn't be here. Chasing a mother who should have been at home, knitting in front of the television—not gallivanting across the country like some rock star on a comeback tour.

New tears filled her eyes. Not from the gas now but from rage. From helplessness. From a lifetime of holding everything together, only to have it all fall apart like this.

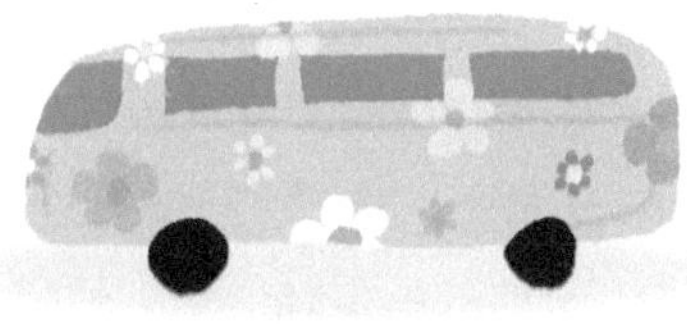

CHAPTER EIGHTEEN

NORA COULD NOT REMEMBER A TIME—ANY TIME—she'd seen her mother helpless.

Leanne Miller didn't fall. She glided, always graceful and upright. Standing firm like a mannequin in a department store window. When Nora was little, she used to stare at her mother's feet to see if they actually touched the ground. And then she'd go out into the backyard, barefoot in the grass, practicing her mother's walk.

Somewhere along the way, that glide had become her mom's armor. Her poise, her power.

Until now.

Nora's breath caught in her throat, watching helplessly as her mother sprawled over another person, pinned by the tide of bodies. People kept tripping over them—stumbling, shouting, shoving forward like a herd of antelope running from a lion. They ricocheted into strangers, some falling to the ground. No one tried to help or stop the stampede.

When Nora tried to breathe, it was through air that was thick with tear gas, with fear, with the crush of human heat.

Nora watched in horror as, curled in on herself, her mother wrapped her arms tight, trying to shrink into the dirt. Each attempt Leanne made to rise was met with another foot slamming into her back or shoulder, sending her crashing down again like a rag doll on top of the other person.

Nora screamed, her voice cracking. "Stop! You're crushing them!"

The air burned her lungs, and her words came out in broken pieces, swallowed by the screech of pandemonium and the music still blasting from somewhere above.

"Stop!" she yelled again, shoving back at the surge of bodies. A man in a denim vest collided with her back, and she nearly lost her footing.

She couldn't fall. She wouldn't fall. Her mother needed her.

Nora dropped to her knees, coughing, grabbing her mom's arm, tugging—pulling her back to the surface, out of the crush. But there were too many people. Too much movement. Too much panic.

"Mom!" she croaked, voice trembling. Her eyes stung, not just from the tear gas but from the sudden, terrifying grief of it all.

This wasn't supposed to happen.

Not to her mother. Not to the woman who walked like royalty, who never faltered. Who was always the one to reach out a hand.

Now, Leanne was the one on the ground.

And Nora had never been so afraid in her life.

Leanne pushed herself upright, just in time for someone to leap over her, using her back like she was part of some twisted game of leapfrog.

"Hey!" Nora shouted, her instincts kicking in. She shoved one idiot midair, and he stumbled, arms flailing, crashing to the ground.

Her mother's face was blotchy, red, wild-eyed. She looked on the edge of panic, tears shining on her lashes. And that—*that*—was worse than anything else. Nora couldn't remember ever seeing her mother cry.

Grabbing hold of Leanne's hand tight, she refused to let go. They began pushing through the mass, both of them suddenly more aggressive and desperate.

And then—

"Nora," a voice called from her left, his voice calm and reassuring and at odds with their current situation. "We've got to stop meeting like this."

With a sharp turn of her head, Nora scanned the madness for the familiar voice.

Joe.

"I hardly think a soda line and a riot are in the same category," she shot back.

Joe gave a lazy shrug, all effortless swagger and practiced indifference. "Depends how thirsty you are."

His grin was crooked, and she should've rolled her eyes at his terrible timing and joke—but relief flooded her chest instead. Seeing him there, solid and focused, made her feel grounded. He lifted his arms protectively, creating space in the chaotic crowd. Taking the brunt of people running into his body but remaining still where she and her mother had been knocked aside.

"Let me help, Nora."

Without hesitation, he reached out, taking Nora's hand in one of his and her mother's with his other. He shifted them slightly behind him—as if he were the prow of a ship. Nora let herself be pulled forward as Joe shouldered past people. She couldn't stop glancing toward her mother, worried she'd fall again. And all the while, acting as a barrier, Joe moved forward with purpose. When Leanne did stumble, Joe caught her, easing her upright before she could be overtaken by dozens of feet again.

For a bizarre second, Nora thought of the Vietnam footage they showed on the nightly news. Young men wading through bomb smoke and screaming, pushing forward through the mayhem of war, unsure if they'd ever get out.

She pushed the images away with a shudder, knowing that a crush at a concert was nothing compared to war.

Then, suddenly, the crowd broke open. The air shifted. Cleaner, clearer, cooler.

They'd made it outside of the stadium.

Leanne bent over, hands braced on her thighs, sucking in heavy breaths like she'd just run a marathon at top speed. Nora's chest squeezed tight at the sight.

"Mom?" Nora pressed a hand to Leanne's back, afraid her mother might have suffered an injury and was breathing with pain rather than residual fear.

"I'm okay." Leanne straightened slowly, wincing as she wiped at the sweat on her brow. "Thank you." Her voice was hoarse but measured, and she gave a grateful nod.

"No problem," he said. He tried to sound cool, but he too was clearly shaken by the crowd crush they'd just escaped. "I owed Nora here." He tilted his head.

"Owed me?" Nora shot him a quizzical glance. "How?"

"For the Coke," he said with a wink.

Heat bloomed beneath her skin, making Nora's cheeks flush.

"You two know each other?" As Nora turned toward her mom, she noticed Leanne's gaze had fully sharpened into parenting mode.

"No," Nora said quickly, at the same time Joe replied, "Sort of."

Leanne's spine straightened a little more, an interrogation queueing up in her mind like festivalgoers at the ticket booth.

But Joe, who interviewed strangers for a living, held out his hand with confidence and offered a charismatic smile.

"Joe Dumas. At your service, ma'am."

Nora's mind whirled at hearing his last name. "Wait. Your last name is Dumas? As in Alexandre Dumas and *The Three Musketeers*?"

Joe let out a short laugh. She thought she detected the slightest blush on his cheeks. "'All for one, and one for all.' Long-lost relation. And look at the three of us now—clearly something out of my great-great-great-something-grandfather's novel. 'Never fear quarrels,'" Joe quoted with a wink, "'but seek hazardous adventures.' Which I guess means I was meant to find you in a mutiny."

Her mother held her tongue, but Nora could practically hear the questions bubbling up behind her eyes. She just knew when they climbed back into the Lincoln, the questioning would start firing off faster than the flame juggling act they'd seen at the Madison Square Garden circus last summer. Starting with, *Was that the hot writer you mentioned meeting?* But her mother broke eye contact quickly, whirling in a circle, her frantic gaze scanning the crowd, no doubt praying for a sign of Eleanor.

Nora rubbed at the gooseflesh on her arms, then brushed a tendril of hair off her cheek, still breathless from the turmoil. It suddenly occurred to her that if anyone had seen Eleanor Bell, it would be the journalist following the Grandma Rocker story like a heat-seeking missile. "How's your story coming along?"

Joe's face lit up. "The Dame of Rock and Roll killed it earlier. Did you miss her set?"

Leanne practically jolted. "You saw her?"

"Yeah," he said with an air of nonchalance. "She was onstage with Shep Moon and his band earlier before they took off."

"They made it out safely?" Leanne asked, her body stiff.

Joe nodded. "Pretty sure. The riot really only affected the crowd, not the bands."

Her mother blew out a long breath, her shoulders lowering. "And she was with Shep Moon's band?"

"Yeah. A full-on collaboration onstage. Like...*planned*."

Leanne muttered something under her breath that sounded suspiciously like *un-fucking-believable.*

Nora blanched. She must've misheard that. Her mother didn't curse. Her mother didn't even abbreviate curse words. And Nora had definitely had a bar of soap in her mouth for saying less.

"What song?" Nora asked.

Joe launched into a verse, his voice unexpectedly rich—low and a little raspy, like he'd listened to too many Sam Cooke records.

Nora raised an eyebrow, trying for cool confidence even as her heart beat faster than Creedence Clearwater Revival's drums. "Let me guess—your other ancestor was a famous musician?"

Joe didn't miss a beat. "Actually, yes. Why?"

Nora's mouth fell open a little. "Seriously?"

Joe pressed a hand to his heart. "As a journalist, I have sworn not to lie in my reporting. But I also can't confirm. If the family legends are true, my uncle was a blues guitarist from Memphis. Played backup for B.B. King once before he died."

"Oh my God." Nora glanced at her mom, who seemed to be breathing easier, then back at Joe. "You're like a walking *Rolling Stone* article."

"Flattery," he said, flipping his collar up, "will get you far. Keep it coming."

Leanne still hadn't spoken. Nora watched her mother's face, reality settling in. Eleanor hadn't just come to a music festival. She'd performed. With Shep Moon. And had become, somehow, some way—the story.

If not for Joe, Nora might have been speechless too. And then he said, "She's got an incredible story. I had a chance to speak to her briefly," taking any remnants of words from her brain.

Time to tell Joe just who the Dame of Rock and Roll was.

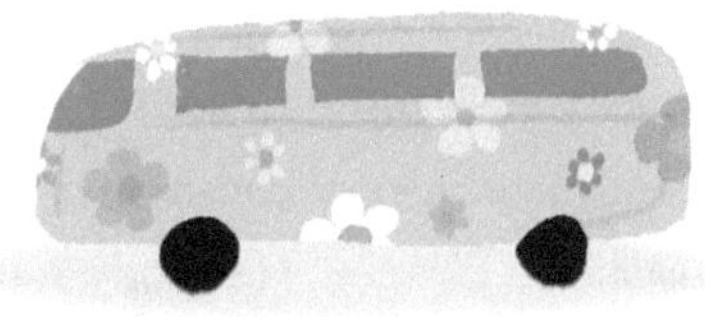

CHAPTER NINETEEN

ELEANOR WAS BACKSTAGE STRUMMING A FEW CHORDS one minute, laughing with the band, feeling light and almost… sprightly, like the girl she used to be.

The next moment, everything was bedlam.

Someone grabbed her by the arm, her shoes slapping against the grass as they rushed her out the back. She'd barely had a chance to pick up Roxy. The stadium loomed behind them, smoke curling into the sky like a question mark.

"Is there a fire?" Her breath caught, and she inhaled slowly through her nose, trying to calm her breathing and her sweet pup.

"No," said one of the band members, peering over his shoulder. "Cops."

"Cops?" Her voice went up in pitch. For the briefest paranoid second, she had the ridiculous thought that Leanne had called the police. Was it even possible that her daughter had somehow tracked her down and sent officers to drag her home like a runaway teenager?

No. The thought was shaken off before it could settle. Every step had felt careful—at least, that was the intention. From what she could remember, she hadn't left much of a trail, and she knew for certain she hadn't told Leanne where she was going.

"Yeah, some folks were causing a scene." He shrugged, unconcerned like riotous outbursts were as common as encore requests.

But it wasn't usual for Eleanor. Her body started to shake as the sudden rush of adrenaline that had come from their performance drained away.

Concerts in her day had been mellow. Civilized. A sea of cigarette smoke, not tear gas. People dancing, not fistfighting. She'd been to jazz shows where the loudest noise came from a high hat. Now, the atmosphere outside the van buzzed with something else—something dangerous.

Megan whipped open the van door, and Eleanor filed inside with the rest of the band members. The van smelled like vinyl and the musk of the road and something more lived-in, like the feeling of freedom after a lifetime of restraint.

Shep sat beside Eleanor, wrapping a casual arm around her shoulders, steadying her. Almost instantly the shakes started to subside.

"Don't worry," he said gently. "Just the system pushing back. You were electric up there. You belong here."

But Eleanor wasn't sure anymore. Her fingers still tingled from the chords she'd played, but her heart thrummed with uncertainty.

Was this what she came for?

Eleanor's gaze was pulled out the window, watching the throngs of people escaping. The van engine rumbled to life, exhaust fumes curling into the air behind them, and she wondered—had she brought herself to the edge of independence…or the end of something else entirely?

Leaning into Shep, she was grateful for his weight and warmth beside her. His steady, solid presence. It had been so long since she'd had someone she could lean on without apology. Without needing to explain. At times like this, she missed Henry so much.

"What are we going to do now?" Her voice had gone soft against the thrum of the crush still pulsing outside the van.

"Wait it out if we can." Shep slid a cigarette from his shirt pocket, flicked open a silver lighter. The flame caught with a metallic snap. He took a slow drag, exhaled a curl of smoke, and passed the cigarette.

Eleanor accepted it with practiced fingers, lifting it to her lips and inhaling. The familiar bite of tobacco hit the back of her throat, burning away just enough tension to make her shoulders drop.

"And if it doesn't calm down?" she asked, glancing toward the tinted windows.

"We grab a bite and head out. Got a show in Atlanta next. You in?"

Eleanor didn't pause, just nodded. The nod coming before any thought had a chance to intervene. The decision was already written in muscle and instinct. She craved the open road. Was drawn to him. And the music, the music thrummed in her veins. The rhythm pulling her forward.

But *should* she go…and did she *want* to go—those were two different questions.

Shep leaned back, one hand draped over the vinyl seat. Outside, the smoke had started to clear, but Eleanor's thoughts still hadn't. At some point, she was going to have to find a pay phone. Call Leanne. Let her daughter know she hadn't been kidnapped, hadn't fallen off the face of the earth. But with every mile she put between them, she forgot a little more of what had once held her back.

Roxy gave a little yip from her lap, her tongue flicking out. Eleanor smiled faintly, fishing a treat from her pocket and placing it gently in her dog's mouth.

"I've got a sandwich left." Shep patted the cooler beside him. "My old dog would've killed for a bite."

Eleanor looked down at Roxy, who was eyeing the cooler like it held the secrets of the universe. "Well, mine might just stage a full-blown mutiny."

"Then it's a good thing I'm a generous man."

She narrowed her eyes, playful. "Generous, or looking to impress?"

He grinned and took the sandwich out of the cooler. "Can't it be both?"

She laughed softly, listening to the crackle of the wax paper while he unwrapped the sandwich. "Just don't expect me to share with you. Roxy takes priority."

"Smart girl. I'd choose her over me too."

Roxy's little pink tongue lolled out, and a string of drool landed squarely in Eleanor's lap. "Oh, you have no shame," she said, scratching behind the dog's ear.

Not until she watched Roxy tear into the club sandwich—lettuce and tomato hanging from her crooked miniature teeth—did Eleanor realize she was also starving. Her stomach let out a low, hollow grumble.

Had she eaten today? She must have. Maybe even a sandwich just like this. She'd been with Shep all day, hadn't she? If he'd eaten, surely she had as well. That's how it worked…wasn't it?

Outside, the disorder still pulsed as she finished the part of the sandwich Roxy didn't want. Feet pounded. People shouted. Fists slapped the side of the van. Bodies rushed past. But Eleanor closed her eyes and leaned her cheek against the cool windowpane, letting the hum of adrenaline and music dissolve into stillness. She was safe in the van with Shep.

Roxy curled in her lap, full and satisfied, her diminutive body already vibrating with gentle snores. Eleanor drifted off, lulled by the rhythm of Roxy's breath, her solid warmth, and the distant drums thumping from the stadium where the musicians continued playing despite the pandemonium. There'd been an incident like this when she'd performed on vaudeville. The Gerry Society busting underage performers and their parents. She dissolved into the memory, recalling how one young singer had asked Eleanor to hide her underneath a colossal paper-mache cake.

Eleanor jolted upright, heart hammering. Her vision swam, the present coming swirling back.

She was alone.

The van—dim and unfamiliar—seemed to press in on her. The walls too close. The silence too deep. Roxy, more bangs than mane, dozed in her lap, twitching. A scrap of paper crinkled in Eleanor's hand.

Staring at it as if it might bite, she unfolded the paper with trembling fingers, but the letters floated in front of her eyes, not making sense. She blinked once, twice, a dozen times, trying to decipher what she was seeing. Finally, the letters aligned, and her brain decided not to punish her, forming words.

Went to grab hot dogs. You looked too peaceful to wake.—S

Her breath hitched.

Who was S, and why had they gone to get hot dogs?

Where *was* she?

The question opened up a vacuum in her chest, a swirl of disorientation and dread. Her hands shook, and the motion jostled the little animal in her lap. The dog's eyes blinked open and she cocked her head to the side, the little mop of hair flipping to one side. Eleanor had a feeling she should know this weird little dog. A tug at the corner of her brain, too weak to pull back the curtain.

She touched its tag. *Roxy.*

And with that one name, her mind began to reassemble itself, piece by fragile piece.

She was Eleanor Bell once more.

She was at a concert.

She was—God help her—the Dame of Rock and Roll.

She let out a long breath, her free hand fluttering to her chest, steadying herself. These moments seemed to be coming quicker, and she feared that the time on the road away from familiarity was the cause.

Outside, the uproar was fading, replaced by laughter and song. Shep would return soon. Roxy snorted and nestled back in.

Eleanor stroked the tiny dog's back, whispering, "I'm still here."

This was a van.

A van owned by her…what, exactly?

Friend? Companion? Beau?

Sometimes, Eleanor saw Shep as the man she'd lost all those summers ago—his laugh familiar, his touch even more so. Other times, she saw him as he truly was—a stranger, two decades her junior, wrapped in rhythm and smoke, cloaked in youth and dreams he hadn't yet given up on.

But what she preferred, what she needed, was to think of him as a chapter. A chapter named *Now*.

Because this trip, this music, this fleeting blur of smoke and song and memory wasn't about reinvention. It was about reclamation.

Eleanor Bell had come here to live the life she never dared claim. The one she'd tucked away with her guitar behind chiffon blouses and silk scarves. The one she'd handed over in pieces. First to duty, then to love, then to motherhood, and then to the silence that came after.

And soon, she'd have to go back.

Back to New York. Back to being just regular Eleanor Bell Strickland. Widow. Mother. Grandmother. Housekeeper of memories and maker of casseroles.

She hadn't grown up imagining she'd be defined by titles with such hollow rings. Somewhere along the way, she had deemed herself unworthy of ambition, of artistry.

And when she did, Eleanor Bell, the musician, disappeared like the wisps of cigarette smoke on a windy night. And in her place stood Mrs.

Strickland, somebody's something—someone's mother, someone's wife, someone's something else, but no longer someone's dreamer.

Closing her eyes, she tilted her head back against the van door. She wished she could fall asleep and wake up in some beautiful elsewhere, free of the weight of memory.

But if she forgot the life she'd lived—the good, the hard, the music that had carried her through—how could she fully honor this chance to feel it again?

Opening her eyes, Eleanor glanced down at Roxy, who gazed at her with lazy affection, her head cocked and tongue cockeyed. That little tuft of hair still made her laugh.

Eleanor patted her silly dog on the head, then eased the van door open.

The air was cooler now. In the distance, music mixed with laughter. Gone was the disorder of the night. A hot dog stand flickered in the sun like a lighthouse, surrounded by people.

Eleanor Bell—musician, widow, goddess of second chances—tucked her hair behind her ears and went in search of a hot dog and the chapter she was living.

CHAPTER TWENTY

THE LOCAL DINER BUZZED WITH A CHARGED ENERGY. The air was thick with the scent of burned coffee, fried onions, and sweet maple syrup and clung to Leanne's clothes as she stepped inside.

A slight tremble still buzzed in her fingertips, and every now and then she found herself gasping for air. There were places on her shoulders, arms, back that ached like bruises, and she was sure when she finally undressed for bed tonight, she was going to see the marks of people's shoes and hands on her body.

Every booth, every counter stool, and every syrup-sticky table was crammed with concertgoers seeking refuge from the smoke and sirens still drifting up from the stadium. They looked as worn out as she did. It was an ironic energy when compared to the panoramic scene of the mountains out the window. A few patrons sported torn band T-shirts, either on purpose or from people grabbing hold of them while trying to stay upright.

She craned her neck around the diner looking for her mother, but there was no sign of her here either.

"Mom, I'm sure she's fine. If she's with the band, they probably had people to protect them," Nora said, her soft touch on Leanne's elbow. "Besides, when Joe spoke to her she was full of spunk."

Leanne nodded, hoping that was true and also feeling jealous that this young journalist had been able to track down her mother for a quote when she couldn't even track her down for a hug. But where the hell had the band gone? When was she going to find her mother? Frustration made her grind her teeth. The mix of feelings only made it harder for her to breathe. She drew in a steadying breath, imagining her mother's hand on her back, telling her to breathe slowly in and out, the way she'd done when Leanne was nervous for a test at school, the same way she'd done when she'd gone into labor with Nora. God, she wanted her mother.

The three of them grabbed stools at the counter's far end. Stools still warm from the patrons who'd just vacated them. Leanne perched on hers, her spine aching from lying on the ground during the panicked stampede. Leanne gripped the edge of her round, red stool, hoping to ease her still trembling hands. Despite the deep breathing, her nerves hadn't entirely caught up to her stomach yet, but she ordered a coffee anyway, grateful for something to hold.

Joe sat beside Nora, their knees just barely touching. The ease between them had Leanne raising one carefully plucked brow. He was handsome in a scruffy, slightly poetic way—rumpled shirt, pencil behind one ear, a leather satchel slung casually at his feet. He didn't look like the clean-cut, polite, all-edges-and-no-depth boys Nora had brought around before. This one had stories in his eyes and was full of questions.

Nora was beaming.

Leanne took a slow sip of her coffee, cringing at the weak and bitter taste. Like it had been on the burner since four a.m. But at least it was something.

"So," she said, tone light but direct. "Tell me how you two met."

Nora's cheeks flushed, her smile faltering for half a second before she swept a lock of her hair behind her ear and gave her mother the same innocent visage she'd perfected as a child.

"I bought him a Coca-Cola at the last concert. That's all." Nora said it with a too-practiced shrug.

Leanne hummed, unconvinced. The way Joe glanced over at her daughter—like he was seeing straight through her nonchalance—told a different story. But Leanne didn't press, not here. Her daughter would never forgive her for pressing in front of an audience.

Leanne folded her hands around the warm mug. "Well, thank you, Joe. Truly. I don't know what might have happened if you hadn't appeared at our moment of need."

Joe tilted his head in her direction. "No problem, Mrs....?"

"Miller," she replied. "Mrs. Miller."

He nodded as if tucking the name into some mental notebook. "Good to meet you, Mrs. Miller." Joe offered his hand across the counter in front of Nora, who sat between them. Leanne leaned left and shook it, interrupted by the waitress swooping in and pouring more steaming coffee into each of their chipped white mugs.

Leanne took a tentative sip, hoping this fresh batch of brew would be better. No such luck. Pure diner sludge. But at least it was warm.

Joe raised his glass of water slightly in a quiet toast. "To fortunate chance encounters."

Nora rolled her eyes, but her smile didn't falter.

Leanne let herself imagine this was what change looked like—not confusion, not collapse, but connection. Small moments. Three people at the end of a counter. A little hope served alongside a grilled cheese and a cup of burned coffee.

"So, you've seen my mother?" Leanne leveled her gaze at Joe over the rim of her mug.

Joe nodded, reaching for the sugar canister. He poured at least half its contents into his cup, followed by a generous splash of cream. He stirred it all with the handle of his spoon like he was mixing paint.

Nora kept her hands wrapped around her mug but didn't drink. She had never been a coffee girl. Though if she copied the way Joe had doctored his up, she might be. That cup was pure dessert.

"I have seen her." Joe lit up, scooting taller in his chair. "More than once actually."

He glanced toward the waitress refilling someone else's mug, then back at Leanne. "At first, no one knew what to make of this elderly woman onstage with Shep Moon. Everyone assumed she was his grandmother." His grin was sheepish, apologetic. "They were so in sync, so relaxed together. Like they'd known each other forever. Honestly, I just figured she was family."

Leanne felt her throat tighten. She wasn't sure why.

"But then she started to sing and play," Joe continued. "And Shep introduced her as Mama Lightning."

"Mama Lightning?" Nora repeated, a small laugh escaping before she could stop it.

"Pretty amazing, right?" Joe nodded the way young people did when they were still awestruck by the world. "Now, the radio guys call her the Dame of Rock and Roll all due to a little article I wrote in the *San Francisco Chronicle* about her that Johnny Carson happened to read and talked about in the opening of his show."

"I just can't believe it," Nora said, glancing at her mother. "I didn't even know she could sing like that."

"I did," Leanne said softly.

The words dropped like a stone in a still pond.

She set her mug on its saucer, prepared for Nora to ask for an explanation. But just when she was about to no doubt ask, the waitress returned, breaking the chain of conversation. Leanne ordered a whole stack of pancakes with extra syrup and a side of bacon, extra crispy.

Nora stared at her with shock. Leanne had never ordered anything that indulgent, and she was certain her daughter had a thousand questions running through her mind. For breakfast, it was always grapefruit, cottage cheese, and black coffee. That was the Leanne Miller everyone knew.

But after the emotional whiplash of the day—the riot, the sheer disbelief of learning her mother was now a stage-singing sensation—Leanne figured she'd earned a stack of sugary pancakes, probably with butter on top and a side of unapologetic, crispy deliciousness. And maybe she'd even add some sugar to the terrible coffee to wash it all down.

Add this to the many things she'd changed up on the trip. Was it any wonder that Nora was confused?

"You knew she could sing like that? I've heard her sing lullabies, but to really sing..." Nora asked, her tone caught somewhere between awe and accusation.

Leanne looked down into her coffee for a minute then raised her eyes to meet her daughter's. "When I was younger, she sang all the time. While making eggs or hanging laundry on the line. Even when she washed my hair in the kitchen sink. I don't think our house was ever quiet. At the very least she was humming along in the background."

She paused, swallowing against the lump that had crept into her throat. "But as I got older, she got quieter. The singing became something I heard only through closed doors. Like the older I got, the more her voice disappeared." Leanne exhaled, long and slow, a sigh laced with something that sounded and felt suspiciously like guilt. Had she said something once, years ago? Rolled her eyes? Laughed at the wrong time?

"Well," Joe said, "she has definitely found her voice again. She blew the roof off with Shep Moon tonight. Honestly? Wouldn't be surprised if a record label calls her."

"And you're making her into your muse for the summer?" Nora's eyes narrowed slightly in that perceptive, protective way that reminded Leanne how brilliant her daughter really was.

Joe lifted his hands like he was under oath. "I am. But this"—he motioned between them—"is off the record. Just here as a friend."

Leanne nodded slowly. "Thank you," she said genuinely. How strange to be grateful to a boy she didn't know for looking after her mother—and her daughter—but she was.

She scanned the diner. The Formica counters gleamed under the buzzing fluorescents. Behind the pie case, nestled next to a cigarette vending machine, was exactly what she hoped for.

"I'm going to check if that pay phone works," she said, sliding off her stool. "I need to call your dad and let him know the latest installment in this rock-and-roll soap opera. See if maybe through his marketing connections he can find a way for us to contact Shep Moon's manager."

"That's a great idea," Nora said.

"If he can't, I might be able to see if can find out through the newspaper I'm interning for," Joe offered.

"Thank you."

Nora smiled at Joe, and Leanne caught it—a glimmer in her daughter's expression at Joe's desire to help.

Leanne slipped off her stool and made her way toward the pay phone. The linoleum floor squeaked beneath her sensible heels. She dropped in the required coins, which clinked down with a hollow finality, and dialed home.

The phone rang. And rang.

No answer.

Again.

Leanne let the receiver dangle briefly in her hand, then returned it to its cradle with a soft click. She stared at the rotary dial, hesitating, her finger poised to spin the operator for Dean's office line. But the image of that honey-voiced secretary flickered through her mind, and the knot it formed in her stomach was enough to make her retract her hand.

Not tonight.

Through the smudged glass, she watched Nora at the counter, laughing at something Joe had said. The two of them were dipping toast into their yolks. Beside them, a glorious stack of pancakes awaited her, the syrup glistening like amber in the diner lights.

Leanne took a breath and straightened her shoulders. She was going to devour the hell out of those pancakes.

And then?

She was going to find her mother.

CHAPTER TWENTY-ONE

"I HOPE YOUR MOM'S OKAY." JOE CHOMPED DOWN on his toast like it owed him money. The butter glistened on the corner of his mouth, and for a split second, Nora considered telling him, but then decided to let him wear it. There was something charming about a boy who could be both confident and unaware.

Nora glanced toward the pay phone. Her mother held the receiver to her ear, one toe tapping anxiously like she could tap a conversation into existence.

"She took a pretty bad tumble," Nora said quietly. "People just kept stepping on her. It was"—she swallowed—"kind of awful."

Joe's brows lifted. "Yeah. People lose their minds the minute tear gas hits the air. Understandable, but still. Their primal instincts kick in, and things turn into a deranged stampede. Your mom's lucky she didn't come out with anything broken. And you're lucky you weren't pulled under."

Nora's shoulders were still tense, expecting the horde to come crashing through the diner doors to repeat the stampede. "I'm glad as hell you turned up. I really hope my grandma is okay."

"The action was mostly near the gate, well away from where your grandma was. From what I understand, all the bands went out the back way in their vans. She's been traveling with Moon's entourage, so I'm pretty sure she is safe."

"Good, that's a relief. We've been so worried about her and to think she could have been in all that chaos." Nora drew in a deep breath and then let it out, her shoulders relaxing, knowing that her grandmother was most likely safe. This entire thing was just crazy. Boy, was she going to have some stories to tell her friends back home.

Then, wanting to change the subject, Nora shook her head, narrowed her eyes, teasing. "So, Joe Dumas, are you following me?"

Joe flushed pink from his cheeks to his ears. He scratched the back of his neck as if it might have helped him find a response other than "yes." "Swear I'm on assignment. Scout's honor." He held up three fingers in a Boy Scout salute. "But, you know, if I were tailing you, it's only because your drink orders are incredibly intriguing."

"There's more to me than a soda order."

He tilted his head. "Challenge accepted. If I wanted to get to know you, what would I have to ask?"

Warmth spread through Nora's chest. "That's your job to figure out, journalist."

Joe leaned closer. "Okay. Then what do you want to do after college, Miss Yale-bound mystery?"

The question hit differently than all the others. She felt the weight of it like someone had set her leather-bound notebook—currently tucked deep inside her bag—onto her chest. That prized possession since junior year, with its cracked cover, worn like an old baseball glove, the edges thinned from the number of times she'd flipped the pages. Inside were bits of her soul scribbled in blue and black ink. Half-finished poems, lines of overheard dialogue, pages of messy, untamed story ideas that had never made it past paragraph three.

She carried the journal everywhere but never talked about it. Not even with her best friend, not even with her mother. That notebook was her proof. Her secret. Her almost-belief that she could be a writer.

"I told my parents I wanted to get a business degree, a minor in English, and maybe go into marketing like my dad," she said slowly. "You know. A practical career. Something clean. With desks."

"But…?"

"But what I really want to do is major in English and write." It was a confession she hadn't meant to make. "Not just copy for toothpaste ads. I want to create stories. Whole worlds. Characters that feel real. Dialogue that cuts to the bone. Stories that move people."

Joe's face lit up like she'd just handed him the Pulitzer. "I knew it."

"You knew nothing," she said, smiling in spite of herself.

"You have the eyes." His tone was sincere and serious.

"What eyes?" Suddenly she wished for a mirror so she could look into her own eyes and try to discover what he might mean.

"The kind that people have who eavesdrop on others in diners and write down what they said later. The kind of eyes that see details—notice how the waitress's earrings don't match, but she keeps wearing them like she doesn't care, or maybe like she does care but wants you to think she doesn't."

Nora's mouth twitched. "Okay. That's…scary accurate."

"Reporter's instinct." His gaze held hers.

She stared back at Joe. This tousle-haired, harmonica-carrying, leather-satchel-wearing boy, asking her questions. Actually *listening* to her answers. His elbows rested on the counter like he had nowhere else to be, and his gaze didn't dart past her to scout the room. He looked at her and talked to her like what she said mattered. Not too many people did that. She wasn't sure a guy ever had.

"I'm just not sure my parents would accept me as a writer," Nora said, her voice low, self-effacing. This was the first time she'd spoken her truth out loud to someone other than herself or the pages of her notebook. Not even Kelley knew this part of her.

She supposed she kept it hidden because there'd been plenty of comments at home about starving artists, and Nora didn't want to give her parents reason to think she'd live in their house until she retired. Yet now she'd confessed it to someone she hardly knew. She moved her eyes back to her mom at the pay phone then reconnected her glance with Joe's, feeling self-conscious for being so vulnerable and open with him.

There wasn't even a hint of a smirk in his gaze. Instead, he nodded, his expression suggesting that she'd told him she was going to fly to the moon and had asked if he would like to pack snacks for the ride.

"You never know; you should talk to them about it." From his serious air, she could tell he meant what he said, but the idea of doing so was terrifying.

She didn't respond because she couldn't think of what to say.

Joe must have sensed she was stuck because he went on. "So, you're getting your business degree at Yale, even though you wish it were English?"

"That's the plan." She lifted her mug and swallowed a sip of bitter coffee gone cold. She really didn't like coffee, but she didn't want to answer his implied question either. "Assuming we find my grandmother before the semester starts. I don't know if I could leave my mom alone to keep up the search."

"Your mom would let you bail on college?"

"Oh, no." Nora shook her head, the ends of her ponytail bouncing against her spine as if it wanted to add an exclamation point to her reply. "She wants me there. She'd pitch a fit if I said I was staying behind, but part of me would definitely feel guilty about leaving her to find my grandmother alone."

"Well, good thing you've already found her. It's just about catching up now."

She nodded and took another look at the phone booth where her mom stood, a long cord stretching from her ear to the receiver's base like an umbilical tether to the life she'd left behind in New York. Even from across the diner, Nora could see the subtle shift in her mother's shoulders when she hung up—disappointment *again*.

"He's not home," Nora murmured. "He never is."

Joe followed her gaze but didn't say anything. She appreciated that. Most people rushed in with a silver lining or a bad joke. Joe just saw her. That alone felt special—precious.

"Sometimes I wonder… I don't know. When I leave for college, what's she going to have? My dad practically lives at the office. I just—"

"You're worried about her." Joe's voice was gentle.

Nora shot him a look, half glare, half surrender. "You're annoyingly good at this, you know."

"At what?"

"Being an investigative journalist."

He grinned. "You're only mad because I'm right. But also, you practically said it out loud."

"Okay, maybe. I wish I knew where to start."

"I think you mean at being human."

Nora didn't know what to say to that, so she pivoted back to the search. "I shouldn't be thinking about myself anyway. I need to think about catching up to my grandmother. I just wish I knew how."

"I might," Joe said. "You're not the only one who wants to be face-to-face with the Dame of Rock and Roll."

Nora let herself smile then, the kind that tugged at the corners slowly and settled in her cheeks.

"I'll request an official interview with her. My last one was a quick chat as she walked offstage," Joe said. "You come with me, and we can both talk to her."

"You mean like a real press pitch?"

"Yeah, why not?" Joe leaned forward, that spark of excitement lighting his eyes like a backstage bulb. "What musician after a contract can resist a good spotlight? Might work better than showing up with a guilt trip and a suitcase. Plus, your grandma kinda likes me."

Nora wasn't surprised. It was hard not to like Joe. "You'd really let me come along?" Her fingers started to tingle at the prospect.

"Of course." Joe shrugged. "We're coconspirators now."

"Journalistic partners in crime. And," she added, "if it doesn't work, we're no worse off than we are now."

He raised his mug like a toast. "To catching grandmothers…and maybe ourselves in the process."

Nora clinked her mug against his. "And to bylines."

"The next festival is in Atlanta. Starts in a few days." Joe glanced at the tab he was folding in half.

"It'll take that long just to get there." Nora blinked. Being on this road trip felt like tripping down the highway always a day behind.

He nodded, unfazed by her dramatics. "I'm actually heading out after this. Figured I'd get a jump on the road so I can be there before it kicks off. I've got a hunch your grandma is doing the same. Might be able to meet up with her for the interview before the festival."

"I hope we make it in time," Nora said, dismayed. Driving to Atlanta would take days. "We've still got to get gas, check out tires, pack, maybe breathe for five minutes—"

"You could always fly with me."

Nora glanced at him like he'd just offered her a backstage pass to meet the Rolling Stones. "Let me guess—you have a private jet stashed off the highway, and it's called *The Dumas*."

"I wish." Joe chuckled, showing off his dimple. "Just a generous pilot uncle who has a deep affection for his charming and underpaid nephew."

"Think our car will fit on the plane?" she teased.

Before Joe could answer, her mother returned, sliding onto the stool beside her and immediately digging into a syrupy stack of pancakes like she was in a competitive eating contest.

Joe tossed a ten-dollar bill on the counter, the edge curling from being tucked in a sweaty wallet too long. "That should cover all three," he said. Then he looked at Nora, his fingers brushing her arm. Just a squeeze. Gentle, sure. But her whole chest lit up like a pinball machine.

"I'll see you ladies in Atlanta, and if I secure an interview, I'll try to make it closer to when you arrive. Otherwise, I'll ask the Dame for a meeting for you both."

And then he was gone—vanishing out the door and into the warm, chaotic hum of postconcert escapees like a character exiting stage left in one of her short stories. She stared at the swinging diner door and smiled. She'd been waiting for an idea to write about. And maybe, just maybe, her story had finally started.

"Very generous of him to help. He seems like a nice young man," her mother said between bites, eyes on the pancakes like she was trying to absorb them into her bloodstream.

"I think he is." Nora tried to play it cool though her cheeks warmed.

"And he's cute," Leanne added, in a singsong voice that mothers have been using to torture their daughters since the dawn of time.

"Mom!" Nora gasped, rolling her eyes with dramatic flair, but her insides had gone all soft, syrupy, like the pancakes Leanne was devouring. She pictured Joe's dimple, that teasing smirk, the way he looked at her like she wasn't just another girl in a crowd but a character in a story he wanted to write an article about.

"I'm so glad he's going to help us get to Grandma in Atlanta."

"Atlanta, huh?" The way her mom asked mid-chew was like Nora had casually suggested driving to Havana rather than Georgia.

"Yup."

Leanne exhaled and sat back. "Then we better get a good night's sleep."

Nora agreed. With all the adrenaline flushed from their bodies after the race to get out of the stadium, exhaustion was setting in deep. "We only have a few chapters left of *The Godfather*. We should finish that up tonight, and tomorrow, I'm cracking open *The Love Machine*."

Leanne crunched a piece of bacon between her teeth. "Don't get any ideas about Joe Dumas being Robin Stone."

Nora pushed back her unfinished coffee, wishing she'd ordered a Coca-Cola instead. "Who's Robin Stone?"

Leanne wiggled her brows in a teasing way that seemed natural at the same time it was foreign. Leanne wasn't the teasing type, yet she'd opened up so much on this trip since they'd left New York. "He's *the* Love Machine."

"Mom!" Nora's mind flashed to the cover of her mother's risqué novel, and she couldn't help teasing. "But what if he is?"

Leanne gave a theatrical gasp, and Nora pressed her hand to her mouth just in time to keep from spraying coffee out her nose. Across the booth, her mom actually laughed—like, really laughed—and for the first time in forever, everything felt light.

Just two women, some bacon, a possibly magical boy, and a road map to Atlanta to find the woman who'd put them on this journey.

PART THREE

Southern Heat

SUMMER 1969

CHAPTER TWENTY-TWO

SOMEWHERE BETWEEN MIDNIGHT AND TROUBLE—OR Denver and Atlanta—hurtling down the dusty spine of the interstate in a van that smelled faintly of patchouli and unwashed denim, Eleanor Bell, a.k.a. Mama Lightning, if the band's enthusiastic renaming had anything to say about it, was rewriting the set list for Shep Moon's band.

The boys were still laughing over how she'd cut three of their psychedelic filler tracks, declaring, "You can't groove if you can't remember what key you're in, sweetheart."

Now they were running through the revised order in harmony, vocals overlapping like kids around a campfire, Shep strumming the guitar while the drummer kept beat with his sticks on the back of the seat. Eleanor sang along with them, her voice warmed up from days on the road and laced with that smoky edge that had started to feel like her own again. Her mind was sharp today, and she was taking advantage of the lifted fog, unsure how long it would last.

They'd driven through most of the night, taking turns at the wheel, though she was relegated to copilot, a role she didn't mind, especially when Megan wasn't behind the wheel. Roxy took her job more seriously—riding shotgun with her ears perked, snorting at every bump, and whimpering when someone dared turn on the radio too loud.

They'd stopped at a diner off Route 66 for dinner, where Eleanor insisted they all eat vegetables for once. Not just Cracker Jacks and Coca-Cola and gas station jerky. Real food. She made the drummer get the meat loaf with green beans, and Shep grudgingly ordered grilled chicken and sliced tomatoes.

Eleanor had gotten the meat loaf too—only halfway through did she remember she hated meat loaf. Always had. But Roxy didn't, and that dog polished it off like it was prime rib.

"Mama Lightning," Eddie, the drummer, called from the back, tapping out a new rhythm. "What do you think of this?"

Eleanor paused, listening. The beat was sharp, a little jagged. Almost like a foal that wanted to gallop but hadn't found its footing yet.

"Maybe a little lighter on the third," she suggested, patting her thighs in a similar pattern. "Don't chase it so hard. Let the song come to you."

Eddie adjusted, tapping again with a slight swing in the downbeat.

"Yes!" Eleanor clapped her hands in time as he mimicked her sound. "That's it!"

The rest of the band let out a cheer, and even Roxy gave a bark of approval, her tail thumping against Eleanor's foot, tongue lolling out of the side of her mouth.

This—*this* was what had been missing. Not just music. Not just the road. But the sense that her voice still mattered. A purpose. That people were listening. That she wasn't a widow with a dog and a fading memory.

Here in this van, sandwiched in the middle of where they'd been and where they were going, with a follicularly challenged dog and a band of long-haired boys who thought she was cool as hell—she belonged.

Her eyes drifted shut, the wind funneling through the cracked window to sweep across her face. The road ahead stretched on, long and winding. Atlanta was calling. And this time, she wasn't following someone else's path.

She was chasing her own damn music.

Just like that, Eleanor realized she'd slipped into this band of misfits like a spoon into sugar. She stroked her hand over Roxy's absurd little tuft of rocker hair—the only hair the dog had, perched on her head like a cotton candy bouffant. "You're a mess," she whispered, smiling, "but you're my mess."

The van was loud and smelly and held together by duct tape and divine intervention, but she felt at home. Like this was her crew. Her chosen family. The kids called her Mama Lightning now, and it stuck in a way that didn't chafe like Mrs., Mom, or Grandma always had. Titles that belonged to thousands, when she wanted one that belonged to just her.

She had the strangest urge to introduce the band to her actual family. But the image came too quickly, too clearly. Leanne standing in the doorway with her mouth in that tight little line, arms folded like she expected bad news. And Nora, eyes half focused on the middle distance, already thinking about which boy would pick her up for a date, twirling the phone cord around her wrist like the tether holding her social life together.

Who could blame them? Nora had just turned eighteen—at the edge of becoming an adult. The world was cracking open at her feet. Eleanor remembered what that had felt like. The delicious ache of possibility.

Only it had been different for her. She was born in 1900, and when she turned eighteen, it was 1918. The Great War was just ending. The flu pandemic was just starting. Women didn't go to Yale. In her case her options were to chase the music and starve or marry a man who could afford meat twice a week. She'd skipped the school but found the latter. But it had required giving up her big musical dreams.

And now? Eleanor stared at the woman in the side mirror, the night wrapping around her like a shawl filled with holes. The woman who looked back wasn't the girl she remembered but an old woman. Lines etched around her eyes where it used to be smooth and supple, making her skin resemble the Grand Canyon more than a level plain. Hair that seemed brittle, silver rather than silky and blond. Age spots on her arms and hands where skin used to freckle in the summer. And her lips, which used to be full and plump, were withered and wilted. Her cheekbones faded into a softness that betrayed the sharpness of who she'd been.

And yet, there was something fierce still burning beneath the surface.

Maybe that's why she left home. Because when she looked at Leanne, she saw herself in the years she had lost—a life full of duty. When she looked at Nora, she saw the self she might have been if she'd chosen differently.

And the cruelest trick of all was that she knew those selves were slipping through her fingers. Her mind was starting to blur at the edges. Little memory lapses had become longer. Sometimes, she forgot where she was mid-song. Sometimes, she forgot names. Even her own. Just yesterday she couldn't remember how to open a Coca-Cola bottle, until Shep had popped the cap off. And though she smiled through it—though she laughed and played and traveled and sang—a terror lived in her bones that left her constantly feeling unsettled.

Because what was she, really, without her memories? A puffing body without a soul.

"You okay?" Shep asked, pencil moving in quick scratches across the open page of his beat-up notebook, lyrics forming faster than the miles unspooling beneath their wheels.

The hum of the van, the lull of late-night headlights, and the faint scent of gasoline and road dust wrapped around them like a familiar old song. His tapping hand kept time against his bell-bottoms, knee bouncing to a rhythm only he seemed to hear.

Eleanor sat curled in her seat, Roxy a warm lump of loyalty on her lap, her arms loosely crossed over the dog as if doing so would keep the words on the tip of her tongue at bay.

She watched Shep. Bright-eyed. Handsome as sin and just as dangerous.

What if she told him the truth? That no, she wasn't okay. That she was scared. That her memory was beginning to fray like the hem of an old apron. That sometimes she forgot the key of a song she'd written herself or the name of the diner they'd just left. That sometimes she said "egg" when she meant "chicken." That cracks were forming in her mind, spreading quietly.

Then, she thought, why spoil the moment? Why anchor this golden, fleeting ride in the weight of her grief?

So, instead, she nodded toward his notebook and raised an eyebrow. "Are you about to turn me into a love song?"

Shep grinned, slow and cocky, a dimple flashing. "Only if you'll let me."

"Dangerous game you're playing." She gave him a droll grin and an arched brow that she hoped—despite her years—could still take a man's breath away.

"This isn't a game, Ellie," he said earnestly. "Not to me."

She let out a breath, slow and cautious. If she exhaled too hard, she might tip the balance, sending everything spilling over the edge. She'd been admired before. Flirted with, courted, loved even, but not like this. Not when she felt like an antique. A relic on tour.

"You better make it original," she said lightly, brushing her fingers through Roxy's ridiculous patch of hair.

"If it's about you, it can't be anything else."

She swallowed. There were things she couldn't say at her age, no matter how free she pretended to be.

"But you hardly know me." Eleanor turned to the window. Her reflection caught her off guard again—silver hair mussed, wrinkles drawn like a topographical map of her life. She stared out instead, into the dark blur of trees and open road.

"I know enough." Shep's voice was lower now, quiet like the hush before a chorus. "I know the way you pretend not to like the attention. And I know how your eyes go soft when you think no one's watching. Like you're remembering something worth hurting over."

"That's not knowing someone," she whispered. "That's a good songwriter filling in blanks."

He didn't answer right away. And the seconds ticked by in heavy silence. "I know you think me flirting with you is some kind of joke. That when we hit Atlanta, I'll wink and disappear."

She opened her mouth to interrupt, to tell him it was fine, expected even.

"But I genuinely like you, Ellie," he said before she could. "Not just Mama Lightning, the Dame of Rock and Roll. *You.* And I'm not afraid of the years between us. Only afraid you won't let yourself be liked."

What Shep said might be true.

Maybe it was the adrenaline from fleeing tear gas and baton-wielding cops. Maybe it was the high that came with writing a song that might actually mean something. Maybe it was just the hum of the highway and the illusion of freedom that comes from being neither here nor there but somewhere in between.

But Eleanor Bell had lived long enough to know you couldn't count on maybes.

This would all end one day—tomorrow, next week, or next month. The songs, the stage, the laughter, the looks. One day, Shep would wake up, and the melody he'd write for her wouldn't be sweet or flirtatious—it would be a ballad of what-ifs and nearlys. A sad song for a woman whose name he'd remember like a ghost note in a forgotten tune. A name she would have long forgotten in the endless sinkhole of dementia.

Still, she wasn't ready to burst his bubble. Or her own.

Not yet.

Eleanor smiled, soft and small, letting the sorrow gather behind the lines of her smile. Without thinking, she reached out, her fingers brushing his cheek with a tenderness that surprised even her, and gave a playful tug at the unruly hair curling above his ear with just the slightest hint of silver starting.

He leaned in to her touch like a boy starved for mothering—or something else. And then he scooted closer, his thigh pressing warm and steady against hers, the heat of his body seeping into her always-cold bones like sunshine through a kitchen window in winter. Definitely something else.

In this quiet vulnerability, she leaned her head onto his shoulder, letting him bear some of the weight she wasn't ready to voice. When she spoke, it was quiet but sure. "Write me a song I'll remember."

Shep smiled. His arm moved in rhythm as he scribbled in his notebook, the scratch of the pencil against paper steady, hypnotic. The van rumbled along the dark stretch of highway, rocking her gently.

And she drifted off.

But it wasn't a peaceful sleep.

In her dreams, they were all there—Shep, her husband, even the man from so long ago, the one who gave her music before she ever knew what love really was. They all stood before her like a jury of ghosts, waiting for a final verdict. Each face was etched with an emotion she couldn't fix but was responsible for. Longing, expectation, disappointment.

And she—Eleanor Bell, musician, mother, memory in motion—looked them all in the eye and said, "I'm old enough now, I don't have to choose. Not anymore. I've earned the right to live what's left of my life the way I damn well please."

And with that, she turned toward the music, toward the light, toward whatever came next.

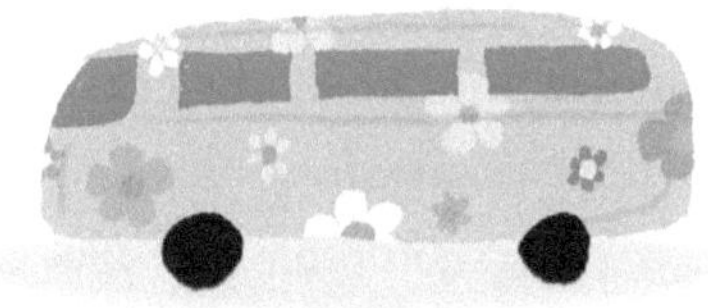

CHAPTER TWENTY-THREE

AFTER THE HAVOC OF THE DENVER FESTIVAL—THE TEAR gas, the panic, the push through the crowd—Leanne and Nora had returned to their motel room and collapsed in a heap of bruised exhaustion. The room smelled faintly of bleach and stale cigarette smoke. A Western, *The Good, The Bad and the Ugly*, was playing on the television, cowboys galloping across a dusty plain in search of justice or stolen gold—Leanne couldn't remember which. Maybe both.

They'd taken turns teasing the mustaches and gruff line delivery. Nora had laughed until she cried when Leanne dubbed one of the bounty-hunter cowboys Sheriff Shifty 'Stache.

Tonight was one of those rare mother-daughter exchanges where nothing felt forced. They'd talked about the road ahead. About Eleanor. About how the hell any of this had even started. Gone was the tension that seemed to constantly fill the space between them, replaced by a comradery Leanne was reluctant to let go of.

Now, hours later, the sun was already high, squeezing through the slits of the green motel curtains, and Leanne was back behind the wheel. Another state. Another stretch of highway. Another gamble that her mother might show up at a music festival like some cigarette-smoking, guitar-playing ghost.

The Lincoln rumbled into a rinky-dink gas station on the outskirts of Kansas. A rusted Texaco sign swung on a crooked pole, and a diner attached to the side of the station promised "Hot Coffee, Cold Pie, All Day Breakfast."

Nora, eyes still puffy from sleep, rubbed her face as they parked. After falling asleep before finishing the book, they'd been reading the last chapters of *The Godfather* aloud that morning, the scenes heavy and blood-spattered. Michael Corleone getting his revenge. It felt fitting somehow—like they were on the last page of something in both fiction and real life.

The red vinyl booths squeaked inside the diner, and the smell of bacon grease and toast wrapped around Leanne like a warm, greasy hug. She welcomed it. A part of her—one that she didn't like to admit—was starting to fall in love with this strange pilgrimage they were on. And after talking to Joe, knowing her mother was safe and even in good spirits, had eased some of the worry, though it never fully left her. She didn't think it ever would now.

At the counter, a waitress leaned against the register, cracking up. "You're kidding," she said to a patron, swiping a rag over the countertop between giggles.

The man she was chatting with wore a trucker hat that said "Keep on Truckin'." He laughed, tipping his coffee mug toward the waitress for a refill.

"I wouldn't have believed it if I hadn't seen it. Old lady and a trucker arguing about whether she could drive his semi." He shook his head. "I swear, she had a mouth on her. She looked him straight in the eye and told him age and gender didn't mean a thing if she had the guts and the gumption."

Leanne's heart stuttered. She leaned forward, her coffee forgotten, her pulse picking up like she was chasing a moving train.

Old lady. Argumentative. Mouthy. Gumption.

She and Nora looked at each other across the sticky table. Nora mouthed one word, "*Grandma?*"

Leanne wasn't sure why it was this, of all things—a story about a truck-stop shouting match—that made her think of her mother. Maybe it was the sheer audacity of the thing. Maybe it was the mention of a mouthy old woman. Or maybe it was the fact that, deep down, she could absolutely picture Eleanor getting into a heated debate with a trucker about why women should be allowed to drive a semi.

What solidified it for her was when he mentioned the old woman had ended the argument by breaking out into song, before she'd been led away by a rocker-looking dude.

Leanne took another sip of coffee, which she'd doctored with sugar and a splash of cream, and side-eyed Nora over the rim of her mug. "So, what do you think? You think Grandma's picking fights with truckers now?"

Nora giggled, stirring her hot chocolate lazily, her marshmallows melting into goo. "Honestly? I'd love to see it in person."

Leanne smirked, shaking her head. "You would."

They ate quietly for a bit—soft eggs, crispy toast, a side of bacon Leanne hadn't realized she'd craved until she took the first bite. It reminded her of being young and free, back when breakfast in a roadside diner felt like the start of something big instead of a rest stop on the way to the next chaotic destination. Back when she didn't worry that her rear end would get bigger just from sniffing greasy food.

Soon enough, they were back in the Lincoln, tires humming as they coasted down the on-ramp to the highway. Nora was fiddling with the radio dial again, skipping past static, jazz, and talk radio.

But Leanne's hand shot out mid-turn.

"Wait—go back."

Nora twisted the dial back one notch. A burst of static, then—

"—folks, I'm not making this up. First reported in the *San Francisco Chronicle*, reports are flying in from all over, and now, hot off the wire, we've got it on good authority that she's en route to Atlanta."

The DJ had a voice that was smooth and magnetic, just amused enough to sound like he wasn't taking himself too seriously but serious enough that a listener would pay attention. Leanne's spine straightened, and Nora turned up the volume.

"They call her the Dame of Rock and Roll, and she's living up to the name. Out of nowhere, she's been lighting up the summer music festival stages with Shep Moon and his band, turning every set into an unforgettable experience." The announcer let out a whistle that startled Leanne enough she came back to herself. "With that silver hair, sweet guitar strumming, and a voice that's nothing short of angelic, she's got fans and musicians falling swiftly under her spell."

Leanne and Nora glanced at one another, and Leanne felt her body levitate, as if she were no longer in the car, just hovering above the leather.

The announcer continued. "No telling how long she'll be out on the road, so if you're anywhere near Atlanta—or heading to the big festival this weekend—keep those eyes peeled and your ears wide open. And hey, if you spot the Rocking Granny tearing it up onstage, give us a ring and let the rest of us live vicariously through your epic experience. This is one act you don't want to miss!"

Shock numbed Leanne's hands, her brain, basically her entire body, and she nearly swerved off the road.

"They're really calling her that? I thought Joe was joking," Nora choked out, twisting toward the radio like she could pull the words out of the dashboard or rewind and have the announcer say it all over again.

"The Dame of Rock and Roll," Leanne slowly repeated the moniker given to her mother, like saying it aloud might help her wrap her head around it. "It has to be her."

"I think so," Nora said, her voice caught somewhere between disbelief and hysterical laughter.

"This is just...crazy." Leanne tightened her grip on the wheel, her knuckles turning white as she eased the Lincoln back onto the highway and gunned the engine like that might somehow ground her in reality. Hard to believe that this was really happening.

The radio announcer continued to speak, his voice full of amused disbelief, the same feelings swimming in her mind. "If you've seen her, folks, let us know. Frankly, we want to meet her."

Nora burst into giggles. "Everyone wants to meet Grandma. What is happening? Is she famous now?"

"Seems we're not the only ones looking for her," Leanne muttered.

The truth of it hit her like a sudden pothole in the road. Her mother—Eleanor—wasn't missing. She wasn't wandering around dazed or confused or lost. She didn't need Leanne to rush in and rescue her. She was out there singing with rock stars, making friends with DJs, and probably starting philosophical debates with truckers over women's rights.

And here Leanne was. Squeezing the steering wheel like she might be able to choke the answers out of it, driving across the country as if she were on some noble rescue mission.

But for what?

For autonomy? For joy?

For herself?

She glanced sideways at Nora, who was still laughing, her ponytail bouncing from beneath her tie-dye bandanna as she kicked her bare foot onto the dashboard. The sun glinted off her sunglasses. Nora looked young and carefree and joyful. Exactly how a girl of eighteen should.

Leanne swallowed hard against the guilt rising in her throat.

All her life, she'd tried to be the opposite of Eleanor. Where her mother had been wild and whimsical and unpredictable, Leanne had clung to order. To routine. To crisp table linens, weekly pot roast dinners, and a perfectly penciled grocery list. She had been safe.

And now? Now Eleanor was on a nationwide stage. Literally.

The words from long ago echoed in her ears like a tune she couldn't shake: *"You're such a square, Leanne."*

At the time, it had felt like an insult coming from her mother. The one person who was supposed to love her unconditionally and not judge her. Now, she wasn't so sure it was an insult but rather a warning.

What was so wrong with being a little different? A little chaotic? A little...*alive*?

Maybe the real problem wasn't that Eleanor had left on a wild adventure. Maybe it was that Leanne had never permitted herself to do the same.

She pressed a little harder on the gas. The wind caught Leanne's hair and flung it around her face as they sped forward into the sun.

Who was she to stop her mother from doing what she wanted? If what Eleanor really wanted was to sing—to chase a dream that had been collecting dust in the corners of a closet somewhere between raising Leanne and growing old gracefully—then who was Leanne to snatch that away?

Especially now. Especially after reading the words in that letter from the doctor's office. Since she'd shared the news with Dean and Nora, researched as much as she could, she hadn't said the word *dementia* out loud. But it was there, floating in the passenger seat like an invisible ghost. Not quite real yet, but close enough to haunt her.

When Leanne cleared her throat, Nora was adjusting the radio dial again, catching another burst of a Janis Joplin track.

"Nora?"

"Yeah?" Her daughter tilted her head, sunglasses sliding halfway down her nose.

Leanne hesitated. Then, taking a breath that felt like peeling off a mask, she said, "What if we didn't make this trip about chasing Grandma to bring her home?"

Nora stared at her for half a beat. "What do you mean?"

"I mean, what if we're not here to stop her? What if we find her and…support her instead? Cheer her on. But only if you're okay with it. I know chasing Grandma has sort of ruined your summer plans."

Nora's mouth dropped open as if her mother had just donned a daisy chain and traded her high-waisted belt dress for a flower-flowing bohemian smock. Leanne's heart stuttered in her chest. She wasn't sure if Nora was appalled or just shocked. If someone had told Leanne when they climbed into the Lincoln and headed out of their driveway that she would say, "Let's cheer on Grandma," she was pretty certain her daughter would have laughed and then said something snarky.

"Do you mean it?" Nora's voice was soft, hopeful.

Leanne let out a breath that she wasn't even aware she was holding, then nodded.

Nora let out a loud whoop, clapping. "I think my friends are going to be totally jealous. I wouldn't give up this summer for all the lake trips in the world. Well, maybe that's an exaggeration. I think it's groovy."

"Groovy?"

"That's what the cool kids are saying," Nora replied, a hint of teasing in her tone.

Leanne chuckled and tapped the steering wheel. "Well then, groovy it is."

They flew past a hand-painted sign that read ATLANTA 1238 MILES, and Leanne felt something crack open in her chest. Not in a painful way. But in the way a window that's been painted shut finally unsticks after you wrestle with it.

"Atlanta, here we come," Leanne said, her voice steadier than expected.

Because the Dame of Rock and Roll might have a whole country of fans now…but Leanne and Nora Miller?

They were number one.

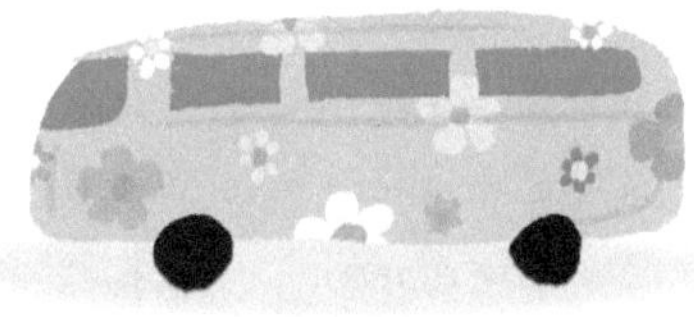

CHAPTER TWENTY-FOUR

NORA STARED AT THE COVER OF *THE LOVE MACHINE*, her cheeks already pink and warm. This wasn't the first time she'd seen it. She studied the cover with secret interest. Two hands. That was all it was. But the way his fingers gripped her skin…tight and desperate, like something dangerous and decadent was about to happen.

Something inside Nora stirred. Something she didn't fully have the vocabulary to name yet. Something that sort of felt like the jolt she'd gotten when Joe had touched her shoulder back at the festival. Or really any time his eyes met hers.

She flipped the book open, fingertips brushing the edge of the dog-eared pages, already smoothed from her mother's prior reads. The words wrapped around her like a pearl necklace she didn't ask to try on but now couldn't bear to take off.

By the end of the first page, her entire face was a bonfire.

"Mom…this book…" she hissed, half scandalized, half fascinated.

Leanne giggled. *Giggled.* Like she was eighteen and Nora was an old lady. "Don't stop now. I can't wait to hear the rest."

Nora groaned but turned to chapter one. Amanda. Fall season.

Bra issues. And God apparently not gifting her with "giant, beautiful breasts."

Nora glanced down at her own chest, concealed in a white camisole. A respectable A cup if there ever was one. Small and simple. Certainly not Love Machine material.

"Maybe I should start wearing falsies," she muttered.

Leanne glanced over, one brow lifted. "I wore falsies once."

"You did?"

"On my wedding day." She chuckled, swiping a piece of hair out of her eyes. "Your grandma told me I was 'false advertising.' Said the merchandise didn't match the sales pitch."

"Oh my God—Grandma said that?!"

Leanne burst out laughing, a full, whole-body type of laughter that made her shoulders shake behind the wheel. "In front of my aunt too. Mortifying."

Nora howled, letting her head fall against the open book. "I'm scarred forever. Sounds a lot like when someone says, 'Why buy the cow when you can get the milk for free?'"

"Not exactly the same," Leanne replied, lifting an eyebrow. "But close, and it was pretty hilarious. I still remember your dad's face when he saw me walking down the aisle in that dress—with those obviously enhanced breasts pushed halfway to heaven."

Nora held up both hands like she was stopping traffic. "Okay, okay! I give. Not another word about Dad looking at your boobs, please."

They both broke into giggles, clutching their stomachs, the Lincoln gliding over the flat southern road.

Nora wiped her eyes and returned to the book. *The Love Machine* was racy, risqué, and positively provocative. The sort of book that didn't even pretend to blush. Men sleeping with women just because they could. Breasts described with the care of fine art. Power, lust, fame.

Made *The Godfather* seem almost chaste. *Almost.* There was a lot of talk in that one of Sonny Corleone's gigantic…

If her father even heard her say some of these words aloud, he might board up her bedroom and send a telegram to Yale saying she'd joined a convent.

But Leanne was cackling beside her, sipping her gas station coffee like it was martini hour.

After finishing chapter one, Nora turned to her and waved the book between them. "Have you read any other books like this one?"

Leanne snickered, then bit her lip as if she wasn't sure she should confess. "Not in front of your dad."

Figured, but Nora didn't say that. "Which one?"

"I read Jacqueline Susann's other book, *Valley of the Dolls*. Fantastic."

Nora smirked. "Maybe I should read that too."

Leanne gave her a side glance. "Maybe you should. When you go to Yale your English minor classes will have you reading all the important stuff. Chaucer, Proust, Eliot, all the dead white men with big ideas and longer sentences. Reading should be fun too."

Nora laughed, reminded of her high school English class. It was a good thing she'd gotten practice there showing up with books that her teacher didn't approve of.

"Don't let 'literary' fool you into thinking that's all that matters. Jacqueline Susann gets a lot of flak, sure, but every housewife in Ossining has *Valley of the Dolls* hidden under the bed next to their Avon catalog."

Nora raised an eyebrow. "Even Mrs. Murphy?" That woman was buttoned up tighter than a toddler in a snowstorm. Nora couldn't even count the number of times Mrs. Murphy had wagged her finger from behind her curtained window.

"*Especially* Mrs. Murphy."

They both burst into another fit of laughter.

The sun danced lower in the sky, casting its golden warmth over the dashboard. And as the wind tousled their hair and Leanne tapped her fingers on the wheel to the rhythm of Dusty Springfield's song "You Don't Have to Say You Love Me," Nora had a thought she hadn't had before: *My mom is kind of cool.*

Nora grinned, picturing it now—those suburban matrons in high-waisted skirts and sensible heels, coiffed hair held tight with Aqua Net, ladling Jell-O molds into Tupperware and cutting perfect brownie squares for the church bake sale. Women who kept a roast in the oven, lipstick on their smile, and a smutty novel tucked inside the ironing basket or beneath their side of the mattress.

The secret rebellion of housewives.

She wondered how many of them were one steamy chapter away from setting their aprons on fire.

And then she wondered…when her own mother would revolt.

Before this trip she'd never really looked at her mom as someone who might want more. Leanne had always just been *Mom*. The keeper of lists, of order. A woman made of sturdy heels and perfect posture. But now…

"Did you always want to go to secretarial school?" Nora kept her tone casual but probing.

Leanne's features softened, and a sentimental stare swept over her face. For a split second, Nora wished to know her thoughts and what made her reminisce in a way that was so not like her usual perfunctory self. But she didn't have to wonder, because her mother started to share.

"Every little girl dreams of being something magical, don't they?" Her laugh was barely audible, more a whisper that carried secrets within memories. "After I realized I couldn't be a mermaid," she laughed softly, "I used to think I might be an artist—though I'm better at stick figures than portraits. Or maybe a singer like my mom.

But when it came time to choose, magic wasn't what made sense. I'm not artistic in that way. I had to choose something that was not just practical but respectable too."

Nora raised an eyebrow, flipping the corner page of *The Love Machine* with her finger. "Maybe that's the whole problem."

Leanne tilted her head. "What do you mean?"

"I mean…maybe the issue isn't that women read these books or want different lives. Maybe the issue is that we're all so scared of looking unladylike, ungrateful, or being too much that we stuff all our desires under the bed with the paperbacks."

Nora wasn't sure from her mother's expression if she was surprised or…impressed.

"Maybe if we stopped worrying so much about being respectable, practical," Nora added, "we'd remember who we actually are. Or at least give ourselves permission to figure it out. Bring some of that magic back."

A silence passed between them—not heavy, just…thoughtful.

"Maybe. You're pretty wise for eighteen." Leanne's voice was soft, contemplative, as she steered with one hand, gripping the map with the other to check their route.

"I'm wise, maybe," Nora replied with a mischievous grin. "But I still want some falsies."

Leanne laughed. "Every girl should try them at least once. Preferably not on her wedding day."

They were still giggling when they pulled into a peach-and-mint-colored roadside motel along Route 66. Neon lights flickered and Adirondack chairs painted in rainbow order lined the walkway. Leanne parked the Lincoln under the soft buzz of the overhead light, their brown paper sandwich bags crinkling in the back seat like firecrackers.

Instead of flipping on the television like they had at every other stop, they each kicked off their shoes and climbed onto their beds, cracking open *The Love Machine.* The room smelled like a mixture of borax and their sandwiches, and someone had left the air conditioner on arctic mode, but they didn't care; they just climbed under the covers.

Tonight, the entertainment was Jacqueline Susann.

Nora read aloud about Robin Stone—midway through the book now—navigating his dangerous dance between Amanda and Judith, both women heartbreakingly self-aware and heartbreakingly blind at the same time. In the chapter they devoured, Robin bought Amanda a luxurious apartment, promising love while planning his subsequent escape. Amanda, wise to the world but not to him, kissed him anyway, knowing what came next.

"I swear," Leanne muttered, "he's like if Robert Redford and a bottle of Brut cologne had a baby."

Nora laughed until she had to set the book down. "I don't know whether I want to date or slap him."

"That means Jacqueline did her job," her mom said, already chewing on the next page.

Later that night, the book closed and their sandwich wrappers tossed in the motel trash, Nora lay in bed, cocooned in the air conditioner's hum and the thrum of the highway just beyond the curtains. She didn't think about college exams or dorm room assignments. Not about the boy who'd broken her heart junior year or the curveball of calculus.

Instead, she thought about telling her mom she wanted to be a writer.

Really telling her.

Not just the vague "I want to get an English degree so I can write" but the truth about the notebook in her bag—the leather-bound one with bent corners and ideas scrawled in margins. The one that held the line she wrote last night, lying in a motel bed just like this one, after Joe said goodbye…

In the electric haze of the open-air concert, with the night thrumming like a heartbeat around us, I turned—and there he was, a stranger with ink-stained hands and eyes that held entire stories, watching me like he already knew how this would end.

With her eyes closed she let the story drift through her, humming like a song only she could hear.

CHAPTER TWENTY-FIVE

SITTING IN THE SHADE OF A CANVAS TENT UNDER THE sweltering Atlanta sun, Eleanor wiped a bead of sweat from her brow and handed Roxy the last bite of her ham sandwich. The diva dog nuzzled into her lap like royalty, tongue lolling, belly full, and wholly unbothered by the heat or the noise. Around them, the festival throbbed like a living, breathing creature—drums pulsed in the distance, bass lines vibrated the dirt beneath her sandals, and the air smelled of patchouli, beer, and the occasional illicit smoke.

She would have thought she'd feel energized after the excitement of sleeping in a van for a week and spending the past few days bouncing from one backstage to the next. Refreshed. Reinvigorated. But no—she felt like a suitcase with a broken handle. Lugged along. Half open. On the verge of spilling its contents into the dirt.

Still, she smiled, one hand absent-mindedly stroking Roxy's spine.

How long had it been? Two weeks since she'd left New York? Already it felt like a month or more. And today was the Fourth of July. Back home, after the town parade, Leanne would be preparing a strawberry and blueberry Jell-O mold while Dean fired up his Weber barbecue for burgers and hot dogs. Kids would be lighting off firecrackers, and Eleanor would have been sitting back to watch it all.

"Ellie." Shep's voice was syrup-slow and sun-drunk. "There's someone I want you to meet."

She glanced up, squinting through the halo of sunlight bleeding into the tent.

Shep glided toward her, flanked by a young man who practically shimmered in the heat. A rolled red bandanna crowned his dark curls, hair spilling out like a halo of effortless rebellion. A turquoise stone caught the sun from where it hung on a beaded necklace. His white fringe shirt was unbuttoned, framing a sinewy brown chest that gleamed with sweat, and his bell-bottoms hugged his hips like they were sewn on.

Silver rings adorned his fingers, a cigarette tucked between them, and when he smiled—full lips, a glint of teeth—she swore the temperature climbed ten degrees.

Jimi. Goddamn. Hendrix. A name she was certain never to forget.

Eleanor stilled.

If she were forty-five years younger, she might've screamed, begged for an autograph, and thrown herself at his Converse. But she was sixty-nine. Did sixty-nine-year-old women swoon over rock stars?

Well. Maybe they should.

She caught Shep's eye. His smirk said, *I know.*

"I hear you're the Dame of Rock and Roll," Jimi said. That voice could melt the ice in a drink before he finished the sentence.

Eleanor straightened her spine just slightly, offering her hand with practiced grace.

"Nice to meet you, young man." The corner of her mouth twitched into a wry smile. "They call me Mama Lightning too sometimes. But that one's a little more scandalous."

Jimi threw his head back and laughed. Roxy barked once, punctuating the reaction.

Funny, but right then, Eleanor Bell, widow, mother, and grandmother—sweaty, sunburned, and sleep-deprived—felt like she *was* forty-five years younger. The exhaustion that had been consuming her only seconds before vanished and was replaced with the energy she'd been hoping for.

"Care for a sandwich?" She reached into her handbag like a magician pulling out a trick. She'd tucked an extra ham sandwich in there earlier, just in case. On this trip, she'd often found herself forgetting to eat and being hungry without access to a meal. This was a survival tactic, she'd told herself. Or maybe a grandmother's intuition.

She held out the sandwich to Jimi like it was a peace offering or maybe a gift to a god.

He chuckled, shaking his head. "No, ma'am. I'm good, thank you."

Jimi accepted an ice-cold soda from Shep instead, popping the cap off with a flick of his thumb.

"Damn, it's hotter than a Marshall amp after a three-hour set." Jimi took a long swig.

Eleanor grinned. "Hot? Honey, this isn't hot. This is just the oven preheating."

Jimi laughed, the sound bright and easy, like a guitar riff sliding into the air.

She watched him over the rim of her sunglasses, still pretending she wasn't fazed even though her heart pounded a rhythm faster than the drummer onstage. Jimi Hendrix was drinking a soda in her tent. Of all the things… Nora would flip out, as the youths said.

"When was the last time you sat still and just let the world happen?" Eleanor settled deeper into her folding chair, doing that herself, her tone curious but edged with something softer.

Jimi paused, tapping his cigarette against the arm of the chair before lighting it. He took a drag and exhaled a lazy cloud.

"Man, that's a real question," he said. "I try, you know? Sometimes,

I'm not even there when I play. Just floating, letting the notes talk instead of me. But sitting still? Just letting it all happen? I don't know… The world moves too fast. People want to put you in a box, tell you what you got to be. And me? I just want to play, keep moving, keep searching."

Then he turned to her, that same smile back.

"But maybe I ought to try it right now. Think I could learn a thing or two from you, Mama Lightning."

Eleanor chuckled, the breeze ruffling through her silver-streaked hair like a whisper. "Dangerous game you're playing, Mr. Hendrix. You sit too long with me, you might not be able to get up."

He raised an eyebrow. "Then I better only stay until my next set, huh?"

The hum of festival fervor faded into the background, replaced by the rustling of canvas in the wind and the distant thump of a bass line rolling. The heat shimmered around them in slow, thick waves, and Eleanor breathed it all in. Sweat clung to her collarbone. Dust clung to her sandals. But none of it mattered.

She watched him tip his head back, eyes half lidded, staring up at the sky as if the clouds were speaking to him. The cigarette dangled forgotten between his fingers. And for one silent breath, neither of them was an icon, rebel, or a story waiting to be told—they were just two souls caught in the middle of a sticky Georgia afternoon, letting the world turn without them.

When he drained the last sip of his soda, he glanced at her sideways, that crooked grin unwavering.

"I like you." His words weren't a flirtation but a fact. "What should I call you?"

She grinned. "I've had a lot of names." She brushed a crumb from her lap. "Eleanor. Ellie. Mama Lightning. The Dame of Rock and Roll."

There was another name too, one she hadn't said aloud in decades—a stage name from a past life. A version of her that once sang under carnival lights, barefoot and invincible. But that girl was tucked away, folded like a love letter at the bottom of a drawer. For now.

"Well, Ellie," he said, standing with a lazy stretch. "It was real good meeting you. I hope I see you out there again. You sing like you mean it."

"That's the only way I know how," she replied, watching him turn toward the sunlight, guitar slung across his back like a sword.

Eleanor drew in a deep breath as Jimi disappeared beyond the tent flap, and as she let it out, her world started to wobble, until Shep came into view, his hand on her shoulder as he stood in front of her and gave her a gentle shake. She blinked at him, blinked at the empty tent around them. Jimi Hendrix had been a dream conjured by heatstroke and too much smoke in her lungs.

"You must have been having one hell of a dream." Shep's grin was teasing.

"A dream." She shook her head, trying to right herself. "Jimi seemed so real." A cinematic quality, like the flickering edge of a film reel right before it flies off the wheel. The doctor had warned her she might soon not know the difference between what happened in her dreams and when she was awake. Was this the start? A shiver passed through her at the thought.

"Hendrix?" Shep raised a brow.

"Yeah, me and Hendrix having a cigarette." She let out a soft laugh, hiding her disappointment.

"Wouldn't that be a hell of a thing?" Shep wiped a hand down his face. "He's up right now. Must have heard him playing."

Eleanor grinned, nodding, watching a bead of sweat drip down Shep's temple. Off in the distance, she could hear Hendrix finish up "Foxy Lady," and then his guitar started playing a familiar tune, "The Star-Spangled Banner," in honor of today's holiday. "Met a lot of musicians back when ragtime was the thing. But Jimi Hendrix would take the cake."

"You've sure lived a life." Shep's voice was half awe, half whiskey.

Megan flipped the tent flap open, and Eleanor squinted into the sun. "A life, I sure have."

But only half of one, if she was being honest.

Because for the past few decades, she hadn't really been living. She'd been existing—cooking dinners, folding sheets, showing up to church with lipstick on and teeth clenched. She'd smiled through grief. Through boredom. Through invisibility. The spotlight had moved on, and she'd quietly packed up her guitar like a guilty secret and buried it beneath her sweaters and sacrifices.

She remembered when it had all started—New York City, 1918. She was eighteen, shaking like a leaf in her borrowed boots, her guitar strapped across her body like armor. That first open mic night, she'd played chords no one understood. Not jazz, not folk—something new. Something too loud, too fast, too alive.

She remembered how the polite silence in the room had felt like rejection. The way the applause had come a beat too late, too tepid. Like the crowd was clapping just to be polite, not because they felt a connection with her music. And so she'd changed the tune, gave them the Bell of Wartime Music like they wanted.

But she'd kept coming back to original sound.

Week after week, heart thudding in her chest, she'd returned to the stage. The regulars began to notice. Heads tilted. Fingers tapped. One man leaned over his gin and said, "That girl plays like a fuse about to blow."

And then someone told… What was his name? Will? Ben? Willy Ben?

No, it was Billy Murray. They told him to come hear her.

The Billy Murray. Star of the phonograph. America's golden-voiced crooner back then. He'd come backstage after the show, still in his camel coat, smelling of whiskey and money.

"Where'd you learn to strum like that?" he'd asked, eyebrows raised.

Eleanor had shrugged, nonchalant, even though her knees were jelly.

"Just how it came out of me." Despite her nerves, she'd been able to play it cool.

He'd asked her to show him the chords. And she had. Right there in the hallway of a smoke-filled speakeasy, she'd handed him her guitar and taught him her rhythm, her pulse. He'd invited her onstage for a show the very next week.

She never forgot the look in his eyes. Like he'd stumbled onto something before the world was ready for it.

Eleanor glanced over at Shep, who was watching her like he had just discovered something rare. If only she could explain to him what it had cost her to tuck that girl away for so long. But instead, she reached down to scratch Roxy's ears. The little dog blinked up at her, blissed out and half asleep.

"You ever miss it?" Shep asked.

Eleanor looked out at the sunbaked horizon where the stage waited, where the crowd pulsed like a heartbeat.

"Every day I didn't pick up the guitar," she said softly, "I missed her."

And for once, she didn't mean the music but herself.

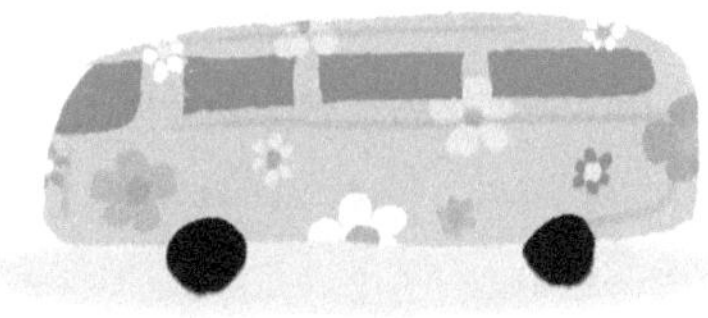

CHAPTER TWENTY-SIX

TRAFFIC HAD BEEN HELLACIOUS, AND ONCE MORE they were going to miss the opening of a festival. After sitting on the highway going approximately zero miles per hour for hours, they called it quits. They were only four hours from Atlanta, but the way things were going, they'd never make it in time to even see the last set.

Nashville it was.

The hotel lobby in Tennessee smelled of lemon cleaner and something faintly metallic—old radiator pipes, maybe. Through the open front door, the late-afternoon heat poured in like the velvet curtains in Leanne's mother's living room, heavy and slow, the low hum of music drifting from down the street.

At the front desk, Leanne thumbed through a spinning rack of postcards with glossy, oversaturated colors and tongue-in-cheek sayings. One caught her eye: "Wish You Were Here—But Then Who'd Feed the Dog?" There was a cartoon guitar lounging in a hammock strung between two cowboy boots, with the neon lights of Nashville behind it.

She smiled at the silly image. Maybe if she couldn't get Dean to answer the phone, she could at least make him laugh through the mail. If he even had it in him anymore to crack a smile.

"Do you have a pay phone?" she asked the clerk behind the desk, who was reading a paperback. The question was starting to feel like a mantra.

"Yes, ma'am." He pointed around the corner toward the vending machine and the ice maker, which was humming like it might start randomly spewing ice at unsuspecting patrons.

"Thanks." Leanne tucked the postcard under her arm and turned toward Nora, who balanced both their overnight bags and hummed a tune Leanne thought she recognized from the radio. Hendrix's "Foxy Lady" maybe.

Their motel room was a worn-out relic from a glitzier time—maybe the early '40s. But the management had let it fade. Brown carpet with gold thread and matching curtains, and that unmistakable cocktail of stale beer and old cigarettes baked into the walls. But it had two beds and a working air conditioner, so they couldn't complain.

Leanne fished for the coins buried in the bottom of her purse, and Nora plopped on the nearest bed, bouncing once, like she was testing the springs, which screamed from overuse.

"It's the Fourth of July. I can't believe it. Should we go listen to some music? Grab something to eat?" Nora's casual voice did not match her hopeful air.

Leanne glanced down at the coins in her hand. At the postcard now perched on the dresser beside a maroon leather Bible. At home she would have been working on preparing for a backyard barbecue. Nora's friends might have been over, the parents commiserating about losing them to college soon. Dean would be handling his Weber, staring satisfied at his charred meat with a beer in hand. A part of her wished they were back home doing the familiar, and yet, here was a chance to make a new memory.

She could call Dean. Wish him a happy Fourth of July. See if he'd been invited by a neighbor. Try to reach him for the tenth time this week. Or she could take this moment—this sliver of shared rebellion with her daughter—and say yes.

Time with Nora won. She dropped the coins back into her purse with a soft clink and smiled.

"Yeah. Let's do it."

Nora beamed, and in that instant, Leanne saw the shadow of the little girl her daughter used to be and the woman she was fast becoming. This rare, flickering beat between then and now felt precious. Sacred, even. Like the last song of a set, when the crowd leaned in, not wanting it to end.

She'd write the postcard tonight. Maybe. Or maybe not. Maybe she'd leave it unsent, tuck it into her suitcase like a souvenir.

Because right now, her daughter was asking her to go out—to a bar, to dinner, to listen to music. Soon enough, she'd be gone to college, gone into the wide world of dorm rooms, academic degrees, and dances, doing these things with friends instead of her mother.

Leanne straightened her blouse in the mirror and swiped on a little lipstick.

"Let's see what Nashville's got for us tonight," she said.

"Let's put on something a little more…fun." Nora was already elbow-deep in her suitcase, flinging shirts and denim and beaded scarves onto the bed like she was prepping for a photo shoot.

Leanne moved more slowly. She opened her modest floral-print overnight bag and sighed. Everything looked like it came from a rack at Proper Woman Weekly. Shift dresses in navy, beige, and one particularly sad pastel pink. A-line skirts stiff from starch. Her low, sensible, nude heels were lined up like obedient little soldiers.

She picked up one of the dresses that looked very much like the one she already had on and held it against herself in the mirror. The look said everything she'd been told a lady should be. Polished, put-together, pleasant. But at a music bar in Nashville, it might as well be a Sunday school uniform.

"I don't really have anything else to wear," she admitted, still holding the dress like it might suddenly bloom into something daring. "Other than my pajamas."

Nora glanced over from her suitcase, a wry smile curling at her lips. "We wear the same size. Try these."

She tossed a pair of well-worn bell-bottom jeans across the bed, followed by a loose pink button-down blouse with pearl snaps and the faint scent of Nora's perfume clinging to the fabric.

Leanne raised an eyebrow. "This feels…youthful."

"It is," Nora said, winking. "So are you. Sometimes."

Leanne laughed, kicking off her shoes. She slipped out of her dress and tugged on the jeans, shimmying them over hips that hadn't worn denim since she'd secretly tried them on in a dressing room at Gimbels last year, and just as quickly discarded them as inappropriate. This time, though, when she buttoned Nora's jeans and tucked in the blouse, something shifted. Not just in how she looked but how she *felt.* A small zip of energy coursed through her—a forgotten spark. Like she'd accidentally put her finger in a light socket labeled freedom.

Her hand reached for her heels on instinct, habit from years of mothering and modesty. But Nora snatched one mid-reach.

"What are you doing?" Nora's mouth was open in scandalized horror.

"I—"

"You cannot wear those," Nora said, laughing. She dug into her things and pulled out a pair of leather sandals with tiny pink flowers embroidered on the straps. "These. Please."

Leanne slid her feet in, surprised by how comfortable they were, how naked her feet felt not tucked into panty hose. She wiggled her toes, the nails painted pink, and then turned toward the mirror, smoothing the blouse, her reflection slowly resolving into someone she half recognized. The woman looking back at her had lines around her eyes, but they were laugh lines. Her hair was up, but loosely, like she didn't care if it came undone. She looked…like someone who had stories to tell. Almost like a stranger.

Nora came to stand beside her, resting her head gently on her mother's shoulder. Their reflections leaned into each other, two generations in sync for a rare breath of time.

"You look really pretty, Mom," Nora said softly.

Leanne met her daughter's gaze in the mirror. Her throat tightened.

"Thank you," Leanne said quietly. "I needed a change."

Nora simply nodded, a knowing smile tugging at the corner of her mouth as if she'd been waiting for her mother to catch up.

Outside, the Nashville evening buzzed with neon and twang. American flags hung from balconies over the bars, and overhead fireworks randomly sparked. Honky-tonk bars spilled music into the streets like broken water mains—steel guitars, fiddle solos, the occasional *yeehaw* echoing off the brick. The air smelled of fried food, diesel, and something sweet—honeysuckle maybe, or the lingering perfume of a woman who'd just passed.

They strolled down the sidewalks, alive with laughter, patriotic pride, and stumbling boots. Leanne had been worried she might feel out of place, but bell-bottom jeans were everywhere. Finally, Nora pointed at a bar that had a line of twinkly lights strung across the doorway and a band they could hear clear as day from the street.

"This one," she said with a decisive nod.

Inside, the bar was a motley buzz of voices and clinking glasses and a singer hollering into the microphone about heartbreak and the highway. After a short wait, they slid into a sticky vinyl booth near the back, where the speaker above them crackled like it might give out at any second. Photos of musicians hung on the walls, and in their booth was a singer named Jet Moon, wildly popular in the 1920s. He had a fiddle propped on his shoulder, and a mega-watt smile that melted plenty of hearts.

The air was thick with the heat of bodies that an overhead fan did little to mitigate. The whole bar was unmistakably southern. Laughter everywhere. Beer in mason jars. A couple two-stepping between the tables ignoring the fact that it wasn't a dance floor.

Leanne took it all in, trying not to look like a tourist in her borrowed blouse.

They ordered fried chicken and two draft beers because that's what everyone else seemed to be doing. Leanne had never been a beer drinker. Wine, occasionally. A dainty sherry at Christmas. But beer? Beer had always struck her as the sort of thing that bloated you and made you burp—decidedly unladylike—and was relegated to men.

Still, when the waitress thudded the cold glass onto the table, Leanne lifted it like she knew what she was doing. She took a sip. Let it roll around her mouth like she was appraising it. Crisp. Bready. A little bitter. Kind of like life.

Nora took a sip and let out a low, satisfied "Mmm," her eyes twinkling. "This is my first beer."

Leanne looked over, genuinely surprised. "Really?"

"It's not like they hand them out in the school cafeteria," Nora joked. "And I didn't exactly attend a lot of parties. And the ones I did, I was always too nervous about drinking. I had water or soda in my cup the whole time."

Leanne laughed, then softened. "Like mother, like daughter, huh?"

No sooner had the words left her mouth than something inside her twisted. She didn't want that to be Nora's future. Playing it safe. Always waiting for permission. Choosing sensible shoes over sandals with embroidered flowers. She wanted her daughter to be brave, to feel the fire of life and run toward the flames—not hide behind a smoke screen, like Leanne had done for too many years.

They ate the chicken with their fingers, grease glistening on their knuckles. Nora picked hers clean to the bone. Leanne managed two pieces before her stomach reminded her she hadn't eaten this kind of food in over a decade.

The band played on—twangy and alive—and Nora bobbed her head to the music, mouthing the words to a song neither of them had ever heard before. She looked radiant, flushed from the heat, from the beer, from life. Leanne couldn't take her eyes off her. In the stillness between heartbeats, she wasn't just a mother watching her daughter grow up.

She was a woman watching another woman become who she was meant to be.

Had her own mother ever looked at her like that?

And it struck her like a clap of thunder between the chords that time was a thief. One day, this girl would be gone. Off to Yale. Off to love. Off to heartbreak and discovery and God knew what else. And this night? This night would be a sweet and sharp memory that might cut her mother when she thought of it too long.

But for now, it was here. A perfect night frozen in southern heat. Her daughter was beside her, wearing a blouse she'd once bought on a whim and never worn. Their laughter threaded through the music like harmony. Time slowed, the world softening around the edges, like they'd stepped out of reality and into something eternal.

Leanne raised her glass and clinked it gently against Nora's.

"To first beers," she said.

Nora beamed. "To second chances."

CHAPTER TWENTY-SEVEN

THEY'D BEEN AT THE FESTIVAL FOR HOURS, AND STILL no sign of Joe or her grandmother.

Nora tried to keep her eyes peeled, scanning every mop of dark hair and every harmonica-stuffed shirt pocket in the crowd for Joe, and every silver-haired, guitar-wielding woman for Eleanor. Eventually, the search gave way to surrender. The sun was high and harsh, baking the international raceway until the ground steamed and the people glistened. The southern air clung to her skin like syrup—thick, heavy, sweet with the scent of barbecue smoke, sweat, stale beer, and a whisper of something earthier drifting from the crowd in rolling plumes. Everyone smelled like rebellion.

Up onstage, beneath a cloudy sky, the young superstars of Led Zeppelin tore into "Whole Lotta Love," and the field erupted. Bare feet stomped in the dirt, bodies pressed close, arms flung in the air like surrender flags to the gods of rock. The band was relatively new and had risen quickly to the top.

There weren't really barriers here. Just people. Thousands of them. A lawless, barefoot sea of denim and fringe. People danced like they didn't have spines, throwing their heads back and air-guitaring with conviction.

Someone bumped into Nora and sloshed beer down her arm. She didn't flinch. Just rubbed it in like it was part of the ritual. Her skin was already sticky anyway, freckled and pink from days under the sun, and her hair curled against her neck like ivy. A layer of grime dusted her shins, and she couldn't remember the last time she'd worn shoes. She also couldn't remember caring less.

Then she saw her mother standing not far off, smiling at a stranger with shaggy sideburns and a vest but no shirt. He handed her a square of something wrapped in foil. Leanne unwrapped it with polite curiosity, already lifting the brownie to her mouth.

Nora's reflexes kicked in like a cat spotting a bird.

"Wait!" Nora cried, lunging through the crowd and snatching the dessert from her mother's hand just a fraction of an inch before it hit her lips.

"What in the world—?" Leanne pressed a hand to her chest.

Nora held the treat up, sniffed once, and then flung it dramatically into the grass. "That is not a church potluck brownie."

Leanne frowned at first, not understanding, and then her eyes widened. "Was that…?"

"Pot. Weed. Jazz cabbage. Whatever you want to call it." Nora planted her hands on her hips. "Do you want to hallucinate a talking dog? Because that's how we get a talking dog."

Leanne stared for a beat—then burst into laughter. Genuine, wheezing, shoulders-shaking laughter.

"You're enjoying this," Nora accused, but she was laughing too. It was ridiculous. The whole summer was ridiculous.

And perfect.

A line of Hula-Hoop dancers traipsed by and Nora cheered them on.

Even the clouds overhead roiled and darkened with a threat to break up the fun, but no one seemed to care. Thunder cracked like a bass drum, and still, the people danced.

Nora closed her eyes. Let the sound wash through her bones. Let the beat settle into the hollows of her chest. She didn't think about Yale. Or home. Or the fact that in less than two months, she'd be surrounded by ivy-covered buildings and boys in blazers trying to argue about politics and philosophy. None of that mattered right now.

Right now, her feet were on the earth. Her voice was belting the chorus. Her mother was beside her, singing off-key. And her heart beat louder than the music.

This wasn't how she'd expected to spend the summer before college. And she'd been bitter at first about missing the lake days with her girlfriends, mourned the loss of a few flirty kisses with someone who smelled like Coppertone and ambition. She thought she'd ease into adulthood like dipping toes in a pool with one last carefree, friend-filled summer.

But instead, she'd been catapulted through late-night motel rooms, jukebox diners, surprise rock concerts, and emotional-whiplash conversations with a mother she was only just beginning to see as human.

And despite what she'd been sure would happen—endless disappointment and resentment—the opposite had.

Nora was alive in a way she hadn't been before. Unguarded. Unfiltered. Unfolding.

And somewhere in this massive crowd, Joe was out there. With ink-stained fingers. With something clever to say. And if she saw him again, there was a good chance she'd tell him that she'd started to write too. That she had a notebook full of lines she hadn't yet dared to read aloud.

But for now, she sang. Danced. Let herself be young and infinite.

Thunder clashed overhead as if the sky had started its own rock band, the clouds on drums pounding out a beat so fierce it made the real band hesitate for just a breath. The electric hum of the amps buzzed through the heavy air, waiting for someone—anyone—to call it.

But no one said a word.

And then, as if the sky itself couldn't help but join the chorus, the heavens opened wide.

Rain poured down in sheets, fat and relentless, turning hair into wet ropes and shirts translucent. Nora might've sprinted for cover in New York, shrieking about her mascara and her hair. Her mother too—prim, polished, poised—probably would've insisted they find shelter before a single drop ruined her perfectly ironed clothes and sensible shoes.

But not here.

Not now.

They just looked at each other and smiled like fools. Full-body, soul-bursting smiles that started in the chest and worked their way out. Together, they tilted their faces toward the sky, arms raised, mouths open.

The crowd whooped and cheered collectively like they'd all decided getting drenched was the most liberating experience they'd ever had. Some of the guys stripped off their shirts—some of the girls too—and used them as flags. Mud squelched underfoot, toes digging into the earth.

Nora's feet sunk into the saturated lawn. The grass squished between her toes, warm and messy and wonderful. There was something raw and elemental about it, like touching the skin of the world.

She looked over and saw her mother—Leanne, who vacuumed in pearls—twirling. Actually twirling. Her damp linen blouse clung to her torso, her hair darkened by rain and dripping, and her face lit up like she'd just remembered what it meant to feel.

This wasn't just rain but a release.

After a few more songs, the band, half out of breath, half afraid their instruments would short-circuit from the weather, announced a break. The crowd roared their approval, already anticipating the next set.

"We should get something to eat and look around for Grandma," Nora shouted over the noise, her voice bright with adrenaline and joy.

Leanne nodded, pushing her hair off her face and laughing as water sprayed from her fingertips. "God, I could eat a whole funnel cake right now."

Nora grinned. "Who are you?"

"Someone who's finally hungry." Leanne looped her arm through her daughter's. "Let's ask for extra powdered sugar."

They trudged through the sloshing crowd together, slipping and sliding but never letting go. People were dancing in puddles, passing bottles, howling at the sky. A couple kissed like they were the last two people on earth, water slipping between laughing lips. A man with nothing but denim shorts and a cowboy hat balanced a hot dog on the brim.

Nora laughed until her ribs hurt.

For just a heartbeat, she forgot about college, the pressure to grow up, and the carefully packed life waiting for her back home. And hopefully Leanne forgot about dinner at five, her full calendar, and about the epic let down of the unanswered phone.

There was no past, no future. Just now. A girl and her mother in the rain, chasing music and magic.

"This is the best." Nora was breathless, turning to her mom, rain still dripping from her lashes.

"It really is." Leanne's voice was somewhere between a laugh and a sigh. "And we have your grandmother to thank."

"I hope we see her soon." Nora hugged her damp arms to her chest. Wild how her mother had gone from being afraid Grandma was in a ditch to supporting her summer of song. "I kinda miss her."

"Me too. And I want to know what she was thinking…coming out here. What her whole goal was."

"Me too—" But Nora didn't get the rest out. Her foot snagged on the thick rope of a nearby tent, slick with mud and rain, and before she could blink, gravity yanked her forward like a rug pulled out from under her.

She hit the ground face-first in a cold, wet splat that squelched louder than any of the amps onstage.

When she lifted her face, sputtering mud from her mouth, she found herself staring up into the amused eyes of Joe Dumas.

"Breaking news," he said, crouching beside her with a grin. "Festivalgoer takes an unexpected dive—emerges with a new appreciation for mudlarking in the wild."

"Mudlarking?" Nora groaned, reaching up for his hand, blinking rain and mud out of her eyes.

He grasped her hand, but the mud had other ideas, and his hold slipped. She flailed. He staggered. Eventually, after enough slipping and laughing to draw attention from three passing drummers, he got her upright.

"Usually done along riverbanks in London," he said, brushing mud off her shoulder with a too-casual hand. "People hunt for buried treasures—old coins, lost trinkets, clay-pipe stems. But with all this festival sludge? I'm part French, so I'd say this counts."

Nora gave him a look. "Last time I checked, London wasn't in France."

He tipped his chin, smug. "Depends on the year and the king. As the descendant of the great Dumas, I'm allowed to improvise historical metaphors."

She rolled her eyes. "You're impossible."

"But unforgettable," he added with a wink.

She glanced down at herself—mud from hair to shins, a clump of grass stuck to her knee, mascara no doubt smudged near her earlobe. She didn't look unforgettable. "I look like a swamp creature."

"Where's your camera?" Joe asked.

From behind them, Leanne held it up like a trophy.

"Mom—no!" Nora lunged, but Joe already had it.

Click.

He waved the Polaroid through the humid air. "So you'll never forget the moment you became a literal rock goddess from the bog." Joe grinned at the photo. "I think I'll call this one 'Perfection Takes a Day Off,' and I'll include it in my exposé on a college girl discovering the joys of spontaneous mud therapy."

"You're ridiculous," Nora muttered, snatching for the photo.

"Who knew a little mud could make you even more unforgettable?"

Nora tried to snatch the photo again, but he stepped back.

"I'll give it back to you on one condition." Joe eyed her with a challenge in his gaze.

"What?" She folded her arms, trying to look intimidating, which was difficult when you were dripping like a soggy sandwich. "You've already met my grandmother, so, not sure I have anything else to offer up."

Joe grinned. "You've got a lot to offer. Here's the deal: Don't edit the mud out of this memory. Don't try to rewrite it later to make it more palatable. It's perfect exactly how it happened."

She paused, eyeing him. He wasn't teasing anymore. There was something real in his eyes. Something that said he liked her messy, wild, unguarded. "Fine," she said slowly. "But if anyone asks, I fell like an angel."

Joe chuckled. "A perfect angel."

She shook her head, smiling despite herself, and turned to toss a look at her mom—ready for her to tease them both, but Leanne wasn't there.

Nora's smile faltered. "Mom?"

She scanned the shifting crowd, a wave of festivalgoers dancing through the mist. Leanne had vanished.

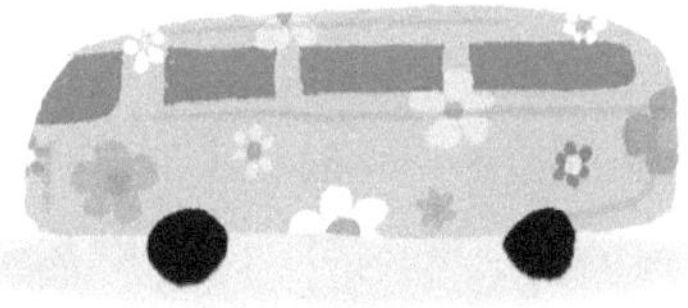

CHAPTER TWENTY-EIGHT

THUNDER CRACKLED LAZILY OVERHEAD AS IF THE SKY couldn't decide if it wanted to be done with its tantrum or not. Roxy burrowed deeper into Eleanor's shoulder bag, her wrinkled little snout barely visible beneath the flap. Eleanor tugged the strap tighter across her chest, shielding the dog from the sudden wind. At least the rain had subsided to a mist.

She stood just under the lip of a canvas tent she'd ducked into on her way back from the facilities—a generous term, given she'd just relieved herself behind a well-worn patch of bushes while trying not to flash the entire festival.

And then her mind went blank, like someone had splashed water on the chalk drawing of her life.

Where was she? A few terrifying seconds of empty space filled her brain. No music. No names. No sense of the timeline. Just trees and thunder and a dog's quiet whimper. But then Roxy yipped—sharp, confident—and the world stitched itself back together again.

Eleanor smiled softly now, watching the vitality and vividness of youth swirl in the storm.

Out in the open, barefoot dancers leaped and spun, summoning the rain, arms open like they were part of the sky itself. Their hair clung to their necks, skirts plastered to their thighs, but none seemed to care. They were laughing—screaming, even—as Led Zeppelin continued to thrash from the stage, the bass line rolling like thunder beneath the actual thunder. The rain wasn't ruining the concert, but rather joined the festivities.

She watched lovers kiss like movie stars in a finale scene, dripping with rain and not giving a damn. Hands tangled in wet hair, shirts transparent, clutching each other as though the downpour only deepened the intimacy. Nearby, a pair of girls lay flat in the grass, heads tilted back, arms outstretched, eyes closed, letting the rain baptize them into a rock-and-roll religion.

A ripple of a shiver wracked her body suddenly. And Eleanor hugged Roxy close to her chest, feeling the tremble of the dog's tiny ribs against her own bones, which ached with the cold that came with being sixty-nine and damp for too long. That creeping chill she couldn't seem to shake with a blanket or even a whiskey was starting to worm its way into her joints.

Still, she stayed.

Because beyond the dreamers, the dancers, and the lovers… were people like her. The practical ones. The ones who sought shelter beneath tents and tarps and tied scarves around their hair and shared warm, dry cigarettes under awnings. One woman passed out foil-wrapped sandwiches and paper cups of red wine. Someone offered to share a plastic tie-dye poncho, but Eleanor declined.

Shep had left a poncho folded in the back of the van for her, some flimsy thing he'd probably bought at a gas station next to the beef jerky. She'd said no, wanting to feel the rain a little longer. Wanting to *feel*—period.

One day, she wouldn't remember the rain, let alone this concert. One day, she might not even comprehend what the word *rain* meant.

A group of drunk boys stumbled past, raising their beers like trophies as if holding them above their heads might keep the rain out. A girl with long braids and a flower crown giggled and tossed them a worn quilt, motioning for them to make a canopy. They cheered like they'd invented architecture.

Eleanor chuckled under her breath. Youth had a way of turning disasters into magic. And for once…she didn't feel like she was just watching. She was part of the fairy tale.

She wasn't Eleanor Bell, the widow from Ossining. She wasn't even just Mama Lightning or the Dame of Rock and Roll.

She was a creature standing at the edge of something wild, waterlogged, with a dog in her arms and a memory, however fragile, stitched into her bones. Right now, she felt less like someone's mother or grandmother and more like a girl again. The girl who once played her heart out on a stage in New York, who sang until her fingers bled and her soul felt clean.

The thunder cracked again, louder this time, like it had revived and the sky was giving a standing ovation.

"Not bad," she whispered to no one in particular. "But I've had better sets."

And then, just behind her, a familiar voice said, "Well, hell. I was hoping to find you."

She turned slowly, heart leaping. But there was no one there.

In sharp contrast to the dreamers and romantics swaying under the rain, a pack of rebel concertgoers stomped through the puddles like soldiers on parade. Their cigarettes drooped, half-smoked and waterlogged, clinging to lips with defiance. They shouted over the storm, "Who needs the sun when we've got this?" as they splashed recklessly, letting thick mud cake the bottoms of their bell-bottoms like badges of honor.

Onstage, one of the bands had refused to yield to the downpour.

They played on, guitars slick with rain, curls plastered to their foreheads, amps hissing with the threat of shorting out. Eleanor cringed. All that water soaking the instruments, a sin if ever there was one. But the music was beautiful in its ruin. The distortion added texture, like a memory half remembered but still deeply felt. There was something unfiltered in how the sound rattled through the sodden air. Imperfect. Honest. Settling into her chest like an old tune she hummed under her breath when no one else listened.

And then she saw her.

A face in the crowd so familiar it struck like lightning, a branching of memories spreading like a wild oak before her eyes.

At first, Eleanor thought she was hallucinating. One of those disorienting flashbacks her doctor had warned her about was a memory bleeding into the present. The face looked so much like her own—strong chin, wide-set eyes, and that unmistakable Bell scowl. She blinked hard, hoping that might adjust her focus.

But in the misty view of tents, that familiar face suddenly reminded her of the circus. Eleanor sank into the memory, which flickered back to a long-ago summer night at Madison Square Garden when the skies had opened above the great striped tent. The air had smelled of popcorn and elephant sweat, the heavy scent of damp tent canvas and crushed peanuts thick as shag carpet. The ringmaster had cracked his whip through the thunder like a bolt of sound itself, but Eleanor had had eyes only for the trapeze girls—swanlike and sequined, bodies glistening, muscles taut and graceful as they sliced through the air with musical precision. What would it be like to fly?

The cymbals crashed onstage, jolting her back into the now.

And that's when she realized the face wasn't a memory.

Leanne.

As she marched through the storm-washed field like she had a mission carved in her spine, her wet hair clung to her face, and her eyes locked onto Eleanor like a heat-seeking missile. Determined. Intent. Unafraid.

A breath caught in Eleanor's throat, equal parts awe and dread.

My girl.

She hadn't seen her daughter like that in decades. Not as a housewife, a mother, or even a dutiful daughter, but as a woman. Fierce. Unraveling. Finding something, maybe even herself, in the rain.

And she was coming straight for her.

No! Absolutely not. She wasn't going back home. Not today. Not yet.

Seattle was next. Then Woodstock. Woodstock, for God's sake. Eleanor was going to end this mad little joyride there with flower crowns and feedback loops, maybe even a stage dive if the spirit moved her and not a moment sooner.

Eleanor spun on her heel, boots squelching in the mud, the hem of her blouse plastered to her back. Behind her, a voice rang out through the storm—shrill, urgent, familiar.

"Mom! Eleanor!"

She didn't stop. She didn't look back. Not even for a heartbeat. Especially not for a heartbeat.

Her heart galloped against her ribs, as she ducked and weaved through a line of wet bodies, darting past a shirtless man screaming something about peace and pudding.

"Ellie, where ya headed?" Shep's drawl cut through the clamor like a lighthouse through fog. Eleanor zeroed in on it, veering toward his voice, her relief practically visible in her shoulders as she ducked into the tent—her sanctuary from motherhood and the monsoon.

"I got a little lost." She smoothed her rain-drenched curls and offered him a sheepish smile. Her cheeks ached from trying to make it look effortless. If he noticed the tremor in her hands, he didn't say a word.

"Lost?" he chuckled. "Looked like you were outrunning the devil himself."

"Something like that."

"Well, I got good news and better news." Shep tugged off his sopping wet bandanna and wrung it out. "Good news is that reporter is back and wants to interview you for a bigger piece. Megan thinks it's a brilliant idea."

"Oh, does she now?"

"Better news is…I told the reporter to come back after the set. Figured you'd want to keep your mystery intact before blowing their minds with that voice."

Eleanor let out a breath she hadn't realized she was holding. "Smart man. And here I thought you only kept me around for my charm."

"Well, that and the fringe jacket," he teased, wagging his brows.

"You are such a rascal." She slapped his arm, light but fond.

He grinned. "Want Megan to let the kid know you're game?"

"Sure. I'll talk to him. But no one else. He's not to bring any of his friends." She was skeptical that the request came the same instant she'd seen her daughter. "Until then, let's keep one of your starry-eyed groupies on sentry duty. If anyone comes looking, especially female, wet, and angry, tell her I'm meditating. Or levitating. Or dead."

"You got it, Mama Lightning." Shep gave a mock salute, and she was grateful he didn't ask her to elaborate.

Eleanor eased down onto the makeshift lounger they'd built from cots, a bean bag, and what looked suspiciously like a drum case. The vinyl squeaked beneath her, and Roxy crawled onto her lap, snorting like a little piglet.

She was safe. For now. But her eyes kept flicking to the tent flap.

What if Leanne knew where to look? What if she saw the stage, saw Shep, saw everything? Her earlier fears of Leanne calling the police resurfaced.

What burned wasn't the fear of being found but the idea that her daughter might show up with judgment tucked into every crease of her face. Like Eleanor hadn't earned this joy. Like she was selfish for choosing this fleeting escape, this music, this reckless, wonderful little rebellion over casseroles and crossword puzzles.

Shep watched her, his own eyes narrowing with quiet curiosity.

"What's got you frowning?" he asked gently. "Besides the rain."

Eleanor leaned back, stroking Roxy's tufted patch of hair on her head. "Just wondering how many more times I get to feel like this before someone tells me I shouldn't."

Shep cocked his head, studying her for a full beat. "That sounded pretty loaded. Want to talk about it?"

The rocker had a talent—not just for creating rhythm or changing chords but for reading people like lyrics. Probably because, while most of the band rode a wave of bourbon and weed haze, he was clear-eyed and stone sober, tuning in to the frequencies others missed.

Eleanor glanced through the sliver of space in the tent flap, the rain still falling in gauzy sheets across the field. "I could've sworn I saw my daughter out there," she murmured, more to herself than to Shep.

The words sounded absurd leaving her mouth. Leanne, knee-deep in mud, soaked to the bone, dancing at a rock concert in Atlanta? And the woman had been in bell-bottoms. Denim! Eleanor nearly laughed. Her prim, pearls-and-pleated-skirt-wearing daughter wouldn't be caught dead without an umbrella, let alone barefoot in a storm.

"No." Eleanor shook her head and brushed a wet curl from her temple. "No, that couldn't have been her. Just my mind playing tricks."

"She into music like you?" Shep asked, his voice gentle.

Eleanor scoffed, the sound dry as old paper. "Not at all. Leanne's… rigid."

The word tasted sharp, too sharp. Like she was cutting into something that shouldn't be sliced so carelessly.

She looked down at Roxy, curled into a tight comma on her lap, and guilt bloomed in her chest like a bruise.

"She was raised to be proper," Eleanor added, quieter now. "Respectable. Clean edges. Good posture. Crisp linens and measured words. Even as a teenager she was the girl who wore gloves to church and never missed a thank-you note."

The kind of girl Eleanor had worked hard to raise.

The kind of woman Eleanor had once promised herself she'd never become and then had done exactly that.

She sighed, a sound dragged up from somewhere deep, like dust from an attic box. "That's on me. I clipped her wings before she even knew she had them." If Leanne had learned to repress her dreams early, to do the practical thing, then she wouldn't have turned out like Eleanor, longing for what she couldn't have. Getting a taste of freedom for it only to be torn away. How wrong she'd been.

Shep didn't say anything. Just sat beside her, drumming one thumb softly against his knee, like he was keeping time with the part of the story she hadn't told yet.

And maybe that was why she liked him.

He let her talk when she wanted to, and didn't push when she didn't.

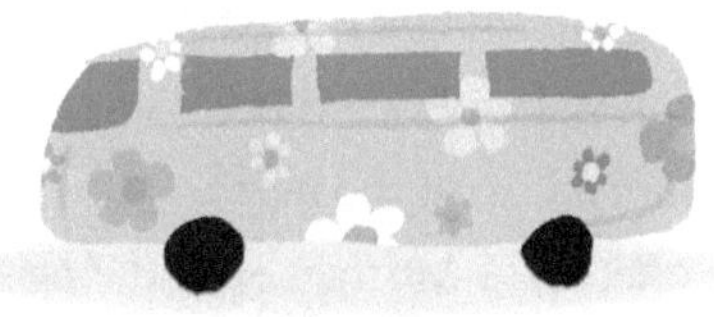

CHAPTER TWENTY-NINE

HOW COULD A PERSON JUST VANISH INTO THIN AIR?

Leanne shoved past a gaggle of sunburned teenagers, weaving through canvas tents and clumps of muddy concertgoers, heart hammering like the kick drum echoing from the stage. She was wetter than a river, her hair plastered to her scalp, her sensible sandals ruined, and her patience stretched thin as the straps of her bra.

But she knew what she'd seen. A silver-streaked bun bobbing through the crowd, a face she'd never forget, and at her side? A naked rat dog with a gem-studded leather collar.

Roxy. Dressed like a rocker poodle.

That was her mother.

Only now, she was gone.

Leanne reached a looped-off section behind one of the bigger tents, guarded by two wiry young men who looked like they'd walked off the Beatles album cover. One had a handlebar mustache and the other wore mirrored sunglasses and had an easy, relaxed smile despite the rain.

"Excuse me." Leanne wiped rain off her brow and squared her shoulders. "I think my mother's back there. Mind if I take a peek?"

The men exchanged a look, then burst out laughing like she'd just delivered the best punch line of the night.

"That's a new one," said Mustache, elbowing his buddy. "Usually it's a girlfriend, or 'I left my tambourine back there,' not Mom."

"I'm serious." Leanne's voice was clipped, the same tone she used when she'd wanted Nora to clean her bedroom. "She's with the band."

"Wait a sec..." said Sunglasses, his smirk widening. "You talkin' about Mama Lightning?"

Leanne shuffled back a step. Mama Lightning? As if this situation couldn't get any weirder, they'd been yanking her chain, pretending her request was silly. "Yes. My mother."

"You don't look much like her." Sunglasses gave her a once-over that made her want to snatch off his shades and make him say it to her face.

The observation landed like a stone in her chest. No one had ever told her that before. Most people said she looked just like Eleanor. The same nose, the same eyes. Now, this stranger was telling her she didn't even resemble her own mother?

She straightened her spine, fisted her hands to keep them from trembling with frustration, and said evenly, "I take after my father." Then, ignoring their snickers, she added, "Look, I've driven all over this country looking for my mother. I've put more miles on my car than it had to start with, and I'm sopping wet out here. I've been to California, Denver, and now Atlanta, following rumors about an elderly woman who I have confirmed is most definitely my mother, who abandoned her life to go on tour with a band. The least you can do is let me walk into this tent and see my mother and her jazzy dog."

"Sorry, no can do," said the guard, barely glancing back, scratching the stubble along his jaw. "Band's about to go on. They'd kill us if we interrupted. You got one thing right, though—Roxy is jazzy."

Leanne's ears perked up. Her mother was about to walk onstage?

Without another word, Leanne spun on her heel, her borrowed bell-bottoms clinging to her rain-lashed legs as she sprinted back into the crowd. The grass squished beneath her feet, and muddy water splashed up her calves, but she didn't care. Not even a little.

She spotted Nora and Joe near a cluster of overturned trash cans and teenagers passing around a soggy joint. They were shouting her name like she'd been missing for days, not minutes.

"Mom!" Nora cried, her brows knit in worry and a fair dose of righteous teenage sass. "You can't just disappear like that. I thought you turned into Grandma and floated off into the rain."

"I'm sorry," Leanne said, breathless. She meant it. Really, truly meant it. "I—I just… I saw her."

Nora narrowed her eyes, but the storm was already melting off her face. She'd clearly been scared. Leanne could see it in the way she clenched her jaw.

For a second, Leanne was thrown backward to when she'd walked into her mother's empty house weeks ago, the silence curling around her like a ghost. The disarray as if she'd only just missed her. That telltale scent of her mother's rosewater perfume had faded into the stale air.

She remembered the way her heart had clenched. The fear that maybe, this time, she really had lost her for good.

Even when they fought, even when they misunderstood each other on a cellular level, Eleanor had always been there. Playing guitar on the porch. Making breakfast while humming old jazz tunes. Saying something outrageous just to get a reaction.

But one day…that house would be sold. That chair would sit

empty. That phone would ring and ring and ring—and there'd be no answer on the other end.

Leanne pressed a hand to her mouth, the weight of it all crashing over her with the same ferocity as the Georgia rain. Tears mixed with the drops streaked down her cheeks, indistinguishable but real.

And then—

She heard it.

A single strum.

The warm, warbling opening to that lullaby. The one Eleanor used to play when Leanne was small, her knees scraped from climbing trees she wasn't supposed to, her eyes heavy with sleep and stubbornness. The melody drifted from the stage like smoke, curling around her bones, softening everything sharp inside.

She didn't need to see her to know it was her mother.

Leanne whirled toward the stage, her breath catching. She shoved through the swaying, rain-slickened crowd, elbows brushing against drenched denim and fringe jackets. Mud squelched beneath her steps. Nora followed close behind, her fingers gripping the back of Leanne's blouse to stay close.

And then—there she was. Eleanor Bell Strickland.

Her mother stood at center stage. The spotlight washed over her silver-streaked hair, held away from her face with a yellow bandanna, casting a soft halo around her head. She wore a pair of purple bell-bottoms, a matching purple top, and bright yellow boots. Her fingers, long, veined, a little trembly now with age, plucked the chords of her guitar. Her eyes were closed. Head tilted slightly. And her face—oh, her face—was a painting of every emotion Leanne had ever tried to bury.

The song wasn't flashy. Wasn't trying to impress. It just *was*. A quiet, aching melody about growing older. About time slipping through your fingers. About waking up and not recognizing the world or the person in the mirror.

Soft and low, the song had been a nighttime ritual, always with the same words, as though Eleanor had been predicting the future. Until one day…it had stopped. And here they were.

Leanne's knees wobbled. Her throat tightened. Tears—hot and quiet—ran down her cheeks, lost in the rivulets of rain.

Nora slipped her fingers into hers. And Leanne squeezed her daughter's hand like it was a lifeline.

"She used to play this for me," Leanne whispered. Her voice cracked in her throat, barely audible over the hum of the audience.

But Nora heard her. Somehow, she always did.

"Me too," Nora whispered back. "I can't believe I forgot."

The two of them—mother and daughter—stood rooted in the middle of a field, dripping in rain, surrounded by strangers, and yet they were utterly, intimately alone in the best way.

The chorus came around again, and this time, the crowd joined in. One by one, voices rose around them, not loud or drunken but elated. As if they'd all grown up with that song too. As if Eleanor Bell had tucked all of them in at night.

Nora sang softly, and so did Leanne. Their voices shaking. Their shoulders pressing together. The lyrics clinging to their lips the way Leanne prayed her mother's memories would stick to the recesses of her mind.

When the last note fell, Eleanor opened her eyes and smiled at Shep Moon like he'd just handed her the world on a platter. He turned to her, eyes crinkling, and lifted her hand toward the Georgia sky.

"The Dame of Rock and Roll, friends," he shouted into the mic, his voice bursting with pride. "Ain't nobody better."

The crowd roared.

Then he turned back to Eleanor and launched into a bluesy, toe-tapping riff. Eleanor grinned, the curl of her lips taking years off her face. She jumped into the rhythm with a strum of her guitar, their bodies moving in unison like they'd been doing it for years, not just a few weeks. As though Leanne's mother had never hidden her guitar in the closet at all.

"This has been the talk of every festival," Joe shouted over the music, his voice electric with awe. "This song's not even on a record yet!"

The crowd surged like a wave, their voices rising in harmony with the chorus. Strangers clung to one another, arms thrown around shoulders, hips swaying in soggy denim and dripping fringe. Everyone knew the lyrics already as if the song had been living in their bones long before they ever heard it.

Eleanor and Shep danced around each other onstage, trading verses like secrets, their guitars slung low and gleaming under the stage lights. They leaned in close, eyes locked, strumming with a chemistry that didn't need words. Behind them, the drummer lost himself in a wild, ecstatic rhythm while the bassist plucked like he was conjuring thunder. The entire band was alive, each musician a wire in a single current.

Leanne stood frozen, rain cascading off her cheeks, unsure if the wetness on her face was from the storm or something breaking open inside her.

Because this wasn't just music. It was destiny on display.

And boy, did it hurt.

Not because the music was loud. Not because Leanne didn't understand the lyrics. But because all of it combined was so right. This stage, this storm, this strange winding road—Eleanor Bell had belonged here all along. Someone had locked the door on her decades ago, only to open it now and watch her run headlong forward.

Leanne felt a quiet quake beneath her ribs. Her hand fluttered to her chest, trying to still a guilt that had just found its voice.

Was it me? she wondered. *Was it Dad?*

Had Eleanor traded a microphone for a mop? A tour bus for

carpool? Had she hung up her guitar to play house because someone had told her that was what a good woman did?

Leanne blinked through the rain at her own daughter. Her brilliant, brave, curious daughter, who stood wide-eyed and openhearted, fully lit from within by joy.

And Leanne knew, right then, that she had to tell Nora.

Tell Nora never to shrink. Never to fold herself into someone else's dream. Never to ignore the fire in her gut, no matter how loud the world got.

And maybe—just maybe—it wasn't too late for Leanne to take her own advice.

Maybe there was still time.

Not to rewrite the past.

But to start living the future.

CHAPTER THIRTY

THERE WAS DEFINITELY SOMETHING WRONG WITH HER mother.

Nora studied Leanne from the passenger seat, stealing glances at her mom, who gripped the steering wheel of the Lincoln like it might suddenly buck her off. The skin of her face was suddenly tight, too quiet, her lips pulled into a brittle smile that didn't reach her eyes.

There were plenty of times her mom had been quiet back home. The queen of doing dishes in silence, folding laundry with a pinched mouth, offering the occasional "mm-hmm" to fill the air. But this trip had been different. Leanne had been talking more. Laughing. Opening up in ways Nora had never expected. And Nora had started to love that part of the drive—the winding roads and the stories that came with them.

But now? Now, it felt like someone had shut the radio off mid-song.

"Mom?" Nora asked gently. "What's going on? Are you okay?"

Leanne blinked as if she'd just been pulled out of a dream—or a nightmare. She turned her head, smiled the kind of smile parents reserve for "everything's fine" lies, and nodded once.

"I'm good," she said too brightly. "Shall we look for her?"

Eleanor.

After her grandmother's haunting performance onstage—the one that had stopped time, cracked hearts wide open, and left the crowd singing like they'd brushed something magical—she'd vanished. Again. Like a magician in full purple-and-yellow fashion disappearing into a magic hat.

One moment, Eleanor had been shoulder to shoulder with Shep Moon, strumming like her fingers were dipped in lightning, and the next—poof. Gone. No last-minute words. No goodbye. No encore. She'd even ditched her interview with Joe, which Nora had been hoping to sneak in on.

They'd scoured the grounds, but the tent where the band had been camped was already packed up, the area nothing more than trampled grass and discarded cigarette butts. Not even the Beatles' look-alikes who'd been standing guard were left.

The few people still lingering offered only vague shrugs and a lot of "Maybe she left with Shep?" speculation.

Nora exhaled hard, pressing her forehead to the cool window as Leanne started the engine. The Lincoln rumbled to life, its radio fizzing to static before settling on an Elvis track.

"I wish Joe were with us," she muttered.

"Me too," her mother said softly.

He had a way of knowing things by asking the right questions. Nora had never met anyone like him—charming, intelligent, and interested in her world views.

But, with a serious glint in his eye, like the story was alive and writhing in his notebook, and he had to pin it down before it slipped away, Joe had taken off after the show, saying something about following a tip. Typical journalist. Always chasing, always hunting the next thread. Nora just hoped that thread led to Eleanor.

Or, at the very least, back to her.

Nora said she understood. Sort of. She was a writer too, at least in theory. The mudlarking scene would make it into her leather journal beside the other lines she'd scribbled in ink so smudged they looked like they were sweating. She knew what it meant to need quiet to think. To feel like your best ideas only visited when you were alone.

What she needed to remember was that however much she liked Joe, he was just a summer crush. Still…Joe would've made excellent company.

He knew all the bands. All the roadie gossip. All the fast ways to track down the next show. And right now, she and her mom were just driving around Atlanta like detectives in a B-rated noir film, stopping at every roadside motel with a VW van in the parking lot, hoping for a lucky break.

For the record, they were not getting lucky.

"Let's try this one." Leanne pulled the Lincoln Continental into the lot of a diner-motel hybrid. A dusty, sun-bleached place with flickering neon that spelled HOTEL—the *E* hanging on for dear life.

She parked next to a blue VW bus that looked promising. Stickers with peace signs and guitars were plastered across the back window. Nora spotted a pair of fuzzy neon blue dice dangling from the rearview mirror.

They got out, stretching from the long ride, and Nora watched her mom peer through the van's window.

Leanne sighed. "I'm not a very good investigator," she said, shielding her eyes from the glare. "I don't know why I thought I could travel across the country and find my mother. Like one pile of blankets or rucksacks will scream Eleanor Bell."

Nora reached out, resting a hand on her mom's elbow.

"But, Mom, you did find her. Multiple times. You found her in California. You found her in Denver. We literally watched her sing onstage here in Atlanta. You did the thing."

"Yes. And then she ran off again," Leanne muttered, wiping her hands against her borrowed jeans. "And I know she saw me. It's like she ran off on purpose."

"Yeah, but we know where she's going and that she's safe," Nora said, her voice gentle, anchoring them both. "Seattle's next. Then Woodstock. She's got a plan. And we're following it."

Nora, unexpectedly, felt like the grown-up. Like the one doling out Band-Aids and pep talks. The way her mom used to do when Nora had tripped on the sidewalk and skinned both knees. Or the time in the fifth grade when little Benny Simmons had pulled her journal from her backpack and read it out loud on the school bus—the journal with the hearts doodled around Sammy Morales's name. Her mom had marched down to the school and given the principal such a firm yet polite earful that Benny never made eye contact with Nora again.

"You're strong," her mom had told her back then. "You write what you feel. And don't let anyone shame you for it."

And now, Nora found herself returning that strength.

"We're going to find her again," she said softly. "Everything's going to be okay. Grandma is probably after that last-hurrah sort of thing."

Leanne turned, and the worry lines softened around her eyes for just a beat.

"I don't know what I'd do without you," her mom said, her voice low, almost hoarse.

"I'm here for the long haul, or at least until the fall semester," Nora said. "Now, let's go see if this place serves fries or just good vibrations."

Leanne paused mid-step in the parking lot, staring at her daughter. The wind whipped through Nora's hair, strands dancing across her face, blinding her from her mother's musing mien.

"What?" She swiped at the flyaways.

"Just admiring you." Leanne tucked Nora's hair behind her ear. "Admiring the woman you've become."

"Wild, willful, and wayward?" Nora infused her tone with a bit of sarcasm.

"I was thinking more wild-hearted, hopeful, and unfiltered, which isn't bad."

Nora grinned and leaned into her mother for a hug. "I'll take that as a compliment."

"You're my height now." Leanne's voice held a strange note of awe. "Let's get some fries. Or pie?"

Nora tilted her head, a contemplative look on her face. She'd been the same height for a few years now. "I like pie."

The diner was nicer inside than outside—checkerboard floor, red vinyl booths, and a jukebox that crackled with Lesley Gore's "It's My Party." The scent of sugary desserts and fresh coffee clung to the air like a second skin.

They took seats at the counter, perched on stools that squeaked under their weight, and ordered two slices of blueberry pie and two coffees.

Nora emptied a cascade of sugar into her cup, then a glug of cream—trying coffee again, this time Joe-style. Her mother, ever the stoic, sipped hers black. She watched Nora doctor her coffee like it was a science experiment.

"I'm just trying to induce a diabetic coma." Nora smirked, adding another spoonful.

Leanne lifted a brow but said nothing.

"Oh, come on, Mom. Give me the speech. 'You're going to rot your teeth out of your head.'"

Leanne laughed and wrinkled her nose. "Is that really how I sound?"

Nora laughed and finally relented, setting the spoon down before the cup turned into liquid candy.

They sipped in comfortable silence for a beat, the sound of pie forks and low conversation filling the background like an old friend humming nearby.

"Well," Leanne finally said, breaking the stillness, "that was a heck of a thing, wasn't it?"

Nora snorted into her overly sweetened coffee. "If someone had told me this was how I'd spend my summer—following Grandma across the country as she played rock festivals—I would've laughed. Or cried. Or called the cops."

"I would've thought they were intoxicated," Leanne replied, shaking her head. "And there's been plenty of things floating around these crowds to justify that theory."

"Maybe that's it." Nora pushed her coffee aside, deciding she'd rather not fall into a coma. "Maybe we ate some funky hot dogs."

"Or sipped on psychedelic soda." Leanne took another bite of pie, lips twitching with amusement.

"Honestly, I think the brownies are safer."

They both chuckled, partly in relief and also in disbelief. This week, the whole world had shifted beneath their feet. The only way to survive was to find the humor. And at least they weren't alone in the journey. The whole world seemed to be following the Dame of Rock and Roll.

Nora leaned back on her stool, her fork chasing a stray blueberry.

"I've never seen you like this," Nora hedged softly.

"Like what?" Her mother licked blueberry juice from her fork.

Nora bit her lip, unsure how much she should say, but then went for it. "Alive."

Leanne tilted her head, eyes on Nora, and her expression made Nora want to pull back the single word like saying it out loud had caused something deep in her mother's chest to crack open.

"Well," she said, "maybe that's what happens when you chase someone who's lost. Sometimes, you end up finding yourself too."

They each took another bite of pie in sync, letting the hum of diner life fill in the blanks between sentences. Forks scraped ceramic plates, a waitress refilled someone's mug, and the radio behind the counter hissed out the twangy and sweet voice of Loretta Lynn. The sounds and smells brought to mind every roadside diner between here and California.

Around them, conversations pinged from sports scores to weekend fishing trips to someone's cousin who just returned from army basic training and was gearing up to be shipped to Vietnam. But then, a nearby voice caught Nora's ear.

"…this old woman just walked out onstage with Shep Moon. Blew the damn roof off if there'd been one."

Nora turned her head slightly, eyes flicking to the booth behind them where a young couple leaned in over a shared milkshake, buzzing with postconcert adrenaline.

"She shredded that guitar. And that voice? Like Janis and Joan Baez had a baby and raised her on cigarettes and whiskey."

Nora snorted softly into her mug and leaned toward her mom. "Looks like Grandma's got some fans."

Leanne shook her head slowly, awe painted plainly across her face. "I just don't get it. If she could sing like that…why did she wait so long?"

Nora lifted her shoulder in a half shrug. "Obligation?"

Leanne drew in a long breath at the word as if it had taken the wind out of her.

She nodded, then got that far-off look again—the one she wore when she was reliving something no one else could see. Then she met Nora's gaze with unusual clarity. "Do you really want to go into marketing like your father?"

"What?" Nora hurried to take a bite of the pie so she didn't have to answer immediately.

"I know you feel like that's the right path," Leanne said gently, "but I want you to choose a path that makes you happy. Not one you think others will approve of."

Nora slowly chewed the blueberry on her fork, letting the fruit burst on her tongue. The syrupy sweetness was suddenly too much—too rich, too real.

She stared down at her plate, then back at her mother. The woman who had spent the last few weeks evolving before her very eyes. The woman who had once walked through life like she was treading on eggshells. The woman who was now wearing Nora's jeans and eating diner pie with a new kind of steadiness in her voice.

A swell of emotion rose in Nora's chest, not just from the question but from the weight of the answer she wasn't sure she should say aloud.

"I don't know," she finally said, her voice quiet. "Marketing sounds practical, and I get why it makes sense to everyone else. But…I've been carrying around this journal, and every time I write in it, I feel more like myself than I ever do when I'm talking about ad campaigns or consumer psychology."

Leanne's eyes didn't widen in surprise. Instead, they softened with understanding. "Then maybe that's worth listening to. That journal—writing—has meant a lot to you."

The jukebox clicked over to a new track—Otis Redding this time "(Sittin' on) The Dock of the Bay"—and mother and daughter just sat there, letting the song fill the silence like the diner counter was the bay and their stools the dock. Outside, the sun was setting low over the parking lot, glinting off the windshield of the Lincoln.

And for once, Nora didn't feel the pressure to rush toward what was expected. Maybe the road ahead wasn't paved, but that didn't mean it wasn't hers.

And now, that path felt bendable for the first time—like a fork in the road she'd been ignoring, with one path leading straight and the other looking more like an adventure. She could still make the turn. Still choose the trail that felt like her, the one that was wild-hearted, hopeful, and unfiltered. There were classes at Yale she hadn't even considered letting herself look at. Ones that whispered of fiction and poetry, of voices and stories waiting to be found.

She swallowed the last bite of pie, the sweet tang clinging to her tongue like a promise. As she cleared her throat, her voice was steady as she finally admitted, "I want to be a writer."

PART FOUR

Singing in the Rain

SUMMER 1969

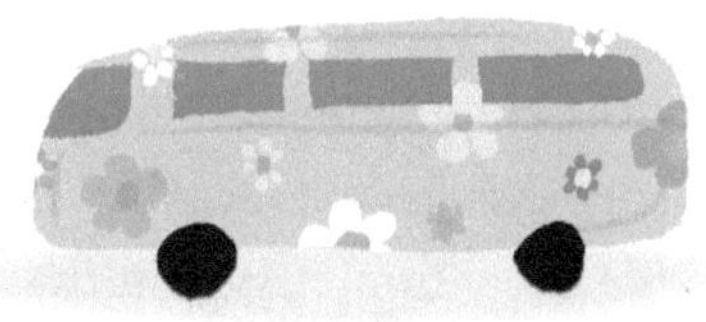

CHAPTER THIRTY-ONE

THE DRIVE FROM ATLANTA TO SEATTLE STRETCHED ahead like a ribbon of possibility, winding through miles of road and miles of thought. Inside the van was a mix of jubilant wonder and groggy comradery. Shep's bandmates hummed unfinished melodies, banging out rhythms on their knees, passing around half-tuned guitars and bags of potato chips like lifelines. Shep was writing lyrics on the back of a diner receipt. The van smelled like sweat, vinyl seats, and the faint sweetness of incense Megan had lit to mask the funk.

Eleanor tried to keep pace with the noise, tossing in harmony lines when asked, offering notes on arrangements, but her thoughts kept drifting back to the stage in Atlanta. To that moment, spotlight hot on her scalp, guitar snug against her hip, when she'd sung the lullaby turned ballad she once wrote for her daughter.

There had been songs before that—so many songs. Youthful, hungry songs. Songs she thought might win her a record deal back when the world still had her name on its tongue. But that song—the one for Leanne—had been something else. Came from somewhere deeper than ambition. Bone-and-blood music. A love letter built from chords.

As she sang, she'd imagined her daughter's face in the crowd. Imagined Nora beside Leanne. She could almost hear their voices rising up in the chorus—ghost harmonies above the crowd.

Eleanor closed her eyes and leaned her head against the side window, feeling a little guilty from having run away from them again. Roxy was curled in her lap, warm and soft as a well-loved pillow. Eleanor's fingers absently traced the dog's smooth back, the rhythm of the van a lullaby of its own.

"Who wants to stop at Graceland?" piped the girl behind the wheel—Maxie, maybe. Or Megan? Eleanor couldn't remember. The names in this van were fluid things. And what was she rambling on about, a land full of grace?

"I've been dying to see it," the girl continued. "And I heard sometimes Elvis comes out and signs autographs. Can you believe it?"

Eleanor's eyes popped open. Graceland. Elvis.

"Let's do it!" Shep whooped from the back, and the rest of the band hooted in agreement.

Eleanor sat a little taller, heart doing something dangerously close to fluttering. She loved Elvis. Ever since he scandalized everyone with the wriggle of his hips onstage. The rawness of his sound. The way he made the whole country question what music could be—just like she'd used to want to do. A fleeting memory, like a whisper, caressed her memory. Her and Nora in the kitchen. Nora must have been five years old at the time, and they were dancing to "Heartbreak Hotel," and Eleanor had lowered her voice, singing like Elvis to Nora's delight. She wasn't about to pass up a visit to the King's palace.

The van screeched off the exit, tires catching gravel, someone in the back screaming joyfully like they were heading to the moon, while Eleanor tried not to curse Megan's driving—at least she remembered her name now.

They wove through Memphis traffic, then slowed, nearing the

estate. Cars were already lined along the curb like worshipful pilgrims. Lawn chairs propped up on hoods. Fans leaned against fences, clutched magazines and Polaroid cameras, eyes trained on the mansion's gate like Elvis might emerge any second with a guitar in one hand and a peanut butter sandwich in the other.

Graceland sat behind those gates like a southern daydream. The mansion was white-columned and wide-porched, with green shutters and crisp symmetry that didn't feel real in the August heat. The iron gates bore musical notes curled into the design, and a sea of fans stood in front of them, some swaying, some singing, some just waiting. The trees out front were heavy with moss and humidity. Someone had tied a scarf to the gate. Someone else had left flowers.

"Incredible," Shep said, breathless. "One day, I'm going to have a place like this. People lining up around the block."

He glanced at Eleanor, his grin slipping from friendly to flirtatious. "Maybe you'll be there with me. Keep the groupies in line."

"Don't tempt me, young man," she said with a laugh, swatting his arm. But the laugh was a thin thing, hollow around the edges. Because she knew—this wasn't her life. This was a borrowed dream. A detour. A firework mid-fizzle.

One day, the road trip would end. The amps would quiet. The curtain would fall.

And she would go home. And then she'd have to leave her home. Live with Leanne or, worse, one of those homes for old people where they went to die but didn't even realize it.

A fog would set in. A version of herself who didn't remember music. Or Roxy. Or even Leanne and Nora.

The thought clutched her chest, a phantom hand.

Still, she pulled herself together as the van sputtered to a stop. She followed the band, who poured out onto the street, joining the crowd. Someone nearby played Elvis on a portable radio, and a little boy with what looked like grape jam smeared around his mouth sang along, not even close to in tune but still adorable.

Eleanor smiled and pressed closer to the gate, just another fan with a heart full of what-ifs.

"He's not here," a young man muttered with a disappointed shrug. "I heard he flew back to Vegas."

A quiet sigh passed through the crowd like a breeze. Eleanor's shoulders sagged just a bit. She'd hoped, selfishly, to see him, not just for the story she could one day pass along to Nora, but because part of her longed to witness a musician who had built the kind of full life she'd never quite gotten to chase.

Shep and his band, undeterred, had pulled out their Polaroid camera, mugging for the lens in front of the iron gates. They leaned into one another, making peace signs and fists in the air, snapping the memory into glossy immortality—hoping the photos would survive the glove box journey to Seattle.

When they were packing up and turning to leave, the massive double doors of Graceland cracked open.

And a child burst out.

A tiny girl with a shock of dark hair and a tutu that didn't quite match her boots. Lisa Marie Presley, shrieking with laughter, bounded down the walkway, her arms flailing like she was ready to fly. A woman—elegant, dark-haired, impeccably dressed even in the heat—chased after her, heels clicking against the walkway with marble-like music.

"Oh my God, it's Priscilla and Lisa Marie!" someone squealed behind Eleanor.

Eleanor blinked, frozen, the sight striking something tender and long buried in her chest. The simplicity of it. The unfiltered joy. She remembered chasing Leanne like that, a giggling toddler in saddle shoes, her little hands covered in whatever mess she'd gotten into. Motherhood had been its own kind of music—messy, all-consuming, beautiful. If she could go back, she wouldn't trade it. She just wished she hadn't been made to choose one or the other. Wished she'd been able to have both.

Then, like something out of a dream, he stepped onto the porch.

Elvis.

Hair thick and glossy, just a little tousled like he'd run his hands through it on the way out the door. Handsome in a white leisure suit, collar open, gold chain catching the Tennessee sun like a spotlight. His skin had the warm flush of someone still in love with his home, and his smile, wide and southern-sweet, lit up the entire lawn.

The crowd gasped. Shrieked. Cameras clicked. A chick—as the youths said—fainted.

Eleanor didn't move. She was too busy trying to keep her heart from bursting out of her chest as he sauntered toward the gate.

Then he looked right at her.

Not just glanced. Looked. Right into her eyes like he was trying to place her.

"You look familiar." Elvis's brow furrowed, head tilting. "Have we met?"

Every head turned toward Eleanor, their expressions shifting from starstruck to curious.

Eleanor froze. She felt suddenly small, painfully aware of the wrinkles in her purple blouse and the way her silver hair clung to her forehead from the humidity. She reached up, smoothing it, shifting slightly closer to Shep—her anchor amid the surreal.

"Oh my God—is that the Dame of Rock and Roll?!" someone gasped. "And Shep Moon!"

Eleanor's spine lengthened instinctively, her narrow shoulders drawing back. But still, she didn't say a word.

Ever her tiny herald, Roxy, gave a sharp, approving yip from her bag—confirming what they were all thinking.

Elvis grinned. Full wattage. He raised his hand in a mock salute.

"An honor," he said, with that drawl that made half the country weak in the knees.

Eleanor nearly swooned. If not for Megan gripping her elbow, she might have.

And just like that, he turned back toward his family waiting for him on the lawn, completely unaware that the world had tilted slightly just because of that modest, yet significant exchange.

The crowd didn't follow him. Instead, they surged forward in her direction. Eleanor's free hand clasped on to Megan, the band surrounding her like her own personal bodyguards.

"Can I get your autograph?"

"Mama Lightning, sign my sleeve?"

"Shep, man, your last set shredded!"

Eleanor exchanged a look with Shep, and he just smirked, passing her a marker as if they'd rehearsed this a thousand times. And maybe they had in their dreams.

She signed her name on a concert program. On a tie-dye headband. On a girl's bare shoulder. Someone handed her a napkin. Someone else a torn-up road map.

Eleanor Bell wasn't just chasing a dream anymore—she was the dream.

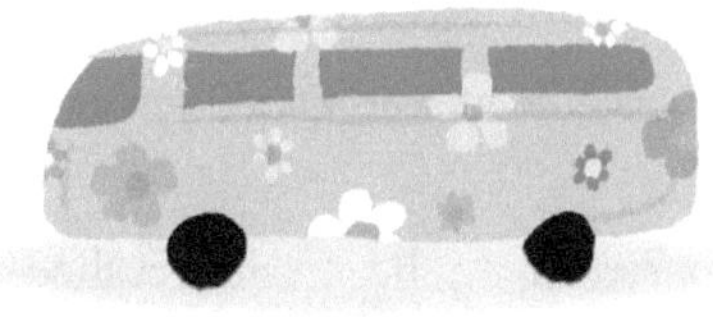

CHAPTER THIRTY-TWO

AFTER NEARLY THREE WEEKS AND NEARLY TWO THOUSAND miles of two-lane highways, back-seat naps, diner meals, astronaut landings on the moon, and Nora's fake, sultry voice as she read *The Love Machine*, making both women giggle like schoolgirls, Leanne finally saw the WELCOME TO WASHINGTON sign flash past the windshield. They'd taken this drive easy knowing the festival was just shy of three weeks away.

Instead, they'd followed the trail of sightings for the Dame of Rock and Roll and Shep Moon, reported in the papers, on the radio, and even an episode of *Johnny Carson* where Eleanor had smiled widely into the camera, seeming perfectly sound of mind. And yet, they were always a step or two behind. Partially because they were following news a day late but also because Leanne wanted her mom to have these moments in the spotlight that she'd so clearly craved. Moments to live to the full extent of her dreams before life so cruelly ushered the memories from her mind. Before her fingers forgot how to strum the notes. Before her voice faltered and shuttered.

And all the time, the barriers between Leanne and Nora dropped, one piece at a time. From the way they smiled and teased, no one would guess that a month ago tempers had simmered and walking around each other had been asking for an eggshell to poke in the bottom of their feet.

And Dean. There'd finally been a few rushed telephone calls that only made her question their future more and more.

Seattle was just a few hours off now. One last stretch. One last push. Then—hopefully—clean motel sheets, a working ice machine, and a bathroom that didn't smell like mildew and broken dreams as several of the gas station restroom stops had.

Nora was curled up in the passenger seat, cheek smushed against the window like a kid's after summer swim lessons. Her dark lashes fanned over her cheeks, her mouth parted slightly, and her fingers still curled around the edge of *The Stud* by Jackie Collins, which had just been published and which they'd found at a bookstore somewhere in Missouri. She'd fallen asleep mid-passage, like she used to do with fairy tales.

Leanne's chest gave a tight little squeeze. How was it possible for someone to look like a child and an adult all at once?

"Bad Moon Rising" fizzled in and out through the radio static, sounding a bit like the universe was trying to hum along, off-key.

And just like that, Leanne's mind drifted. Not gently either. It crashed backward through time—through school drop-offs, PTA meetings, meat loaf Mondays, and beach weekends with Dean, where the sand was always too gritty and the vacation was always too short. "Just in case the office calls," he'd say, propping up his briefcase like it was the third member of their marriage. Every hotel concierge had been instructed to get him immediately should the firm interrupt.

They'd built a beautiful life, hadn't they?

The house with the white shutters. The country club membership. The Japanese maple in the backyard that Leanne still wasn't entirely sure how to prune.

She had a closet full of pastel dresses and a kitchen stocked with Tupperware she'd bought from Marjorie down the street, but she'd forgotten how to hear herself think somewhere along the way.

What good was any of it—any of the things—if the person living inside the picture-perfect life didn't even know what they wanted?

This road trip, this cross-country detour through music festivals and mystery, had cracked something open inside Leanne. An untempered, aching desire to be more alive. She'd danced barefoot in the rain in Atlanta. She'd worn bell-bottoms that weren't even hers. She'd drunk cold beer and eaten fried chicken with her daughter in a dive bar in Tennessee and felt more like herself than she had in two decades.

She glanced at Nora again, her chest rising and falling softly. There were more times on this trip when she saw her daughter not just as a child but as a curious, passionate, powerful young woman who was just beginning to shape the life she wanted. Something she hadn't seen or felt before they'd climbed into the Lincoln to find Eleanor.

Leanne wasn't sure what scared her more—that Nora would end up just like her or that she wouldn't.

Because if Nora carved her own path, what excuse would Leanne have for never carving her own?

She adjusted her grip on the steering wheel, fingers flexing against the smooth plastic. The road ahead was long and winding, and for once...that seemed like a good thing.

The entirety of Leanne's adult life had been one long inhale—waiting for permission to exhale. And now, perched in her mid-forties with a stretch of highway unspooling before her and her daughter asleep beside her, Leanne realized she'd been holding her breath for twenty years.

Nora's generation—God love them—wasn't doing that. They were loud and fearless and curious, marching with daisies in their hair and defiance in their throats. They were rewriting the rules in real time, tearing down what no longer served and building something entirely new.

Leanne admired them. Maybe even envied them. A kind of terrified admiration that thudded against her ribs like John Bonham's drumsticks on a Led Zeppelin snare. That thought made her laugh. She'd never even known Led Zeppelin existed until this summer. So much had changed on this trip.

But pushing back? Speaking up? Choosing herself?

That was terrifying.

She wasn't ready to admit it aloud. Hell, she wasn't even sure she was prepared to admit it in her head, but she was afraid. Afraid of being afraid. Afraid of what it would mean to finally name what she wanted, only to find that no one in her life had room for her wants.

Afraid of being alone.

Because Dean wasn't a man who embraced change. He'd worn the same pair of brown wingtips since Dewey was governor, and when those finally wore out, he'd bought another identical pair. He still read the morning papers in the same order with his coffee, still insisted on his handkerchiefs being ironed. If she shook the foundation of their marriage even a little, there was a good chance it would crack wide open.

And in September, Nora would go off to Yale, off to find herself and change the world and fall in love with a young man who quoted Camus and played his guitar in the quad.

She and Dean were supposed to celebrate their twentieth wedding anniversary that same month. And if Leanne decided to speak up, there was a chance that celebration wouldn't happen. A chance that her seemingly picture-perfect life would simply dissolve. The truth finally revealed.

And without Dean, without Nora, and soon without her mother…

She would be alone.

Utterly, painfully, irrevocably alone.

But she didn't want to be sixty-nine like Eleanor, wake up one day, and realize that the next day she may not know who she was. Or that she hadn't fulfilled a dream she'd put on hold. Even if she didn't quite know what that dream was. She'd never given herself a chance to figure that out.

That feeling of fear that must have been against her mother's chest… Leanne suddenly found it hard to breathe. She gripped the steering wheel tight, feeling the blood drain from her face. Her breaths came rapid, her heart pounding, and she started to gasp. Fear itself choking her.

With a sharp turn of the wheel, Leanne sent the Lincoln skidding onto the shoulder, gravel crunching beneath the tires. The car lurched to a stop. She wrenched out the keys and flung the door open, the humid night air slapping her face as she stumbled out and bent over, hands on her knees, gasping for air that refused to come.

"Mom?" Nora's voice was thick with sleep, but her hand was firm and warm on Leanne's spine, rubbing gentle circles the way Leanne had once done for her after nightmares.

Leanne closed her eyes. She'd heard that same tone nearly every day since they set out on this road trip. But this time, it landed differently—because this time, it was earned.

"I…I can't breathe," Leanne managed, clawing at her neck, trying to force the air in with her own hands.

Nora didn't flinch. She didn't panic. She just stayed. Grounded. Present. Her palm moved steadily along Leanne's back like the metronome of a lullaby.

And slowly, inch by inch, Leanne's heartbeat began to settle. Her lungs stopped acting like they were trying to climb out of her chest.

"Are you sick?" Nora's voice cracked.

Leanne shook her head, the tears beginning to sting behind her eyes. "No," she whispered, her throat hoarse. She stood upright slowly, like a building reassembling itself after an earthquake. "I let my mind get the better of me."

Nora narrowed her eyes. Didn't move. She crossed her arms, blocking the path back to the car like a bouncer outside a speakeasy. Her jaw was set in that familiar way that was all Dean—sturdy, unmoving. But her eyes—those wide, waiting, seeing eyes—were pure Eleanor. Not pushing, not accusing. Just…ready.

Leanne could feel the tears start to slip. "I was thinking," she admitted, "about everything. Your grandmother. Your dad. You. Me." She gave a wet, humorless laugh. "And I'm terrified. Of waking up at nearly seventy, looking around my perfectly arranged life, and realizing I never lived a single minute of it for myself. That I was so busy trying to hold the seams together, I never stopped to ask if the dress even fit me."

A breeze rustled the tall pines lining the edge of the highway. Somewhere in the distance, a truck rumbled past.

"You still have time," Nora said softly. "Grandma's living proof of that."

Leanne let out a long, shaky exhale. "I know."

Leanne glanced at her daughter, seeing a child mirror of her younger self, but braver. "And I'm terrified that I've tried to shape you into myself. And I feel like I've lost my chance to do something more, to…"

"Well, don't be." Nora gave a crooked smile. "I mean, the jury's still out on whether I have a complex about baking chicken casseroles and setting the table perfectly, but I'll survive. I'm good. I'm excited for Yale. I'm excited to spread my wings."

"I'm glad. And I'm sorry," Leanne said. "If I ever made you feel like you had to live the way I did. Safe. Small. I want more for you."

"You've shown me more," Nora said. "This trip? You've changed. And so have I."

Leanne tugged her daughter into a hug, burying her face in Nora's hair. She smelled like rain, wild air, and youth—like summertime before curfews, like independence in a bottle. Leanne was transported back to their living room years ago, Nora's petite frame sitting cross-legged on the carpet while she brushed out her hair in long, patient strokes. They used to make up stories then. Magical ones. About queens and explorers and women who defied the world.

But she didn't tell her daughter what was really eating her alive.

She didn't say that she was afraid her marriage was dissolving in slow, quiet increments—that she'd sacrificed her voice on the altar to keep the peace. That Dean had dictated their life so completely, she'd nearly forgotten she had agency at all. That even the timing of their intimacy had never really been her own.

"How did you get so wise?" she whispered into Nora's hair.

"I'm not wise. I'm just willing to leap."

"Like your grandmother."

"Like all the women in our line," Nora whispered. "Like all women should."

They climbed back into the Lincoln. Nora wiped her cheeks and flicked the radio dial just as a warbling Elvis tune slipped through the speakers like a memory dusted off and dressed for company.

"Oh my God!" Nora squealed, twisting the volume knob. "I love this one."

Leanne chuckled. "Elvis was all the rage when you were little. The King of Rock and Roll. The man who changed sock hops."

"Why'd they call those dances sock hops anyway?" Nora asked, toeing off her shoes with a stretch.

Leanne smirked, tapping the steering wheel. "They came a few years after high school for me, but according to my cousin, who was a sock hop queen, it was because once you got to the gym, off came the saddle shoes. Nobody dared scuff the waxed floor. Not unless you wanted Sister Margaret breathing fire."

"Wait, the same Sister Margaret who was forced to retire last year?"

"The one and only. I think she was ninety-three."

Nora cackled, tilting her head out the window like she was drinking in the night sky. The Lincoln rumbled forward again, its headlights slicing through the dark, winding highway. The road stretched out ahead—uncertain, winding, open.

Just like the future.

CHAPTER THIRTY-THREE

THEY'D PULLED INTO THE MOTEL SO LATE THE NIGHT before that Nora hadn't seen much beyond the faded neon VACANCY sign and the silhouette of pine trees looming like sleepy sentinels in the dark.

But now—morning.

Nora sat at a weather-stained picnic table, notebook open, pen moving. The lake stretched before her like a silver platter from her mother's china hutch. Mist curled from its surface as the sun peeked over the hills. There was a stillness to the lake that was a mix of something eerie and tranquil all at once. Birds chirped from overhead, and the air smelled like pine needles, dew, and a hint of motel coffee drifting from a cracked window behind her.

Her bare feet pressed into the cool, damp grass, and she let the sensation ground her. Anchoring her to this moment. To this place.

She wasn't writing a story. Not a poem, scene, or even a character sketch. She was just writing an amphigory of what was. The slant of the light. The way the water caught it like glass. The ache in her lower back from sleeping half-curled in the Lincoln. The heartbeat of being alive.

Freewriting had been encouraged by her teachers, but writing without purpose wasn't an indulgence she'd allowed herself. Normally, her pen worked in desperate bursts to capture something before it vanished. A story idea. A snippet of overheard conversation. A one-liner that might someday become a first sentence. But now…she was just observing. Soaking in the world like her mother soaked in a hot bath after vacuuming the whole house from top to bottom.

This was what it meant to be a writer. To notice. To translate air color and sensation into ink.

She wanted, more than anything, for whoever might read this notebook someday to sit down on this exact bench—feel the splintering wood under their thighs, the morning air's chill, the tickle of dew on their ankles—and *know*.

The door creaked open behind her. And she saw her mother poking her head out, hair still tousled from sleep, brow furrowed. She looked panicked for a second, not like she had last night on the side of the road, but still, it was an emotion that she could pick up quickly.

They'd all been too spooked by Eleanor's vanishing act. On edge now like every absence might be permanent.

"I'm right here," Nora called gently, lifting her notebook with a wave.

Leanne strolled across the gravel lot, her gaze lifting toward the lake, which sparkled beneath the rising sun. "Wow," she breathed, squinting into the morning light. "I didn't see this last night. It's beautiful."

Nora closed her notebook apace, the soft snap of the cover more of a reflex than anything else. She wasn't ready to share what she'd written—not yet. The idea of calling herself a writer still made her throat feel too tight, and she feared she might choke on the word. Writing was still sacred, and she wasn't ready to hand it over for inspection.

Lucky for her, her mother didn't ask.

Instead, Leanne tilted her head back and closed her eyes, allowing the sun to warm her face. The light caught in her eyelashes and gave her a glow Nora had never really noticed before. She looked…peaceful.

Nora smiled. She knew exactly what that felt like.

They hurried through their morning routine, neither of them wanting a repeat of the long lines they'd endured at past festivals. Nora pulled her hair back into a loose ponytail, slipped on her sandals, and tried not to think too hard about whether Joe would be there.

It had been weeks since she'd seen him. Weeks since he'd vanished into the music-scattered sunset with his camera, notebook, and maddening ability to make her laugh at exactly the wrong time. But she hadn't felt too far from him, looking for the *Chronicle* at every newspaper stand they saw, reading his byline and smiling. She hadn't meant to fall for anyone over a single summer. Especially not Joe, destined to vanish once they returned to school that fall.

But her stomach flipped anyway, and she knew—just as she knew when a song was about to crescendo, that if she saw him again, it'd be like pressing play on something she couldn't pause.

They paid for their tickets and pushed through the gates, the thump of bass rumbling in their chests.

The concert grounds were already a blur of movement—bodies swaying, hands lifted, long skirts twisting in the breeze. Cigarette smoke curled lazily through the air, blending with spilled beer, damp grass, and illicit herbal scents.

Up on stage, Santana had his guitar slung low, coaxing wild, feral sounds from the strings like the instrument was a living, breathing thing. His fingers were a blur of motion, his head nodding in time with the drums. He was electric. Alive. Pure genius.

Nora and Leanne found a spot near the center of it all, unfurled a blanket, and sank down, both of them instinctively pulling off their shoes to dig their toes into the grass.

For the first time, they weren't in a rush. They weren't darting through the crowd looking for Eleanor. They were here, simply existing in the now, knowing the show wasn't over, and neither was the story.

Leanne leaned back on her elbows and smiled at Nora. "We'll find her."

"I know," Nora said.

And just as she was about to close her eyes and soak in the next guitar solo, a familiar voice drifted from behind her.

"Well, aren't you a sight for sore eyes?"

Nora glanced up, and there he was—Joe, notebook in hand, a pencil tucked behind his ear like some roving journalist straight out of a French new-wave film.

"I never really got that phrase," she said, shielding her eyes from the sun. "'Sight for sore eyes.' Are your eyes hurting or something?"

He chuckled, tapping the pencil against his temple. "Only my ego. But I'll survive."

She laughed too, the sound light and unguarded, and hopped to her feet, brushing grass off the back of her jean shorts. "Mom, I'm going to take a walk with Joe."

Leanne didn't even open her eyes, just gave a lazy nod, one hand folded beneath her head while she basked in the afternoon sun and the dulcet riffs of Santana.

The crowd thickened as they wove between booths—macramé vests, tie-dye headbands, patchouli-scented everything. Music floated through the air, bleeding from one tent to another. A couple kissed with reckless abandon near a hot dog stand, and someone in the distance let out a whoop that could've been joy or just the mushrooms kicking in.

"How's the story chasing going?"

"Kinda stalled," Joe admitted. "I was able to get through to Shep's manager, and your grandmother agreed to an interview, but then she vanished. Again."

"A lot like she's been doing with us."

Joe chuckled. "Exactly, but—"

A man in a rainbow poncho and round John Lennon glasses leaped in front of them, nearly tripping over his own sandals. He held up a pair of pink fuzzy handcuffs like a prize from behind door number three.

"Ever tried love handcuffs?" The man's eyes gleamed.

Nora's eyes rounded. "Love handcuffs?"

"They're symbolic," the man said with a little shimmy. "But also literal."

Joe raised an eyebrow, a teasing challenge in his gaze that she couldn't help but be drawn to. "I'm game if you are."

"Oh, God," Nora muttered, rolling her eyes. "Fine. For the bit."

She held out her wrist, expecting a quick clip and an even quicker laugh. The man slapped the cuffs on both of them—ticklish pink fuzz and all—then cackled and bolted into the crowd like he was training for the music festival's first annual handcuff heist.

Nora looked down at their wrists. "Wait… Did he just—"

Joe tugged gently, the chain between them clinking. "Yup."

"Oh my God, we're going to be stuck together for hours. We don't have a key! How are we going to explain this to my mom?" Nora groaned, still tugging at the chain between them. "Somehow, I don't think she's going to find it very funny," she added, cheeks flaming as festivalgoers passed by, chuckling at the sight of them joined together by fuzzy pink handcuffs.

Joe raised an eyebrow, the very picture of calm mischief. "I guess you could say we're…in this together?"

She shot him a look.

A sparkle lit his eyes and he nodded extra seriously. "Too early for bad puns?"

But then she laughed—half from panic, half from the ridiculousness of it all. Joe joined her, shaking loose some of the angst.

"We need to find that guy. Chase him down. Get the key."

Joe grinned. "Wow, we're just stacking up missing persons like it's a full-time job. Your grandma, the mystery band, and now…Fuzzy Poncho Man."

"Definitely way too soon," she said, though the smile on her face stayed.

There was something electric in the air now—besides the cigarette smoke and the heavy scent of clove and fried onions. The music shifted, a vinyl-scratch twist of fate as the ironic opening riffs of "Break On Through (To the Other Side)" roared across the speakers, and Nora froze.

Maybe this was it.

Her breakthrough.

To the side of herself she kept hidden beneath perfect grades and polite smiles. The one who scribbled poems in the margins of textbooks and didn't always want to follow the rules.

"Actually," she said slowly, the edges of a grin forming. "On second thought…maybe we play this out. See where it goes?" It was the most let-loose thing she could have ever said.

Joe looked surprised. Then his lips curved, slow and full of something that made her stomach tumble.

"You sure?"

She didn't answer with words. Instead, she lifted their cuffed hands high in the air, laughing as people around them whooped and danced in the mud. She swayed to the beat, singing along with Jim Morrison, loud, off-key, and completely uncaring.

And then, like it was the most natural thing in the world, Joe tugged her gently toward him—one hand on her hip, the other still bound to hers—and kissed her.

This wasn't her first kiss, not by a long shot. There'd been plenty of awkward spins of the bottle, and one high school boyfriend who thought being "passionate" meant trying to swallow her whole.

But this kiss wasn't rushed or awkward or desperate. Rather like stepping into a story she hadn't realized she was already writing.

Like breaking through to the other side.

CHAPTER THIRTY-FOUR

GOLD CREEK PARK, NESTLED JUST OUTSIDE SEATTLE, hadn't changed much since the last time Eleanor had gazed beyond the field at towering pines. Nearly fifty years had passed, yet the air still carried that same loamy scent of moss and damp earth. Breathing it all in, she was relieved that it was all so familiar. Her brain had given her one more gift to savor. A hush hovered beneath the clouds, the quiet that existed only in places where time had kindly slowed its march.

Even the trees on the periphery seemed to remember her, their branches spreading wide, beckoning her in for a hug.

She swore one of them still had the heart she'd carved back in 1920—Jet, whose smile she could hardly summon but whose kiss still lingered. And good Lord, the clouds looked like they'd never quite left, still sprawling and stubborn in the sky like cotton candy stuck on fingers.

Shep's arm slung casually around her shoulders, warm and anchoring. The park was filled with concertgoers, and a stage had been erected for the Seattle Pop Festival.

"What are you thinking about?" His voice was low, as if he knew she was somewhere else entirely and didn't want to startle her from her reverie.

"I'm thinking about the last time I was here," she murmured, scanning the tree line. "I'd just fallen in love."

He glanced down at her with a crooked grin. "And now?"

"Now I'm thinking about how this park, unlike me, hasn't aged a day. And somehow, I feel like I've stepped straight through a crack in time. Like the air here has a memory, and it remembered me." She bumped him gently with her hip. "Standing here with a handsome musician, his arm around my shoulder, the sun playing hide-and-seek with the clouds… Looks like déjà vu is at it again."

"We're in Seattle." Shep squinted at the sky. "I don't think the clouds ever let the sun win."

"Hmm." Eleanor's mouth curved into a smile. "Seems like there's a full-on custody battle up there."

He laughed, but it was soft, full of affection. "Was it this gloomy when you were here last?"

"Not gloomy," she said, shaking her head. "Moody, maybe. Mysterious. Like the sky knows something the rest of us don't."

Then she slipped her arm around his waist, leaning into him without thinking. They'd grown closer over the last few weeks, and she was glad to have met him. To have him sharing this summer of love and music with her. "You're a good boy, Shep Moon."

He feigned offense. "You make me sound like a golden retriever. I'll have you know I'm a forty-three-year-old man."

Eleanor laughed. "You don't look at day over twenty-nine."

Nestled in her satchel, Roxy let out a yip of protest—reminding them who the real golden girl was.

"Don't worry, girl; he's not going to take your place," Eleanor said with a laugh, stroking Roxy's peach-fuzz head while the dog gave Shep another side-eyed glare.

"One of these days, I'm going to win her over," he said, holding out a tentative hand.

"She's particular." Eleanor arched a brow. "Just like her mama."

"Well, that explains a lot," Shep said, grinning. "Particular's my favorite kind."

They ambled across the grass, the stage still a distant hum behind them, the smell of festival food mingling with the scent of damp bark. The strumming of guitars and harmonica wails had become a constant backdrop for Eleanor. And she worried when she returned home that she'd keenly feel the loss of music. Worried too, that when she returned to New York, her final stop wouldn't be home at all but somewhere else. An institution. Wherever they put aging people who were slowly losing their minds.

On the whirlwind of music and road-tripping, it was easy to brush off the little things. A loss of a word. Forgetting where she was. But in her own environment, people would notice.

"Tell me about him," Shep said after a quiet beat. "The man you loved, that you were here with."

Eleanor closed her eyes, the past flickering behind her eyelids like an old home movie. The hem of her skirt lifted in the wind. The tinny pitch of a slightly out-of-tune upright piano. The press of someone's hand on the small of her back. The summer heat had been a thick blanket. The music, everything.

"The clothes were different," she said, voice low. "The hair. The pace of things. The way you kissed someone felt…earned. And the instruments were all heavier. Except for the guitars. And the drums, of course."

She tilted her head, watching a pair of imaginary young lovers slow-dance in the grass.

"Actually, maybe not much has changed at all," she murmured. "Just the people."

"You think you've changed all that much?" Shep asked gently.

Eleanor looked at him, her expression unreadable. "I wouldn't call it changing," she said. "I'd call it burying." *Or getting lost.*

Shep's brow furrowed.

"I buried myself. Buried my voice. Buried people I loved and pieces of myself I didn't think anyone would want." Her hand curled protectively around Roxy. "Then, one day, I woke up and didn't recognize the woman staring back at me. And learned that pretty soon I wouldn't remember the woman I was."

There was a pause. Even the birds seemed to hush. That was the thing with aging. The years passed in a blur, and the little bitch suddenly stole your youth.

"Is your old flame still alive?" Shep asked, his voice quiet.

Eleanor shrugged, the motion halfhearted. "I don't know. After that summer… I left with a note from him in my hand that said, *Until next time.* I went back to marry the man I was supposed to. The man who was safe. I didn't keep up with the other one. Couldn't. The letters stopped. The silence stretched. And then there was Leanne. And laundry. And casserole dishes. A depression. A war. Suddenly, there wasn't any room for wondering."

"You're lucky to have loved more than once." Shep's words were faint.

"What about you? Have you ever loved anyone?" Eleanor asked.

"I'm loving someone right now." He grinned wickedly in her direction.

Eleanor pinched him in the side. "You're a devil."

"Anything to please," he said, rubbing his ribs.

She looked away toward the trees, where the light filtered through the moss as if it were stained glass. Her heart ached in that familiar, distant way.

"Well," Shep said, his voice softening, "maybe we dedicate our next song to him."

"I think I'd rather let bygones be bygones," Eleanor said softly, her voice like the slow strum of a guitar string after the chord has faded.

"Well, if you change your mind…" Shep leaned in, brushing a kiss to her temple. "You let me know, darlin'."

The opening notes of "Light My Fire" filtered through the park like smoke—velvety, intoxicating, impossible to ignore.

Eleanor straightened, mischief back in her spine. "Enough of this melancholic moping," she said. "Dance with me."

"You got it." Shep didn't hesitate. He caught her hand like a spark, twirled her once, and pulled her in close.

And for one blissful, untethered moment, Eleanor forgot about her aching joints, her fraying memory, and the looming return to New York. Her world became this music, this man, this dance. The cool breeze kissing her cheeks, the grass tickling her ankles, the drums vibrating through the soles of her sandals. She was twenty again, reckless and laughing and dizzy with possibilities.

"Come on, baby, light my fire," Shep sang into her ear, low and teasing. "You can pretend I'm him if you want."

Eleanor scoffed. "Thousands of much younger women would be thrilled to help you with that little fire of yours."

"Sure," he said with a shrug, "but I don't want to be put on a pedestal. I don't want to be worshipped. Well…" He grinned. "Not in the way they want to worship me."

"Oh, poor you," she teased.

"You're the first woman I've met in a long time who didn't give a damn about all that. You saw the music. You heard it. And you shared it. That means more to me than anything."

"Musicians are people too, you know."

"Exactly," he said, like she'd just solved a puzzle no one else could crack.

Eleanor shuffled her feet in time with the beat, her hips giving a playful sway as she winked at Shep. He mirrored her move, letting out a deep laugh that made her cheeks warm.

"Careful now, Ellie," he warned, twirling her again. "You keep that up, and you're liable to break my heart."

She flashed him a grin full of life and sass and something dangerously close to love. "I was breaking hearts before you were even a thought."

They were drawing attention now—festivalgoers slowing, forming a loose circle around them. Some clapped along, while others simply stared, their smiles wide.

"We're being watched," she murmured, breathless.

"Then let's give 'em something to talk about."

Before she could so much as arch a brow, Shep dipped her low and kissed her.

And not just a stage kiss. Not a chaste little peck for show. No—this was a *kiss*. One that short-circuited thoughts, silenced years, rewrote history in one molten, unapologetic press of lips.

Eleanor froze. Startled. Stunned. But then she felt the slide of his fingers through her silver-streaked hair, the warmth of his hand against her spine, and the unmistakable truth of his mouth: bold, unhesitating, hungry in the most humble of ways.

She remembered that kind of kiss. Not from her husband. His had always been polite, gentle. As if he was afraid to let his passion show. But this…

This was the kind of kiss she'd once believed in. The kind that made her toes curl in her sandals. That reminded her she was still here, still worthy of desire, still made of heat and hunger and every damn note in a musical line.

Shep kissed like he played guitar—reckless in all the right ways. Fingers dancing with instinct, rhythm in his bones, soul in every motion. And Eleanor, caught between memory and electricity, kissed him back with everything she had left to give.

When they finally broke apart, the crowd erupted in whoops and applause. A whistle cracked the air, and there came a shout. "Get it, Mama Lightning!"

Shep grinned like a fool, dazed and delighted. "Who-eee," he breathed, eyes glassy. "Now that was some kiss."

Eleanor's fingers lingered at the collar of his linen shirt, steadying herself. She wanted to say something witty that reminded him she wasn't just an old lady playing pretend—but the words tangled in the warmth still radiating through her.

So she let the silence hold.

Finally, she exhaled a smile and said, "Thank you for letting me relive my younger days, Shep." She met his gaze, softer now, something almost solemn beneath the sparkle. "I'll never forget it."

Except...she knew she would forget. Maybe not tomorrow, maybe not next week, but one day.

And that, perhaps, was the most heartbreaking part of all. Knowing she'd lived an experience worth remembering, and still, it would slip through her like water through her fingers.

Not because it didn't matter. But because even the most beautiful memories couldn't outrun the storm gathering in the labyrinth of her brain.

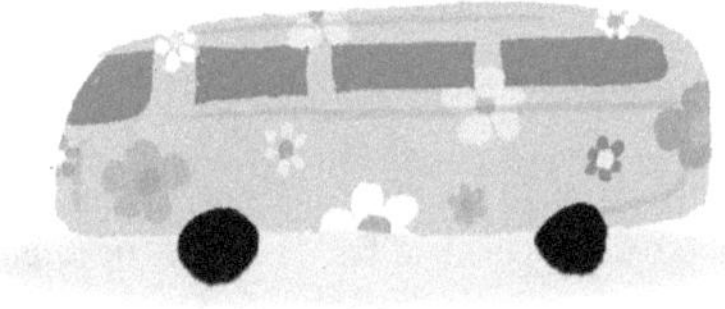

CHAPTER THIRTY-FIVE

LEANNE MADE HER WAY BACK TO THE MOTEL ALONE, the sound of her sandals sticking faintly to the pavement with each step. The evening air had cooled, but the day's heat still clung to the asphalt, rising in little waves around her ankles. In a strange way, this felt like a test. A dress rehearsal for what the future might look like—her, by herself, learning to walk without someone else setting the pace.

After Leanne had used a bobby pin and a pair of tweezers to pick the lock on the handcuffs they'd managed to get themselves locked into, Joe had asked Nora to stay a little longer. They would grab a bite, maybe find some pie and coffee, maybe not come back until much later. And Leanne had waved her not-so-little girl off with a smile, swallowing the sharp pang that caught her in the throat. Nora deserved something like this—a summer story, a boy with ink-stained fingers, a memory that would live in the margins of her life forever.

A luxury Leanne had never let herself indulge in.

There had been a boy, once. Back before secretarial school. A young-looking Humphrey Bogart who drove too fast and smelled like tobacco and motor oil from his mechanic shop. Her parents hadn't approved, of course. He wasn't "serious" enough. He wasn't "the future." So she had done the right thing and let him go.

God, she was so tired of doing the right thing.

She rounded the corner of the motel and spotted the phone booth—mercifully unoccupied. The glass pane was streaked with dust, and someone had scribbled a peace sign in black marker across the metal. She stepped inside, clutching the coins with her damp palm like they were tickets to the moon.

The receiver stared back at her, daring her to lift it from its hook. Was it even worth it?

Dean probably wouldn't answer. Or if he did, it would be short, hurried, like she was in the way. There was always a meeting, or maybe he'd decided to go to the club for dinner. Or she'd call his office, and he'd have left five minutes ago and was on the train, or he was about to leave and rushing out the door. And really, what could she possibly say from three thousand miles away? The conversation she wanted to have was not appropriate or fair to conduct over a long-distance delay.

But the silence between them had grown louder than any argument she could imagine.

Leanne released the breath she'd been holding and slipped in the first coin. Then another. Asked the operator to connect her.

Rang once.

Twice.

And then—his voice.

"Hello?"

Leanne froze. That voice, so familiar and foreign all at once. The air in the booth seemed to vacuum itself out.

"Leanne?"

She swallowed. "Hi," she said softly. "Dean." His name strange on her tongue. Stranger still that it had only been a few weeks, yet she felt she was calling from another life.

"Where are you?" he asked. Not unkindly. Not warmly. Just… expectantly. Like he was still trying to fit her into his schedule.

"We're in Seattle," Leanne said into the receiver, her voice sharper than she intended. "At the Seattle Pop Festival."

There was a beat of silence on the line. Then Dean said, "Seattle? I thought you were going to California."

She bit the inside of her cheek. That had been weeks ago. "I told you when I caught you last. And I've sent you postcards from each stop we've been at."

Another pause. A faint rustle—papers being shuffled, maybe. Like he was searching for the postcards in a pile of mail. "Well," he said, "this is the first I've heard of it."

Of course, he never listened when the details didn't involve him. And the mail, well that had always been her domain.

"We found my mother," Leanne said, in case he didn't remember her mentioning it as he'd hung up the last time.

"So why aren't you returning to New York already?"

There it was. The question cloaked in command. The unsaid *Wrap it up, would you?* He didn't ask how Eleanor was. Didn't ask how Leanne was. Or Nora, for that matter. Just…logistics. Always so clean and efficient with him. Cut and dry. Emotions were inconvenient.

As if everything—people, marriage, even grief—could be penciled in like another weekly board meeting. And so he expected her home. Wanted his dinner on the table by five o'clock. And it was almost Thursday, and that's when they had sex.

"She's happy," Leanne added, softer now. "My mom."

"She'll be happier when she's back in New York," Dean said, the certainty in his voice cutting like a blade.

But Leanne wasn't so sure. When they returned to New York, Dean wasn't the only one she'd have to have a challenging conversation with. Where serious life decisions would have to be made. What did her mother want? What was the plan when her mother couldn't live alone anymore? What was the plan when she didn't remember who she was?

Leanne's fingers tightened around the receiver, knuckles white. The phone cord coiled like a snake around her wrist, the plastic slick with sweat. Heat climbed up her neck, and her breath quickened.

How could he speak with such authority about a person he barely knew?

The thought rose in her chest like a wave—and this time, she didn't stop it. "Sometimes people are happy doing things they love," she said aloud, her voice firm, no longer trying to keep the peace.

"What's that supposed to mean?"

Of course, he didn't understand. Of course, he bristled the second she questioned anything—his routines, needs, and expectations. He liked her pliant. Predictable. And she had been for so many years.

But not anymore.

"It means"—she kept her voice steady now, finding the confidence to tell him what she needed to—"we're going to have a serious conversation when I get home."

She had no idea what that conversation with Dean would look like. But she had a couple weeks to form the words. And frankly, a couple weeks for him to figure some things out too.

"What's that supposed to mean?" he asked again, his voice, at last, edged with something other than indifference.

"It means things need to change." Leanne hung up the phone.

Not because she was trying to be dramatic. But because she didn't owe him more than that. Especially when he wasn't even concerned. He was only concerned with one thing: himself.

And if that wasn't a clue about how their future would unfold, then she'd been wearing blinders for twenty years.

Leanne stepped out of the phone booth, the summer air pressing against her skin like steam. Across the parking lot, a young couple was necking on a bench, tangled in each other like they didn't care who saw. Leanne offered them the ghost of a smile and kept walking.

Next door, a dive bar with flickering neon signage called her in like a confessional booth.

She wasn't one for bars. She wasn't one for drinking, really. But that was mainly because Dean didn't think it was appropriate for his wife to imbibe too much. He preferred she stick to sherry or the occasional white wine cocktail at parties.

Tonight, she didn't care what Dean preferred.

She stepped inside, her borrowed sandals clicking against the sticky floor, and slid onto a cracked brown vinyl stool. The air smelled like cigarette smoke and regret. A Patsy Cline song crooned from a battered jukebox in the corner.

"What'll it be?" The bartender was wiping a glass with a towel that looked like it had seen better decades.

"Whiskey," she said, surprising even herself. "Neat."

He raised a brow but poured it without question. Leanne took the glass in both hands and stared at the contents, letting it catch the dim light like gold.

The first sip burned in the best way.

This wasn't a polite glass of wine. This wasn't a husband-approved cocktail on a coaster. This was a shot of fire that went straight to her belly and told her she was still alive.

Leanne grabbed a handful of peanuts from the communal bowl, the shells gritty against her fingers. She cracked them open and tossed them back like a woman who knew what she was doing—even if she didn't.

"Another," she said when the first glass was empty.

The bartender grinned and poured her a second. Leanne spun the shot glass slowly on the bar top, watching the whiskey swirl like liquid courage. She thought of all the nights she'd played bartender to Dean.

Perfectly measured old-fashioneds, soda water for herself. The good little wife. The quiet little shadow.

Not tonight.

Tonight, she was the woman at the bar. Drinking the real thing. Starting to feel real herself.

"Actually," she said, her voice low but clear, pushing the still-full shot glass forward, "can you make that an old-fashioned? And...have this one on me."

The bartender's brow lifted, amused. "Sure thing."

He knocked back the shot with a practiced flick of his wrist, then set to work mixing the sugar and bitters, the clink of the spoon a steady rhythm behind the bar. The orange-peel twist caught the light like a flame.

Leanne brought the cocktail to her lips and took a slow sip. *Strong.* A little sweet, a little bitter. Like the truth she was finally letting settle on her tongue.

She turned on her stool to take in the rest of the bar—the sagging booths filled with truckers and locals, a jukebox warbling "Crazy" in the background, the scent of stale beer and cheap cologne clinging to the air. The atmosphere wasn't glamorous, but it was real. Honest in a way that country clubs and charity luncheons never could be.

And maybe that's what she was craving now. Something real. Something hers.

As she took another sip, her eyes caught on her reflection in the mirror behind the bar. She barely recognized the woman staring back. Wind-tousled hair, no lipstick, bell-bottom jeans she'd borrowed from her daughter. A little rumpled, a little tired.

But *alive*. The same word Nora had used to describe her.

She wondered what her life might look like if Dean couldn't—or wouldn't—change. If he insisted on going back to the way things were, pretending this summer had never happened.

Would she agree, shrink herself down again, tuck her dreams behind his desk calendar, fit her joy into the sliver of space he allotted her between dinner and Thursday-night sex?

Leanne didn't think she could.

She hadn't come all this way, literally and figuratively, just to hand her independence back like it was something borrowed.

No. This time, she'd keep it. The first half of her life had belonged to everyone else. Parents. Husband. Expectations. But the second half? That was going to be hers.

"Damn straight," she murmured. She lifted her glass to her own reflection. "To me." Then she drank.

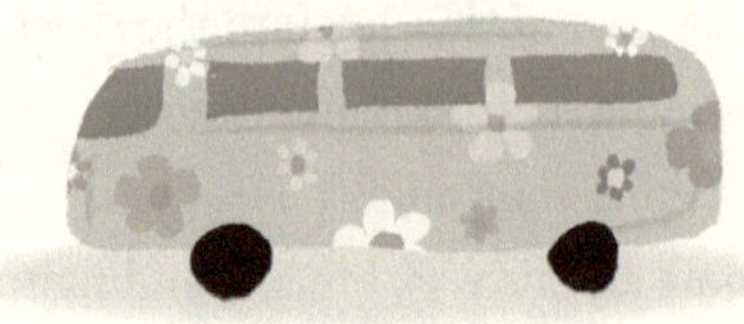

CHAPTER THIRTY-SIX

NORA WAS STILL RIDING THE HIGH FROM THE CONcert, her cheeks warm from laughter, her skin buzzing from the electricity of the crowd, the kiss, the music. Who needed drugs when the whole day had been a natural high?

She couldn't stop smiling. The whole thing—dancing in the mud, the handcuff joke, Joe's ridiculous historical references—had been the type of keepsake memory that rooted itself deep. A moment she already knew she'd carry for the rest of her life, tucked beside her heart like a pressed flower in a book. How many memories like that did Eleanor have? Enough she'd wanted to relive them. Nora smiled, grateful that instead of staying home, she'd gone with her mom on this epic journey.

Now, she and Joe sat on a picnic bench behind the motel, stars freckling the black sky above them, a velvety darkness experienced only this far from city lights. Crickets chirped in the grass, and the faint hum of a vending machine buzzed nearby.

Nora leaned against Joe's side, savoring his warmth, which bled into her skin like sunshine after a long winter. Casually and confidently, he slung his arm behind her, fingers brushing the curve of her shoulder in a rhythm that matched her heartbeat.

The way life unfolded was funny.

Not that she was some sage of wisdom. She was barely eighteen, fresh out of high school, but these past few weeks on the road had taught her more than any textbook ever could.

She'd learned about her grandmother's wild, radiant past. About the ache in her mother's silence. About the generational push-and-pull between autonomy and expectation.

But most of all, she'd learned about herself. About how many versions of Nora she'd been carrying around. The perfect daughter. The good student. The maybe-marketer. But another version of Nora wanted to write stories, kiss boys with kind eyes, and laugh so hard that her stomach hurt.

And maybe that was the biggest lesson her grandmother had given her. The best things in life happened when plans were tossed to the wind. When a person stopped gripping the wheel so hard and just... let the music play.

Nora rested her head fully on Joe's shoulder, her hand brushing the fabric of his sleeve.

"I can't believe we're heading back to New York tomorrow," she said softly, not wanting to break the spell.

Joe's voice came low, close to her ear. "Woodstock?"

"Of course. Wouldn't miss it." Nora smiled into the dark.

She didn't just mean the music. She meant the whole thing. The journey, the wildness, the unexpected softness of sitting under the stars with someone who made her laugh. She meant him too—even if she couldn't quite say that out loud.

There was still time before school. Still time before her mother started packing up the Lincoln and her life went back to meal plans and check-ins and "How was class today?" But right now, she was sitting on a splintered picnic bench with a boy who smelled like cedarwood and ink, the two of them staring at the stars. Nora wasn't sure she'd ever be able to look at the nighttime sky again without thinking of this moment.

"There's still a couple weeks before Woodstock." Joe's fingers lightly skimmed her wrist. "What are you guys going to do in the meantime?"

Nora exhaled, letting her head lean into his shoulder. "I don't know. Mom hasn't really said. We could head back home, regroup, then go to the concert. But I don't think Grandma's doing that."

He tilted his head toward her. "Nope. Word is Shep and the band have a few gigs lined up. They've invited her to come with."

"They what?" She worked to keep her mouth from falling open.

Joe grinned. "She's kind of a star now. They're calling her their secret weapon."

Nora laughed, her cheeks warming with pride. "I still can't believe any of this is real."

"I can," Joe said. "You've got the kind of family people write songs about."

"More like operas," she muttered, and they both cracked up.

Then he asked, "You ready for college?"

Nora bit her lip. "Yes. And no." She glanced up at the stars. "I think I'm more ready for the things they don't grade you on. Like…figuring out who I am when I'm not being told what to do every second."

Joe's arm slipped around her shoulders, and she didn't flinch or pretend to fix her hair. She just let it happen. Let herself melt into the closeness.

"I get that," he said, his voice softer now. "It's going to be hard for me to head back to class after I've been on the beat this summer. I've got your grandma to thank for all the bylines I've had. Only two years left though."

"And a great start to a portfolio. She'll love that," Nora smiled. "All thanks to a rockin' grandma who decided to vanish from the suburbs and hit the stage."

Joe let out a low laugh. "Now that's a headline."

Nora looked at him, really looked at him, feeling time fold around them like the soft hum of a vinyl spinning its last track. "Sometimes I think this whole summer's been a dream," she whispered. "Like we got dropped inside someone else's story."

He brushed a hair from her cheek. "Well, if it is...I hope we don't get to the end just yet."

She didn't know what the future held—not for her, her writing, and definitely not for whatever this was with Joe. They'd both be in college come fall. But not the same college. Not close enough to hop over and say hello either.

So when he tilted her chin up, his thumb brushing against her cheek with the same gentleness he used on his notebook pages, Nora didn't flinch. She didn't panic. She didn't pull away.

This time, she leaned in.

She met him halfway, lips soft and certain, and let the kiss happen. Let herself feel it. The slow-burn heat of his mouth on hers, the press of his fingers at her waist. He'd kissed her at the festival, but this seemed different. Joe kissed like he wrote—intentionally, curiously, with just the right mix of confidence and restraint. Maybe it was the French blood in him. Or perhaps it was just that he was different. Either way, when his hand traced the line of her arm and stopped just under her ribs, her breath caught. Not from nerves, but from the dizzying realization that she actually wanted this.

Wanted him.

And maybe, just maybe, wanted to stop being the perfect girl with the perfect grades and the perfectly laid out life.

So she said it before she could second-guess herself: "Where's your room?"

Joe froze, blinking at her like she'd just quoted Poe in the middle of a Beatles concert.

"Are you…sure?" Even in the dim light, she could see the slow bob of his neck when he swallowed.

Nora nodded slowly, the damp heat of the day clinging to her skin. "I like that when I'm with you, I can let go. I don't feel like I have to follow every rule."

He studied her face like he was sketching her from memory. And then, ever so slightly, he nodded.

"C'mon," he said, taking her hand.

They practically ran back to the motel, hands clasped, hearts thudding, half-laughing from nerves and anticipation. Nora was grateful to see his room was on the opposite side of the building from where her mother was staying. The last thing she needed was for Leanne to hear anything that might make her barge in wielding maternal concern like a weapon.

Joe opened the door and held it for her, the very picture of a gentleman—if gentlemen wore band T-shirts and had smudges of pencil lead on their fingers. The room smelled faintly of aftershave and newspaper. His bed was made. His bag was tucked in the corner. A stack of books and half-scribbled notes was spread across the desk like a chaotic love letter to his future career.

Nora stepped inside, breath catching.

Then, before she could overthink it, she pulled off her top and pressed herself against him.

Joe didn't hesitate. He caught her in his arms like he'd been waiting all summer. His mouth found hers with heat and hunger, his hands firm at her back, grounding her. Nora let her fingers explore his shoulders, chest, and the line of muscle beneath his shirt. Who knew that buttoned-up, word nerd Joe had a body like this?

He stripped off his shirt, tossing it aside, his smile both cocky and surprised. "You're full of secrets, Nora Miller."

She laughed low and breathless as he guided her toward the bed. The mattress squeaked with their added weight and her heart hammered against her ribs. This was reckless. Wild. Uncharted territory. And yet—this was also her choice.

"I have a condom," he whispered, his forehead pressed to hers.

"Good," she murmured, tracing his bottom lip with her thumb. "You're going to need it."

Then she pulled him down, letting herself feel, fully and unapologetically, the intimacy she knew she'd remember for the rest of her life.

PART FIVE

Peace and Music

SUMMER 1969

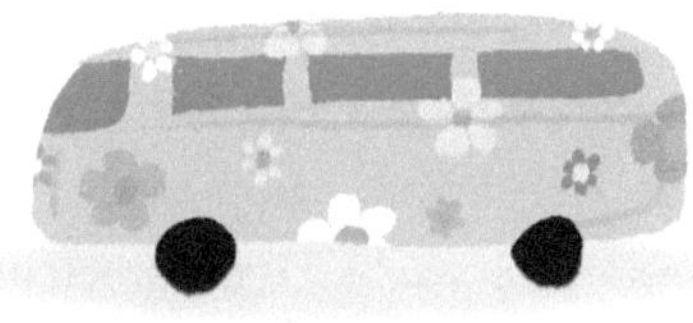

CHAPTER THIRTY-SEVEN

ELEANOR HAD NEVER MINDED A CROWD. IN FACT, SHE used to say the bigger the crowd, the better she sang. The roar of applause had been her fuel back in the day, and these past few weeks, it had started to feel that way again. She'd fed off the energy like the rabbits fed ravenously off the vegetable garden she'd once tried to grow.

But this was something else entirely.

Woodstock wasn't just a crowd but a sea of humanity. A pulsing, sweating, swaying continent of barefoot youth, all moving in rhythm under the golden August sun, arms raised to the gods of music and mud.

They were packed in tighter than sardines, sprawled across the rolling green of Max Yasgur's farm. Half a million people, they said. Half a million! And if anyone had asked Eleanor even a month ago if she'd be here—at nearly seventy years old, dragging around an uncanny canine and letting her hair flow free—she'd have laughed them right back into their bell-bottoms.

But here she was.

And even though the music was electric, the energy intoxicating, and the vibes mostly good…Eleanor was also hungry.

Not metaphorically. Literally.

Her stomach growled like a bass line as she perched beneath a makeshift canopy near the main stage. The smells in the air—herbal, body odor, hot dogs, wet denim, damp earth—swirled together into something heady and unforgettable. Woodstock perfume, she thought wryly. Bottle it up and sell it for a dollar.

Shep had proudly brought her a bowl of lentil soup from the Hog Farm Free Kitchen earlier. He and the rest of the band had been giddy about the "brown rice and vegetables" movement like it was some kind of culinary revolution.

Eleanor had taken one look and thought, *If I wanted to eat like a monk, I'd have joined a commune twenty years ago.*

She took a polite bite. Earthy. Mushy. Kind of like wet cardboard with a hint of cumin. What she wouldn't give for one of Henry's steaks grilled medium rare and big fat baked potato topped with butter and sour cream.

She'd smiled and thanked Shep, because he was trying and because he was adorable in a rocker sort of way. But now, hours later, with her stomach twisting and Roxy napping in the crook of her arm, all she wanted was a nice, juicy hunk of farm-raised beef. Maybe a wedge salad topped with blue cheese crumbles and extra crispy bacon. Something with crunch and meat and an honest-to-God metal fork.

That was the downside of all this freedom. Chasing the music, soaking up the spotlight, and running away from everything that tied you down was liberating. But at the end of the day, a girl still wanted a good home-cooked meal.

Three more days.

Just three more days, and she'd be back in Ossining, back in her house with the creaky floors and the doilies she used to hate but had somehow grown fond of. Back to her pink refrigerator. Back to a mattress that didn't leave her spine shaped like a question mark. Back to real food—something not cooked over a camp stove or ladled from a communal pot by a stoned teenager in bell-bottoms and no shirt.

And yet…her stomach twisted at the thought.

Home wasn't just a place. Home was a reality. A responsibility. A structure. A routine. And routines, Eleanor had come to realize, were just cages dressed up in pearls and wallpaper. Routines were things she wasn't sure she could keep up with, not after this summer and not with her diagnosis.

Home meant facing the music.

How long would Leanne let her live alone? What if something happened…

The thought of slipping out of her mind, no longer being in control of her life, of possibly forgetting what that life was, of maybe not knowing how to buckle her shoe, or even knowing what a shoe was sent a shiver of fear and dread so hard down her spine that she gasped and hugged her guitar closer.

Eleanor hadn't given herself time to process what the doctor had said. On purpose. But quiet spells like this, where she leaned into her fears, let them come to the forefront of her mind, threatened to ruin her day, week, and the rest of this concert.

So, instead of joining Shep and the others for their autograph session, she wandered. Drifted past a tie-dye stand, a booth selling incense and handmade candles, and a teenager balancing a tambourine on his head.

Roxy yipped from her bag, tail wagging as if to say, "Finally, some fun."

The dog had been a surprisingly great companion—patient, quiet, and oddly intuitive—but even Roxy was getting fidgety. They hadn't stayed in one place long enough to let the dust settle. Open mic nights, dive bars, grassy fields under the stars. The road had become a rhythm Eleanor loved. But now the tempo was changing.

Eleanor had felt it when they'd crossed the border into New York yesterday. A heaviness in her chest. Like someone had draped a wet wool blanket over her shoulders.

The weight of expectation.

Of reality.

Of a life she'd never quite chosen but had waded through for decades.

And just like that, it was pressing down again. The floral wallpaper. The casseroles. The "How was your trip?" phone calls she didn't want to answer.

Eleanor wove through the spirited crowd, her eyes scanning the mess of humanity that had gathered like a vibrant tide at the world's edge. Tie-dye T-shirts and army jackets. Buttons that said "Make Love, Not War." Necklaces strung with beads and shells. Protest signs tucked under armpits or held aloft between sets. The spirit of Woodstock wasn't just about the music—it was about rebellion, healing, and defiant joy.

Would Leanne and Nora be here like they'd been in Atlanta? She'd felt bad rushing off but didn't want them to drag her home just yet. Let her finish this summer out on her own terms.

She paused in front of a henna artist's table, her eye catching on a stack of hand-drawn designs curling across yellowed pages like ivy. Intricate mandalas, sunbursts, and—what was that?—a treble clef nestled in a tangle of vines.

"Thinking about getting some henna?" The artist brushed a strand of dark hair behind her ear. She looked to be maybe twenty, barefoot, her hands already stained with designs of her own.

"Yes." Eleanor smiled, tapping the sketch of the music symbol. Wouldn't Leanne have a fit if she saw her with a tattooed hand, even if it wasn't permanent? She could already hear the scandalized gasp and see the hand flutter to her pearls that she wore like a collar, keeping her strapped firmly in her housewife world. Although, she hadn't looked like that when Eleanor saw her. No, her daughter looked as if she'd had her own revolution this summer, and the idea made her smile. "I think I'd like this one. Right on the top of my hand."

"Great choice," the girl said, reaching for the applicator. "Music's a universal spell."

Eleanor offered her hand, palm down. The paste was cool against her sun-warmed skin, a soft tickle as the girl began painting the curling design in deliberate strokes.

The henna artist hummed some nameless melody, sweet and low, and asked casual questions about Eleanor's experience so far. Where she was from. What bands she'd seen. If she was with anyone.

And for once, no one recognized her.

How oddly refreshing.

No "Mama Lightning!" No requests for autographs or photos or "Tell us what it was like on tour with Shep Moon!" Just her and a stranger, and the gentle art of being human together.

"You'll want to let it dry before you touch anything," the girl said, inspecting her work. "It'll flake off in a few hours and leave the stain behind. Looks good."

Eleanor stared at her hand. The symbol glistened in the sunlight, a declaration inked in temporary permanence. "Music's always been my truest part," Eleanor said softly. "This...is lovely. Thank you."

"Peace and love, Grandma," the girl said with a wink.

Eleanor laughed and she stood, stretching her stiff joints. "Love, my dear," she said, her voice warm, "is the only revolution that ever worked."

And with that, she slipped back into the tide of the crowd, her henna-painted hand lifted gently to her heart.

With each step toward the tent, Eleanor's thoughts grew hazy, a strange fog closing in. One second, she was walking confidently, the rhythm of the music pulsing beneath her feet in an unspoken map of the grounds. The next, she wasn't sure where she was.

The crowd had thickened, bodies connected in a prism of sweat and color. Bare shoulders brushed against her skin, arms lifted to the sky, blocking her view. She couldn't see the tent anymore. Couldn't see the band. Could barely hear herself think over the roar of the crowd and the drone of an electric guitar.

Her breath hitched.

She turned in a slow circle, disoriented, Roxy trembling inside her shoulder bag. The pup's plucky head popped out, eyes scanning, perhaps hoping to spot a familiar face.

"Mrs. Bell?"

Eleanor didn't register it at first. She was Mrs. Strickland, formerly Miss Bell. But being called Mrs. anything sounded too formal, too far removed from the woman she'd become.

"Mrs. Eleanor Bell?"

Eleanor Bell… That was her name. Once. She turned.

A young man stood there, maybe in his early twenties, holding a notebook in one hand and a pencil tucked behind his ear like a cigarette. His dark hair curled slightly from the heat, and he was dressed in that half-casual, half-collegiate way that reporters often wore when they were trying to blend in. But there was no mistaking his intent.

"Can I help you?" Eleanor kept her voice guarded but polite.

"I don't know if you remember me, but I interviewed you a few weeks back. I'm Joe." He was a little breathless, and his wide-eyed expression was the same one she'd used when she gazed at Jimi Hendrix onstage. "Your family's been looking for you. They're, uh…well, they're really concerned."

Eleanor's stomach clenched. She resisted the urge to bolt. She didn't know where she was. And she didn't know who he was. Didn't recognize him at all. Barely remembered every reporter who'd drilled her with questions this summer. But she knew she didn't want to be found, even if lost.

Instead, she lowered a hand to Roxy's head, stroking her soft skin. A calming habit she'd developed on the road. The little dog gave a reassuring yip and lick to her palm.

"There's nothing to be concerned about." While Eleanor whispered the words to Roxy, they were more of a reassurance to herself.

"I believe you," the young man replied, jarring her that he was still there. "But still...they've been out here for weeks. I think—well—I think they're in awe of you."

"Awe?" Eleanor lifted an eyebrow. "You sure you've got the right family? My daughter was born buttoned-up. If she's feeling awe, it must be at the absurdity of it all."

"I'm guessing she's not the same woman you left in New York," the reporter said, tilting his head slightly.

That gave Eleanor pause. There was always the possibility for change for anyone, even Leanne. Hadn't she witnessed it firsthand, Leanne in bell-bottoms and sandals?

He smiled just a little. "I can take you to say hello. If you'd like."

Eleanor didn't move. Not yet. Her eyes scanned the crowd again—colors, drums, voices, guitars.

She'd been so sure that coming out here meant reclaiming a piece of herself. But maybe it wasn't about reclaiming. Maybe it was about sharing.

Her hand flexed over Roxy's head, needing the grounding of her dog's presence.

"How do you know Leanne?" Eleanor asked, squinting at the young man. "Are you from Ossining?"

"San Francisco, actually," he said, voice gentle. "I'm a friend of your granddaughter's. Nora. We met on the road. And you and I had an interview a while back."

Eleanor raised a brow, weighing his words. He'd mentioned that a few minutes ago, but she failed to place him. "Is that so?"

He nodded, earnest as a puppy. "Nora and Mrs. Miller have been looking for you. For weeks. Crisscrossing the country all summer. All the way from California to here."

Eleanor exhaled slowly, pressing her lips into a thin line. The weight of those words, that journey, sank in, but she wasn't ready to hold them. Not yet. Her heart fluttered in her chest like a bird trying to escape a cage.

"Well," she said, smoothing Roxy's ears, "you tell them I'm okay. And that I'm not ready to talk. Not just yet. I think I need to go lie down."

"Do you want me to walk you back to your tent?"

She turned her head to glance around the sea of bodies—half a million people spilling across a muddy hillside, shirtless and barefoot, flowers in their hair, music drifting on the breeze like incense. There were no signs. No directions. Just endless canvas tents, all blending together like melting Popsicles.

She suddenly remembered that she had no idea where her tent was. Or if there even was one anymore. The concerts were starting to blur together. California, Denver, Atlanta, Seattle, now here. Her memory was a swirling kaleidoscope, missing pieces falling through the cracks.

But pride was a nasty little companion.

"I can find it," she said, chin lifting with stubborn dignity. "On my own."

Joe tilted his head. "It's really no trouble."

There was something in his gaze, steadfast and kind but also unwavering. Eleanor got the impression he was the type who didn't back down when someone needed help. The sort of young man who would've made a good soldier—not that she would have wanted him shipped off to war.

Eleanor gave a resigned sigh. "Fine. But don't you dare tell my daughter I was lost."

Joe held up both hands in mock surrender. "On my honor."

Roxy yipped softly in her bag. Clearly the dog didn't believe him either.

Eleanor smiled despite herself.

CHAPTER THIRTY-EIGHT

THERE WAS JUST OVER TWO WEEKS BETWEEN THE Seattle Pop Festival and Woodstock. The idea of returning to Ossining, New York, and then immediately hitting the road again for Woodstock had not, in any universe, appealed to Leanne. In fact, it was the exact kind of unpredictability she usually worked her entire life to avoid. But the alternative—facing Dean, unpacking reality—was somehow worse.

So, instead, she and Nora took the scenic route.

They wound through Montana, staying at a little log cabin inn that boasted hot springs and elk sightings. Nora nearly cried from laughter on a hike when one of the elk chased a tourist who got too close. They spent an afternoon horseback riding in Glacier National Park, their legs sore for days, and even tried their hand at panning for gold in a touristy little mining town. Nora declared they were both too glamorous for frontier life. Leanne declared she'd take aching frontier muscles any day of the week over awkward dinner parties for people she didn't particularly care for.

They stopped in South Dakota to see Mount Rushmore, where Nora remarked that the presidents looked judgmental. In Nebraska, they ate the highly recommended sour cream and raisin pie, which Leanne loved and Nora said she'd be fine never having again. In Kansas, they rode the Ferris wheel at a county fair and munched on candy apples. And with *The Stud* finished, they sang Janis Joplin at the top of their lungs as they crossed into Pennsylvania.

The last two weeks, actually the entire summer, was the kind of liberation Leanne didn't realize she'd been starved of. And the bond between her and her daughter had strengthened to what she hoped amounted to unbreakable.

When they pulled into the farmland outside Bethel for the Woodstock concert, she could hardly believe her eyes. A tidal wave of people spread across the hills like a multicolored quilt. Barefoot bodies, shirts in vibrant swirls of colors and shapes, tents pitched like little mushroom caps. The smells got her the most. At every concert, they'd experienced the cornucopia of scents—herbal patchouli, hoppy beer, and damp earth—but in the last two weeks, she'd forgotten what that smelled like. Now, the odors filled her nose in sharp reminder, and her stomach twisted with a mix of wonder and mild panic.

And the sheer size of the crowd… In all the concerts combined, she wasn't sure there had been this many people.

She couldn't help but think back to Denver. The blur of motion, the weight of bodies pressing her down, tear gas stinging her eyes, the way her heart had thundered in her chest as she lay in the mud gasping for breath. Nora had been terrified. And so had she.

Also, being back in New York meant there was no more "we'll figure it out when we get home" regarding her unavoidable conversation with Dean. Because here they were. Technically, home. And Dean was only a ninety-minute drive away. There was also the inevitable discussion she'd need to have with her mom.

The thought made her stomach churn.

She'd been putting off "the talk," the confrontation with Dean, the point where she'd ask for change or, worse, ask if there was still anything left to ask for. And with three more days of festival ahead, she was more than happy to keep kicking that can down the road until after nightfall.

Her mother hadn't said a word to her, not directly anyway. But Leanne had seen her.

Seen her up on that stage, smiling. Glowing. Alive in a way she hadn't been in years—maybe ever. A silver-haired woman with her guitar slung low and a voice that wrapped around the crowd like a comforting hand-knit sweater, every thread a memory.

And Leanne, standing at the edge of it all, could only think: *She's doing fine without me.*

And that was the part that hurt most of all.

She could listen to the interviews. She could read the newspaper blurbs and magazine features and see the black-and-white photos of her mother grinning under stage lights. *Mama Lightning: The Dame of Rock and Roll.* Eleanor looked happy. Radiant, even. Was it possible that her doctor had gotten the diagnosis wrong? Was that too much to hope for?

But then Leanne remembered her mother's home. The strange little notes, the disarray. The episodes of forgetting. She couldn't shake the feeling that there was something under the surface. A shadow behind her mother's smile. Maybe it was just her imagination. Or perhaps it was a knowing that only a daughter could feel in her bones.

Because when the truth finally came for her mother, when the lights dimmed and she stropped strumming her guitar, Leanne feared it would be too late to navigate the new normal. And she was terrified that no one—especially not her—would be ready.

She sighed, adjusting the loose linen top she'd picked up at a roadside artisan shop in Montana. The embroidery still smelled faintly of cedar. Her cutoff shorts with frayed edges were Nora's, and her sandals, worn smooth by the rocky trails in the Badlands, wrapped around her ankles in crisscrossed leather fringe.

She looked nothing like the woman she'd been two months ago. Not even close.

Dean wouldn't recognize her—not just the outfit but the woman inside it. No pearls. No lipstick. Her skin was tanned and freckled, her hair down, lightened from days outside. She even moved differently, as if the music played softly in the back of her mind, giving her an added sway. She hadn't worn makeup in weeks. Hadn't missed it either. In fact, she felt almost like she was glowing with youth.

Nora had changed too.

She had a radiance about her now, an ease, a softness that hadn't been there before Seattle. And Leanne had a hunch it had something to do with Joe. He'd gone home to California after the last concert, due back at his newspaper internship for a couple weeks, but he was supposed to meet up with them again today.

Leanne watched Nora adjust the flower crown in her hair, humming a tune that sounded a lot like the one her grandmother had sung with Shep Moon. There was a peace about her now that hadn't been there before, like someone who'd finally exhaled after holding their breath for too long.

Maybe they both needed this summer more than they ever realized.

Freckles and a suntan weren't exactly fashionable in the suburban housewife set. They preferred pale skin, pink lipstick, and freshly pressed dresses—like they'd just stepped out of a *Women's Day* magazine and into a casserole contest.

Leanne didn't give a damn about that anymore.

This trip had cracked something open inside her. What had started as a quest to find her mother had morphed into something else entirely. A slow-burning revelation. A mirror held up to her life—not the polished version but the real one. And in that reflection, she saw a woman living for everyone but herself.

Well. Not anymore.

She still wasn't entirely sure who she was, but she knew who she wasn't.

Gone was the woman who ironed dress shirts and vacuumed in pearls. Who scrubbed the baseboards while dinner roasted and whose morning began with slicing grapefruit and ended with folding Dean's socks into perfect little rolls.

She didn't want to be a woman whose whole identity was in her roast chicken and her ability to poach a damn egg.

There were better things to do. Like wearing sandals and shorts and dancing in the rain. Like sleeping in. And God, when had she last done that? Not since Nora was born. Not since before secretarial school. Not even as a teenager. While other girls spent their Saturdays gossiping and painting their nails, she'd been up at six—reviewing vocab cards and ironing her pleated skirts.

Even her mother, in one of her rare moments of maternal clarity, had told her to relax. "You've got the rest of your life to be responsible, Leanne," she'd said, swatting a record sleeve against her thigh. "You don't get a second chance at seventeen."

Leanne had rolled her eyes at the time, certain her mother was being ridiculous. Eleanor Bell Strickland giving out life advice? Please.

But now, standing here at forty-five, the music pulsing in the background and the scent of fried dough and cigarettes curling through the air, she finally understood.

Her mother had been right. The thing that scared her the most was how much time she'd spent trying to be perfect when what she really wanted was to feel something. To be someone.

And maybe, just maybe, it wasn't too late.

She wanted to sleep in, dammit.

Not just on Saturdays. Not with one eye on the alarm clock and a to-do list already ticking in her brain. No—she wanted to wake up when her body felt like rising. To stretch luxuriously in a bed she didn't have to make the minute she climbed out. Maybe she would wander barefoot onto the back patio with a mug of hot coffee and let the birds serenade her instead of the sound of her husband clearing his throat and asking where his tie was and when his toast would be ready.

Leanne wanted a life where she wasn't poaching eggs for anyone but herself.

And wasn't that something?

Onstage, Janis Joplin belted out "Summertime," her voice raw and glorious, curling into the late-afternoon sky like a promise. The sun was low and golden, brushing everything with magic, making her believe life could be different.

Leanne swayed to the beat, the grass damp beneath her sandals, her cutoffs soft and worn. Beside her, Nora swayed too—smiling, yes, but also scanning the crowd with that dreamy, distracted look.

She was looking for Joe.

Leanne bit the inside of her cheek to keep from smiling too wide. Young, summer love. So intoxicating. So fleeting. So dangerous.

God, she hoped that young man didn't break her daughter's heart. Because Nora, for all her newfound fire and grit, still had that softness to her. That hopefulness. That trust. And heartbreak—well, that had a way of hardening a gal if she wasn't careful.

Leanne had the scars to prove it.

She slid an arm around her daughter's shoulders, pulling her close just for a second. Nora didn't pull away. They both stood there in the golden light, mother and daughter, two women at two very different crossroads, both wondering what came next.

And for the first time in a long while, Leanne didn't dread the question.

CHAPTER THIRTY-NINE

NORA WAS PRACTICALLY VIBRATING OUT OF HER SANdals.

She couldn't stand still. Her toes dug into the trampled grass, eyes darting over the sea of swaying bodies, scanning for one particular head of dark curls, for one crooked grin that made her stomach flip like a jukebox record.

Joe Dumas.

Two weeks since Seattle. Two weeks since they'd kissed under the stars, since he'd slipped the handcuffs off her wrist and made her forget about every boy who came before. Two weeks since they'd made love, not once but three times, while the world hummed outside like it didn't dare interrupt.

They'd said goodbye that night, and the next morning, he was gone—off to finish what he'd started, with a promise to see her soon. Returning to her room, she'd brushed her hair, trying to act like her bones weren't still trembling, while her mother slept.

Two weeks since she'd last spoken to Joe.

No letters. No calls. Just his promise, "I'll see you at Woodstock."

Except…how was that even going to happen?

There were more people here than she'd ever seen in her life. Half a million strong, someone had said. A wall-to-wall patchwork of color and bare feet and bodies packed on the hills like barnacles on the bow of a ship. Every inch of grass was wrapped in blankets and good intentions. The air was thick with smoke—some legal, some very much not—and the sweet, tangy scent of herbal oils and sweat lingered over everything.

She and her mom had ditched the Lincoln miles back, abandoning it on the shoulder with a thousand other cars that looked just as lost. They'd hiked through mud and hills and people carrying banjos and babies and half-eaten corn on the cob. When the stage was finally visible, it felt like they'd just crossed the finish line of a marathon.

And now? Now, she was starving. Everything at the Food for Love stand had sold out hours ago, save for a few soggy hot dog buns and a sign someone scrawled in charcoal: "God bless the PB&J."

The first bite of the peanut butter and jelly sandwich nearly made Nora tear up.

Absurd, really. Two slices of white bread slathered with sweet strawberry jam and crunchy peanut butter that cemented itself to the roof of her mouth. But something about it hit her with a wave of nostalgia so hard it nearly knocked her over.

Tasted like childhood summers in Ossining. Like cannonballs into the neighborhood pool, like sand in the peanut butter during picnics at Orchard Beach. Like lemonade in plastic cups, sunburned shoulders, and the occasional bee chasing her sandwich. Simple. Familiar. Cherished.

Nora relished every bite, chewing slowly, savoring the memory as much as the flavor.

The only thing that would've made it better was a basket of golden and crispy french fries dipped in a pool of ketchup. But the fry vendor had sold out hours ago, and from what she'd heard, it would be a miracle if there were enough potatoes left in the entire country to feed this many people. Half a million and counting. She wasn't holding her breath.

She tugged at the hem of her new T-shirt—one she'd bought at a vendor's stall, her mother covering her so she could shimmy it on over her bra. The words Peace & Music swirling in hot pink letters across her chest. Her cutoff shorts clung to her hips, her legs speckled with dust and sun. Her hair had gone wild with the humidity and hours of dancing, but she didn't care. Not anymore.

Up onstage, Joe Cocker was belting "With a Little Help From My Friends," and the lyrics reverberated through the air, clinging to the clouds and raining back down in drops of happiness.

And then—there he was.

Joe Dumas, notebook tucked under one arm, pencil behind his ear, curls as wild as her heartbeat when she spotted him.

Nora smiled, full and open, trying to calm the pounding of her heart. "Well, don't you have impeccable timing?"

He gave a sheepish shrug, all boyish charm. "I try my best."

She was suddenly nervous. Didn't know whether to slap him on the back or throw her arms around his neck and kiss him. To pretend it hadn't been two weeks of wondering if she would ever see him again. The silence between Seattle and now had been a canyon she didn't know how to cross. But here he was, standing on the other side of it.

"I'm really glad to see you," she said.

His grin softened, and for a heartbeat, the noise of Woodstock fell away.

Her mom was watching from the blanket, squinting at them like she could see something they weren't saying. Nora's stomach did a little flip. She didn't need a third party narrating this reunion.

"Mom," she said, turning quickly, "would you like me to get you a

Coke?" Considering she had met Joe over a soda, it seemed the perfect excuse.

Leanne smiled, nodding with just enough subtlety to say, *Go on. I get it.*

And just like that, Nora reached for Joe's hand, the crowd pressing around them, the music swelling, and the moment was hers.

"Wait—before we go grab that soda," Joe said, rubbing the back of his neck. "I have to tell you something. And it's probably best your mom hears it too."

His tone was suddenly serious, which made Nora's stomach drop like a jukebox needle skipping across vinyl.

"What is it?" Leanne straightened up on the blanket, eyes scanning the crowd like she half expected Eleanor to be crowd-surfing unconscious toward the med tent.

Which—honestly? Morbid. But Nora kind of felt the same way. They hadn't seen her in days. Sure, she'd caught snippets of radio interviews while they drove, the sound scratchy and full of static, Eleanor's voice drifting in like it was already halfway to memory. But that wasn't the same as seeing her. Talking to her. Hugging her.

God, Nora had never wanted to hug her grandmother so badly in her life.

Joe's ears went pink. "I saw Eleanor. I mean—Mrs. Bell. Or Strickland. Sorry."

Leanne laughed, and the tension in her shoulders unspooled just a little. "It's okay, Joe. Seems my mother has a lot of names these days. Was she okay?" Leanne's words tripped over each other.

Joe's shoulders settle. "She was perfectly well. Said she wanted you to know that. That she's doing great. Enjoying the ride."

Nora let out a breath she didn't realize she'd been holding. But before she could get too comfortable, Joe added, "She also said to let you know…after this concert's over, she's ready to go home."

Nora's whole body stilled. Three more days.

She knew, of course, that this couldn't last forever. That music festivals didn't rewrite the rules of time. And it was August. The fall semester at Yale was right around the corner. But hearing it spoken aloud—that it was the end of the road—hit her harder than she'd expected.

Three more days, and then she'd be packing up for Yale. Trading in concert tees and open highways for syllabi and study sessions. Lecture halls and libraries. Term papers and textbooks.

This summer had been…everything.

Messy and loud and alive.

And there'd still be a couple weeks left to hang out with Kelley and her other friends.

She reined in her sudden emotion and forced a smile. "Well. I guess we better make the next three days count then, huh?"

Joe looked at her with a soft kind of knowing. "I think that's exactly what she wants you to do."

Leanne nodded slowly, her eyes glossy in the sun. "Thank you for talking to her. I just… I wish we could've talked to her ourselves."

Joe offered a sympathetic smile. "I tried to bring her with me. Told her you were close by. But she said she wanted to rest. Said she wasn't ready yet."

"I can understand that." Leanne's voice caught a little on the last word.

Nora turned to glance at her mother, the weight of those words settling in her chest. What wasn't she ready for?

Before she could ask, Joe nudged her elbow gently. "Ready for that soda now?"

"God, yes."

They peeled away from the crowd, and Joe slipped his fingers through hers like it was the most natural thing in the world. Like no time had passed at all. Nora's breath hitched, and every ounce of anxiety she'd carried for two weeks about whether or not he'd forgotten her melted away like ice in a paper cup.

She leaned into him, legs moving in tandem, hands swinging between them. The music hummed around them like a second heartbeat. Joni Mitchell was now crooning from the main stage, and Nora's body instinctively moved to the rhythm.

She was going to miss this. All of it.

The music, the dancing, the carefree joy of strangers swaying shoulder to shoulder. The barefoot mornings with her mother, the way they'd sip diner coffee and read books like whispered secrets. The early light casting long shadows across picnic tables while she filled her notebook with half-formed thoughts that felt like magic.

And Joe.

She was going to miss Joe more than she wanted to admit.

So she made a promise to herself, right then and there—she would savor every second with him over the next few days. She'd press each memory between the pages of her mind like dried flowers. She'd do the same with her mother. Because soon, she'd be packing her bags for Yale, stepping onto a different path entirely.

And nothing, absolutely nothing, would ever be quite the same again.

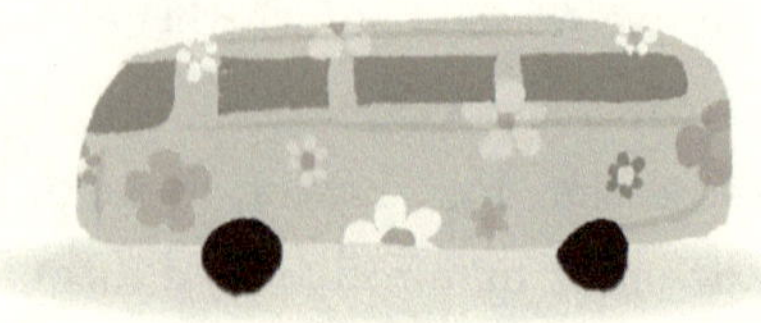

CHAPTER FORTY

WHITE SURROUNDED HER ON ALL SIDES. THE SKY above was washed pale and overcast, a canvas stretched too tight. Under her feet, a sea of woven blankets sprawled like clothes on a teenager's bedroom floor, looking for the right outfit—colors clashing in psychedelic swirls and frantic dots, paisley puddles tangled with sun-faded stripes. It was chaos. Pure, undiluted, joyful chaos.

And it made her toes itch.

Eleanor kicked off her sandals, letting her bare feet sink into the fabric. The soft fibers pricked against her soles, grounding her in something she couldn't name. Her toenails, usually painted a bright crimson or electric blue, were bare. Just pale crescents now, forgotten. She crouched slowly, knees cracking, and touched one toe with a calloused finger as if it might tell her something. Why hadn't she painted her toes?

Her gaze caught on the brown music symbol painted across the back of her hand. When had that gotten there?

She pressed her thumb to the ink, surprised it didn't smudge. The henna had stained into skin. When she curled her fingers, the note danced. How strange. How beautiful.

"We're up, Mama."

The voice jolted her like a flashbulb. She looked up, startled. A young woman with long, beaded braids and a yellow woven halter top stood before her, hands on her hips, a tambourine dangling from one wrist like a forgotten accessory.

Eleanor's mouth parted. "Am I your mother?"

The girl stared at her, caught somewhere between confusion and amusement. Then she let out a quick laugh, too loud for the softness that had settled between them. "You're a funny one. No wonder Shep likes you."

Eleanor's body jolted like a radio catching signal at the mention of Shep's name. Her brain did a little two-step—slow, glitchy, like a record trying to find the groove. She may as well have been asleep for a hundred years, and her synapses beginning to stir, whispered, *You're here. Wake up, Sleeping Beauty.*

This wasn't just any patchwork of blankets beneath her bare feet—these were their blankets. The ones Shep's band had spread across festival fields for weeks, collecting crumbs, stories, and sleep. This wasn't just any stage. This was their tent. And she hadn't painted her toenails because they'd been on the road. Gas station to gas station, bar to bar, festival to festival.

And the girl in front of her, of course, her name was Megan. Kind, scattered Megan, with her tambourine and bangles and ever-mismatched socks.

"Sorry about that." Eleanor laughed, masking her passing lapse like a pro. "You know how it is...preshow jitters."

Megan smiled but didn't press. Instead, she gently tugged the bag holding Roxy off Eleanor's shoulder and handed her the guitar in its place.

"Knock 'em dead, Grandma. Roxy and I will cheer from the side."

Grandma. Mama. Everyone had a name for her, and none of them were her name. Not really. They were masks. Titles that came with expectations, not essence.

And then—

"Ellie! Come on!"

Finally. A name she recognized.

Eleanor turned toward the sound. Shep stood at the edge of the stage, one arm extended like a lifeline, grinning in that maddeningly charming way he had—half rascal, half Romeo.

Eleanor took his hand, and he hoisted her up. Her foot skidded slightly, and she stumbled off-balance, off-kilter. Odd. She'd never had balance issues before. She blamed it on the stage surface which was slick with sweat and who knew what else, and the fact that her body was running on minimal sleep, maximum adrenaline, and maybe a little too much black coffee.

Still, as the lights hit her face and the crowd murmured like a wave just about to break, she steadied herself.

The crowd erupted. They weren't shouting her name, though. They were shouting the myth.

"Mama Lightning!"

"The Dame of Rock and Roll!"

And just like that, she was annoyed again.

Like they'd turned her into a roadside attraction. A relic. A gimmick.

But she didn't have time to stew. The sheer size of the audience hit her like a wall of sound. This was by far the largest crowd they'd sung for. An ocean of bodies stretching so far and wide that she couldn't even find the end. Like the earth had cracked open and spilled humanity onto this one muddy hillside. Arms waved like seaweed in the current, and the roar was constant and deafening, matching the thrum of blood in her ears, the race of her heart.

She and the band launched into their usual opener, the one that got feet stomping and hands clapping, and Eleanor hit every chord from muscle memory. She was a machine. A vessel. A woman in the eye of the storm.

And then someone from the crowd shouted the request she hadn't known she was wishing for until the words rang out. "Play the one you wrote for your daughter!"

The words cut through the noise like a clear bell, and the band turned to her for the cue. She gave a slow nod, fingers finding the strings, the first soft strum rising like a secret in the wind.

And that's when she saw her.

Right near the front of the crowd, impossibly close, stood Leanne.

But not the Leanne she remembered. Not the pressed-pleated, pearl-buttoned version who lived in the suburbs of Ossining with a calendar full of PTA meetings and roast dinners. This Leanne was different. Her jeans were cutoffs, threads fraying at the edges over the bare skin of her thighs. Her top was loose, bohemian, swaying in the breeze. Her hair was down, her skin flushed, kissed by a summer of wandering.

And her eyes were wide and wet, her cheeks streaked with tears. Not grief. Not fear. Joy. Pure, radiant, unfiltered joy.

Eleanor's throat tightened. She hadn't realized how much she needed that look. That permission. That recognition. That love.

She strummed the next few chords like they were breathing for her daughter. When the chorus swelled, she pointed directly at Leanne—let the crowd see her, let Leanne feel her mother's love.

Standing beside Leanne, Nora was impossible to miss.

Eleanor's heart gave a heavy thud against her ribs as if the strings of her guitar had found a way to pluck her from the inside out.

She opened her mouth, sang the next line—those familiar, aching lyrics—and something sharp tugged against her thumb. She glanced down. Her finger was tangled in the guitar cord. Odd. How had that happened?

Her gaze traveled to the microphone, hovering just in front of her mouth like a floating question. She blinked. The lights felt too bright. The stage felt too high. Her own voice was too loud in her ears.

"Leanne," she said aloud, barely a whisper into the microphone. She stared down at the woman in the crowd who looked so much like her daughter—and yet not like her at all. The Leanne she remembered had a stiff posture, lips pressed thin. This Leanne was barefoot in the grass. Hair wild. Eyes bright. Wearing joy like a badge of rebellion.

The music didn't stop. The crowd kept singing. They knew the words, had memorized the rhythm, and had absorbed the song into their bones over the summer.

Another jolt rolled through Eleanor's body, like her mind catching up to her mouth, and suddenly, it clicked back into place. *You're onstage, Ellie. This is your song. These are your people.*

She laughed, full-throated, into the mic, and sang again—this time louder, with a wink in her voice. "Guess I've got a fan in the front row today."

The crowd roared.

No one looked at her strangely. No one leaned in with worry. No one whispered, "Is she all right?"

Only cheers. Only support. Only love.

And then, just as the bridge began to build, she watched Leanne be lifted into the air. Palms pressing her upward. The crowd passing her like a note in class, delicate, full of secrets, handled with care.

Eleanor's instinct flared—*Be careful with her; that's my baby*—but it passed quickly. Nora was laughing, cheering, hands raised. The two of them aglow like living sunshine.

And then she was there. Leanne. On the edge of the stage. Forty-five years old, eyes shimmering like they had when she was four and Eleanor used to sing this very song to lull her to sleep.

Except this time, Leanne wasn't drifting off.

She was awake.

And Eleanor, guitar steady in her hands, strummed a chord so true it made her knees go weak.

This—*this*—was the moment she'd been singing toward her whole life.

CHAPTER FORTY-ONE

WHEN SHE WAS A CHILD, LEANNE HAD BELIEVED HER mother was immortal.

Not in the comic book sense, but in the steady, unshakable way parents seemed to exist. Always there. Always reachable. An ever-present feminine spirit who knew how to fold sheets just right and who sang lullabies even when she was tired. Even as an adult, Leanne had taken it for granted that Eleanor would arrive if she called and asked her mother to come over for Sunday dinner. If she wanted to walk the promenade at Orchard Beach, her mother would lace up her shoes and go.

But now, watching Eleanor onstage—losing the lyrics, blinking like she wasn't sure where she was—Leanne had felt a cold realization tighten in her gut.

One day, her mother wouldn't be there. That familiar face, those eyes that had seen her through every version of herself, might someday look right at her and not recognize a thing.

Before she could dwell on the ache forming behind her ribs, hands lifted her into the air.

Leanne gasped—not in fear but in wonder. A few weeks ago, the thought of crowd-surfing would have terrified her. And admittedly, there was a slight tingle of fear they might drop her now. But she'd spent a summer watching people move like waves, and now the hands beneath her were steady, guiding her forward with care.

And suddenly, she was there.

On the stage.

Beside her mother.

Eleanor's guitar was slung low, her shoulders hunched slightly, bracing for the next chord. Leanne could see it up close now, how her hand trembled on the strings, how her eyes flicked across the crowd like she was still orienting herself.

Leanne wanted nothing more than to pull her mother into a hug, bury her face in her neck like she was still a little girl, and whisper, "It's okay. I've got you."

But to do that would stop the music. Would shatter the spell.

So instead, Leanne stepped beside Eleanor, placed her hand lightly over her mother's where it gripped the microphone and began to sing.

The lyrics came like breath. Like memory. Like home.

Her mother's hand was warm. Fragile in a way it had never felt before. Leanne squeezed gently, her voice finding the harmony, their words weaving together in the air like ribbon.

Together, they sang.

The song unfurled across the sky, and at last, Leanne saw what her mother had seen all these weeks—the sea of people, the energy, the joy. The eyes shining back.

Terrifying.

Beautiful.

Standing under the heat of the stage lights, with the crowd rippling in front of her like an ever-changing sea, Leanne understood how this became addictive.

The attention. The electricity. The sound of hundreds—no, thousands, hundreds of thousands—of voices echoing back lyrics that had once belonged only to a mother and her daughter. It was intoxicating. A moment that would imprint on a person's soul.

Her eyes scanned the crowd until they found Nora.

There she was, tangled in the music and in Joe. Arms swaying in the air, her head tilted back in laughter, until Joe's arm slipped around her shoulders like it belonged there. And maybe it did.

Leanne's heart squeezed.

That night when Nora had finally crept into the motel room long after midnight, hair windblown and cheeks flushed, Leanne had recognized the blissful disarray of young love. Only after several minutes did she realize the couple on the picnic bench, locked in a kiss under the stars, had been Joe and Nora.

She wanted to ask what had happened. Wanted to pull her daughter into the warm circle of motherly knowing and ask all the questions. But she didn't. Nora would tell her when she was ready.

And for now, it was enough to see her daughter smiling like that. Light spilling from her face like it was her own personal sunrise. After all the drama of high school, the heartaches, the self-doubt—this was the kind of joy every mother prayed their child would find.

Behind her, the drummer went wild, pounding the beat into the sky like thunder. Cymbals clashed in a gleeful frenzy. The guitarist let loose a solo that curled around the audience like the hug she desperately wanted to give. Someone passed Leanne a tambourine, and she took it without hesitation, slapping it against her thigh in rhythm.

A laugh burst from her chest, loud and bright and so thoroughly free it startled even her.

Leanne wasn't a musician. Not like her mother. Not like the rest of the band. But she didn't need to be. Because what she felt wasn't performance it was harmony.

She caught a glimpse of her reflection in one of the chrome microphone stands. Hair loose. Face bare. Freckles bright against flushed skin. A lacy top. Cutoff jean shorts. The Leanne she'd left back in New York—polished, restrained, invisible behind layers of responsibility—felt a million miles away.

And good riddance.

All around her, people danced. Colorful clothes swirling, fringe swaying, sweat glistening on open, joyful faces. Didn't matter who you were or where you came from.

No one was thinking about war. Or dinner. Or making sure the laundry was folded just right.

There were only a million hands in the air.

Swaying.

Beating like a single heart from one soul.

Peace and music, she thought. *This is what it means to be alive.*

Being up onstage was the cherry on top of this wild, messy, magical search for her mother.

The final brick in the foundation Leanne was building to finally honor herself.

As the song's last note drifted into the sky, Leanne turned and wrapped her arms around her mother. The hug was tight, warm, unshakable.

"I love you, Mom," she whispered into Eleanor's ear, and her mother squeezed back, her frame smaller now than Leanne remembered but still pulsing with that electric kind of strength.

"What's your name?" the lead singer, Shep Moon, asked, breathless into the mic.

Leanne stepped toward the microphone without hesitation. "Leanne." Her voice came out clear and proud.

"Your mom's one hell of a lady." Shep's grin was genuine and proud, and it made Leanne wonder just how deep her mother had become entrenched in this world and how much she would miss it when they left.

Leanne turned, pride rising in her chest like a tide. Eleanor gave a sheepish shrug, a smile tugging at her lips.

"That she is," Leanne said softly.

Before she could say anything else, Shep's band kicked into a new jam, the guitar riff roaring through the crowd. Another woman appeared from the wings, gripping Leanne's hand with the urgency of someone who'd done this dozens of times.

"I'm Megan. Come on, let's get you a band T-shirt," Megan shouted over the music.

Leanne hesitated, glanced back at her mom, then let herself be pulled gently to the side of the stage. But she wasn't going anywhere—not really. She wasn't about to fade into the crowd, away from her mother, not after coming this far and finally finding her. Not when they were finally in the same place, at the same time, singing the same damn song.

She stood just offstage, watching Eleanor lean into Shep, her voice folding into his, as natural as breathing. The two of them radiated joy, rhythm, something unnameable and transcendent.

Megan riffled through a box and held up a T-shirt. Stretched across the front in a psychedelic font, it read "I Heard the Moon. Summer of '69."

Leanne took the shirt, her fingers smoothing over the cotton.

The summer Leanne's mother ran away.

The summer Leanne's mother ran toward herself.

The summer Leanne finally stopped being afraid to do the same.

Leanne smiled. "Do you happen to have an extra one for my daughter, Nora? She's somewhere out in the crowd."

"Mama Lightning must be so thrilled to have her family here," said the young woman beside her, riffling through the box again to pull out another T-shirt. "Watching her perform like that..." She trailed off, gaze drifting wistfully toward the stage.

"We're just happy she followed her dream." Leanne hugged the T-shirts.

"We're happy too. This summer wouldn't have been the same without her." Megan's voice held something unspoken in it, a fondness. And the way she watched Shep sing made Leanne wonder if the girl had more than admiration tucked behind those eyes.

"Do you play?" Leanne asked.

Megan snapped her attention back to Leanne. "Me?" She laughed. "No, no—I'm just the manager."

Leanne raised an eyebrow. "Just the manager?"

Megan shrugged, cheeks pink. "Well, yeah. I don't play an instrument or anything."

"Honey," Leanne said, a smirk curling at the corner of her mouth, "if there's one thing I've learned this summer, it's that the person who manages things is never *just* anything."

That earned a genuine smile from Megan. "They wouldn't have made it without me."

"Exactly."

Just like Dean wouldn't have made it without her. Without the perfectly timed breakfasts. The ironed shirts. The polite, composed dinner parties where she played hostess with a practiced smile and a glass of white wine she never finished. Without the life she'd shaped around his needs like clay.

Except now? She was done managing.

Let someone else keep the trains running on time.

Leanne was ready to miss a train or two. Maybe hop a different one entirely.

She tucked the shirts under her arm and turned her gaze back to the stage, where her mother, her wild, impossible, fearless mother, sang her heart out beneath the Woodstock sun.

And for once, Leanne didn't feel like the grown-up in the room.

She felt like someone just beginning.

She was ready to live.

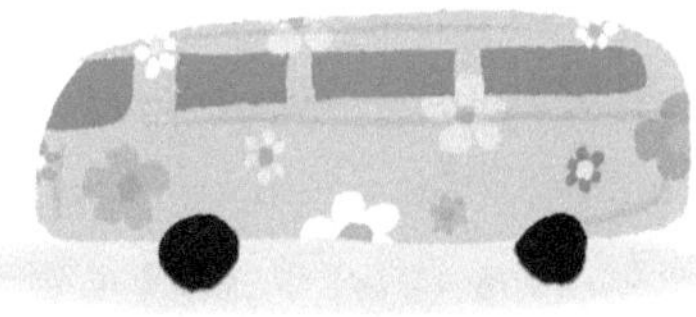

CHAPTER FORTY-TWO

NORA SCRIBBLED A FEW LINES ACROSS THE PAGE OF her notebook, her pen moving quickly, words pouring out. Something about a girl with thunder in her veins and a boy who kissed like rock and roll, unpredictable but somehow always right on time.

Mind-blowing. Magical.

The start of something. Or another practice page in what she was starting to think might be a novel.

"Is this seat taken?"

She glanced up, blinking against the sun, to find Joe standing there, notebook under one arm and a vinyl record under the other. His dark curls were still damp from the shower, and he smelled faintly of soap and something woodsy.

Her cheeks flushed, and she shut her notebook with the pen marking her spot.

The thought of him in that shower—with her—sent a ripple down her spine.

"I've always got an open seat for you." Nora patted the seat, aiming for casual, though her pulse had other plans. Joe settled beside her, and she swore her entire side lit up just from his nearness.

"I picked something up for you yesterday." He held out the record.

She took it carefully as if it might combust in her hands. A Jimi Hendrix album—*The Jimi Hendrix Experience*—the iconic bright yellow cover with the band encircled in brilliant colors. But what stopped her was the sharp black marker scrawl across the front.

"'To Nora,'" she read, stunned. "Jimi signed this?"

Joe shrugged, grinning. "I figured it might be a decent way to remember the summer."

Her fingers traced the loops of Hendrix's signature like it might disappear. "This is insane."

"I know. You're welcome."

She stared at him for a beat longer, heart thudding. "Robin Stone has nothing on you."

Joe raised an eyebrow. "Robin Stone?"

"From *The Love Machine*," she said, cheeks warming. "He's supposed to be the ultimate fantasy, right? Powerful, sexy, mysterious…"

He gave her a crooked smile. "Sounds like a real catch."

"He doesn't hold a candle," she said, lifting the record. "This is better than fiction."

Joe nudged her knee with his. "You're better than fiction."

Nora grinned, then leaned over and kissed him, soft and slow. Not because of the record. Or the famous signature. But this sunlit, music-filled, wild, impossible summer that felt more like a dream than anything she could've written.

And the boy who, somehow, kept making it feel more real.

Because clearly, this summer hadn't given her enough to remember already. The truth was, it had already tattooed itself across her bones. She was pretty sure this summer was going to shape the rest of her life.

"Thank you," she said softly, still staring at the signed record like it might disappear.

Joe shifted beside her, cracking open the sleeve. Inside, in the upper left-hand corner, was a ten-digit number scribbled in pen.

"Jimi gave me his phone number?" she teased.

Joe chuckled. "It's mine," he said casually. "In case you want to call."

Her heart hiccupped. The way he said it, either this was the softest breakup in history or hope hanging on a telephone wire.

"Do you want me to call?" she asked.

Again, he smiled, and there it was, that dimple in his cheek, like punctuation on a promise. "I do," he said. "But I didn't know if you wanted me to stick around long enough to see where the story goes."

She glanced down at her notebook, suddenly hyperaware of how she'd been borrowing little bits of him—his jokes, eyes, that smile—and filtering it through fictional characters. He didn't know. Couldn't know.

Right?

"The story of us?" she asked, voice soft.

"Something like that," he said. "I mean, you're headed off to Yale. And I'll be in school. So…"

So.

So this might be it.

A summer song.

A long, slow fade-out.

Her fingers curled around the edge of the record sleeve, grounding herself.

She wasn't naive. She knew how these things went. People went to college. They grew, changed, and moved on. She'd probably meet a brooding philosophy major with shaggy hair and bad posture and fall head over heels just because he quoted Kerouac at exactly the wrong time. Because Kerouac was French Canadian, and knowing he spoke

French would probably only remind her of Joe, and she'd be looking for a rebound.

But when she thought about never seeing Joe again, never hearing him say something ridiculous just to make her laugh, never watching him scribble notes in the margins of his notebook like his life depended on it, her chest ached.

Joe Dumas had certainly left an imprint.

And she didn't want to erase it just yet.

"Well, enough of the sadness," she said, giving the record a fond pat like it was a friend she wasn't ready to say goodbye to. "I think we should just enjoy ourselves for the rest of the day. What do you think?"

Joe raised an eyebrow. "I think that sounds like the perfect plan."

There was still one final day of music left, and Nora had a feeling her mom wasn't going to let them miss it. Her grandmother wasn't scheduled to perform again, but Eleanor had made them promise not to leave until the very last chord was strummed, the last body swayed, and the last guitar wailed. This was the finale—the exhale at the end of a wild, wonderful, unexpected adventure.

And truthfully, Nora wasn't ready for it to end either.

She wasn't ready for reality to swoop back in with its structured schedules, meal plans, lectures, and internships. A reality where Joe wouldn't be one of the first people she saw in the morning, grinning over a bowl of questionable muesli with Santana playing in the background.

Though she was absolutely looking forward to a toilet without a line and air that didn't constantly smell like smoke and herbs.

She stood, brushing a crumb from her sundress, and leaned in to kiss Joe on the cheek. "Thanks for everything."

His eyes softened. "Anytime."

He laced their fingers together like it was second nature, and they started the walk back toward the motel.

"Meet you back out here in a sec?" she asked when they reached the walkway.

"You bet."

Inside the motel room, her mom was zipping up her suitcase even though they weren't leaving until tomorrow morning. Of course, she was. Leanne had always been the type of person who packed early and double-checked the map twice.

Still, she looked different now. Free in a way Nora had never quite seen before. Like maybe this road trip had unraveled something inside her too.

Something that wasn't going to be packed back up again.

There was a certain set to her mother's mouth, a quiet resolve that made Nora's chest tighten. That wasn't just end-of-summer tiredness. That was the weight of a woman bracing for reality.

Nora lingered in the doorway, watching Leanne smooth the bedspread one last time, even though she'd rumple it again tonight when they went to bed.

"Last day," Nora said softly.

Leanne looked up, her smile warm but tinged with sadness. "Yeah. This really has been…incredible. I'm going to miss being out on the road with you."

"Me too." Nora didn't sugarcoat it. "I'm going to miss *you*, Mom."

The words cracked something open in Leanne's face. Tears pooled instantly, and she blinked hard, looking up at the ceiling like she could will them back into her skull. But Nora saw them.

Instead of calling her on it, Nora stepped closer and wrapped her arms around her mother.

The hug caught them both by surprise.

They stood there in the middle of the motel room, holding each other like it was the most natural thing in the world. Like the months—maybe years—of tension hadn't happened.

Nora didn't know how long they stood there, but eventually, tears pricked her eyes, and she pulled back with a sniff, fanning her face with both hands.

"Why am I so emotional?" she half laughed, her voice thick.

Leanne chuckled through her own tears. "Because our epic trip is coming to an end."

But it was more than that. Nora could feel it. This wasn't just goodbye to a road trip. This was goodbye to the version of herself that had climbed into the Lincoln Continental weeks ago, full of expectations, pressure, and plans.

Goodbye to the freedom of the open road. The freedom of reinvention.

And she didn't quite know how to let that go.

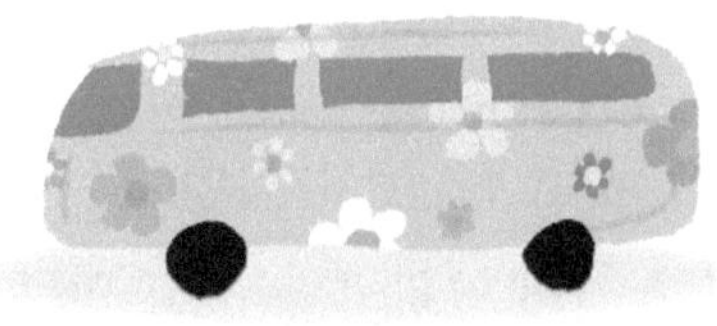

CHAPTER FORTY-THREE

ELEANOR NEVER DID CARE MUCH FOR GOODBYES. That was part of why she'd slipped out of her house weeks ago without leaving a single note for Leanne. Goodbyes were tidy, clinical, expected. But a real, messy, music-filled life was never that neat.

Henry had known that about her too. Maybe that's why he'd died the way he did—quietly, in his sleep, no warning, no hospital beeps, no tearful farewells. Just there one night and gone the next. A part of her had always wondered if he'd done it on purpose, sparing her the weight of a goodbye.

That familiar heaviness filled her chest, watching from the edge of the tent while the last stragglers of Woodstock rolled up their lives into bedrolls and duffel bags. The festival was winding down, the music fading into memory. Shep and his band were buzzing about Colorado, their next stop. Another gig, another town.

They'd asked her to come.

And oh, how tempting it was. To keep riding the high of late nights and impromptu jams, of being known not as someone's mother or someone's wife but as Mama Lightning, the Dame of Rock and Roll.

But her bones ached in places she'd forgotten existed, and her mind was starting to slip more than she wanted to admit. Faces blurred. Time blurred. Sometimes, so did her name.

No. It was time for her to go home. Time to face the diagnosis her doctor had given her. Time to plan out what the rest of her life would look like before she lost the capacity to do so.

Shep didn't know it yet, but this was goodbye.

Eleanor slipped Roxy into her worn leather bag and tightened the strap across her chest. The pup nestled in without a fuss, like she knew and also was resigned to their fate.

Eleanor stepped out into the maze of tents and faded flags. The old Irish goodbye—no fuss, no fanfare. Just a quiet exit stage left.

She picked her way through the colorful sprawl, the patchwork quilts and daisy-chained teenagers, the smell of lingering weed smoke, and extinguished campfires. Her sandals crunched against discarded bottle caps, wrappers, and crushed grass.

The air was different now. No longer did it hum with bass guitars or crooning voices or crackle with energy. Soft. Mellow. Like the closing notes of a perfect song. Eleanor refused to cry, walking away from the stage, from the band, from the wild and beautiful thrill that had defined her summer.

Because she refused to believe that this was an ending. Rather, it was an encore.

Scanning the crowd, Eleanor realized she wasn't exactly sure where to meet Leanne and Nora. She was certain someone had told her—Leanne, probably—but the memory had floated away, soft and slippery, like a lyric she was sure she once knew.

Panic made her heart skip a beat. But then, the world appeared to have finally done her a favor. She glanced up to see Leanne standing right there, arms crossed, eyes a contradiction between relief and wariness.

"I wasn't sure you were going to come," Leanne said.

"Why not?" Eleanor kept her voice light though she already knew the answer.

Leanne's smile tilted gently. "You looked awfully comfortable out here on the road. That rock star of yours didn't seem too eager to let you go."

Eleanor followed her daughter's gaze, glancing back toward the tent where Shep was still playing with his bandmates, head thrown back in laughter, completely unaware that she'd slipped away. He probably just thought she'd gone off to the restroom.

"All good things must come to an end," she whispered.

Leanne cocked her head. "Do they really have to?"

Eleanor hesitated. "I suppose not. But for this old gal..." She smiled, a half lie on her tongue. "I'm ready for the next stage."

Her throat tightened around the syllables, the finality of her statement. The next stage—what a cruel phrase for what was waiting. Not a stage with lights or applause. No encores. No set list. Just the slow, inevitable erasure of everything she knew. Everything she was.

She took Leanne's hand between both of hers. The softness of her daughter's skin startled her. Youth was so easily forgotten when wrapped in an aging body. Her own hands looked foreign sometimes. The thinning skin, the map of blue veins, the delicate brittleness of bones that used to strum a guitar without effort.

And then Nora was there, slipping into place like a missing puzzle piece. Joe Dumas was with her, hands in his pockets, eyes scanning the crowd like he'd already written this scene in one of his articles.

Three generations reunited at the end of a summer that had changed them all.

"Hey, Grandma," Nora said, and that word didn't sting quite as much anymore.

Eleanor gave her a soft smile. "Hey, sweetheart."

She looked at Nora and Leanne—her girls—and let the moment root inside her.

Even if she forgot it one day, she hoped this summer would live on in them.

Her eyes shifted to Joe, standing tall beside her granddaughter. They made a sweet-looking pair, Eleanor thought. Nora with her hopeful eyes, Joe with his tangled curls. They had that electric energy about them that could be spotted a mile away, one that burned hot and fast. Still, Eleanor hoped her granddaughter wouldn't tether all her dreams to just one boy. College was coming and, with it, a wide-open world Nora had only just begun to taste.

"Joe," Eleanor said, pausing beside him, "didn't you say you had one more question for me?"

He grinned. "Was it everything you dreamed of?"

Eleanor looked out over the fields, now dotted with tents being folded, guitars being zipped into cases, the last notes of music still drifting faintly in the warm air.

"It absolutely was, young man," she said. "And more."

They began walking, the crowd flowing around them like a river with no beginning or end. And somewhere along that winding path, Eleanor leaned into her daughter.

"You've spent so much of your adult life being something for everyone else," she whispered. "Don't forget to be something for yourself too, honey."

Leanne blinked fast. For a second, Eleanor thought she might argue. Her daughter had always had that defensive streak. But instead, she just nodded and gave Eleanor's hand a squeeze. Her throat bobbed like she was swallowing something too big for words.

Then Eleanor turned to Nora and whispered, "And you, young lady… Don't be afraid to leave. But don't be afraid to come back either."

Where her mother had reacted quietly, Nora threw her arms around her grandmother, giving her a tight hug.

"Thank you, Grandma," she said, pulling back with a grin. "You're a living example of that."

Eleanor smiled so hard she felt it all the way through her bones. This new outlook on life might have taken her a lifetime to figure it all out, but she'd finally gotten there. And now she got to leave a few truths behind, tucked in the hands of the two women who mattered most.

They reached Joe's car first.

"A pleasure meeting you, Joe," Eleanor said, her voice laced with warmth.

"Likewise, ma'am," he replied, his grin boyish, his eyes full of something like hope.

"Take care, Joe," Leanne added.

"You do the same."

Nora shifted on her feet, glancing sideways in that unmistakable *please don't embarrass me* kind of way that only teenage girls could master.

Eleanor caught the cue and turned to Leanne without missing a beat. "Come on, darling," she said with a wink. "Let's give them a minute."

Leanne laughed, falling into step beside her mother, and for once, didn't argue.

Eleanor leaned into her daughter as they ambled a little farther down the road, leaving Nora and Joe behind in the soft, golden light of the afternoon. The crowd around them moved in a lazy tide, the festival winding down into quiet hums and goodbye hugs.

"He seems like a nice young man," Eleanor said, nudging Leanne gently.

"I think he is," Leanne said with a soft sigh. "I just hope this doesn't end like every other relationship Nora's had. She falls hard, fast…and then it's heartbreak city."

Eleanor chuckled, a knowing twinkle in her eye. "Well, if she truly wants to be a writer, a broken heart will give her enough material to fill volumes."

Leanne tilted her head, surprised. "How did you know she wanted to be a writer?"

Eleanor glanced up at her, squinting against the setting sun. "Isn't it obvious? That notebook is practically glued to her hand. She's been scribbling stories since she could form a sentence. She's always lived half in the real world, half in some imagined one."

Leanne smiled, a swell of emotion catching her unprepared. "She just told me this summer. Said she doesn't think she wants to go into marketing after all."

Eleanor nodded with approval. "That's a dream worth chasing. The real ones usually are."

They walked in companionable silence, the breeze tugging gently at the fringe of Eleanor's shawl.

"Joe, on the other hand…" Eleanor mused, breaking the quiet. "He'll probably fade."

"Maybe," Leanne said with a shrug. "But maybe not. You never know with these things."

"No, you don't. But either way, he's a chapter. And those matter too. And what about you and Dean?" Eleanor's voice was gentle, almost like she was afraid of pushing too far.

Leanne's smile faltered. Her features shifted, sobered. Eleanor immediately wished she could pull the question back into her mouth.

She had tried so many times over the years to broach the subject of Dean and Leanne's marriage, but it had always felt like knocking on a door no one wanted to open.

"Things are going to change," Leanne said finally. "I just don't know how yet. I know what I want. And I know I'm going to tell him what I want. It'll be up to him what happens next."

"Or," Eleanor said softly, "you could tell him what happens next."

Leanne let out a surprised laugh. "No one tells Dean anything."

"Maybe that's the problem." Eleanor's voice was edged with just enough bite to get her point across. "No one ever has. Maybe hearing what he needs to hear—from you—might finally wake him up."

There was a pause, like something delicate was shifting.

Eleanor sighed. "The doctor telling me I was in the early stages of dementia wasn't what I wanted to hear. But it…it forced me to stop putting things off. To stop pretending I had all the time in the world."

Leanne looked at her mother then, truly looked. "Music?"

"Yes. Art. Creation. Expression. Doesn't matter what form it takes—singing, writing, painting, baking a cake… If it stirs your soul, that's what you're meant to do. That's how you leave your mark."

Leanne's face lit up, the spark of realization flaring in her eyes. "I love to bake, and I've won many contests with my confections. But I've been thinking of going on strike when I get back home."

Eleanor gave a knowing smile. "But that would only punish you."

"Yeah," Leanne murmured. "Yeah, you're right." She glanced down at her hands, then back at her mother. "Thank you, Mom."

Eleanor nodded, her smile small but steeped in something deeper. Pride. Sorrow. Hope.

"Go live your life, sweetheart. Or it will keep living you."

CHAPTER FORTY-FOUR

THEY CLIMBED INTO THE LINCOLN CONTINENTAL, THE top down, the sky above them wide open and blue. The breeze ruffled their hair like it had missed them and was welcoming them home.

The drive back to Ossining would take a little over an hour. First stop: Eleanor's house. They'd ensure everything was in order and that Eleanor had what she needed, with a plan to discuss the next steps. Then, it would be back to Leanne's own front door. Back to the house with the trimmed hedges and perfectly folded towels. Back to Dean. If he wasn't avoiding her by burying himself at work. Again.

The highway unspooled before them, black asphalt and trees lining the median familiar but different, the way a place always looks after you've seen something new. After you've changed.

From the back seat, Nora leaned forward and touched Leanne's shoulder. "Mom? Would you mind if we went to Orchard Beach before we go home?"

The question made Leanne's heart catch. It had been years. She used to take Nora there when she was little, just like her mother had taken her. They'd go after school or on weekends, get ice cream from the vendor by the boardwalk, dip their toes in the Long Island Sound, and watch the boats drift like ghosts beneath the lighthouse's steady gaze. But around the time Nora had entered high school, the visits had become few and far between until they petered out completely.

She turned to Eleanor. "Would you mind?"

Eleanor grinned. "I wouldn't mind at all. I used to take you there when you were young. You always danced in the sand."

Leanne smiled. She remembered those days with almost painful clarity. How the wind would whip their sundresses around their legs and her mother laughed like the world hadn't told her to hush.

And she remembered trying so hard to give that to Nora too. Little borrowed pieces of joy passed down like recipes.

Now Nora wanted to go back. To taste it again. And Leanne realized she did too. There was no telling when they'd get a chance to repeat a trip with the three of them, if ever.

"Orchard Beach it is." Leanne turned the car toward the shore.

They drove the extra hour past their house, following the coastline until the road curved and the scent of the ocean filled the air.

The day was perfect for the beach—bright sun, a soft breeze coming in off the Sound, and just enough of a crowd to feel alive without being overwhelming. Nothing compared to the madness of Woodstock and the roar of half a million voices.

They didn't bother changing into bathing suits. Instead, they kicked off their sandals and ran laughing into the water like kids—like they were racing time itself. The surf licked at their ankles, cool and refreshing. Spindrift spraying and tickling their knees. Eleanor held up the hem of her flowy skirt as she waded in, grinning like someone who had nothing left to prove.

They held hands and kicked at the water, the splash of it catching the light like glitter.

They reminisced about that time Nora had been knocked over

by a rogue wave—and how, in a heroic attempt to rescue her, Leanne had gone under too. All limbs and laughter and seaweed in their hair. They'd giggled until their sides ached, hugging each other, wet and sandy and full of joy.

Later, they made their way to the ice cream stand. Nora chose her forever favorite, mint chocolate chip. Eleanor and Leanne each went for chocolate, the same as always.

Leanne stood at the edge of the boardwalk, watching her mother and daughter holding hands and skipping along the shore, their skirts fluttering, their voices carried on the wind like a song, and Roxy chasing behind. The world doubled. She closed her eyes, picturing Nora little again—toothless smile, sandy knees, arms stretched wide with wonder. But the illusion flickered. Nora was a young woman now. Beautiful. Grown.

Nearly two decades of mothering, of being needed in a way that filled her completely, and now, in just a few days, her daughter would leave for college. They would load up the Lincoln and drive to Connecticut and Yale's vast Gothic buildings, where Nora would begin the next chapter. And Leanne would wake up in a house that echoed a little more than it used to.

Of course, it wasn't really goodbye. Nora would call, she'd visit, they'd write. But it was an ending, nonetheless.

And what a wonderful person her daughter had become.

Leanne swiped at a tear before it could fall. This was a strange kind of joy—being proud and also breaking a little inside. To see your child step into the world and realize they don't need you in quite the same way anymore.

To know she'd finally gotten her daughter back, only to be preparing to let her go.

She was going to miss her. That was the hardest thing of all.

Leanne didn't know who she was without being a mother. She

didn't know who she was without being a daughter. Her identity had always been shaped by her roles in other people's lives. And now, with one preparing to leave and the other fading before her eyes, she would have to sort out what all that meant. Who she was when no one else was asking her to be something.

They wandered the shoreline with their melting ice cream cones, the sweet, chocolatey cream trailing down the sides, sticky and comforting in that summer way. The ocean breeze tangled their hair, and the scent of brine, sugar, and distant charcoal grills wrapped around them with nostalgic tenderness. They were doing everything except walking back to the car—lingering, stretching out the magic a little longer, like savoring the last lick of an ice cream cone. That slow, reluctant goodbye.

When they finally sat, it was on a soft stretch of sand worn smooth by a hundred years of tide. They didn't speak much. Just watched the sun melt into the horizon, casting the sky in molten pinks and oranges. The lighthouse winked to life like a single, solemn eye, and they all knew what it meant.

As children, that beam of light had been the signal that the day was done. The call to pack up their towels, laughter, and bare feet and head home. And it was like that now too. A quiet, unquestionable cue: *Time to go.*

Leanne had never been one to wallow. Not really. And she wasn't about to start now, even though her chest squeezed with emotion.

"Time to face the music," she murmured aloud, a slight, wry smile curling on her lips.

"What's so funny?" Nora brushed sand from her knee.

"I just said it's time to face the music," Leanne replied. "Funny, right? We've been chasing music all summer, and yet now it feels like the real meaning of that phrase is what we've been avoiding."

"Oh, I'm not so sure." Eleanor sat cross-legged beside them, her hand still faintly stained from the fading henna, Roxy snoozing in her lap. "I think maybe we were avoiding everything before. And this summer, we did, in fact, face the music."

Leanne glanced at the horizon one last time before it darkened. Maybe her mother was right.

Maybe they had already faced the things they were avoiding, though they all still had unfinished business to attend to. And maybe now, they were finally ready for the next verse.

"There's another idiom that means something similar," Nora said thoughtfully, twirling the end of her ice cream cone between her fingers. "Pay the piper. Why do you think facing the consequences always ends up tied to musicians or music?"

Eleanor chuckled, the sound weathered and warm. "Because music tells it like it is. It's memory. Confession. Truth dressed up in melody and metaphor. Music is sharing stories—pain, joy, betrayal. Music is honest...but it can also lie."

Leanne raised a brow. "Lie?"

Her mother nodded, brushing sand from her skirt, eyes still fixed on the darkening water. "Oh, sure. Music can make you believe something that isn't true. A love that's not real. A memory that's rosier than it was. It romanticizes the ache. Sometimes, it hides the truth in a pretty chorus just to make it easier to swallow."

Nora went quiet, taking that in.

And Leanne felt the truth of her mother's words settle between them like fog rolling in from the sea. She thought about the soundtrack of her own life—lullabies sung beside a crib, old love songs playing in the car while her husband drove in silence, radio jingles while she wiped down countertops.

Now she had new songs. Ones from a summer of rediscovery, long drives, loud guitars, and quiet epiphanies. A new rhythm to live by.

"Maybe," Leanne said softly, "it's because when you finally stop dancing around the truth, you have to listen. You have to really hear it."

Eleanor hummed her agreement. "And when you do? That's when the real music starts."

CHAPTER FORTY-FIVE

THEY RINSED THE SAND FROM THEIR FEET AT THE PUBLIC outdoor shower station, the cold water making Nora yelp and laugh. Then came the ritual—slipping their shoes back on, brushing off calves and hems, the beach already starting to feel like a memory even as it shimmered behind them.

Nora glanced at the two women she came from—her mother walking just ahead, her grandmother humming softly and adjusting Roxy's bag over her shoulder. And suddenly, she was struck by time. How it passed, how it shifted people. She imagined her mother, once her age, walking away from this same shoreline. Her grandmother too, would she have been barefoot and wild decades before, the hem of her skirt clinging damply to her legs, or would she have hung back? There seemed to be two sides of Eleanor Bell Strickland. Which was real?

The thought made her heart ache with wistful tenderness she hadn't experienced before.

Nora was different now. This summer had changed her. In so many ways, she felt older than she had just two months ago. Older than the girl who'd crossed the high school stage with a nervous smile and a diploma in her hand. But in other ways, she felt achingly young. College loomed like a whole new universe, one she wasn't entirely sure she was prepared to enter. A dorm. A roommate. Classes. Choices. Self-reliance. All of it exhilarating, all of it terrifying.

At the car, Nora glanced over her shoulder toward the shore. "I'm going to miss this. Promise me when I'm home for Thanksgiving, we can take a day and come back to the beach."

"It'll be freezing," Leanne said, smiling. "But I wouldn't dream of saying no."

Nora smiled back. Not so long ago, there'd been a time when her mother might've said no without thinking. When there was a list of rules and unspoken expectations. No cold beaches. No off-schedule adventures. That list seemed to have vanished somewhere along the way, maybe back in Atlanta, Denver, or the middle of a muddy music festival.

"I'll knit us some scarves," Eleanor added. "Peace and music scarves."

Nora laughed, turning to lift her grandmother's hand, still adorned with the faded swirl of henna. She brushed her thumb gently over the design, mesmerized that her grandmother had the spunk to tattoo her skin, even if temporarily.

"You're a real rebel, you know that?" Nora asked.

Eleanor winked. "I suppose you can try to take the rebel out of someone, but it doesn't mean they'll forfeit who they are."

"Tell me something rebellious you did," Nora said, nudging her gently.

"Besides running away at the age of sixty-nine?"

Nora laughed. "Besides that."

Eleanor's eyes twinkled. "When I was about your age, I set out to be a musician. But most people in the industry didn't like my style."

"What was your style?"

"Picture Jimi Hendrix," she said, "but make him a young blond in a demure ankle-length day dress with saddle shoes, when the music of choice was jazz or the blues."

Nora's eyes widened. "That is a sight I would've liked to see."

"Well, it wasn't a sight the world was ready for. They tried to shape me. Mold me. And I let them for a while. Until I got tired of playing music their way...and I gave up."

"You were a woman ahead of your time."

"Perhaps I was." Eleanor's gaze drifted to Leanne, her eyes alight with mischief. "Are you going to change before heading home?"

Nora glanced at her mother, struck by how beautiful and youthful her mother looked, years younger than forty-five. Not in the polished, presentable way of church luncheons or PTA meetings—but in the real, undone kind of way. Her face was bare, untouched by makeup, her hair wind-tousled and full of life. The ocean air had painted her cheeks with the sun. She still wore Nora's cutoff jean shorts and a brand-new T-shirt that read "I Heard the Moon"—a tribute to Shep's band and a play on the Apollo 11 landing on the moon with Neil Armstrong and his crew. The shirt was still stiff, not yet broken in, but somehow it suited her. Like slipping into something softer, more honest.

Nora watched her mother, seeing a woman teetering between past and future. A woman who had walked back into herself.

"No," Leanne said, her jaw set. "I rather like this shirt."

Nora didn't know what to make of that. Her father was going to combust when he saw her mom.

For the first time in Nora's memory, her mother's face held a kind of lightness—her eyes sparked with something entirely new. The years of quiet exhaustion, of tamped-down wants and unspoken disappointments, had been peeled away mile by mile on the road, revealing the woman who had always been buried just beneath the surface.

And for a split second, a question lodged like a thorn in Nora's chest. Had she helped put that version of her mother in hiding?

The resentment between them—the distance that had grown over the years like ivy on a house—had felt unmovable. But now she wasn't so sure. Maybe the divide hadn't been written in stone but chosen. Repeated. Reinforced. Like all the unspoken things they'd allowed to grow too heavy to carry.

Still, deep down, Nora knew it hadn't just been her.

There was something her mother had never shared, something older and heavier than anything Nora had caused. And she didn't want to press. She wasn't sure she was ready to hear it.

She loved her dad. He was a good man—when he was around. And maybe that was the problem. Over the years, he'd faded into the background of their lives, all in the name of building something bigger than himself. Bigger than them.

Most of her friends' dads had done the same. And for the longest time, Nora had accepted that that was just the way things were. She'd never stopped to wonder what it cost or the weight her mother must have carried, alone, every day.

A month ago, Nora would've rolled her eyes. Told her mom to stop making everything so heavy. As if endurance was owed. As if being tired wasn't allowed.

But now? Now she saw it. All of it.

The guilt twisted inside her like a bottle cap. How blind she'd been. Well, no more. Her mother deserved more. She deserved joy. Ease. To be the woman she'd become on this road trip. They all did. And Nora was going to make sure she, her mother, and her grandmother stayed that way.

Eleanor gently patted her daughter's hand. The gesture was small but substantial. So simple it might've gone unnoticed if not for how it made Nora's chest ache.

Her mother, usually so composed, so careful, allowed herself a heartbeat of vulnerability, resting her head, just briefly, on her own mother's shoulder.

Nora felt like an observer in a sacred space, watching something private unfold. The pat. The lean. The movements were almost imperceptible—but they carried the weight of so much more.

Affection had never come easily between her mother and grandmother, not in the way Nora had always longed for. But something about this summer had softened the edges, had cracked something open.

And for the first time, Nora let herself believe that maybe it wasn't too late for them to find their way to each other.

PART SIX

Homeward Harmony

SUMMER 1969

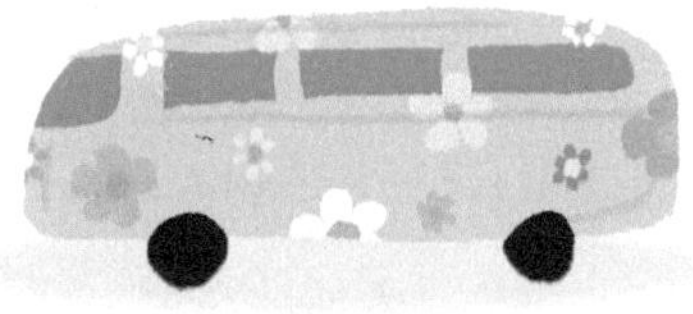

CHAPTER FORTY-SIX

SEVENTY-TWO DAYS HAD PASSED SINCE ELEANOR HAD last stepped foot in this house. Seventy-two days of music, of movement, of chasing echoes of the girl she once was. The Lincoln coasted to a stop in the familiar driveway, and a different kind of silence settled in. Heavier. Thicker. Not the quiet before a song but the hush after one ends, leaving her to wonder what came next.

She didn't move at first. Her hand rested on the car's door handle, fingers curled tight. Inside that house waited her past, her grief, her aging bones, and the space Henry had once filled like a bass line—steady, low, reliable.

The scent of old denim and cigarette smoke still clung to her jacket, souvenirs from the road. She hadn't washed it on purpose. There was something sacred in the smell, a reminder that said she'd lived this summer, not just passed through it.

But now she was home. Or was she?

She'd been too tired to retrieve her car from the airport, and Leanne and Nora had promised to fetch it tomorrow.

Eleanor hesitated, bracing for the flood. The weight of the silence, the ghosts that might rise like smoke the second she crossed the threshold. Would the walls feel smaller than before? Would the rooms trap her, press in around her, remind her that the music was fading from her mind the same way it had faded from this space?

No.

She took a breath. She would not let it be like that.

She wanted to step inside and feel Henry's presence, not as a void but as a warmth. She wanted to remember the joy—the nights they danced barefoot in the kitchen, the lazy Sundays spent on the porch with records spinning and coffee cooling too fast. She wanted to see Leanne again, no longer the woman weighed down by expectation but the girl who used to leap across the living room, her fingers chasing chords across ivory keys, hope in every note.

She wanted to turn on the record player, let the needle hum and crackle to life, pour herself a cup of tea, and sink into her old chair like her life was still whole, still steady.

She just wanted normal. Or something close enough to pretend.

But Eleanor knew, deep down, that life would never be normal again. Whether she stayed in the car or stepped inside her old house, the truth would follow her like a shadow. Things had changed, even the ones that hadn't. She still had dementia. Still carried that ticking clock inside her chest, her head.

The funny thing was, sometimes she knew what was happening. But other times she did not. And worse—she knew exactly what would eventually happen and couldn't stop it. Eleanor had watched her grandmother go through the same thing. Her own mother spared losing her mind by a tragic early death.

The part that frightened her the most was the lack of control in her undoing.

Roxy put her paws up on the dash, tongue lolling out as she stared at the familiar house.

Eleanor turned her head slowly, her neck stiff from the long drive and weeks of travel and performing. Leanne sat beside her, shifting the car into park with a soft click, her face a mixture of exhaustion and resolve. Nora offered a quiet smile in the back seat, and Eleanor could still smell the ocean in her granddaughter's hair—sun, salt, freedom.

The memories of the road, the concerts, the sunsets had become some of the most cherished in Eleanor's life. But she'd also realized that the life she'd led before mattered too. Perhaps most of all. The people she was with now were the loving parts of her existence. She hoped that when the darkness came to claim her completely, it wouldn't take away Leanne and Nora first. That she'd be granted more time in the light before the fog rolled in for good.

The doctor had said there would be "lucid moments."

God, let there be an abundance.

Leanne swung open the creaking car door and stepped out of the car. Through the car window, Eleanor watched her daughter circle to the back, open the trunk, and gently lift out Eleanor's worn travel bag and her guitar. The sight of it struck something in her chest. Her fingers itched to play. Would she still remember how?

Eleanor reached for the door handle, her hand hovering there, trembling.

"A wise woman once told me not to be afraid to leave," Nora said from the back seat, "but also not to be afraid to come back."

Eleanor turned slightly, her spine stiff but her smile soft. "Wise?"

Nora grinned. "Very."

Eleanor arched a brow. "Walk me to the door, then?"

"Of course." Nora popped her door open and climbed out, rounding the car just as Eleanor hesitated.

She didn't want to do this—not really. Not to go back inside. Not to face the silence. Not to face what came next. But she knew she had to. Some things in life were unavoidable, and no matter how far she ran, the inevitable was that life would catch up to her in the end.

Nora opened the passenger door and held out her hand. "Sometimes it's better to do things together."

Eleanor nodded, her throat thick. She placed her hand into her granddaughter's. Her own hand looked small in Nora's grip—weathered and veined, worn by time. But strong too.

When she tried to pull away, Nora only tightened her hold. "We don't have to let go just yet, do we?"

"I'll hold your hand anytime you want," Eleanor whispered.

Roxy rushed to the door, scratching to be let in.

Leanne was already on the porch, Eleanor's bag in one hand and her guitar case in the other. "Mom, do you have your key?"

Eleanor reached into her handbag and froze. Her fingers fumbled uselessly through lipstick tubes, loose change, and receipts. A knot twisted in her chest.

Then—relief.

"In the suitcase," she said, remembering suddenly. "Tucked it in a side pocket."

Eleanor knelt beside her trusty old suitcase, the same one she'd taken on her honeymoon, unzipping the leather, and dug through until her fingers brushed yarn—soft and worn from years of use. The key was still threaded through the crocheted heart Leanne had made in second grade. Uneven stitches. Faded red. Her girl had been so proud.

Eleanor lifted it slowly, held it in her palm, and grinned at the treasure.

"You still have that?" Leanne's smile was tremulous.

"Never leave home without it."

They opened the door and stepped inside. The house smelled

exactly as it had when she left. A blend of patchouli and something faintly floral, maybe lavender, maybe memory. The scent wrapped around her like an old shawl, familiar, comforting, and just a little heavy with time.

Roxy raced in wild circles through the house, overcome with joy to reclaim her kingdom.

Leanne quietly set her mother's bags in the bedroom while Nora wandered into the living room, flipping through Eleanor's old records. In the kitchen, the sound of the kettle clinking against the stove signaled Leanne's silent offering of tea, the universal balm.

Eleanor moved to her dresser and pulled open the top drawer. Tucked inside was an old scrapbook she'd started when she was barely more than a girl. The pages were thick with song lyrics scribbled in ink and pencil, ticket stubs from smoky bars, and black-and-white photographs of her wide-eyed younger self holding a guitar. Before Henry. Before Leanne had even been a thought.

She carried it into the living room, settling onto the purple velvet couch that had cushioned her through countless evenings. The fabric was soft beneath her palms, worn in all the right places. She patted the cushions on either side of her.

"I want to show you two something," she said.

Nora looked up from the records. Leanne poked her head around the corner, steam curling from the kettle behind her.

Eleanor rested the scrapbook on her lap. "This is something I should've shown you both long ago. Maybe why I left would've made more sense. Why I needed to take this tour. Why I had to go."

She glanced at Leanne first. "I never regretted meeting your father. I never once regretted having you. Being your mother has been the honor of my life." Her voice faltered, but she pushed forward. "But… sometimes people have regrets toward the end of plans they never finished. And I wanted—needed—to live the life I gave up. Just one more time. Before I can't remember what it felt like."

Before either of them could respond, a knock sounded on the front door.

Eleanor's brows lifted, surprised. She eased the scrapbook closed and stood, crossing the room slowly, her knees protesting just a little. She opened the door to find a young delivery man standing on the porch, a bouquet of roses cradled in his arms.

"Delivery for Eleanor Bell?"

She nodded, her voice caught somewhere behind her ribs. "That's me."

He handed over the bouquet with a polite smile, tipped his cap, and turned back down the steps.

Eleanor didn't need her glasses to read the little white card tucked into the petals. The handwriting was unmistakable, rough and looping from someone who held a pen like a guitar pick.

Until next time.

Her breath caught. The roses were pale pink, edged in crimson. Familiar.

She lingered in the doorway, one hand clutching the blooms, the other pressed lightly to her chest. She didn't say a word. She didn't need to.

Because she knew exactly who they were from.

Memories are delicate, fragile things—needing to be nurtured and loved, conjured when the longing to relive the most wonderful chapters of a life is overwhelming.

And Eleanor was reliving all of hers, then and now, and she was beyond grateful that time had gifted her that much.

A second chance. A final chorus. A song that would echo forever in her heart.

CHAPTER FORTY-SEVEN

THE LINCOLN CONTINENTAL RUMBLED TO A STOP IN the familiar gravel driveway, its engine ticking as it cooled beneath the setting sun. The air smelled of cut grass and warm earth, thick with the sweetness of the massive magnolia tree that stood in the yard. Leanne sat still, hands gripping the steering wheel, feeling the weight of what waited beyond the front door.

They'd made sure Eleanor's house was tidy and her refrigerator and pantry fully stocked before leaving. Leanne wanted to see her mother taken care of, but she was also procrastinating the inevitable.

The past few weeks had been a dream. One of those rare, golden stretches of time where reality bends just enough to let in the light. Giggling late into the night over shared secrets and sweet pie with Nora. Eleanor, vibrant and sharp, singing into microphones and dancing barefoot in the grass. There had been music and laughter and quiet revelations in the early morning haze. A disappointing number of years had gone by since Leanne had felt that tether of belonging, years since she'd allowed herself to feel anything at all.

And now, she was parked at the edge of her life again. As if this summer had not existed at all.

She exhaled, resting her forehead briefly against the steering wheel, the cool, stitched ridges pressing into her skin. A fleeting stillness. A breath before the plunge.

"Mom? Are you okay?"

No more running. Leanne glanced up, forcing a grin her daughter was sure to see through. "Exhausted. But I'm okay."

Nora nodded, eyeing her skeptically but accepting Leanne's answer.

When Leanne stepped out of the car, the heat greeted her, both familiar and unwelcome. The uncomfortable feeling wrapped around her shoulders and pressed against her back, trying to guide her inside. The outside of the house looked different and the same all at once. The white clapboard siding was maybe a little more weathered now. The porch swing swayed slightly in the breeze, still groaning that tired creak. The windows blinked back at her like half-lidded eyes—watchful, waiting.

She'd walked up those steps a thousand times, yet her legs felt heavier today. Every step would carry a decision she hadn't quite made.

Through the window, she saw the flicker of movement. A figure—tall, broad-shouldered—crossed the kitchen. Dean.

Her stomach tightened. They hadn't exactly been on good terms when she left. The cold silences, the look he'd given her before she shut the door behind her, the phone call where she'd said they needed to make a change. It all sat between them now like a wall neither of them had been willing to climb. Maybe time apart had softened the edges. Or maybe it had carved the distance into something permanent.

Leanne reached for her and Nora's suitcases in the trunk, the scent of sun-toasted leather rising to meet her like a ghost of old travels. A cicada buzzed in the trees above, its long, rattling cry a kind of unraveling—thin threads of her resolve slipping through her fingers.

And then, the front door creaked open.

She froze, one hand still on the handle, when Dean stepped out onto the lighted porch.

Her breath caught in her throat.

He was...*barefoot.* A white T-shirt clung to him, soft and wrinkled from the laundry basket or maybe from being worn too long. His jeans were loose at the waist, riding low on his hips like he didn't care how they fit anymore. This was not the Dean she remembered. Not the polished, tailored man who wanted his shirts ironed twice and buttoned his cuffs even on Sundays.

This Dean looked...unarmored. As if whatever he'd been holding in had finally cracked.

The sight of him like that—unguarded in the afternoon light—hit her harder than any well-crafted apology ever could. Because she knew what he looked like at his most vulnerable. She'd seen it in slivers in the early morning before his first coffee, in the soft quiet of their honeymoon, in the seconds after Nora was born.

But she hadn't seen it in years.

But there it was again. And not just for a flicker. The softness she thought he'd buried for good was exposed for all to see.

For a split second, neither of them moved.

She swallowed hard.

"Dean," she said, her voice steady but just barely.

His eyes locked onto hers. And for the first time in longer than she could remember, they weren't hard. There was no veneer, no carefully measured tone. No quiet resentment simmering just beneath the surface. Just bare, unspoken emotion—fragile, unsure. Like he didn't quite know how to stand in front of her without all the armor he'd worn for years.

A heaviness settled against her chest, tightening her throat.

Then, slowly, he nodded.

And just like that, the summer was over.

But something else—unfamiliar and tentative—was just beginning.

"Dad?" Even Nora seemed to sense it, her voice cutting through the hush as she stepped around the car with a mixture of surprise and caution.

"I've missed you guys so much." Dean's voice cracked as he crossed the porch. He didn't hesitate with Nora. She flew into his arms, her laugh light and surprised when he hugged her close, the both of them trying to make up for all the weeks he'd been absent, even before they'd left.

Then he turned to Leanne, and she caught sight of a day's worth of stubble on his chin. The man who would sometimes shave twice a day just to keep his face smooth…

They stood in front of each other, silent for a beat too long. The air was thick with everything they hadn't said, everything they didn't know how to say.

"I've got to go call—uh—Kelley," Nora said suddenly, her voice a little too loud. She grabbed her bag and rushed inside, giving them privacy in a way that felt too practiced for an eighteen-year-old. She knew. She'd always known.

Leanne lifted her gaze, searching his. "You're not wearing shoes," she said—the only words that made it out.

He glanced down and then back at her with a faint, self-deprecating smile. "Yeah. Weird, right?"

"I just…can't remember the last time I saw you barefoot," she murmured.

He took a deep breath, the movement visible in his chest. "I've been thinking about what you said. On the phone."

Leanne's hand tightened on her purse handle. She hadn't said much. Nothing revolutionary. Nothing directive. Just that they'd talk when she got back. That things needed to change. Her tone had carried more than her words. Maybe that was what had stayed with him.

"I should've been there," Dean said, his voice breaking the silence again. "For the phone calls. For everything."

Leanne said nothing.

Because finally, he was talking.

"Even more than that..." Dean's voice was low, almost like he was speaking to himself. "I should've been with you. In this car. Driving across the country, helping you find your mom. I'm deeply sorry that I put my job above you. Above Nora."

Leanne stayed still. Watching. She wasn't sure she'd ever heard Dean apologize for anything in his life—certainly not about work. The silence stretched between them, soft and strange, like a familiar song played in a new key.

"I think..." she hesitated, her voice gentler than she expected. "I think it's good you weren't."

His brows lifted in confusion, but she went on.

"Nora and I"—she smiled faintly—"we really needed this. My mom and I did too. This trip wasn't just about finding her. But seeing each other again. All of us. Of finding ourselves."

Dean nodded slowly, eyes cast down.

"But," she added, "it would've been nice if you'd answered the phone."

"I know," he said, no defensiveness in his tone. "I'm really sorry. I've realized... I haven't been the best husband."

It was on the tip of her tongue to correct him. Because he hadn't been a bad husband—not by anyone's outside standards. He was reliable. A good provider. They had a house, two cars, retirement savings, and college savings for Nora. She'd been able to disappear for nearly two months and not once worry about the bills.

Dean wasn't cruel. He didn't yell, hit, or overdrink. But he was absent. Emotionally. And sometimes physically. He had been a ghost in his own marriage.

She said none of that. Instead, she watched him. Wanted to see what he thought he'd done wrong.

"I want to do better," he said. "I want to make an effort."

He ran a hand through his hair—a move she'd seen a thousand times—but it felt different now, barefoot and bare-faced in the doorway. Vulnerable. Human. A far cry from the starched-shirt version of himself she'd come to expect. And yet, somehow, all the more attractive for it.

After a brief pause, he said, "Nora's leaving soon." His voice was quieter now. "And then it'll be just us. You and me. In this house."

He didn't say it like a promise.

He said it like a question.

A question she wasn't sure yet how to answer.

"You are right. There are a lot of things that need to change," Dean said quietly, his voice thick with something like resolve. He tugged at the hem of his T-shirt. "And I'm starting with this."

He gave a small, almost sheepish shrug. "I want to be more casual with you, Leanne. More open. Honest. This"—he gestured down at himself—"this isn't just about clothes. It's about showing up. Being real. Stripping away all the armor."

Leanne's chest ached. He'd never talked like this before.

"There's a reason we fell in love," he continued. "There's a reason we got married. And I think…I think we need to find it again. I love you. I always have. But I know I've neglected you. And I'll spend the rest of my life making that up to you if you let me."

Tears pricked at the corners of her eyes. She hadn't even had to say a word—Dean just knew. All the things she thought she'd have to fight to get across, he was already holding in his hands like fragile glass, careful not to drop.

"I like the sound of that," she whispered, stepping into his arms. She wrapped herself around him and pressed her lips to his, soft and slow. Their first real kiss in longer than she could remember.

They had never been perfect. But what they had was real. However flawed. While bent in places, their foundation had weathered storms. They had endured.

For better or worse, Leanne decided she was the kind of woman who stayed. Who fought. Who held on when the world told her to let go. Because she loved Dean. Even after everything—even after the silences, the distance, the growing pains—that truth remained. And that love was worth fighting for, if they were both willing.

They had lost sight of each other somewhere along the way. Forgotten how to be partners, how to be friends. But love wasn't just in the remembering. Love was in the choosing.

And standing there, arms around him, heart cracked wide open, Leanne chose them. Again.

CHAPTER FORTY-EIGHT

SAYING GOODBYE SUCKED.

Nora had never been good at it—probably because she hadn't had much practice before this summer turned into one long, slow farewell tour. Goodbye to high school friends who swore they'd write but wouldn't. Goodbye to teachers who looked relieved to be rid of students for the summer. Goodbye to her sleepy little town, the one she used to think she'd escape from but now realized had a grip on her like an old, worn but comforting quilt.

Goodbye to music that stretched from sunrise to midnight, to guitars strumming under wide-open skies, to the indulgence of days with no real beginning or end—just a continuous loop of sound, laughter, and possibility.

And now, the hardest goodbye of all. To the house where she had learned to walk, to read, to dream. To the walls that held her childhood in their quiet corners. To the two people who had always been there, standing in the doorway, watching her leave—smaller now, somehow, as if they were the ones being left behind.

And then there was something—someone—else.

Joe Dumas.

Joe had been a highlight at the concerts. Scribbling in his notebook and writing himself right into her summer and her heart. They had shared long nights of whispered conversations about the world, about music, about all the places they wanted to go. His typewriter and her wild ideas. His ambitions and her rebellion. And then, just like that, the summer had ended, and possibly so had they.

"You'll write to me, right?" she had asked.

"I'm a journalist," he had said, like that was answer enough.

But she knew better. He would write. But maybe not to her.

They had talked on the phone a few times, voices stretching across the distance like a thread that kept fraying at the edges. But knowing they lived on opposite coasts of the country—how different their lives were about to become—Nora had done the one thing she swore she wouldn't. She didn't call him back that last time.

Maybe that was its own painless farewell.

Because now, goodbye to him too.

And hello, Yale.

Nora stepped out of her dorm and onto campus, where the air had that crisp, academic kind of coolness. Somewhere between intellectual superiority and a late-September breeze. The Gothic buildings loomed, ivy curling up their stone facades like they had been here before history itself. Students shuffled past, notebooks tucked under arms, backpacks sagging under the weight of knowledge—or, at least, really heavy books. The boys wore blazers with turtlenecks like they were auditioning for future roles as professors. All of them looked significantly more confident than she felt.

Unlike them, she wasn't just starting college; she was stepping into history. As one of the first women allowed to attend Yale, she could feel the weight of that settling over her like an unspoken challenge. Noticed the glances from some of the older professors, the way a few male students still seemed to shilly-shally when they saw a girl walking on campus with a stack of books in her hand, their brains struggling to recalibrate. It wasn't hostile, exactly. Just...uncertain. Like no one had quite figured out yet if they were supposed to welcome the change or resist it.

The girls had long, straight hair, parted in the middle, or curls held in place with careful indifference—an indifference they worked hard to perfect as if it could offset the weight of history pressing down on them. They were the first. The first women to walk these halls, to sit in these lecture rooms, to take up space in a place that had never been meant for them. And they knew it. You could see it in the way they held their books a little tighter, their expressions schooled into effortless cool, their laughter never too loud, their presence never too demanding.

If they acted like they belonged, no one would question if they did.

She squared her shoulders. Let them stare. She hadn't come here to blend in.

She took a breath. This was it.

She adjusted the waistband of her stiff new bell-bottoms and smoothed her blouse, the fabric light and airy, chosen to make her look effortlessly put-together. Her hair curled just right—the result of an entire can of hair spray and a silent prayer.

She checked her schedule. First class. No idea where she was going. Which was frustrating because she had practiced walking the route yesterday, memorizing landmarks, convincing herself she had it all figured out. But now, as she stood in the middle of this overwhelming, ancient, book-filled kingdom, her brain had gone completely blank.

But she was here. And if she could survive saying goodbye—to her town, her home, her past, and him—she could survive this.

Maybe.

Nora drew in a deep breath, squared her shoulders, and walked in the general direction of somewhere.

When she came back from the concerts, sunburned and half dizzy from a freedom that only existed in the spaces between songs, she packed up her room. Folded her old life into boxes. Got ready for college. But before she left, she did one more thing. She called her adviser at Yale and told them she wasn't going to minor in English; she was going to major in it. No more playing it safe and going into marketing. She was going to be a writer.

She had a few people to thank for that. Herself, most of all, because, in the end, she had to be the one to make the choice. But also her parents, who had always believed she could do anything, even before she believed it herself. Her grandmother, whose stories had been a kind of alchemy—turning ordinary afternoons into adventures, filling quiet moments with whole worlds waiting to be discovered. And Joe.

Joe, who had held up a mirror and made her see that the life she had planned wasn't the same as the life she wanted. Who had asked the right questions, made her think, made her wonder if maybe the "responsible thing" wasn't about playing it safe but about being brave enough to chase what set her soul on fire.

And she had learned something: Art was a responsibility too.

It was an artist's quiet, relentless obligation to put something into the world that hadn't existed before. To take what was inside and shape it into something real. And for her, that meant words. Sentences. Stories. Meshing them together like brushstrokes on a canvas, letting them form something beautiful on the page.

This was her path. And for the first time, she wasn't afraid to follow it.

Nora smiled, striding in the direction she hoped class was. She had about a fifty-fifty shot of being right, which, statistically speaking, was not terrible.

"Let me guess," a voice drawled behind her. "You're the kind of girl who likes Coca-Cola."

She stopped dead in her tracks. That voice. That impossible, infuriating, unmistakable voice.

Her head snapped up, and sure enough, there he was—Joe Dumas, grinning like he had just gotten away with something. Which, knowing him, he probably had.

"What—" Her brain short-circuited. "What are you doing here?" She glanced around, half expecting some sort of elaborate prank, maybe a camera crew, or worse—some stranger in a lab coat ready to inform her she had officially lost her mind.

Joe shrugged, completely nonchalant, like he wasn't supposed to be across the country. "Funny thing, they had an opening in their journalism department. And what do you know? I just so happened to be on the waitlist."

She narrowed her eyes, clutching her notebooks like they were a life raft. "You never told me you applied to Yale."

"Yeah, well, nobody likes to advertise their rejection letters, do they?"

"Fair."

She blinked at him, still trying to process how the boy she had said goodbye to—dramatically, might she add—was now standing here, fate deciding to play a practical joke on her.

Then, before she could overthink it, she grinned, broad and unrestrained.

Joe slung an arm around her shoulder as if they had done this a thousand times before and the last few weeks of missing him had never happened.

"Come on," he said, steering them toward the heart of campus. "Let's go figure out what they call the center of this place. Quadrangle? Courtyard? Something fancy, I bet."

"Ivy League nonsense," she agreed.

Funny how just like that, the world tilted itself back into place.

"I feel like I should pinch myself," she said, still half convinced he might be a mirage. "Or maybe you."

"Don't do it," Joe warned, leaning in slightly. "I'm incredibly fragile. One good pinch and I might dissolve into pure charisma."

She snorted. "Well, I think Yale just got a whole lot better."

"I couldn't agree more," he said, eyes glinting. "Though, for the record, if you decide you're sick of me at any point, feel free to flick me off—like rust on a can. No hard feelings."

She laughed. "I think I'd be a bit more civil than that."

But then she stopped walking, stopped everything, reaching for the front of his shirt, gripping the fabric in her fists, and pulling him down toward her.

She rose up onto her tiptoes.

And kissed him.

Joe made a small sound between amusement and approval, like he hadn't entirely been expecting it but also had never wanted anything more.

When she pulled back, she flashed him a bright, carefree smile, her heart doing a little flip at the pure happiness shining in his eyes.

"Yeah," she murmured, breathless. "This is going to be pretty groovy."

He exhaled a laugh, shaking his head. "Understatement of the century, babe."

Just like that, the future stretched ahead of her in ways she'd never even dreamed. Bigger, messier, wilder than the careful plans she once thought she had to follow. And all it had taken was chasing her grandmother across the country, watching her step onto stage after stage, fearlessly belting out the songs she was born to sing. Somewhere between the long drives and late-night diner stops, between the music and the adventure, Nora had realized that dreams weren't something she needed to wait for. They were something to run toward, arms wide open, heart pounding, ready to make them a reality.

And now, standing in the middle of Yale's storied campus, with Joe by her side and the whole world ahead of her, she knew one thing for certain—this was only the beginning.

EPILOGUE

Instrumental Outro

AUGUST 2019

MADISON SQUARE GARDEN, NEW YORK CITY

NORA PRIDED HERSELF ON EASILY SHIFTING WITH THE tide. Adapting to new situations and making a plan B if needed. Hell, if life hadn't taught her that, certainly her career in publishing had. And dancing beside her daughter and granddaughter at a Jonas Brothers concert was most definitely the plan B.

In the immortal words of the Rolling Stones, "You Can't Always Get What You Want." But the current wisdom being belted onstage by the JoBros (Ellie's affectionate name for the boy band), who were covering the DNCE song, reminded them to why not just have their "Cake by the Ocean." Nora preferred the more innocent and literal connotation of eating carbs beachside as she had in her youth, versus the sexualized overtones that had overtaken the song's popular meaning, but alas, music was meant to be interpreted by the listener. Ironically, the Rolling Stones album featured cake on the cover.

When Woodstock 50 was canceled just a month earlier, Nora had scrambled to find a replacement. She'd promised Ellie a concert, and she intended to deliver. The Jonas Brothers' *Happiness Begins* tour felt fitting. Born from their reconciliation, it symbolized the journey from youth to adulthood and coming together stronger, united. Ellie was ecstatic, and Nora liked the meaning behind the tour. Not to mention they were Ellie's current musical crush.

The truth was, no revival could replace that epic summer of 1969. And perhaps that was a good thing. After all, Anne had been right; 1999 had turned into a disaster. Some moments in history were best left to memory and reminiscing, rather than repetition.

Thousands packed the arena, dancing, singing, waving their hands in the air. Nora loved the thrill of a concert. The way the music thumped in her chest as though it were becoming a part of her very being. Boy bands weren't necessarily her vibe, but watching Ellie now reminded her of Anne in 1990 seeing New Kids on the Block. Music brought people together.

Some things never changed—teen girls screaming, the glow of stage lights, bass reverberating through the arena. And then, some things were entirely new. Instead of lighters, they lifted their cell phones, flashlights swaying like tiny stars as they sang. Nora marveled at the mix of old and new, the timeless and transformed. Every generation found its own beat, but the rhythm of love and rebellion never changed.

Ellie beamed toward the main stage, glitter makeup around her eyes, her youth and joy blazing bright. The Jonas Brothers danced their way down to a smaller stage out in the crowd, coming to stand right in front of them.

"We're taking requests!" the one in the middle shouted, with a wag of his dark hair off his forehead.

"Please Be Mine," Ellie shouted at the top of her lungs, clapping and hopping up and down on her feet.

The same young man pointed at her, a smile curving his lips as they started to sing. Ellie practically vibrated with happiness.

Anne nudged her hip playfully against her daughter's. Nora realized what tonight was all about. The joy of music, the bond between three generations of women growing tighter with every lyric they shouted together.

It wasn't Janis Joplin, Jimi Hendrix, or Creedence Clearwater Revival, but this was the next generation's soundtrack, and Nora was passing the torch.

Nora pulled out her cell phone, snapping photos of Anne and Ellie before turning the camera for a selfie of all three. Then she asked a nearby concertgoer for one more. Later, she'd add this one to her refrigerator beside the pictures of her and Anne at New Kids on the Block and then at Lilith Fair, the faded Polaroid of herself with her mother at Woodstock, and the one of her grandmother at a beach concert when music brought the light back to her faded eyes. A collage of memories, time forever captured in the stillness of their smiling faces.

These were memories to cherish. Of all the gifts the years had given Nora, the ones she treasured most were the connections between the women in her life.

Tears of happiness, of loss too, pricked her eyes. Nora brushed them away. Now was not the time to tumble into the past. Now was the time for sweetness. For music. For making memories that would never fade, even when the song ended. For passing the melody on, one generation to the next.

AUTHOR'S NOTE

Every historical novel I write begins with a question, and then comes the research. Researching is one of my favorite parts of bringing a cast of characters and their world to life. The purpose of this author's note is to share some of what I discovered along the way, the choices I made in weaving fact with fiction, and a gentle reminder that while this story unfolds during a time vividly remembered by many, it remains a work of fiction brought to life with a bit of creative license.

The summer of 1969 was a turning point for rock and roll—an unrelenting season of music, mud, and magic. Across the country, festival stages sprang up in fields, parks, and fairgrounds, drawing crowds in the tens of thousands. Every festival named in this book actually took place: Newport Pop Festival in California (June 20–22), Denver Pop Festival (June 27–29), Atlanta International Pop Festival in Georgia (July 4–5), Seattle Pop Festival (July 25–27), and of course, the legendary Woodstock Music and Art Fair in New York (August 15–18). I also researched the New Orleans Pop Festival (August 30–September 1), but its timing clashed with Nora's fictional matriculation to Yale, so it stayed on the cutting-room floor. And these were just a handful—1969's calendar was overflowing with music.

Rock and roll itself had been building toward this moment for over a decade. Elvis Presley had helped usher listeners from the big band era into a new sound—his guitar licks and hip-swaying moves both scandalized and enthralled audiences. By the mid-1960s, the genre had exploded, carried forward by bands like the Beatles and, in 1968, the arrival of Led Zeppelin, whose rise in popularity was as meteoric as the music was loud.

There are dozens of documentaries and even more nonfiction books chronicling this magical, musical summer, and it was a joy to dive into them—not just for the stories but for the photographs, posters, and grainy video clips that captured the moment the stages lit up and the music began. Through those images, I could almost watch my fictional characters crisscross the country, chasing the sound from one festival to the next.

These festivals were both ambitious and chaotic. Promoters scrambled to secure farmland, fairgrounds, or stadiums, building stages in a matter of days and stringing together enough speakers to reach crowds that sometimes doubled the expected size. For example, Woodstock was half a million strong, when organizers had expected fifty thousand to two hundred thousand attendees. Tickets were printed and sold through record stores, head shops (stores that sold posters, records, incense, and paraphernalia like rolling papers), and even by mail order, though many fans simply showed up, cash in hand—or slipped in without paying at all. Parking lots overflowed into fields, and the long walk to the gates was often its own preshow, lined with makeshift vendors selling tie-dye shirts, beaded necklaces, and questionable sandwiches. Inside the grounds, food was whatever could be hauled in—hot dogs, hamburgers, fried dough, and paper cups of soda or beer—though some festivals ran out entirely, leaving hungry fans to barter for snacks. At Woodstock, the Hog Farm commune famously served vegetables, beans, and rice, and other volunteers handed out peanut butter and jelly sandwiches by the thousands, keeping the masses fed while music drifted through the air.

Drama wasn't confined to backstage: At the Denver Pop Festival, tensions boiled over when police moved in on the crowd with tear gas on the final night, sending concertgoers scrambling for safety and marking the event as the last U.S. performance for *The Jimi Hendrix Experience* (his bassist, Noel Redding, left shortly after). And yet, when the music started, all of it—the mud, the mess, the missed cues—faded into the roar of the crowd.

While the wild music festivals of 1969 form the backdrop of this novel, at its heart it's about three women—Eleanor, Leanne, and Nora—and the ways each of them is transformed over the course of one unforgettable summer. In addition to transformation and self-discovery, memory is a significant theme in the novel. Our memories define not only who we are but also the people who surround us and the world we live in.

Eleanor has recently been diagnosed with early-onset dementia. She has decided that if she's going to lose her memories of a youthful musical career she pines for, she's going to give it one last hurrah before the curtain closes. Alzheimer's disease was first identified in 1906 by Dr. Alois Alzheimer, who described certain behaviors and the presence of abnormal plaques in the brain. The term *Alzheimer's disease* was coined in 1910, though it didn't come into everyday use until the late 1970s. Before then, people showing symptoms at a younger age were typically diagnosed with *early-onset dementia*, while similar symptoms in older adults were often labeled *senile dementia* and considered a natural part of aging. I am by no means an expert in the disease or its distinctions. Still, I drew from my own experiences with family and friends who have faced both early-onset Alzheimer's and dementia associated with aging. I also found deep insight and humanity in *Memory's Last Breath: Field Notes on My Dementia* by Gerda Saunders, a memoir I highly recommend.

Leanne is the quintessential 1950s–1960s housewife, her life defined by the needs of her husband, her child, and her home. But as she sets out on the road—chasing after her mother and trying to bridge the growing distance with her college-age daughter—she begins to sense an absence she can no longer ignore: herself. She's spent her entire adult life living for others, and now, for the first time, she must confront the question of who she is and what she truly wants. Mostly, Leanne is afraid of being alone—of facing a world where she isn't needed, with nothing to show for it except the deeds she's done for other people. Somewhere along the way, she lost sight of who she is, and now she must decide if it's too late to find herself again.

Nora is every bit the typical teenager—freshly graduated from high school, eager to spend the summer gossiping with friends, flirting with boys, and perfecting her tan before heading off to college. In the fall of 1969, she will be among the first women ever admitted to Yale University, blazing a trail for the generations who follow. What she didn't expect was to spend her last free summer on a road trip with her mother in search of her grandmother. Initially sour about her plans being derailed, Nora is quickly intrigued by the lure of the music festivals—and, deep down, she does care for her grandmother. Along the way, she finds the courage to change her major to what she truly wants, discovers a spark of romance with a journalism intern, and sees the world differently through the books she and her mother read together on the road. I chose *The Godfather* by Mario Puzo, *The Love Machine* by Jacqueline Susann, and *The Stud* by Jackie Collins—popular, scandalous novels of the era and the perfect reading material for both a middle-aged woman in search of herself and a young woman on the cusp of her own adventure. I read each one of them too!

In addition to researching the music festivals, women's lives during the 1960s, Yale University's decision to open its doors to women, and Alzheimer's disease, I also explored what it would be like to take a road trip during that era—the cars and highways, gas stations and roadside motels, the food, and all the small details in between. I immersed myself in the fashion, the products that lined store shelves, the decor, the slang, and so much more.

In the frame of the story, Nora decides to take her granddaughter to the revived Woodstock in 2019. However, that festival was ultimately canceled due to the inability to get permits and other snafus. I mention in the prologue and the epilogue the Woodstock 1999 festival, which devolved into absolute chaos. I suggest you watch the documentary *Woodstock 99: Peace, Love, and Rage* to witness the absolute change in vibe from the 1969 concert. I also mentioned Lilith Fair, a traveling music festival put on by Sarah McLachlan between 1997 and 1999 that showcased female artists. The vibe of Lilith Fair was much more in line with Nora's memories, and though it doesn't take place on the page here, I think it's worth exploring. There is a fabulous documentary, *Lilith Fair: Building a Mystery*, that explores the show. Just a couple weeks before Woodstock 50 was supposed to take place in 2019, it changed venues from New York to Maryland and then was ultimately canceled. Bethel, New York, however—the same place where Woodstock was held in 1969—did have a fiftieth anniversary celebration, which included a few of the same musicians who played there fifty years prior, although it was more about the history than the music. The anniversary celebration was considered divisive, given it conflicted with the revival that had been canceled. So instead, Nora takes her granddaughter and daughter to see the Jonas Brothers during their *Happiness Begins* tour in Madison Square Garden, another important place in her past but one also symbolizing the passing of the musical torch and a new age of music.

It takes months of research to bring a period vividly to life on the page, and inevitably, a few details may slip through the cracks. Mea culpa!

READ ON FOR A LOOK AT ANOTHER NOVEL BY ELIZA KNIGHT!

Chapter One

NEW YORK CITY
Summer 1963

IF IMPELLED TO IDENTIFY SOME OF THE SKILLS SHE HAD mastered since graduating summa cum laude from Barnard College and coming to work at Lenox & Park Publishing a few years ago, Bernadette Swift would declare she was an eliminator of subject-verb disagreements, a clarifier of pronoun antecedents, a proponent for perfect comma placement, and a liberator of clichés and ambiguities from the page.

At the moment, however, her boss seemed to have missed the nameplate on her tidy desk that read: BERNADETTE SWIFT, COPY EDITOR.

Instead of holding out a manuscript for review, he had a wrinkled, white oxford button-down shirt in his hand—with a coffee stain on it.

For over a millennium, women have been in charge of cleaning the stains off men's clothes. Coffee in particular is epically difficult to remove from starched white fabric. But Bernadette wasn't Mr. Wall's wife, or even his secretary. Neither of those facts could be stated aloud at this moment, however; not if she wanted to keep her job.

So, she kept silent as she watched his mouth moving. Watched his eyes scanning—and not just her face either. And she thought about how for the last biennium, she'd been charged with getting his coffee, then for what felt like longer than just a few years, taking his shirts to be laundered when he inevitably spilled his dark roast down the front because he was a cloven-hoofed artiodactyl of the *Suidae* family. In other words, an utter swine.

She'd learned from her veterinarian father all the correct biological genera, and she enjoyed tacking them onto human behavior.

Although, that wasn't really fair to pigs, now was it? The ones she'd grown up with on her family farm had been adorable, even when covered in muck. Especially Amaranth, who'd been her pet named after her favorite color—though obviously a pig could never be quite as pink, but she'd always been a lover of big words, squeezing them in wherever she could, even if on a beloved swine.

To be clear, Mr. Wall was never adorable.

Meaty fingers snapped in her direction, yanking her back to reality. "Miss Swift? Did you hear me?"

Unfortunately.

Bernadette glanced around the bustling copyediting room at the typewriters clacking, men sporting Beach Boys floppy hairstyles bent over stacks of galley pages with their red pencils in hand, pages of *Webster's Third New International Dictionary* being flipped, everyone busy and not looking in her direction.

Maybe they were blissfully unaware of what was transpiring. They dedicated a lot of time to pretending she—the sole female junior copy editor—didn't exist. Her male colleagues were never asked to perform such menial tasks for their boss. Tasks that were not part of the job description of a copy editor. Which she was. A fact that Mr. Wall often disregarded. One day, he would not dismiss her so easily, when it was her name on the placard outside the CEO's office and her desk pristine on the inside.

Bernadette met her superior's eyes, watery blue like a child who'd been overzealous in dowsing their watercolor paints in an attempt to bring the pigment back to life. She wanted nothing more than to grab on to each end of his waxed, dark handlebar mustache and yank the smirk off his face. Instead, she sat on her hands, with their neatly trimmed and pink-painted nails, and said, "Yes, Mr. Wall."

Generally, Bernadette had a nearly infinite amount of patience. Working in an office surrounded by men who treated the copyediting department like a boys' club meant she needed it. But there was something about her boss that had the power to bring up what her female friends called her "nicey-nice shield." That deactivated a part of her that wanted to rebel against being asked to perform tasks her male colleagues were never subjected to simply because of their gender.

So far, she'd tamped that urge down and allowed herself to be a doormat. Once a precedent was set, it was hard to change.

Besides, she could push back against injustice, or she could keep her job. And she liked her job, except when she was dealing with Mr. Wall or others of his ilk. So, she rose from her chair, the creaking sound drowned out by the work carrying on around them. Her fingers brushed Mr. Wall's as she reached for the shirt, and it was hard to keep a shudder at bay.

"I need it back by lunch. I've got a meeting." Mr. Wall's gaze traveled toward her lips, and she pressed them inward as if to ward him off.

"Try smiling a little more." He gave her a lascivious grin. "Women are prettier when they smile."

What a cliché. She'd have drawn a fat red line through that quip in a manuscript and written, "Try to be more original."

Wall turned away without so much as a thank-you. "And get me your pages by four o'clock," he said over his shoulder as he headed to the door and the corridor beyond.

Bernadette frowned as she held the sullied garment out in front of her. Any outsider seeing her bustle off to handle the coffee stain would assume she was Mr. Wall's personal assistant. Although even secretaries weren't in charge of laundering garments. At least according to their written job descriptions. All these tasks seemed to be excused by one little line that someone, undoubtedly a man, seemed to have added to every description: "and other duties as assigned."

The line would be more accurate if it said, "and other duties as assigned, provided the employee in question is a woman."

READING GROUP GUIDE

1. Eleanor, Leanne, and Nora represent three different generations of women in 1969. How do their perspectives on freedom, responsibility, and identity differ? Did you connect more strongly with one of them?

2. How does the tension between independence and obligation play out across the three generations? Do you think these tensions still exist for women today?

3. Music is both Eleanor's passion and her fading memory. How does the novel portray music as a force of healing, identity, and rebellion?

4. What role does nostalgia play in the story—both for the characters living in 1969 and for us as readers looking back?

5. Nora is about to enter Yale as part of the first class of women undergraduates. How does her struggle for self-definition compare to Eleanor's and Leanne's?

6. Leanne begins the summer defined by her roles as daughter, wife, and mother, but along the road trip, she is forced to confront her

own fears, desires, and identity. How does her personal journey toward self-discovery unfold, and what does it reveal about the costs—and possibilities—of stepping outside the roles society assigns to her? Do you see parallels for women making similar choices today?

7. Eleanor forgets (or chooses to forget) to tell her family she's leaving. What do you think motivated that choice—fear, defiance, or something else?

8. Do you think Eleanor was selfish for leaving without telling her family or brave for reclaiming her independence?

9. The novel deals with illness and memory loss. How does Eleanor's condition heighten the urgency of her choices? Did it change the way you thought about aging, legacy, or creative expression?

10. Many readers may find themselves in Leanne's shoes—stuck between caring for aging parents and raising children. Did her story resonate with your own experiences or the experience of someone you know?

11. The novel is steeped in the music festivals, fashion, and spirit of 1969. Did it remind you of any road trips, concerts, or coming-of-age summers from your own life?

12. The summer of '69 is a formative period for all three of the women in this story. Is there a period of your own life that felt transformative? How so?

13. The book emphasizes how it's important to love yourself to be able to love others. What are some ways that you care for yourself? How do you practice self-love and care?

A CONVERSATION WITH THE AUTHOR

From music festivals to the start of women being admitted into Yale, there is so much history woven into this book. Where did you start your research? Take us into your process.

I always begin with a single question: *What would it have felt like to live in this moment?* From there, I cast a wide net and dive into newspaper archives, reading and listening to interviews, and in this case, talking to people who lived during the festival period. I watched documentaries and, of course, read everything I could find about that year. For this book, I pored over festival lineups and old concert footage, studied Yale's decision to admit women in 1969, and read firsthand accounts from women who were part of that inaugural class. I also dug into everyday details like cars, music, food, hotels, gas stations, fashion, and the slang of the time, because those little touches make a world come alive on the page.

Nora, Leanne, and Eleanor are all such vivid female characters. Who were they inspired by?

They are entirely fictitious, but I designed them with inspiration drawn from both women of the 1960s and women of today. Eleanor embodies the boldness of women artists and musicians who refused to give up their passions despite obstacles, and she carries the theme of memory: what we hold onto and what slips away. Leanne reflects the many mothers of the era who quietly held families together while longing for more of themselves, representing the journey of finding yourself when the world has defined you one way for so long. And Nora represents the rising generation of young women standing at the edge of great change. Brilliant, questioning, and eager to carve their own paths, capturing the theme of embracing your dreams even when the future feels uncertain. Together, they form a chorus of women's voices across generations that will resonate with readers of all ages.

What about the '60s inspired you? Why did you choose to write in this era?

The 1960s was a decade of social, political, and cultural transformation, and music was at the heart of it all. It was an era when young people believed songs could change the world, and in many ways, they did. I chose 1969 in particular because it felt like a turning point. The end of one decade, the promise of another, and the summer where both joy and turbulence were everywhere you looked. It was the perfect backdrop for a story about women redefining themselves.

If you could attend any of the festivals mentioned in the book, which one would you choose and why?

I would choose Woodstock 1969. Not just because of the legendary lineup, but because it became such a symbol of peace, community, and possibility. To be there, standing in a field with hundreds of thousands of people who all believed in something bigger than themselves, must have been extraordinary. That said, I wish I'd been able to attend Lilith Fair in the 1990s. The musical lineup, the comradery, and the themes of female empowerment are so my vibe, and I would have absolutely enjoyed the heck out that scene.

So many amazing artists and songs are interwoven into this story. What are some of your favorite tracks that Nora, Leanne, and Eleanor would have heard that summer? Take us into your playlist.

Eleanor would have been electrified by Jimi Hendrix, songs like "Foxy Lady" speak to her spirit and sense of defiance. Leanne might have connected most with Janis Joplin's "Piece of My Heart," a song that carries both vulnerability and strength, mirroring her own quiet struggles. And Nora, standing on the brink of adulthood and eager to break free, would have felt the pull of The Doors' "Break On Through (To the Other Side)." As for me, some of the tracks I loved weaving into the atmosphere of the book were Led Zeppelin's "Whole Lotta Love" and the Rolling Stones' "You Can't Always Get What You Want"—songs that perfectly capture the mix of rebellion, longing, and possibility that defined the summer of '69.

All three of the women in this book ultimately form memories closely tied to music. Do you have a favorite music-related memory?

The first concert I ever went to was when I was ten, and it was New Kids on the Block. What an experience—and oh my, did I have a crush on Marky Mark (a.k.a. Mark Wahlberg)! Another fond memory is standing in the middle of the HFStival as a teenager, singing along to Green Day's "Good Riddance (Time of Your Life)" with my best friends. There was something magical about that shared moment of our voices blending, hearts pounding, all of us lifted by music that seemed to understand us better than we understood ourselves. Music was also ever-present at home. My dad had 1960s radio playing nonstop, and my best friend and I used to blast the local oldies station on the drive to high school. On a more personal level, I played piano for years, and now I get to watch my youngest daughter carry on that love of music with the flute—first with "Bohemian Rhapsody" at a concert and now with her own solos in marching band. Those experiences cemented for me the way music becomes both personal and collective, intimate and universal, life-changing even, a feeling I wanted to capture in the book.

ACKNOWLEDGMENTS

While writing a book can feel like a solitary endeavor, no book is ever truly written in a vacuum—unless, perhaps, it's in those very early days when the draft is so hideous we authors would rather hide it from the world. Or maybe that's just me.

To that end, there are many people I wish to thank for helping bring this story from my desk to the shelves.

My deepest gratitude to my wonderful agent, Kevan Lyon, who has championed my writing for over a decade. Your unwavering support means the world to me. To my editor, Shana Drehs, and the incredible team at Sourcebooks—thank you for your faith in me and this book. You are true heroes.

Hugs and heartfelt thanks to my dear friend Heather Webb, who walked and talked this plot into being during a writer's retreat and later cheered me over the finish line alongside Kris Waldherr, E. Elizabeth Watson, and my bestie, Madeline Martin—this time at a retreat deep in the woods. These women poured me wine, offered wisdom, and gave me the push I needed when I needed it most. Thankfully, the only drama came from the page and not the bear that was lurking nearby!

Critique partners are so important, and I am beyond grateful for the fabulous eye of mine, Sophie Perinot. Thank you so much for all of your help with this book!

Thank you so much to Sarah Burris, an early beta reader and a most fabulous librarian! I so appreciate you taking the time to read and offer critique and to share your family's stories with me.

I'm also grateful to all those who shared their memories of music festivals and 1960s adventures—including my dad! Your stories breathed life into these pages.

To my husband and daughters: Thank you for enduring endless hours of me rambling about history and music, for reading draft chapters, for attending events with grace, and for selling my books to perfect strangers. You are my rocks.

To my sister-agents, the Lyonesses, my Tall Poppy sisters, and every friend and supporter I may have overlooked in my edit-induced haze—please know your encouragement has meant everything.

And last but never least, thank you, dear reader. Without you, I'd still be telling these stories only to myself—sharing them with you is infinitely more fun.

ABOUT THE AUTHOR

Michael Devaney, SRQ Headshots

Eliza Knight is an award-winning *USA Today* and international bestselling author. Eliza is an avid history buff, and her love of history began as a young girl when she traipsed the halls of Versailles. She also writes contemporary revenge fiction under the pseudonym Michelle Brandon. She is a member of the Historical Novel Society, Novelists, Inc., the Women's Fiction Writing Association, and Tall Poppy Writers. She is also the creator of the popular historical blog, *History Undressed*, and the host of the *History, Books & Wine* podcast. An MFA graduate of Drexel University, Eliza is an adjunct professor of creative writing. Her books have been translated into multiple languages, and her coauthored title *A Day of Fire* has been optioned for television. She lives on the Suncoast with her husband, three daughters, a dog, a crab, and a turtle.

www.ingramcontent.com/pod-product-compliance
Lightning Source LLC
LaVergne TN
LVHW100505110826
845146LV00002B/517
9781464255113